At the Wedding

ALSO BY MATT DUNN

Best Man
The Ex-Boyfriend's Handbook
From Here to Paternity
Ex-Girlfriends United
The Good Bride Guide
The Accidental Proposal
A Day at the Office
What Might Have Been
Home
A Christmas Day at the Office
13 Dates

At the Wedding

MATT DUNN

LAKE UNION
PUBLISHING

Text copyright © 2018 by Matt Dunn
All rights reserved.

Published by Lake Union Publishing, Seattle

www.apub.com

Amazon, the Amazon logo, and Lake Union Publishing are trademarks of Amazon.com, Inc., or its affiliates.

ISBN-13: 9781503902466
ISBN-10: 1503902463

Printed in the United States of America

For my nieces and nephews: Ida and Pål,
Trisha and Nikita, Keyur and Aman, Vinay and
Shivani, Jay and Om. Hint, hint!

At the Wedding

'Will you marry me?'

Jed froze, mid-chew, and stared at Livia across the table, not quite believing what he'd just heard. The restaurant, just off Barcelona's famous Las Ramblas, was packed, full of tourists devouring plate after plate of delicious tapas, just like the two of them were – the perfect end to a perfect day's sightseeing in this most perfect of cities. And while the place was noisy, it wasn't so noisy that he hadn't been able to hear his girlfriend clearly.

He swallowed his mouthful of *patatas bravas*, then washed it down with a large swig from the beer bottle he suddenly remembered he was holding and that he'd nearly dropped in shock. And then, and only because he couldn't think how else to reply, Jed said simply, 'What?'

'You heard!'

'Why on earth do we need to . . . *ow!* Jed rubbed the spot on his arm where Livia had just pinched him. 'What did you do that for?'

'Pinch you? Or propose?'

Jed had started to sweat, though he knew that was nothing to do with the spicy potato dish that he'd been happily working his way through. Livia's proposal had come out of the blue – as much as these things did when you were in love, and had been since you'd first set eyes on each other, *and* had a baby on the way – and for a moment, he almost wished he *had* been expecting it. Because then, he'd have known how to respond. 'The, um, second one,' he said, though given how Livia was drumming her fingers on her heavily pregnant stomach, he suspected he already knew the answer.

'It's *time*, Jed.'

'And they say romance is dead,' he said, doing his best to make a joke, though he could tell Livia was serious.

'*You* will be, in a minute, if you don't hurry up and answer the question.'

'Marry you?' Jed stared at her, doing his best to ignore the sense of dread bubbling up inside him. 'Do you mean, *ever?*'

'I mean this weekend,' said Livia, as if pulling a rabbit out of a hat. Then she reached across the table, placed a finger underneath his chin and shut his just-dropped-open jaw with an audible click.

'Here?' said Jed, after an uncomfortably long pause. 'In Barcelona?'

'Here in Barcelona.'

'Just the two of us?'

'I believe that's the traditional number of people involved when it comes to marriage.'

'No, I meant . . . what about our friends? And Liam. There's no way I can get married without my brother there. And there must be a ton of stuff to organise before—'

'Relax. They'll all be here. Everything's been arranged.' Livia was beaming at him, as if she'd presented him with the keys to a Ferrari rather than what felt like a fait accompli. 'All that's left is for you to stand there and say "I do". Or whatever the Spanish equivalent is.'

'Oh-kay . . .'

'I think it might be "*Olé!*"'

Jed forced a smile at Livia's attempt at humour. A part of him was wishing this was all a joke, but after ten years together – ten years *today*, in fact – he knew her much better than that.

He glanced at his mobile on the table and double-checked the date on the screen, silently praying it might be April 1st, wondering why he couldn't just come out with the answer Livia wanted. No, expected. And, in fact, *deserved*.

'Oh-kay,' he said, again.

'Is that a yes?' said Livia, so hopefully that Jed immediately felt terrible for not biting her hand off straight away. But there were rules for this kind of thing, weren't there? Rules of engagement. The main one being, both parties had to think getting married was a good thing. Or, in the absence of that, could vocalise a reason why it wasn't, and quickly. But Jed was too petrified to do anything quickly. Too scared of what this would all mean. Desperately worried about disappointing her. Both now, and as her husband.

It may not have been a leap year, but it *was* 2018, so he suspected any objections on the basis of her not being *allowed* to propose would probably fall on deaf ears. Besides, in true Livia style, everything had been arranged. Any issues anticipated. People invited. How could he possibly say no?

He told himself nothing had changed. She was still the same Livia he'd fallen for all those years ago. The same Livia he wanted to spend the rest of his life with. The same Livia who – up until about a minute ago – he'd assumed was fine with the way things were. And then, conscious she was still waiting for him to say something, he reached across the table and took her hands in his, though partly to stop his own from shaking.

'Yes,' he said, as sincerely as he could. And – though Jed loved Livia more than anything – a lot more cheerfully than he felt.

Chapter 1

'So Jed didn't have any idea?' said Izzy, and Patrick looked up from the article on Barcelona's best museums he'd been about to read to her from the in-flight magazine, then broke into a broad grin. His girlfriend was staring at him, wide-eyed, as if Livia's ruse was the most audacious, ridiculous and amazing thing she'd ever heard. But, he supposed, if you'd only recently turned twenty-two, it just might be.

'None whatsoever,' he replied.

'But what if he'd turned her down?'

'Then we'd be flying to Barcelona for a dirty weekend, instead of their wedding.'

'Fuck me!' said Izzy, a little too loudly for Patrick's liking given the young family sitting in the row behind them, and he winced. It was her go-to expression for surprise, anger, disappointment – even after the best part of three months together, he still hadn't got used to the way she freely bandied it about. Although the amount of times she used the phrase as a request almost made up for that.

He rolled his eyes, then, as the 'Fasten Seatbelts' sign pinged on, indicated she should look out of the window. 'And speaking of Barcelona . . .' he said, fondly.

'What?'

'There it is.'

'Cool,' Izzy said, then she frowned. 'It's very . . . regular.'

'That's the Eixample,' he explained, pronouncing it 'eye-sham-pla', like a local might. 'It's Catalan for "extension". One of the earliest examples of town planning. The grid design was intended to . . .' Patrick stopped talking. Even in the indistinct reflection in the aeroplane window, he could tell Izzy's eyes had glazed over. 'You see that big street down the middle?'

Izzy stifled a yawn theatrically. 'What about it?'

'That's where all the shops are.'

'Oh. Right.' Suddenly interested, Izzy leaned in closer to the window, letting out a louder-still 'Fuck me!' when she banged her forehead on the glass, and Patrick had to hide a smile. Already window-shopping, even from up here. Though the real thing, he knew, would come later.

He reached across and rubbed a thumb affectionately over the spot where she'd bumped herself, resisting the inclination to offer to kiss it better. Izzy *loved* shopping. This weekend had already cost him a fair bit and they hadn't even landed yet. Patrick could almost feel his credit card running through a series of warm-up exercises in his wallet. He was sure the depth of his pockets was one of the reasons Izzy put up with a 'granddad' like him – her description whenever he refused to dance with her, or go to concerts to see bands whose members were younger than Anna, his daughter, or eat at restaurants where the music was so loud they had to shout at each other across plates of food presented as if they were some kind of porcelain catwalk, or eat anything served from the back of a van (or 'food truck', as Izzy would always correct him, as if that made a difference). But Patrick knew that if you wanted nice things, you had to pay for them, like the vintage Tag Heuer Monaco watch he sported on his wrist, or the classic Porsche 911 convertible he kept in the garage beneath his central London apartment and only ever drove when it wasn't raining (which, in England, meant he didn't drive it that often). But while the watch and the car made him look good, Izzy made him *feel* good. She put a smile on his face, gave him a spring in his step – apart from when he was too stiff after a night of their between-the-sheets exertions, that was. No, Patrick was sure she'd been a good investment. Even though – unlike the watch and the car – she might be a depreciating asset. Or at least depreciating his finances.

'How do you know Jed again?'

'Through Livia. She and I used to . . .' Izzy's raised eyebrow made him catch himself. 'Livia worked for me, in answer to the assumption you look like you're making. We were here in Barcelona for a conference, and Jed happened to be in the bar we all ended up in, and the two of them . . . I don't know if it was quite love at first sight. Livia's too . . . *sensible* for that. But that was ten years ago. And she's a good friend.'

'How good, exactly?'

Izzy was pouting at him, and Patrick sighed. 'She'd hardly have asked me to give her away if we'd—'

'Okay, okay,' said Izzy, begrudgingly. 'And who else will be there? Assuming this wedding actually happens.'

'Why wouldn't it happen?'

'No reason,' said Izzy, in the same innocent tone his daughter sometimes adopted, usually just as she was about to impart some bad news. Or ask him for money, which, since his divorce settlement, amounted to the same thing.

'Well, it's just a small affair. Eight of us, including the happy couple, I think.'

'Why only eight?'

'I guess it'd have been hard to get more than that out here and still keep it a secret from him.'

'So nothing to do with in case Jed had said no?'

Patrick almost laughed out loud. 'I don't think there was ever any danger of that. The two of them are . . . well, there are couples, and then there's Jed and Livia. You'll see.'

'I can't wait.' Izzy yawned again, then flung her arms up in an exaggerated stretch, nearly punching Patrick on the nose. 'So the eight will be?'

'Well, there's us, and obviously Livia and Jed. He's nice. Does something in IT.'

'Tech.'

'What?'

'It's not called IT nowadays, granddad. It's *tech*. Short for—'

'Information Technology. I know. Which, actually, so is IT.'

'*Was* IT.'

Patrick sighed. 'You'll be telling me "wireless" isn't the thing you sit around and listen to as a family next.'

'What?'

'Nothing,' said Patrick, quickly. Sometimes he forgot just how much younger than him Izzy actually was. 'Sorry. *Tech*.'

'Always happy to teach you new stuff.' She leaned across, kissed him slowly on the lips and rested a hand suggestively on his upper thigh. 'And not just in bed.'

Patrick gave her a look, though given the one she returned, he then had to do his best to think of something else, and quickly. The stewardess was checking everyone's seatbelts were fastened for landing, and the last thing he wanted was for anyone to be staring at his lap right now.

'Oh, and the best man is Jed's younger brother,' he said, gently but firmly sliding her hand away from his groin area. 'He . . . actually, I'm not sure exactly what he does. But he's famous. Or used to be.'

'For what?'

Patrick thought for a moment. On the odd occasions he'd flicked through one of Izzy's glossy magazines, it had seemed to him that nowadays you didn't have to be famous *for* anything – and besides, he wasn't sure what Liam's talents actually were. 'He was on *Big Brother* a couple of years ago. His name's Liam . . .'

'Not Liam *Woodward*?'

Izzy had widened her eyes, and Patrick fought to keep down what he was surprised to recognise was a pang of jealousy. He'd seen the way Liam was with women, and the last thing he wanted was for Izzy to fall under his spell this weekend. 'That's right.'

Izzy let out a squeal of delight. 'He's *gorgeous*. Though he's also the kind of person who'd ask how much something cost in a Poundland.'

'Pardon?'

'That's how one of the tabloids referred to him. It means—'

'I can guess what it means.' Patrick chuckled. 'It's actually a pretty good description.'

'You didn't tell me we were going to a celebrity wedding.'

'We're not. It's Jed who's getting married.'

'*His* big brother!' She mimed an exaggerated belly laugh, as if to underline how poor her own joke was, and Patrick couldn't help but chuckle. Izzy's sense of humour was one of the things he liked about her. One of the many things, he'd been surprised to realise the more time they'd spent together. Unlike Liam, she was more than just a pretty face. Or a killer body.

'He's very good-looking,' she continued. 'At least, he was. He hasn't been on TV for a while, as far as I'm aware.' Izzy narrowed her eyes. 'And does Liam have a girlfriend?'

'Liam *always* has a girlfriend. Sometimes more than one. Often someone else's.' He glanced around the plane, keen to change the subject. 'Oh yes. And I mustn't forget Rachel. She's Livia's best friend. And her boyfriend's Rich.'

'Coming from you, that's quite a—'

'No, his *name's* Rich. I don't know him that well. But she's lovely.' He lowered his voice. 'And don't look now, but she's sitting about six rows back.'

'Which one?' Izzy had popped her seatbelt open, raised herself out of her chair and swivelled round, causing the returning stewardess to reprimand her sharply. Patrick shook his head, wondering which part of 'don't look now' Izzy hadn't understood. 'The brunette,' he said, taking a quick peek himself. 'Staring wistfully out of the window. Next to the . . . oh.'

'Oh?'

Patrick glanced round the rest of the plane and quickly put two and two together. 'The vacant seat. Where Rich should presumably have been sitting.'

'Oops!' To his relief, Izzy had turned back round to face him. 'She's pretty.'

'Is she?'

Izzy gave him a look. 'Anything I should know?'

'About?'

She arched an eyebrow. '*History?*'

'Huh?'

'Which of these women have you . . . ?'

'None of them! I was married, remember?'

'Hmm.'

'What's that supposed to mean?' he said, though Patrick knew full well. After all, being married hadn't stopped his wife from straying.

'Nothing,' she said, reaching over to grab his hand, a bit like his daughter had when he'd walked her to her first day at school. While he was a little nervous about introducing Izzy to his friends, surely she wasn't feeling insecure about meeting them all for the first time? She was the most confident twenty-two-year-old he knew. The most confident *person* – outwardly, at least – he knew. He was sure they'd love her. Everybody did. Maybe, under different circumstances, and if he hadn't just been chewed up and spat out by his ex-wife and her divorce lawyers, even *he* could.

His stomach rumbled, and he wished he'd had more to eat this morning than the on-board 'hot bacon baguette' that hadn't actually been that hot (and Patrick wasn't sure had been bacon, either) that'd had to serve as a substitute breakfast. But Izzy had made them late this morning – she made them late every morning she stayed over at his – though he knew he shouldn't complain. The last two years of his marriage, he and his ex-wife had stopped having sex (or rather, his ex had stopped having sex with *him*) – something Izzy was more than making up for.

'So, why *didn't* Jed?' she said, after a moment.

'Why didn't Jed what?'

'Ask Livia. To marry him.'

'You'd have to ask him.'

'I will!'

'Don't you *dare*.'

Patrick ignored Izzy's mischievous grin, and as she turned her attention back to the view through the window, he double-checked his seatbelt. The plane was making its final approach, its wings almost skimming the huge container ships sitting in Barcelona's port, and he gripped the armrests tightly. He'd never been a big fan of flying – no, scratch that, he didn't mind the flying, it was the landing that always got him spooked. Those people who applauded whenever a plane touched down safely? He'd lost count of the number of times he'd had to stop himself from joining in, or even leading a standing ovation for the pilot. Once you were allowed to stand.

He braced himself, both dreading and desperate for the moment the wheels hit the tarmac – surely they were nearly down by now? – and in the split second before he shut his eyes tightly, he caught Izzy's pitying look. Younger people were different. Fearless. And sometimes, the twenty-plus years between them felt like a lifetime.

Finally, to his relief, he felt the wheels make contact with the runway, so softly he barely noticed it, and he opened his eyes and peered out through the window into the morning sunshine. He hadn't been here for a good few years, and the airport had changed. A modern, glass-and-steel terminal building now sat opposite the old one – evidence that the city was moving forward. Looking to the future. Patrick knew the feeling.

He'd always loved coming to Barcelona. Every time he landed here and saw the city's name spelled out in that classic, widely spaced lettering on the side of the old terminal, he felt a wave of – what? A sense that he was where he belonged, perhaps. Something about the place – a small big city, with a beach, amazing architecture, a fantastic climate and great food and wine – made him daydream occasionally about moving here. He'd even considered it, after the divorce, after he'd had to sell the company to pay his wife what he owed her for her infidelity. Though he suspected it might be one of those things that was nice in theory, but maybe a bit difficult in practice. A bit like he'd feared dating a twenty-two-year-old might be. Though, so far, he'd been surprised to discover that had been the opposite.

They taxied towards their stand, Izzy already unbuckling her seatbelt, anxious to get off the plane and get on with the weekend, and Patrick smiled to himself. She'd been good for him, reminding him that life was for living – that his divorce, though it was the end of something, could actually be the beginning of something else.

He waited until they'd come to a complete stop, listened for the familiar, comforting *ping*, then double-checked the 'Fasten Seatbelts' light had gone out, but only when the captain announced they'd arrived did he feel safe enough to undo his buckle. Hauling himself stiffly up, he retrieved their bags from the overhead lockers, wincing at the weight of Izzy's carry-on. At least they were here with hand luggage only, which in itself might be enough to limit her shopping, though he doubted it – Izzy seemed to see limits as a challenge rather than a recommendation. He preferred to travel with as little baggage as possible, and he'd already made sure he'd allowed some extra space for her. Patrick didn't want to end up paying for Izzy's excesses. Like he still was with his former wife.

No, he reminded himself, as she scampered off the plane in front of him, he wouldn't make the same mistake with Izzy. Forewarned was forearmed, after all. Besides, the two of them were . . . well, to tell the truth, Patrick hadn't yet decided what they were. A fling maybe, or simply (as a number of his friends had told him) a reaction to what his wife had done to him. In the meantime, a 'bit of fun' was how he saw the two of them. And how Izzy did too, he was sure, given the childlike joy she seemed to respond to every new experience with.

Then again, he'd been sure he and his wife were happy. And – as the same friends had often reminded him – look how *that* had turned out.

Six rows back, Rachel leant down and retrieved her handbag from under the seat in front of her, still a little miffed at missing the stunning city views everyone on the right-hand side of the plane had spent the last five minutes oohing and aahing at. It was just her luck to be sitting on the opposite side to where all the good stuff was going on – all she'd been able to see from her window had been the wide blue expanse of the Mediterranean. And while that would normally be something to behold, right now she could do without thinking about the sea – or more specifically, that there were apparently plenty more fish in it. Something she'd been told a little too often for her liking.

Still, at least they'd landed now, and she had something else to think about: her best friend's *wedding*! Livia's excited text last night – that Jed had said yes – meant it was all systems go. Though not for Rachel, sadly. Springing this weekend on Rich, her boyfriend, had turned him into her *ex*-boyfriend. When she'd told him about her plans, he'd told her he didn't like where they were going, and while she'd assumed he meant the city (perhaps, Rachel had initially, naively believed, because he'd never forgiven Barcelona for knocking his beloved Arsenal out of the Champions League), it had turned out he meant with their relationship. She was 'too set in her ways', apparently. 'Not impulsive enough.' Which she found shocking and ironic: shocking that this had come from a man who planned his (and therefore *their*) weekends around the Premier League fixtures list; ironic how it had taken her booking a surprise trip to somewhere they'd never been before for him to decide to tell her that.

Though the real irony was, she'd seen this weekend as a 'save-cation' for the two of them. Things hadn't been great recently, but Rachel had hoped a romantic city break to see two people in love make the ultimate commitment to each other might give their relationship a shot in the arm. Instead, Rich had freaked out, and her shot in the arm had become a bullet in the head.

After the ensuing argument, with Rich's 'it's not me, it's you' ringing in her ears, an angry Rachel had decided she'd show him she *could* be impulsive by coming on her own – and as she'd shed a silent tear or two over the vacant seat where Rich should have been sitting, Rachel had vowed to herself she'd get him back. Though she wasn't sure how yet.

There had been one upside to the space next to her. It had separated her from the thickset, bald, Chelsea-FC-tattooed, fifty-something man sat in her row who'd been trying to make conversation up until the drinks trolley arrived. Then, fortunately, and despite the early hour, he'd been more interested in seeing how many overpriced cans of lager and miniature tubes of crisps he could get through during the two-hour flight (answer: a lot), and though he'd been piling his empties on the seat between them – a seat Rachel had paid for, but she'd been too scared to point that out – at least it had meant she could just stick her earphones in and try to catch up on some sleep. To tell the truth, she'd been struggling to understand his strong Cockney accent: when he'd leant over and said 'Pringle?' she'd thought he'd been using some rhyming slang to enquire about her relationship status, before realising he'd simply been offering her a crisp.

She stared out of the window, pleased to see the sun glinting off the airport building. The hotel where Jed and Livia were getting married had a pool, and thanks to the flattering new bikini she'd ordered from Asos (though that had taken a fair few trials and errors – thank goodness for free returns), a visit to her local spray-tanning salon and a rather painful waxing session, the agony of which had at least taken her mind off the pain of her and Rich's break-up, she wouldn't feel too self-conscious to spend a good part of the weekend lounging around it absorbing some much-needed warmth.

As the plane continued its journey towards the terminal, Rachel pulled her phone out of her handbag and switched it from flight mode – after all, you couldn't be too careful, and the last thing she wanted if they crashed was the black box to have recorded that it had been *her* fault. She stared at the screen, willing a message from Rich to appear, but instead the 'Welcome to Spain' text from her service provider merely informed her she should call 112 in case of emergency, though she suspected not having a date for Livia and Jed's wedding didn't count.

Rachel peered around the plane, careful not to make eye contact with Patrick, or even that woman – no, *girl* – he'd brought with him, desperate to avoid sharing a taxi into town with the two of them pawing at each other. She liked Patrick, as everyone did, but as for – Rachel couldn't remember her name, but surely she was just a phase . . . Patrick's mid-life crisis . . . a reaction to his wife leaving him – no, there was little point investing any time in her. She'd be gone soon. At least, that was what everyone hoped. For Patrick's sake.

The loudspeaker above her head crackled into life and Rachel looked up expectantly. 'Welcome to Barcelona,' said the pilot's disembodied voice, 'where the temperature's an extremely pleasant twenty-two degrees. We're just taxiing to our stand now, so please keep your seatbelts securely fastened until we've come to a complete stop.'

Rachel looked furtively to her right. Her row-mate had already unbuckled, and she tutted to herself disapprovingly. Why couldn't people do what they were told? Rules existed for a reason. What if the plane suddenly lurched, and a suitcase – or even worse, *he* – fell on her?

Then, as if making some momentous decision, she took a deep breath, reached down and surreptitiously undid her own seatbelt, her breath quickening at the thrill, then she caught herself. If *this* was what she found exciting then Rich had been right. It *was* her. And there was no reason why that couldn't change. Starting right now.

She stood up and reached for the overhead locker, only for the stewardess to hiss a sharp 'Sit down!' in her direction, so Rachel did as she was told, fastening her seatbelt again for good measure. 'Right now' would have to wait another few minutes, at least.

Jed awoke with a start, his first thought that yesterday's proposal had simply been a bad dream, though when he swivelled his head to the right, the smile on a still-sleeping Livia's face told him otherwise.

He watched her for a moment, struck by how beautiful she looked, even though the mouthguard she wore to prevent her from grinding her teeth gave her the air of an out-cold boxer. Jed had loved Livia since the first moment he'd seen her, though at the same time, he'd always been mystified as to why someone like her would be interested in someone like him. Had feared it would only be a matter of time before she saw through him, realised he wasn't good enough for her and he'd be out on his ear. And while somehow he'd managed to survive a decade in the role of boyfriend, he couldn't help but worry the promotion to 'husband' was way above his pay grade.

Careful not to wake her, Jed wrestled his way out from under the sheets, silently cursing the bed's super-tight tucking-in at the corners. He often wondered why hotels insisted on doing this – it always made him feel like those mental patients you saw in films being strapped down for their own safety, or a prisoner restrained while waiting for their lethal injection. Perhaps the latter was an appropriate image, as given what was going to be happening later today and the way he was feeling right now – particularly with the hangover he was currently nursing – he could do with being put out of his misery. That was something else he didn't dare admit to Livia, especially after the 'skinful' he'd had last night, as she'd pointedly described it when he'd eventually rolled into bed. Then again, as he'd tried to tell her, given her condition he'd been drinking for two, an excuse that hadn't done him any favours, and it was only afterwards he'd realised that 'celebrating' might have been a more appropriate description. And rather more appreciated.

Gingerly, he hauled himself upright, and watched his fiancée for a moment, making sure he hadn't disturbed her. It had used to be that she could sleep for England, and her napping abilities had been phenomenal – in the car with the roof down, on the Tube with her head on his shoulder, even once on a ski lift during the five-minute, windswept, icy-cold ride it had taken to get to the top of the mountain – but since she'd fallen pregnant, he'd often woken up in the middle of the night to find her wide awake and staring at him, something he'd begun to find disconcerting. And while Jed liked a lie-in – a thing he suspected would be a distant memory after the baby arrived – why he was awake so early this morning was beyond him. Usually he needed the sound of the alarm. Something to jolt him out of his slumber. A bit like Livia's proposal had done yesterday.

He shuddered at the memory. It had been the biggest shock he'd had in a long time. Apart from coming home six months ago, when he'd been met by an anxious-looking Livia in the hallway, and his 'How are you?' had produced a one-word reply: 'Pregnant.' Though that had been something he'd actually felt like celebrating – once he'd got his head around it, which, admittedly, had taken a while. He was still trying to, if he was honest. Which was another reason why yesterday had thrown him.

Silently, he unplugged his phone from where it had been charging on the bedside table, tiptoed to the bathroom, softly closed the door behind him and checked his messages. He contemplated texting Patrick and Liam, and had even typed out the *H, E* and *L* of 'help', before he decided against it. They'd be making their way to the hotel right about now, and the last thing he wanted was for either of them – Liam, probably – to show Livia *that*. Besides, from what he could work out, they'd both been in on her plan, and he wasn't sure he'd forgiven them for that yet. Or – where his brother was concerned – that he ever would.

In any case, right now Jed was worried he was somewhat beyond help. He was already committed to her – surely she knew that? They were having a *baby*. But how on earth could he possibly explain to Livia how he was feeling, what he feared about marriage, without risking this weekend – and everything else – coming tumbling down around him?

With a sigh, Jed stared at his reflection in the mirror above the sink, shocked at the tired-looking, hungover person he saw staring back at him, and tried fixing a smile on his face, hoping that if he at least *looked* happy, it might lift his mood a little. He still didn't know what he was so upset about (though he'd spent a good part of the previous evening staring into his beer trying to work it out) – being blindsided, or the fear that this might be the beginning of the end. *Of course* he loved her – people didn't stay together for ten years, and didn't (or perhaps, shouldn't) have babies, if they weren't in love – but marriage . . . In Jed's experience, that wasn't always a positive step. Besides, it was what every-one did. And Jed had always prided himself that he and Livia wouldn't be the ones doing what everyone did.

His stomach rumbled, but he couldn't really go down to breakfast without Livia. And even if he woke her up now, it'd take her a good half an hour before she could even contemplate facing the outside world, especially today, with their closest friends due to arrive any moment. He could go for a swim, he supposed – the hotel's pool had looked pretty inviting in the brief glance he'd got of it as they'd checked in yesterday – but it was more of a plunge pool than something for serious swimming, and what would be the point, particularly given the plunge he was taking later. Besides, he needed to get rid of his hangover, and a run was the surest way of making that happen.

Making his way quietly back into the bedroom, he found his running shoes in the bottom of the wardrobe, bristling at the sight of the dark grey suit and freshly laundered shirt hanging above them that Livia had packed for today's ceremony without him knowing. He'd been about to complain yesterday, and tell her that she didn't need to dress him, that he might not want to get married in that particular suit, but he'd decided against it. The fact that she hadn't thought to check whether he wanted to get married *full stop* hadn't prevented Livia from proposing, so why on earth would she care how he felt about what he'd be wearing? Besides, they were in Barcelona, not the back of beyond. He could just go out and buy something else if he didn't like what she'd brought, as she'd oh-so-casually informed him in response to his raised eyebrows, though Jed had stopped short of telling her the only reason he owned *that* suit was for any potential funerals.

He checked his watch again, and wondered whether Livia's undoubtedly militarily precise plans for the day meant he even had time for a run. Not that he knew what was going on. Aside from hanging round the hotel this morning to make sure everyone got here okay (though what he could do about it if they didn't was beyond him), then a trip into the centre of town to run some errand that Livia had been very coy about, she hadn't shared any information about their schedule, apart from the fact that everything was on a 'need-to-know' basis, and she had it all arranged. When he'd pressed her, she'd shared brief details about the officiant who was marrying them, the catering (the kitchen was providing a special menu, no doubt at some specially inflated price) and even the post-dinner dancing (the hotel had a DJ every Saturday, apparently, so there'd be no extra charge for that) – but stressed that all *he* needed to know was that everything was kicking off around six, so Jed hadn't dared to ask further. When he thought about it, he was amazed Livia had managed to both find the time to sort this all out *and* be able to keep it from him. Though he didn't really want to think about it. Which was another reason why a run was a good idea.

Retrieving yesterday's T-shirt from the pile of clothes on the chair in the corner, he located his swim shorts in the depths of his suitcase, pulled on his trainers, then rummaged around in Livia's handbag for the map they'd got from tourist information yesterday. *A run along the beach*, thought Jed, studying the glossy, department-store-sponsored fold-out. That was what he needed. As was some rehydration.

The minibar provided him with a complimentary bottle of ice-cold water, which he gulped down most of, though as he replaced it in the fridge door, the clinking of glass against glass stirred Livia awake.

'Morning,' she said, in a tone that immediately made Jed feel as if he was doing something wrong, before fumbling for her watch on the bedside table, then bringing it right up close to her eyes. Livia couldn't see a thing without her contact lenses in, and for once, Jed was grateful, sure she'd immediately read something into his surly expression.

'Morning,' he replied, as breezily as he could, which, when he played it back in his head, wasn't that breezily at all, though he hoped Livia might put his gruffness down to the hangover that she probably knew he had.

'You're up early?'

'Uh-huh,' said Jed, neutrally. He didn't feel like explaining what it was that had jolted him back into consciousness. That wasn't a conversation he wanted to get into just yet. 'Thought I might just go for a quick run.'

'On our *wedding day*?'

She sounded amused – perhaps at the phrase – rather than cross, but even so, Jed felt a sudden flash of irritation, though he knew better than to start an argument right now. A pregnant Livia could be . . . unpredictable. As she'd ably demonstrated yesterday.

'I won't be long.'

'Jed . . .'

'Honestly, love.' He padded over to where she lay, leant down and kissed her on the forehead, then – as if worried she'd even read something into that – kissed her again on the lips. 'Back before you know it.'

'Okay.' Livia peered pointedly at her watch again, as if making a special note of the time, in the way someone might in a massage parlour to tell the therapist they'd be expecting the full hour. 'Try not to get lost.'

'Yes, dear,' he said, with more than a trace of sarcasm, though he quickly followed it up with a smile, and as Livia pulled the duvet up to cover her face, Jed slipped out through the door.

He shook his head as he made his way along the corridor, then forcefully jabbed the lift button, Livia's words ringing in his ears. Right now, the thought of getting lost was actually quite appealing.

Downstairs, Liam was waiting impatiently by the hotel's reception desk. As usual, he'd left it to the last minute to book his flights, and it had turned out to be cheaper for him to fly out on Friday on some airline he'd never heard of (and, to his annoyance, who'd quite plainly never heard of him, given their refusal to give him an upgrade), stay in a budget hotel in the old town, then head across to the venue this morning. And while the prospect of an extra night in Barcelona was something that would fill most people with joy, it hadn't turned out to be much cop. He'd spent yesterday evening on a bar crawl in a futile attempt to find a date for tonight's wedding, and the lack of anyone who recognised him in the four or five places he'd been to (and his lack of Spanish – it was hard to live up to your reputation as a smooth-talker when you only knew the words for 'hello', 'two beers, please' and 'where are the toilets?') had meant he'd drawn a blank on that front.

Still, he supposed, he shouldn't be surprised. He doubted the series of *Big Brother* he'd appeared on, where he'd come second (something he'd been immensely proud of until Jed had – rather unkindly,

Liam thought – pointed out that second place only meant you were the best of the losers), would have been shown here in Spain. Or anywhere else, for that matter – as for the Dutch girls on a hen night he'd tried to chat up . . . well, even though they'd spoken better English than he did, he'd had to tell *them* he was a celebrity. Which kind of defeated the point.

Next, he'd turned to Tinder, but the girl he'd met up with hadn't looked at all like her profile photos, and when Liam had – perhaps being rather ungentlemanly – pointed this out, her suggestion that he buy them both drinks until she did had sent him hurrying (via 'the toilet') for the door.

In the end, he'd given up at around midnight, returned to his room, and (in the hope he might learn a bit more of the language that way) watched *Alien* in Spanish on the tiny television set bolted to the wall above the far end of the bed while working his way through the entire contents of the minibar, which was why he was currently nursing the hangover from hell. To cap it all, he'd checked out of his thin-walled, non-air-conditioned hotel first thing and come to Livia and Jed's much posher venue early to try to sleep last night's excesses off, but the receptionist – an extremely pretty Spanish girl with a name he couldn't pronounce despite repeated attempts (which gave him an excuse for repeated glances at the name badge pinned to her ample chest) – was telling him his room wasn't ready yet.

'Are you sure?'

'I am.'

'Could you look again?' – Liam nodded towards the laptop in front of her, then frowned at her badge – 'Arant, um . . .'

'Arantxa!' said the girl, emphasising the 'sha' part, then unclipping her name tag and brandishing it right in front of his face in a way that suggested Liam had been doing a little bit too much *looking again* for her liking. 'I have checked. Your room is still . . .' She paused for a moment, as if trying to remember the word. 'Dirty.'

'Dirty?' Liam smirked, then thought better of what he'd been about to say. 'Okay. In that case, is there somewhere I can go and' – he fixed her with his best, most winningest smile – 'lie down for a while? Your room, for example? I'm sorry. Did I say that out loud?'

'The pool,' said Arantxa, flatly, and Liam's smile wavered.

'The pool?'

'Through there.' She nodded towards the double doors behind him. 'There are sunbeds by the side. You can wait there until your room is cleaned.'

'How long will that take?'

Arantxa shrugged. 'There is a bar there too, if you want a drink.'

'It's a little early, no?'

'Which is why I cannot check you in yet,' she said. 'They serve coffee. But, if you want, with brandy in it. The dog's hair.'

'What?'

'If you have a hangover,' Arantxa said, in a way that suggested the 'if' was redundant, and Liam opened his mouth to protest, then realised he probably looked the way he felt, and in fact, with the amount he'd drunk last night, he feared they could probably bottle his sweat and make a cocktail with it.

'Coffee with brandy it is, then,' he said, thinking, *What the hell.* After all, it wasn't every day your brother got married, and while the poster advertising 'All-day Breakfasts' in the window of the Irish pub across the street (and showing a picture of the biggest fry-up Liam had ever seen) had caught his eye, he couldn't guarantee he wouldn't bring anything he ate straight back up again, whereas a coffee and brandy might just give him the pick-me-up he needed. 'And it's "hair of the dog",' he said, as if imparting a valuable lesson.

'Hair of the dog,' said the girl, glancing at the telephone that had just started ringing on the desk in front of her, as if it were a lifebelt she'd just been thrown. As she hurriedly moved to answer it, Liam reached down and placed a restraining finger on the handset.

'Will you come and get me when the room's ready?'

'Someone will,' said Arantxa, politely removing his hand, and as she muttered '*Hotel Catalonia, buenos días*' into the receiver, Liam tried not to take it personally that she'd sounded relieved she might not have to have anything more to do with him.

He picked up his luggage and made his way towards the pool, but as he strode away from the desk, he felt a hand on his shoulder. Hoping it might be the receptionist to tell him the call had been to say his room was ready after all, Liam swivelled round, though the smile he'd fixed on his face wasn't exactly mirrored by a scowling Jed.

'You . . .'

'Bro!' He dropped his bag and enveloped his older brother in a huge hug, then let him go again quickly; Jed's arms had stayed by his side. 'Congratulations?' Liam suggested, taking a precautionary step backwards.

'You *knew*?' growled Jed, more of a statement than a question, and Liam held his hands up.

'Liv made me promise. She made *all* of us promise.'

'You could have warned me.'

'*You* could have said no. Then again, you'd have missed out on the chance to have me as your best man.'

'I don't need a best man.'

Liam's face fell. 'Guysmaid, then.'

'That's not even a thing!'

'Which is why I'm your best man.'

Jed had opened his mouth as if to say something, then quickly closed it again, so Liam picked his bag up, put an arm round his brother's shoulders and steered him towards the pool area. 'Come on, bro. Happy days. Remember what you always used to tell me when we were growing up?'

'That I couldn't believe we were related?'

'No! That it takes forty-two muscles to frown, and only seventeen to smile.'

'How many does it take for me to throw you in this pool?'

Liam tightened his grip. 'Hey. Take a chill pill, will you? I think it's fantastic news.'

'How is it *at all* fantastic?'

'Firstly, it's you getting married, rather than me, which means – seeing as there's not a woman alive who I'd let tie *me* down, not unless we were playing some kind of kinky sex game – it's the closest I'm going to get to being where the action is at a wedding. Secondly, like I said, I'm the best man, which means I'm guaranteed a shag this evening with one of Livia's bridesmaids.'

'Livia's not having any bridesmaids. Is she?'

Liam shrugged. 'And . . .' He hesitated, and Jed shook his head.

'Thirdly?'

'Oh. Yeah. Thirdly.'

'Well?'

'It's a great excuse for a party!'

Jed extricated himself from underneath Liam's arm. 'Since when have you ever needed an excuse for a party?'

'True.' Liam grinned, then he punched Jed lightly on the shoulder. 'It's at this point I'd normally say something like "Cheer up, it might never happen", but it *is* happening. And in less than . . .' He glanced at his watch, then frowned. His head still felt very fuzzy, which was making the maths a little hard right now.

'Ten hours,' said Jed, desperately, and Liam caught himself. His brother was sounding anxious, and though he couldn't put his finger on why, Liam feared it was more than just pre-wedding jitters.

'What's your problem?'

'*Marriage*, Liam.'

'Huh?'

'Hello?' Jed reached across and rapped Liam on the forehead with his knuckles. 'Our dad?'

'Yeah, but you're nothing like him.'

'I've got his DNA, though, don't I?'

'Relax. It'll be fine. A walk in the park.'

Jed was staring at him, the expression on his face suggesting it'd be more like a walk in Jurassic Park. 'Not everyone has your blind confidence that you can just march into any situation and, you know, *do it.*'

Liam sniggered, then he remembered Jed was being serious. 'Trust me.'

'How can you be so sure?'

'You and Liv are as good as married anyway.'

'Evidently not, as far as she's concerned, otherwise she wouldn't have felt the need to pull this little stunt . . .' Jed glared at him. Liam's smile was widening. 'It's *not funny*, Liam.'

'It is. A bit. Isn't it?'

Jed stared at him for a moment, and shook his head. 'I'm happy you're finding this all so amusing,' he said, then he spun round on his heel and marched out through the hotel's front door.

Liam smiled to himself as he watched Jed go. Though as he slung his bag over his shoulder and headed through the double doors that led to the pool, it occurred to him that his brother hadn't actually looked happy at all.

Livia was contemplating another half an hour in bed when her phone bleeped: Rachel, texting to say her bus was just leaving the airport – so she messaged her back with a simple *C U at breakfast*, then hauled herself upright. Jed wasn't back from his run yet, so she supposed she could wait for him, but like she'd told him earlier, this *was* their wedding day, and she wanted to make the most of it. Besides, she had things to do.

And – thanks to a certain miniature someone jumping up and down on her bladder – she was desperate to pee.

She did what she had to in the bathroom, then opened the blinds and peered out of the window, squinting at the morning brightness. The sky was cloudless, and already a deep blue – another hot one, Livia suspected, so she pulled on her shorts and forced a T-shirt down over her stomach, admiring her trim legs in the mirror. When she'd joined the gym a year ago, Jed had teased her it wouldn't last, but she'd kept going regularly, even after she fell pregnant – though she hated that phrase. 'Fell' suggested it had been accidental, and – unlike today, perhaps – both she and Jed had gone into this with their eyes open.

She considered putting make-up on, but she'd be getting dressed and made up properly later for the ceremony, and given how her condition was beginning to make every activity an effort, the last thing she wanted to do was go through that twice. It was bad enough that she felt the size of a hot-air balloon, although from the front, she could just about pass off as normal, if she covered her bulge (having realistically passed the 'baby bump' stage a month or so ago) with something. Like Jed, for example.

Her stomach rumbled, and she realised she was starving; last night's meal had been fine, but that was the problem with tapas – lots of small portions, rather than one big satisfying plate. The *patatas bravas* had been particularly spicy, and Livia could still smell the garlic on her breath, but at least she didn't have a hangover. One of the advantages of her condition – if you couldn't drink, you couldn't feel lousy the next morning . . . though in her early stages, the morning sickness had been a cruel substitute. Mind you, by the look of him earlier, Jed had more than made up for her abstinence. Although she supposed she owed him that.

She smiled to herself, though she still felt a little guilty for duping him into today's events. But being pregnant was a good excuse to behave . . . well, if not badly, impetuously, perhaps. Livia had been worried everything had been about the baby of late, so she'd hoped surprising Jed with this might make things more about *them*, again.

Mark the ten-year anniversary of them meeting with a real milestone. Remind him how much she loved him. And help them to remember that they used to love being spontaneous, had taken such pride in being impulsive. Before their lives *really* changed.

Still, he'd be fine with everything once it was all over – Livia was confident about that. Jed was one of those people who often needed a helping hand, a little direction, a polite 'shove' to get him moving. When they'd first set eyes on each other, in that bar here in the backstreets of the Gothic Quarter, she'd had to flirt her backside off to get him to come over and buy her a drink. Livia had even ended up dancing on the table to try to attract his attention. Though yesterday hadn't felt as risky as dancing on that table had back then. This time, she'd been confident Jed was a sure thing.

He'd been the same when she'd suggested they move in together, and then where the baby was concerned, initially responding to her suggestion they think about starting a family with a plaintive 'We are a family, Liv. You and me,' then eventually agreeing that he *did* want kids, and that if not actually trying for a baby, they'd at least stop trying *not* to have one. And when she'd announced she was pregnant, once he'd got over the initial shock (and admittedly, that had taken a while), Jed had been so happy. Excited. Perhaps even more enthusiastic than *she* was, when the enormity of what was happening had hit her. Livia was sure he'd be the same with getting married. And while a part of her might have wished he had already done the decent thing by getting down on one knee without her having to ask, in typical Livia-and-Jed fashion, it had been up to her to instigate things.

Hurriedly, she smoothed on a bit of lipstick – she had *some* standards, after all – then collected her room key and made her way downstairs, mouthing a cheery *hola* at the older Spanish ladies who'd just got into the lift with her, and whose faces had lit up when they'd spotted her distended stomach. Livia *loved* Barcelona – the people, the climate, the food – and she knew Jed felt the same way, which was why it had been the perfect set-up: coming back to the place they'd first met, a city they both adored, on their tenth anniversary, with her six months pregnant . . . and then, when she'd dropped the bombshell – how the others already knew, and were flying out to celebrate the day with them . . . As Jed had said yesterday, how could he possibly have said no? Even though, for just a moment, when she'd seen the look that had flashed across his face, that was exactly what she'd feared he was going to do.

And doing it this way was perfect – a throwback to the days when they used to surprise each other with trips to mystery destinations, wild days out or unexpected presents. And though that last one had backfired recently, when Livia had presented Jed with a watch that had cost more than his car and he'd made her take it back, there was no way he was going to think a small affair like *this* was too ostentatious.

Besides, Livia had never been a girly girl. Not the type to dream of a big wedding, dressed in some meringue-creation of a dress, hordes of annoying nieces and nephews running riot around some draughty old church while she and Jed said their vows in front of a congregation of relatives they hardly knew and a God neither of them believed in, before an orgy of eating and drinking they'd have to foot the bill for. No, this way was much better: just the two of them, and their three closest friends and their partners (though that term was usually rather fleeting where Liam was concerned), a brief ceremony where they'd exchange a few, meaningful words and the rings she and Jed would be picking up later (Livia had already ordered those from a shop here in Barcelona, not wanting to risk Jed spotting them in her luggage), then dinner, a bit of a dance . . . It would be perfect. Back in England, they could do the legal stuff, then hold a party for everyone else. Assuming everyone else was speaking to them after being, as Liam would say, NFI – Not Fucking Invited.

The lift doors pinged open, and her fellow occupants stood back to let her go first, so Livia nodded her thanks and waddled through the ground-floor reception. The hotel was beautiful – an old townhouse (they called them 'palaces' here, and given the grand sweep of the stairs, the ornamental fountain in front of the desk and the loftiness of the reception area, she could see why) in the Gothic Quarter, with a pool out on the terrace where they could relax for the day (and next to which they'd be holding the ceremony later). Breakfast, a discreet sign at reception informed her, was in the courtyard restaurant, and as Livia pushed her way through the heavy glass doors, the waiter rushed over to help her.

'Table for two?' he said, glancing at her stomach, his English as perfect as everyone else's in this most cosmopolitan of cities.

'Not just yet. I hope!'

He beamed at her, then led the way to a table in the corner, and Livia couldn't keep the smile from her face. She loved the way the Spanish evidently adored children – from the moment they'd arrived, she'd been treated almost like royalty by everyone she'd met simply for being pregnant. To his credit, Jed had been the same, so excited when he'd realised what it meant, and not just that she was always the designated driver whenever they went out for the evening. When the baby came – and it wouldn't be long now, Livia realised nervously – he'd melt. She just hoped that she would too.

The waiter pulled the chair out for her, then offered her his hand to help her sit, and Livia took it gratefully. 'Breakfast is a buffet,' he said, indicating a long table against the far wall of the courtyard, which was piled high with plates of cold meat, cheese and fruit, and baskets of pastries in front of a selection of heated silver trays. 'You can have everything you want.'

'*Gracias*,' said Livia, resting a hand on her belly. Finally, she was beginning to believe that.

Chapter 2

'*Hola!*' said Liam, louder than perhaps strictly necessary, and, startled, the woman briefly glanced round at him before turning her attention back to her Kindle – an invitation, in Liam's mind, so he quickly jumped onto the next-door bar stool. This was the problem with e-readers: you couldn't tell what someone was reading, or – more importantly in this case – what language they were reading in, but sitting with one on your own suggested a lack of a partner, so it was definitely worth a shot.

'Do you speak English?' he asked.

With a sigh, the woman adjusted her sunglasses. She was gorgeous, Liam thought – flowing auburn hair, olive skin and the kind of figure that he was sure got her a lot of attention, something she probably welcomed, given the low-cut, curve-enhancing dress she'd somehow managed to pour herself into. First the receptionist, now *this* beauty – Barcelona was going to become a regular trip for him, if all the women looked like this.

'No,' she said firmly, finally, without even turning round, and for the second time this morning, Liam's confidence took a kick right where it hurt.

'Ah. Right. Sorry to have disturbed you.' He made a show of clambering dejectedly down off his stool, then he hesitated, one foot on the floor. 'Hold on. If you don't speak English, then how did you know to say no when I asked you if you did?'

The woman sighed again, louder this time, and when Liam showed no sign of going anywhere, slowly shook her head. 'What makes you think I was answering your question?'

'Huh?'

'Or at least, that one.' She reluctantly put her Kindle down on the bar, then removed her sunglasses, revealing her deep brown eyes. Which, Liam noticed, were narrowed at him.

He made his best confused face. 'I'm sorry. I don't . . .'

'You were trying to start a conversation, I think?' she continued, her voice an exotic purr. 'No doubt leading up to asking me if you could buy me a drink? Perhaps get to know me better? Maybe even hoping we could go back to your room?'

'Well, I . . .' Liam thought about protesting, but the only grounds he'd have for that would be the fact he didn't, as yet, *have* a room.

'Whichever one, the answer would have still been no.' The woman swivelled round to face him. 'I was just saving us both some time,' she said, slipping elegantly down from her stool.

'But . . .'

'What now? Were you about to tell me you were sorry you disturbed me?'

Liam nodded. He *was* sorry. Though not perhaps for the reason the woman might think.

'Well, so am I,' she said, picking her Kindle up before stalking off towards a sunbed in the corner.

As he watched her walk away past the pool, Liam found his sunglasses in his shirt pocket and slipped them on, using the movement as an excuse to subtly check his breath in his cupped hand, then – slightly less subtly – sniff at his armpits. *Oh well*, he told himself, *maybe she's gay*. Or married – though that wasn't necessarily a problem where Liam was concerned. He'd dated all kinds of women – perhaps 'dated' wasn't quite the right word – and it never ceased to amaze him how little the marriage vows meant to some of them, particularly when they realised he was *famous*. And while recently, perhaps, his standards had been slipping a little, Liam put that down to a lack of availability, rather than anything that was his fault. After all, he was getting older, and so was his 'audience'.

He caught sight of his reflection in the mirror behind the bar, still liking what he saw. He and Jed had been blessed genetically, he knew. And while Jed had perhaps let himself go a little since he'd been with Livia – preferring running at some ungodly hour before work (usually around when Liam was coming home from a night out) to sculpting the perfect six-pack in the gym, and paying less attention to what he wore (though he had Livia to do that for him now) – Liam still took pride in his appearance. Worked hard. And worked it hard too. Though that had become a little more difficult since he'd hit his late twenties. And since people seemed to be forgetting who he was.

Or perhaps not. A couple of women – English, he'd guess, given how pink they'd both gone, and yet they were still sitting right in the morning glare of the hot Spanish sun – were perched on stools a few seats away from him, behind the kind of cocktails you'd get if you asked a child to design one: garish pink liquid with all sorts of cocktail umbrellas and sparklers, and obscenely shaped pieces of cucumber, sticking out of the glass (though it was more of a bucket, which was possibly a good idea, seeing as that was what you probably needed to be sick into after drinking the thing). One of the women was trying to take an 'arty' photo of him in between their two glasses, and the blonder of the two (though it was a close-run thing) seemed to be trying to attract his attention.

'No photos!' he said loudly, holding a palm up as if shielding himself from the paparazzi, then he grinned. 'Actually, if you want one, you just have to ask nicely and I'll—'

''Scuse me?'

The other girl had swivelled round, and Liam took advantage of his sunglasses to give her a quick once-over. The two of them could be sisters . . . Now *there* was a thought.

'If you wanted a photo, you only had to ask.'

'No, you're all right,' said the girl with the camera, and Liam frowned.

'Huh?'

'I were just trying to get a pic of us drinks, and you were a bit in the way, is all.'

Liam tried hard to keep his smile from flickering, wondering if he'd misunderstood, but it was still English they were speaking – if a very heavily Northern-accented one – and not Spanish.

'Right. Still, *photobomb!*' he added, making a 'ta-da!' face and adding a quick jazz-hands for extra effect.

'That's what we was trying to avoid,' said the other girl.

'Sure. Good one!' Liam hesitated, then pulled off his sunglasses. He'd always thought celebrities who insisted on the cap-and-sunglasses combo when out in public just looked like themselves in a cap and sunglasses, rather than it acting as some impenetrable disguise, but maybe it *did* work. Either way, he didn't want to take any chances. 'Well, that's kind of you. When you're in the public eye, people usually just barge up to you without even asking, stick their phone in your face, and before you know it, you've got a million likes on Instagram . . .'

The woman with the camera nodded non-committally, then she did a double take. 'Hold on. Aren't you . . .' She nudged her friend – or sister. Liam was still holding out hope. 'Sooz. Look. It's that fella.'

Liam put on his usual 'you've got me' expression, though he didn't have to maintain it for long.

'What fella, Debs?'

'The one from the telly.'

'Maybe 'e's that dancer.'

'Anton . . .'

'Dec?'

'That's two people. They're not dancers. And anyway, 'e's not either.'

'Hang on a mo . . .'

Sooz peered at him, more closely this time, so Liam flashed her a smile. 'I know, I know,' he said, resignedly. 'The guy from *Big Brother*.'

Debs shook her head. 'Nope. That's not it.'

Liam stared at her in disbelief, a little intrigued to see where this might go, although the last time he'd done that, someone had confused him with one of those posh twats from *Made in Chelsea*, and Liam had had to spend the rest of the evening (and an awkward hour or two the following morning) putting on his best upper-class accent and pretending that was exactly who he was.

'It is, actually.'

The two women looked at each other, then back at Liam. 'Nah,' said Sooz.

'Maybe 'e's one of them lookalikes?' suggested Debs. 'Like Sal down the caff's boyfriend.'

''E's good, 'e is. It's like 'im and that Justin Bieber were separated at birth.'

'Knows 'e's good-lookin', though.'

'I'd snog 'im.'

'Me too!'

'You did. Last Christmas,' said Sooz. 'Sal were *livid*.' She sighed. 'I miss going to that caff!'

As the two women cackled at each other, Liam contemplated slipping his sunglasses back on and withdrawing gracefully, though given that Sooz was climbing off her stool and making her – rather unsteady, Liam noticed – way towards him, he feared he was too late.

'It is you, innit?' she said, her face so close to his he could smell the alcohol – and whatever foodstuff laced with around a ton of garlic she'd consumed last night – on her breath.

'It is,' he admitted. 'Liam Woodward. From *Big Brother*. I came second.'

'Makes a change from most men,' guffawed Sooz.

'You'd know, you old slapper!' said Debs.

Liam laughed politely. It had been a pretty funny comment, after all. And one he could file away and use in the future, he knew. 'So, like I said, I'm trying to have a weekend away from being a celebrity, so . . .'

'What did 'e say?' Debs had abandoned her stool now, and was staring rather aggressively in his direction, and Liam swallowed hard.

'Sorry, I . . . I just wondered whether you could possibly keep your voice – well, *voices* – down a bit. I'm here for a wedding and I don't want anyone recognising me. Don't want to spoil the bride's big day by being the centre of attention.'

He winked conspiratorially at them, and Sooz narrowed her eyes at him – though one had narrowed somewhat more than the other, giving Liam an idea of just how drunk the women were. Impressive for this time of the morning, thought Liam, though given that they were dressed for a night's clubbing rather than a morning by the pool, he decided they'd probably just got back and were here for a rather overdue nightcap.

'Gotcha!' said Sooz, after a number of seconds that Liam was sure stretched into double figures. 'Say no more. Can I 'ave a pic, tho?'

'Sure,' said Liam, automatically.

'Great! Debs?' Sooz had marched up to stand next to him, and as Liam obligingly put his arm round her, Debs got her camera at the ready, though before he knew what was happening, Sooz had reached up and grabbed his cheeks in her palms, wrestled his face to within an inch of hers, and to his surprise Liam found himself being kissed – rather sloppily, and extremely unpleasantly – on the lips.

'One for the grandkids,' announced Debs, and as Sooz let him go, Liam hoped she hadn't seen him wipe his mouth with the back of his hand.

'Whoa!' he said, holding both palms up, as if trying to stop a rampaging bull. 'Unexpected item in the gagging area!'

'You never said no tongues!' said Sooz, accusingly.

'I never said "tongues" either, to be fair,' protested Liam.

As they studied the photo they'd just taken and erupted into fits of giggles, he climbed down from his stool and – careful to avoid eye contact with the woman he'd attempted to chat up earlier, who appeared to be doing her best not to burst out laughing – made his way along to the far end of the pool. The walkway was narrow, and he wouldn't bet on Sooz and Debs being able to navigate it without falling in, so he suspected he was safe.

He yawned, and looked at his watch. Still most of the day to kill before tonight's main event, and no sign of Jed coming back from his run, though he had a feeling his brother probably needed a bit of time on his own right now. He could perhaps go and disturb Livia, nick some of her breakfast, but Sooz's kiss – on top of his hangover – had made him feel a little nauseous. Plus, Livia would undoubtedly have things to do, which meant she'd probably try to find *him* things to do too, and right now, a nap by the pool was looking more of a sensible idea. Particularly given the way the loungers were beginning to fill up. And who they were beginning to fill up with.

With a smile to no one in particular, Liam peeled off his T-shirt, dragged his sun lounger into a position where he could watch for women (and watch out for Sooz and her friend), laid himself down and promptly fell asleep.

'Stop!'

Patrick almost jumped out of his skin. Despite the fact that 'go as fast as you can' seemed to be what they taught you here on day one at taxi school, he'd been enjoying the familiar scenery on the drive in from the airport, but Izzy had just shouted so suddenly, so loudly, that Patrick feared they must have run someone over.

'What is it?' he said, anxiously bracing himself against the back of the driver's seat as the black-and-yellow cab screeched to a halt.

'Over there.' Izzy was gesticulating excitedly out of the window, so he followed her gaze, half expecting to see some poor crumpled soul writhing in agony on the pavement. 'On the corner.'

'Aha.' Patrick breathed a sigh of relief, and willed his heart to stop hammering. 'Gaudí's masterpiece.'

'What?'

'The building. Casa Milà. Designed by Gaudí and built between 1906 and 1912. More commonly called La Pedrera, which means "the quarry", because some people, perhaps rather unkindly, thought the stone facade looked a bit like a—'

'Not that ugly thing.' Izzy was already unbuckling her seatbelt. 'Over there. It's a Stella McCartney.'

'Hold on. We have to get to the—'

Too late, Patrick realised he was addressing an empty seat: Izzy had already leapt out through the door. With the word 'hotel' dying on his lips, Patrick climbed stiffly out of the cab, handed the driver a bundle of euros, extracted their luggage from the boot and set off in pursuit. He paused briefly to look up at the architectural gem in front of him, then, reluctantly, followed her into the shop.

'Can I help you?'

The black-suit-clad assistant had addressed him in English, and Patrick immediately felt a bit put out. Did he look English? He hoped not. In his experience, the English abroad seemed to be a badly or underdressed bunch with too much fleshy white cleavage on show, and that was just the men. Then again, he supposed, it was probably the international language. Plus, judging by the rest of the shop's clientele, mainly Asian or Arabic in appearance, there were very few Spanish people shopping here.

'My . . .' Patrick hesitated. 'Girlfriend' always sounded so child-ish, 'partner' made her sound like a colleague at the law firm he'd once owned, and he didn't dare risk 'wife' in case Izzy overheard – not that they'd ever talked about it, but his refusal to even consider getting mar-ried again wasn't something he wanted to risk an argument over, espe-cially at someone else's wedding. 'The young woman who came in here a moment ago.'

'Upstairs,' said the man, then he nodded at Patrick's bags. 'You can leave them with me?'

Patrick did as he was told, then made his way up the spiral stair-case to find Izzy frantically rifling through a clothes rail in front of the store's large picture window. He watched her for a moment, her forehead furrowed in concentration in the same way a brain surgeon's might be in the middle of a particularly tricky operation. Shopping was Izzy's 'thing' – both personally *and* professionally. They'd met when he'd been for a personal shopper session in Selfridges – a birthday present from his daughter, perhaps despairing at Patrick's recent purchase of what she'd described as a pair of 'dad jeans' – and while he hadn't liked many of the items Izzy had suggested for him (and still hadn't worked up the nerve to wear the majority of them), sensing the session might indeed get 'personal', he'd bought them anyway. Patrick hadn't wanted to disappoint her, and his credit card had been an easy way to ensure he wouldn't. And he'd taken pretty much the same approach ever since.

He cleared his throat, and she looked up at him momentarily, as if he were disturbing something important. 'See anything you like? And by that, I mean anything better than the three outfits you've brought with you?'

He'd said it with a playful smile, but Izzy gave him a look. 'This,' she said, after a moment, reverentially holding up a scrap of material on a hanger like Indiana Jones might reveal some holy artefact he'd just unearthed. 'It's from the new collection.'

'Right.' Patrick squinted at the dress. Or blouse. Or it might even have been underwear. He wasn't sure. 'And how much is it?'

Izzy shrugged. 'I didn't look.'

Patrick didn't dare. 'Did you want to try it on?'

'You're sure?'

She broke into a grin, and he swallowed hard. Her assumption that getting permission to try it on meant he'd buy it if she wanted it grated a little, but he feared the alternative was for her to pout and sulk all day. And it would be hard enough being at a wedding without that.

'It can't hurt.'

As Izzy scampered off into the changing rooms, he sank into a nearby armchair and checked the time. Livia would be wondering where they were, plus they had to fit in the surprise city tour he'd arranged to show Izzy 'his' Barcelona, and then there was the small matter of lunch – Patrick had the venue (and the menu) all lined up – followed maybe by a bit of pool time. And, knowing Izzy, a bit of 'room' time too.

He glanced round the shop's minimalist interior, and noticed he wasn't alone – to his left, a man around his age wearing a watch encrusted with so much bling Patrick would be surprised if he could raise his arm was doing a bad job of stifling a yawn, while in the chair opposite him, a much older man was glued to his mobile phone as his . . . wife. . . daughter . . . mistress? – Patrick wasn't sure – ran through various poses in front of the enormous mirror that covered one entire wall, snapping a series of selfies on hers.

Not knowing where to look, he glanced at his watch again, feeling a little self-conscious. He'd been too busy working to have a midlife crisis, too focused on work to pay attention to his marriage, apparently, which was probably the reason he was here with Izzy. Trying to convince himself he hadn't 'lost it'. Or perhaps, as he often feared, trying to convince everyone else.

'What do you think?'

Izzy had materialised in front of him, and Patrick had to fight hard to stop his mouth from flapping open. 'Wow. That's . . . I mean, it's very . . .' He swallowed hard. 'There's not a lot to it.' *Especially when you consider how much it costs*, he thought, catching sight of the price tag.

'I know!' said Izzy, as if that was a good thing.

He glanced around the shop. The man on the phone had suddenly perked up, and was doing a bad job of pretending not to look in their direction, whereas the other one was out-and-out staring. And it didn't take Patrick long to realise why.

'Shouldn't you be wearing a bra?'

Izzy shook her head vigorously, causing her breasts to jiggle under the thin layer of material in a perfect demonstration of Newton's third law of motion. 'Then you'd *see* it, silly.'

'As opposed to seeing your, you know . . .' He knew better than to finish the sentence. 'All I'd say is . . .' He hesitated, given the beginnings of a frown on Izzy's face. 'You might just embarrass the bride.'

Izzy gave him a look. 'She's six months pregnant, and she still had to ask her boyfriend to marry her. Don't you think she'll be embarrassed enough already?'

'Sorry. Perhaps "embarrass" was the wrong choice of word.'

'What would the right choice be?'

Patrick pretended to think for a moment, though in truth, he'd known the answer the moment she'd emerged from the changing room. 'Well, seeing as you look amazing, perhaps "upstage" would be more appropriate.'

Izzy leaned down and kissed him, slipping her tongue cheekily into his mouth for the briefest of moments, then, as she turned to the mirror and admired her reflection, Patrick folded his arms and regarded her. The thing was, she *did* look amazing. Wasn't that the point? And so what if the – he decided to go with 'dress' – cost more than their flights had? After all, as Jed had reminded him a while back, if you drove a Porsche, you didn't get it serviced at Kwik Fit. Like the car, Izzy had a maintenance cost too, and Patrick much preferred paying maintenance for something he could still enjoy rather than some*one* – given how much his ex-wife still got from him every month – he couldn't.

As Izzy scampered back into the changing room, he caught the older man's eye. 'If you don't buy it for her, I will,' said the man, with a seedy smile, and while Patrick's first instinct was to punch him in the face, he knew he ought to take it as a compliment.

With a sigh, he hauled himself up out of the chair, reached for his wallet and made his way towards the till.

'Rach!'

At the sound of Livia calling her name, Rachel looked up from where she was hauling her overstuffed wheelie through the hotel's lobby, then squealed in delight, so Livia hurried across and enveloped her friend in a huge hug. It may simply have been due to the early start, but Rachel was looking flustered, her normally impeccably made-up face bare, her hair scraped back into an untidy ponytail, as if she'd been through some sort of drama already this morning. Though as Livia knew all too well, that wouldn't be anything unusual.

'Hey, Liv!'

She let Rachel go, then laughed at the 'oh my god!' face she'd just made.

'What?'

'You're getting *married*!'

'I know!'

'Where's the groom?'

'Gone for a run. Or so he said.' She glanced at her watch, then towards the hotel's front door. 'I'm beginning to think it's more a case of done a runner.'

At the Wedding

'Not Jed.' Rachel smiled. 'And especially given . . .' She nodded at Livia's stomach. 'Not that I'm suggesting you . . . or he . . .'

'I'm joking, Rach.'

'I knew that!' Rachel raised her eyes to the heavens. 'He was happy about it, though?'

'Happy?' Livia thought for a moment. To tell the truth, 'happy' wouldn't have been her first choice of adjective, though Jed had never been the most demonstrative of people. 'I'm going to go with "still getting used to the idea".'

'He said yes, though?'

'He did. In so many words.'

'Well, that's the important thing.'

'It is.' Livia nodded. 'Assuming he says something similar this evening!'

Rachel let out a short laugh, then her smile suddenly faded. 'You're not worried about that, are you? Jed would never . . .'

'No, but . . .' Livia shrugged. *Many a slip 'twixt the cup and the lip.*'

Rachel narrowed her eyes. 'I heard you say something about a Twix but I didn't really . . .'

'You know – it's not over till the fat lady sings.' She grinned. 'Not that I'm planning on singing this evening.'

'Thank goodness!' said Rachel, a little too quickly for Livia's liking. 'Sorry, I didn't mean . . .' She shook her head, then mimed zipping her mouth shut. 'I wouldn't rely on me to make a speech this evening. Anyway, good on you for asking.'

'Maybe it'll give Rich some ideas, eh?' Livia nudged her, then she peered over Rachel's shoulder. 'Where *is* Rich?'

'Let's just say he kind of responded to *my* surprise for this weekend with the opposite reaction to Jed.'

Livia clamped a hand over her open mouth. 'He dumped you?'

'Seems that way.'

43

'Oh, *Rach* . . .' Livia leant across awkwardly and gave her friend another hug. Rachel's life seemed to be a succession of events like this, and what was worse was she could never see them coming. Which was ironic, because everyone else always could. 'Is now an appropriate time for me to tell you we never liked him anyway, and that you're better off without him?'

Rachel stared at her for a moment, then she forced a smile. 'Perhaps not *right* now.'

'You okay, hun?'

Rachel shrugged dismissively, though Livia feared she was on the verge of tears. 'I've been better. But, then again, I've been worse. Besides, today is all about you!' She repeated her earlier 'oh my god!' face, then forced a flat-lipped smile. 'You're getting *married!*'

'Looks that way!'

'So where's the rest of the wedding party?'

'Well, Liam arrived yesterday, though I haven't seen him yet – he's probably trying to sneak out of some poor girl's bedroom without waking her.'

'The rumours about him are true, then?'

'They are. As I'm sure you'll find out when you meet him. Especially when he finds out you're here on your own.' Livia raised both eyebrows like a ventriloquist's dummy might, though Rachel's reaction was hardly the most enthusiastic. 'Patrick . . .' She peered towards the hotel doors. 'I thought he was on your flight?'

'He was.' Rachel shuddered. 'With *her*.'

'Izzy?'

'Is that her name?'

'The *D* at the front is silent, apparently,' Livia said, wryly. 'I thought you might have shared a taxi here?'

'No, thank you!' Rachel gave her a look. 'In fact I, um, hid from them in the check-in queue. And pretended I hadn't seen them when we got off.'

'What on earth for?'

'The less time I spend in the company of fit twenty-something girls, the better. Especially right now.' She stuffed her hands dejectedly into her pockets. 'I'd hoped this was going to be one of those weddings where children were banned.'

'Rach!' scolded Livia, though she laughed, despite herself.

'In any case, the bus was cheaper. If slower.'

'Which is why I'm surprised you're here before them.'

'Maybe they had something to do on the way?'

'Shag, probably. If Patrick's heart can take it.'

'Which is another reason I'm glad we didn't come in the same cab.'

Rachel laughed – genuinely, it seemed – and Livia smiled. She suspected it was the first time her friend had laughed in a few days. 'You all checked in?'

'I am.' Rachel brandished her key card in the air, in the manner of a football referee sending someone off. 'So, what's the plan? For today, I mean.'

A waiter walked past carrying a plate of *jamón*, and Livia eyed it appreciatively. 'Well, when Jed comes back, he and I have to go and pick up the rings, so you've got a few hours if you wanted to go and get in some sightseeing. Kick-off's not until six, and I'm sure the boys will want to take Jed off somewhere for some pre-wedding drinks, so we've got plenty of time for a catch-up round the pool this afternoon . . .'

'Sightseeing?'

'Why not? You're in *Barcelona*, baby!'

'Maybe.'

'No, it's definitely Bar—'

'I know!'

'You've been here before?'

'No, but . . .' For the third – or was it the fourth time? Livia was losing count – Rachel made a face as if her world was coming to an end. 'You know. Sightseeing. On my own.'

45

'It's what the selfie was invented for. Besides, you always complained Rich never wanted to do anything except sit at the bar or watch the football, which meant that was always what *you* ended up doing.'

'I suppose I have always wanted to see more of the world.'

'Rather than just the World Cup? You're a free woman now, Rach. The world's your oyster.'

'Says the woman about to get married. I *miss* him, Liv.'

'Even so. You just get on with your life, enjoy Barcelona, have a lovely weekend without Rich. Meanwhile, he's going to be sitting at home, probably questioning whether he's done the right thing, wondering what you're up to, so he checks your Facebook, looks at your Instagram, and he sees you having a great time, going to all these amazing places, rubbing it in his face . . . If that doesn't send him grovelling to meet you at the airport with a huge bunch of flowers when you get back home, I don't know what will. And then . . .'

'Then?'

'You either have the satisfaction of telling him where to go, or taking him back on *your* terms. Either way, you've still had a fab weekend out and about in Barcelona, rather than simply moping around in your hotel room.'

Rachel stared miserably down at her feet, as if weighing up which suicide method to choose, then she took a deep breath. 'Well, in the absence of anything better to do . . .'

'That's settled then. But first . . .'

'First?'

'I'm seriously considering a second go at the breakfast buffet. If you'd like to join me?'

Rachel glanced over towards the front desk. 'I've just checked in, so I don't think I'm allowed.'

Livia rolled her eyes. 'Rich isn't here. If anyone asks, we'll just tell them you're having his tomorrow's breakfast today.'

Rachel hesitated as she tried to process Livia's reasoning, then she shook her head. 'No, that's fine. I'm not all that hungry, actually.' As if on cue, her stomach rumbled, so loudly a man reading a newspaper nearby looked up at them. 'Then again, it seems that perhaps I *am*, so . . .'

'Excellent!'

Livia hugged her friend a third time, then, before she could change her mind, she took Rachel's wheelie in one hand, grabbed her arm with the other and steered her through to the courtyard.

Jed pounded along the pavement, enjoying the freedom he always felt when running, while appreciating how the amazing Barcelona weather made today's run such a contrast from his usual, grey-skied, chilly-breezed pre-work session. He'd taken a wrong turn on his way back from the beach, and even though he'd lost his bearings more than once, was sweating like he'd just emerged from a sauna *and* was constantly having to dodge around shoppers and through tour groups on what he hoped was his way back to the hotel, he felt like he could just keep on going.

That had occurred to him too. It would be a way to avoid everything wedding-y that was no doubt going on back at the hotel. Right about now, Livia was probably holding court, drilling Rachel in her responsibilities, forbidding Liam to get too drunk (and good luck with *that*), while possibly instructing Patrick in the exact speed she wanted to be walked down the aisle later, and God only knew what she'd be asking *him* to do. But Jed knew he'd have to go back eventually. And he was already worried Livia would be wondering where he was.

As he ran along by the kerb – a tactic he'd worked out to avoid being knocked over by the surprising number of older-than-usual skate-boarders treating the pavements as a skate park – a taxi slowed to match his pace, and he was just debating whether to give the driver the finger or to flag it down when a familiar voice boomed out of the window.

'Fancy a lift?'

Jed turned to see Patrick waving at him. 'Only if you're heading to the airport!'

'That can be arranged!'

The taxi had stopped, so Jed did the same, and slumped against the side of the car. 'Bloody hot,' he puffed, then he wiped his palms on his shorts and squinted up at the sky. 'I'd shake your hand, but I'm sweating like the proverbial—'

'From the run, I take it, and not your anxiety about what's happening later?'

'What's happening later?' deadpanned Jed, enjoying the momentary look of panic that had just appeared on Patrick's face.

'You bastard!'

'Look who's talking!'

'Fair point.' Patrick shook his head slowly. 'I'm not sure whether "congratulations" is appropriate, rather than "sorry" . . .'

'For not telling me, you mean, rather than the fact that I'm, you know . . .' Jed stopped talking, not sure he could bring himself to say the words yet. 'Yes, well, Liv can be . . .'

'Persuasive?'

'She can. And was.'

'So it *is* congratulations?'

Jed made a face. 'I'll let you know.' He mopped the sweat from his forehead with his sleeve, then peered into the back of the cab. The girl he'd just noticed, sitting there half-hidden behind a large Stella McCartney shopping bag, was stunning. And very young. 'And you must be Izzy!' he said. 'Sorry – didn't see you there.'

'Hi.' Izzy was looking him up and down, and Jed had to resist the temptation to suck his stomach in. 'Well, *I* think it's congratulations,' she added, staring pointedly at Patrick, who just rolled his eyes.

Jed grinned again, then glanced at his watch. 'Shouldn't you be at the hotel by now?'

'Shouldn't *you?*'

'No, I mean, I thought Livia was expecting everyone . . . earlier.'

'Sorry.' Patrick jabbed a thumb at Izzy's shopping bag. Or it could have been at Izzy – Jed wasn't sure. 'We made a little detour.'

'Hey, I'm just glad you're here. I could do with a bit of moral support. Though the amount I'm planning to drink this evening, I might need a bit of *actual* support.'

'No worries. Wouldn't have missed it for the world.' Patrick swung the taxi's door open. 'Hop in.'

'Best not.' Jed indicated his sweatiness. 'Besides, it's not far,' he said, pleased he finally recognised the street opposite as the one that led to his hotel. 'I think.'

'Suit yourself. How's Livia?'

'Feeling very pleased with herself, I think.'

'She's a woman who knows what she wants.'

'Isn't she?' said Jed. It was one of the things he found so attractive about her. Though recently, Livia seemed to think she knew what *he* wanted too, and he wasn't quite sure how he felt about that.

'And smart move on her part,' continued Patrick, pulling the door shut again. 'Doing this here.'

'Why's that?'

'Look above you.' Patrick shielded his eyes with his hand as he peered up at the clear blue sky. 'The sun is shining, and it's twenty-five degrees.'

'What's that got to do with anything?'

Patrick gave him a look, then indicated for the driver to head off. 'Means you won't get cold feet,' he called, cheerfully waving a hand out of the window as the cab picked up speed.

Jed waved a less-friendly greeting back, then – despite the heat – set off quickly after them. Being here, where the sun always seemed to be shining, made him feel alive – though that wasn't a view shared by his heavily pregnant girlfriend . . . sorry, *fiancée*. Livia had been struggling with the heat almost as soon as they'd stepped off the plane. She'd been struggling with a lot of things – despite the picturesque scenes round every corner, and the weather here in the city, his hopes for one final pre-baby romantic anniversary weekend hadn't seemed to be doing him any favours: an offer to take her on a cycle rickshaw tour of the city had been scuppered less than five minutes into the trip, when head-ing down a particularly bumpy cobbled street had necessitated a swift U-turn followed by a breakneck pedal back to the hotel to find a toilet; a suggestion they spend yesterday afternoon relaxing on the beach was pooh-pooed by Livia's comment that she didn't want some small child to think she was one of the inflatable toys; his idea that they should just hang the 'Do Not Disturb' sign on the door, order room service, turn the air conditioning up and spend an intimate evening together in their hotel room had elicited the observation that she'd booked din-ner 'somewhere nice', followed by a pointed glance at her belly and an amused 'Besides, if you think I'm ever letting you near me again . . .' Though it was only when she'd dropped the bombshell at the restaurant yesterday evening that Jed knew why she'd been so keen the weekend went according to *her* plans.

The worst bit was, Jed hadn't known how to respond. He'd thought he and Livia had an understanding. But she'd cornered him, put him on the spot, and in the end, he'd said the only thing he could have said, then put a face on and finished his dinner as if being proposed to was an everyday occurrence, when he should have simply told her how he felt. And he was regretting not doing that now.

They'd ordered cava – well, for him, and a sparkling water for her – and had toasted the 'good' news, then Livia had needed a lie-down, so he'd left her in the room with a curt 'Just going for a walk', and had in fact only walked as far as the hotel's bar for an ice-cold glass of *cerveza* or six (which hadn't done him any favours, either when he'd arrived back at the room a couple of hours later, or this morning). And when he'd protested that sitting on his own at a hotel bar hadn't been much of a stag night, Livia had teased him that for someone who'd seemed quite happy to never get married, Jed should think himself lucky to have had *that*. Besides, she'd told him, he could celebrate properly tomorrow, with his brother and their friends, after they'd made their vows. He'd bitten off his response to that.

He slowed down, wary of bumping into any oncoming tour groups, and jogged round the corner. The hotel was up ahead, where Livia was no doubt simultaneously wondering where he was while demolishing the breakfast buffet, but instead of hurrying inside to meet her, he found himself continuing on past and into the Gótico's main square. He *could* sneak up to his room, grab his passport, hightail it to the airport – right now, that felt like a much easier option than just sitting down and opening up to her. But running out on Livia would mean running out on their unborn child . . . His heart swelled with pride at the thought he was going to be a dad soon. Why couldn't he find it in himself to feel the same way about Livia's proposal?

He double-checked his watch against the clock on the front of the town hall and forced himself to stop running. In a few hours, he'd be *married*. In a few months, he'd be a father. Either of those things was scary enough on its own, but thinking about them both . . . Jed was all for new beginnings, but why did he suddenly feel his life as he knew it was coming to an end instead?

As he performed a few perfunctory stretches against the wall of the building, an uneasy feeling began spreading through his stomach. Perhaps it was last night's spicy *patatas bravas* coming back to haunt him, more likely it was nerves, but either way, Jed decided the best thing to do was to try to walk it off. Once more round the block, at least. He'd cool down, calm down, then he'd head back to the hotel, take Livia to one side, and tell . . . no, *explain* to her why this was all such a bad idea. Maybe she'd understand. Get that this wasn't something he'd be good at. Marriage was . . . well, if you had a history of alcoholism in your family, and someone was forcing you to work behind a bar, you'd be nervous. Convinced you'd do a bad job. Sure you'd fail. Wouldn't you?

With a last, guilty glance at the time, he took a deep breath, then set off past the hotel and back in the direction he'd come from.

Rachel rode the elevator up to her floor, smiling neutrally at the male hotel employee standing uncomfortably close to her in the cramped lift who'd insisted on helping her with her luggage, despite it simply being a wheelie, and one that she'd managed to transport here all the way from England on her own. Surely the final fifty or so metres were the least of her worries, and especially since the lift was doing all the work?

At first she'd been flattered when a tall, not-bad-looking man dressed head to toe in black had rushed to hold the lift doors open, then taken her case from her, even asking for her number in a rather sexy Spanish accent. Then she'd noticed several other people milling round reception dressed in similar outfits, so she'd asked her companion whether he was here for a funeral *at the precise moment* she'd spotted his nametag and realised they – and therefore he – worked here, and that it was her *room* number he'd been after, simply so he could show her to it. Still, she conceded, despite her mortification, in the absence of Rich to carry her bag it was nice to see someone being the gentleman, even if they were only doing it through professional obligation.

Obediently, she trailed after the man along the corridor to her room, relieved to find it wasn't right by the lift – being woken during the night by the sound of other people coming back from having a good time was the last thing she wanted.

'*Aquí*,' he announced, producing a key card from his pocket with a flourish.

'I can see that,' said Rachel, sniffily. 'And they already gave me one at reception, so . . .'

'No – *aquí*. Here.'

Rachel held up her own key card. 'And here. A key. I already—'

'You don't understand. *Aquí*. It's Spanish. For "here".'

'I knew that,' said Rachel quickly, awkwardly trying to recover some composure, even though she didn't actually speak a word of Spanish. 'So, thanks, but I'm fine, if you could just . . .'

She made to push past him, but the man was too quick for her. 'I show you your room,' he insisted, clicking the lock open and leading her inside.

He hoisted her case onto the luggage stand at the end of her bed, wincing slightly at the weight, then strode across to the other side of the room, turned round and looked at her earnestly, as if about to divulge some great secret. 'The bathroom,' he said, opening a door which Rachel would probably have guessed led there anyway, before marching in and briefly turning on the taps on the various fittings as if to prove they weren't an optical illusion. 'The shower, the bath, and . . .' He cleared his throat, as a tour guide might before pointing out the *Mona Lisa*. 'The toilet.'

'Got it,' said Rachel, grateful for the lack of a demonstration, not knowing what the appropriate response to him pointing out the bleeding obvious might be.

The man beamed at her, then strode back into the room, picked up the TV remote control and pointed it towards the set hanging on the far wall. 'The television,' he said, as some inane-looking Spanish gameshow appeared on the screen.

'Really?'

The man nodded – obviously her sarcasm had been lost in translation – clicked the set off again, and peered around the room as if looking for any more hotel 'mysteries' he might be able to shed light on. Rachel folded her arms. She'd been in a hotel before. Most people had. And in any case, even if you hadn't, it wouldn't be that difficult to work out what was what.

'Aha!' said the man, as if he'd just remembered the most important thing of all, and Rachel sighed to herself. Why wouldn't he leave?

'Aha?'

'The air conditioning!' He picked up another remote from beside the bed and aimed it at a unit above the door, which sent an icy blast in Rachel's direction.

'And where exactly do I sleep?' she said, giving the man a look that she hoped matched the air temperature.

The man pointed at the bed, then pulled his hand back as if he'd accidently stuck it into a fire. 'I think you are having a laugh, yes?'

Rachel shrugged. 'Well, one of us is,' she said, moving across to the door and opening it, though instead of leaving, the man simply stood in front of her, his hand out at waist height, palm upwards, as if waiting for a low five.

Rachel rolled her eyes. He may have been expecting a tip, but she was damned if she was going to pay him to leave. 'I don't have any change,' she said after an awkward moment, though his 'I do' in response threw her a little.

'Thank you,' she said, as cheerily as she could muster, then she disappeared into the bathroom, waiting until she heard the shutting of her door – though it was more of a slam – before coming back out again. Rich could be like that, she reminded herself – expecting a medal for simply putting a cup away, or washing up a teaspoon, not that she'd had many occasions to award him one. But whenever she'd tried to take him to task about it, he'd just flash her that mischievous smile of his, say something charming and she'd turn to putty in his hands.

Men! she thought, exasperatedly. She'd be better off without them all. Maybe she would get that cat and . . . Rachel puffed air out of her cheeks, not liking the mental picture of her life-to-be that plan painted. She sniffed hard, then unzipped her wheelie and peered at the wardrobe, debating whether to unpack, even though she was only here for the one night, and only had the one wedding outfit with her (well, two – a girl always needed a spare, just in case of any last-minute accidents, or clashes with other guests. Though given how this was possibly the smallest wedding she'd ever been to, that was unlikely).

She collapsed onto the bed and stretched her arms out, instantly regretting booking a 'king deluxe' – all that extra space just seemed to rub her nose in the fact that she was here alone – and tried to stop herself from bursting into tears. Not at the room – it was beautiful, with the comfiest bed she'd ever lain on, but the views of Barcelona's gothic streets from her balcony were so stunning she immediately wished she had someone here to share them with. And later, after the wedding, when it was supposed to be the eight of them on the top table . . . Well, now it was just the seven: Jed and Livia, Liam and whoever it was he'd brought, Patrick and his 'child bride', and her, with (for the second time today) an empty seat next to her. But the alternative had been to not come, and to let her oldest friend down. And Rachel would never do that.

She pulled out her phone and checked the screen. No text messages apart from Livia earlier, and nothing from Rich, though she supposed she shouldn't be surprised. They'd hardly parted on the best of terms, and besides, he'd rarely messaged her when they'd been together, apart from the odd 'running late' message (which usually meant the match he'd been watching was). Had hardly ever called. Though some people were just like that, she knew. Weren't the romantic type. Rich had been more . . . macho. Old-fashioned. Her 'bit of rough' (as he'd liked to describe himself) – into football, and going to the pub, and . . . just those two things really.

In truth, she'd seen him as a bit of a project. Thought he'd had potential. But he'd turned out to be a little too 'rough' for things to go as smoothly as Rachel had wanted, which was possibly why her plans to make everything right between them here in Barcelona had ended up having the opposite effect.

With a sigh, she hauled herself upright, found the information card on the bedside table, logged onto the hotel's Wi-Fi and checked her emails, but there was nothing from him there either. Perhaps the Rich chapter of her life *was* over.

She strode to her balcony, and peered down at the couples seated at the various tables in front of the café opposite, then caught sight of Patrick getting out of a taxi and waved. Patrick gave her a cheery smile, whereas Izzy – or Dizzy, as Rachel would forever think of her, thanks to Livia's comment – responded with a suspicious glance. Rachel thought about heading downstairs to say hello, but she'd just have to run the awkward gauntlet of more 'where's Rich?' questions, and quite frankly she could do without that. No, she decided, the best thing would be to head out into the city. See Barcelona, and without Rich constantly demanding they stop for a beer, or complaining that the museums were boring, all the time with one eye on his watch, anxious not to miss kick-off. Besides, she reminded herself, absence was supposed to make the heart grow fonder. So maybe she would take Livia's advice, post as many photos as she could of her having a good time – or at least, pretending to – without him, and then . . . he'd be putty in her hands when she got back.

She hoped.

And if not? Maybe the single life wouldn't be too bad. At least if you had no one there to constantly disappoint you – well, you wouldn't feel constantly disappointed, would you? Besides, meeting someone new was exhausting, and right now, Rachel wasn't sure she had the energy to go through it all again. In any case, this was . . . whatever the decade after the noughties was called. Life was different now. Lots of people lived on their own. Had babies on their own. A friend of hers at work had done it – and finding a suitable donor had seemed like less hassle (and been cheaper!) than when Rachel had bought her new iPhone.

Besides, she had to face facts: most of the other men she knew – Jed and Patrick aside – were like little boys. Maybe Patrick was too, seeing as he was dating a little girl. And even Jed – someone Rachel thought was probably as good as it gets where men were concerned – still hadn't been mature enough to get down on one knee in front of Livia, despite that being what Livia quite plainly wanted *and* she was pregnant.

Though if Livia could take matters into her own hands – and didn't care who knew it – then surely Rachel could do what she liked. Live how she wanted. Have a baby if she decided to (though she would probably start with a cat. It made more sense). And all of that would begin with her embracing the single life while she was here.

So she'd quickly unpack, put on some make-up, change into her comfortable shoes and spend the next few hours happily taking in whatever Barcelona had to offer, followed by a late lunch in a restaurant of her choice rather than Rich insisting they found a pub where the football would be on, back here for a relax round the pool, then she'd change into her evening's finery and watch – no, *help* – her best friend get married. All in all, that sounded like a pretty good plan.

With a newfound resolve, she stepped back into the room, shut the balcony doors behind her, hung her dress(es) carefully in the wardrobe and got herself ready to face the world, determined not to waste another second. This was *Barcelona*. Exotic, trendy, hip, beautiful, romantic *and* the sun was shining . . . How could she not have a good time?

A leaflet on the desk beneath the TV was advertising 'Hop on, hop off' bus tours, and Rachel scanned through it, deciding this would be *perfect*. With a last quick check of her reflection in the mirror, she grabbed her sunglasses, slipped her copy of *Lonely Planet Barcelona* into her bag, hurried back downstairs and out into the street, and made her way excitedly towards the bus stop.

Chapter 3

'You made it!' squealed Livia, embracing Patrick tightly.

'Wouldn't have missed it for the world,' he said, then he stood back, took her by the shoulders and looked her up and down. 'You look . . .'

'Huge?'

'Well, yes, there's that, obviously. Though "radiant" was the word I was originally gunning for.' Patrick smiled affectionately. 'We ran into the blushing groom in the taxi.'

'Not literally, I hope?' Livia grinned at him. 'He was heading back, yeah?'

Patrick laughed. 'Why wouldn't he?'

'No reason,' she said, doing her best not to sound guilty but – judging by Patrick's expression – failing miserably.

'Hey – good on you for asking.'

Livia shrugged. 'Don't ask, don't get! I think you taught me that.'

'Well, now the pupil has overtaken the teacher.'

Patrick took a step back as Izzy cleared her throat behind him. 'Is this a private love-in, or were you ever going to introduce me?' she said.

'Sorry.' He slipped an arm around Izzy's shoulders. 'Livia, this is—'

'Izzy. Of course.' Livia smiled warmly. 'Welcome to the Hotel Catalonia.'

'*Such a lovely place,*' sang Patrick, and Izzy frowned.

'It's a song,' he explained, embarrassed. 'By the Eagles . . .'

Izzy wasn't looking as if that information had helped, so Livia leant over and gave her a hug. 'Patrick's told me all about you.'

'He has?' Izzy shot him a suspicious glance. 'When?'

'Whenever,' said Patrick, in an end-of-conversation tone.

'Right. Well, congratulations,' said Izzy, grabbing hold of Patrick's arm.

'We're not married yet.'

'I meant for getting him to marry you. *And* having his baby. That's pretty mega . . .'

'Well, technically, it's *our* baby.'

'Even so,' continued Izzy. 'Girl power!'

'Right,' said Livia, wondering if Izzy had even been born when that was a thing. 'When did you get here?' She addressed the question to both of them, but Izzy seemed distracted by the view of the pool though the double doors.

'A couple of hours ago.' Patrick stifled a yawn. 'Same crack-of-dawn flight as Rachel.'

'Who beat you here, by the way.'

'We went for breakfast.' He pointed at the Stella McCartney bag balanced on top of his wheelie. 'Plus Izzy wanted to go shopping. On the way in from the airport.'

'I needed something to wear for tonight.'

Patrick lowered his voice to a stage whisper. 'The three outfits she brought with her obviously weren't appropriate.'

'I won't wear it if you're worried I might upstage you.'

For a moment, Livia wasn't quite sure how to answer that, though she couldn't detect any malice in Izzy's tone. Wasn't this how the youth were nowadays, though? Used to just telling it like it was? Though in Izzy's case, Livia feared she could turn up this evening dressed in a bin bag and she'd still upstage her.

'No, please do. In any case, I'll be walking down the aisle with a stomach with its own gravitational field. *Everyone* will be upstaging me.'

59

Izzy smiled politely, then glanced back towards the double doors, as if anxious to be outside, and Patrick laughed. 'You're acting like you've never seen the sun before.'

'Hello?' Izzy made a kooky face. 'I live in *England*, remember?'

'Go on, then,' he said, letting go of her, and as Izzy scampered off towards the pool, he caught Livia staring at him disapprovingly. 'I know, I know,' he said, resignedly.

'She seems very . . .'

'Young?'

'I was going to say "keen on you", but now you come to mention it . . .' Livia laughed. 'What does Sarah think?'

Patrick shuddered. 'As you can imagine, my forty-something ex-wife absolutely loves the fact I'm seeing someone not much older than our daughter.'

'And Anna?'

'Is actually fine with it. Though that could be more down to the fact that she gets to use Izzy's staff discount at Selfridges.' Patrick grinned sheepishly. 'But the heart wants what the heart wants.'

Livia glanced out to the pool, where Izzy had already stripped off to what could be either her underwear or a bikini – it was hard to tell given how little of it there was – and stretched herself out on a sun lounger. 'You sure your heart's the part of your body that's making the decisions?'

'Hey, I'm not making any decisions. It's just a bit of fun.'

'Does Izzy know that?'

'How could she not?'

'Because you haven't told her?'

He nodded out at the pool, where Izzy had begun doing some strange yoga poses. 'She may be young. But she's not so innocent. And she's smarter than she looks.'

'Thank goodness. Oh, I'm sorry, did I say that out loud?'

'Yes. You did.'

'Patrick—'

'And here's Jed!' Livia's fiancé, sweating heavily, had just appeared through the hotel's front door, and before Livia could say any more, Patrick had waved him over enthusiastically. 'You're just in time.'

'For what?' puffed Jed.

'Stopping Livia from giving me a lecture about Izzy.'

'As if,' protested Livia.

Jed burst out laughing, and when Patrick couldn't help but join in, Livia wasn't sure whether it was at her expression or from his happiness at escaping a talking-to.

She'd have to find an appropriate moment later, she knew. Because this was the thing about men. Sometimes, they just needed telling.

Liam's sixth sense had just begun to fire, and when he opened his eyes, he almost fell off his sun lounger in surprise. The girl doing some weird stretching exercises two sunbeds away was *stunning*. Maybe a little younger than he'd normally go for, but hey, he was on holiday.

He pretended to be asleep for a while, enjoying the show, then, as she unhooked her leg from around her neck and pulled a bottle of sunscreen from her bag, he sat up, rubbed the sleep from his eyes and cleared his throat.

'Did you need a hand?'

'What?'

'With the sunscreen. If there's anywhere you can't, you know . . .' He cracked his knuckles in the way a masseur might, then fixed his winningest smile on his face. 'Reach.'

'It's a spray,' said the girl. 'It reaches *everywhere*.'

'Lucky sunscreen.'

She regarded him over the top of her expensive-looking sunglasses – Dior, Liam noted, though they could be fakes: the city's streets were full of vendors selling knock-offs. But as he used the privacy of his own five-euro

mirrored 'Ray-Bans' to give her the once-over, he quickly decided there
was very little fake about this girl. He stretched his arms exaggeratedly,
using it as an opportunity to both show off his physique and check out
the surrounding sunbeds. It was still early, and many of them were still
empty, which would suggest she'd chosen to sit near him on purpose.

'You here on holiday?' he continued.

'Just for the weekend.'

'Me too.'

The girl looked at him for a moment – or maybe through him.
It was hard to tell, given the way her eyes, and a lot of her face, were
obscured by her oversized shades. Maybe she was star-struck – it happened from time to time – or simply playing it cool. Then again, she
could just be admiring her reflection in his lenses. Liam was sure if he
looked like that, *he* would be.

'Here for a wedding, actually,' he added, after a pause that had
given her more than ample opportunity to reply.

'I'm guessing it's not yours?' She sprayed a couple of puffs at her
chest, and began to massage the lotion into the top of her breasts –
something Liam would have bet money on her doing on purpose. Not
that he was complaining.

'God no!' he said, perhaps a little too quickly. 'I'm Liam, by the way.'

'I know.' The girl had lowered her shades and narrowed her eyes
at him, so Liam gave her his best TV smile. 'We're here for the same
reason.'

'Oh. Right.' It took a moment to work out what she'd meant,
but once he had, Liam almost rubbed his hands together. This was an
opportunity if ever he'd seen one. An open goal, waiting for him to step
up and tap the ball into the back of the net – like he'd done so many
times before. 'And you are?'

'With someone.'

'Seriously?'

'I hope so.'

'Hey.' He held both hands up, trying not to make a show of his disappointment. 'I was just being sociable. I'm the best man.'

'Really.' The girl gave him another look, as if to say, 'I doubt that,' but Liam decided he'd soldier on regardless. Just because she'd said she was with someone didn't mean that someone was *here*. Or that she'd *stay* with them, once Liam had a chance to work his magic.

'I thought you might be one of the guests. It's my job to look after everyone. Make sure they have a good time.'

'Oh, I don't need anyone's help for *that*.'

I bet you don't, thought Liam. 'So, who's the lucky man?'

'Jed, isn't it? I would have thought, as the best man, that would have been something you'd have known?'

'No, I mean *your* lucky man?'

The girl took her sunglasses off, put the end of one of the arms in the corner of her mouth and began sucking it absent-mindedly. 'Why do you assume it's a man?' she said, suggestively.

Liam swallowed audibly. 'I just . . . I mean . . .' He shut his mouth, conscious he was doing his best impression of a goldfish trying to breathe out of water. 'Not that there'd be anything wrong with—'

'In any case, *I'm* the lucky one.' The girl was rubbing lotion onto her thighs now, and Liam was finding it hard to concentrate. 'So you're Jed's brother.'

'I am. Younger. Which means he's my *big brother* . . .' he said, with a wink, and the girl smirked.

'You did well, keeping all this from him.'

'Oh, I'm good at keeping secrets.' Liam paused to give his remark time to sink in. 'Besides, there was no point telling him. He might have said no, if he'd had a chance to think about it. Then we'd all have had a miserable weekend.'

'Not very loyal of you, though.'

Liam shrugged. 'There's loyalty, and there's being a part of playing the world's best prank on someone.'

'Prank?'

'There was no way Jed wanted to get married. And now – well, he doesn't have the choice, does he? Especially with Livia up the duff!' Liam grinned. 'My speech'll almost write itself. And think of the mileage I'll get out of this in years to come.'

The girl shook her head slowly, and Liam told himself it was probably in admiration at how they'd all got one over on Jed. 'Right,' she said, then she slipped her sunglasses back on and reclined on her sun lounger, so Liam tried to act as casually as he could and did the same on his.

In truth, he was finding her distracting. She really was quite sexy, with a small tattoo on her hip that disappeared into her bikini bottoms and that he'd be keen to have a closer look at. Maybe this evening. And maybe *with* her girlfriend . . . First, though, there was the small matter of the no-man's-land stretch of empty sun lounger between them he had to deal with, so he nodded at her bottle of sunscreen.

'Could I get some of that?'

'Help yourself.'

'On my back.' Liam took the opportunity to peel his T-shirt off, flexing his biceps and pulling his stomach in as he did so. 'If you wouldn't mind . . .' he said, flipping over to lie face down on the next-door bed.

'Sure.'

The girl regarded him for a moment, picked up the bottle, leant so close that Liam could smell the coconut from the Hawaiian Tropic she'd been coating herself with, and made a few artistic sprays over his torso, then started to giggle – not quite the reaction he'd been hoping for. Even so, the effect of her almost touching him was . . . anyway, Liam was glad he was lying on his front.

'You never did tell me your name.'

'It's Izzy.'

Liam frowned. Either her voice had suddenly dropped a couple of octaves, or the shadow he could feel looming over him belonged to . . . well, Liam was pretty sure it wasn't her girlfriend – or if it was, he'd better get out of here *fast*.

He whipped his head round so quickly that, for a moment, he feared he'd cricked his neck, though when he removed his sunglasses, he was relieved to see someone he recognised. 'Patrick?'

'Hey, Liam.' Patrick was reaching down to shake his hand, so Liam reached up awkwardly, trying to ignore the feeling he'd been caught with his trousers . . . if not quite down, he'd certainly been about to unbuckle his belt. 'Nice to see you.'

'I'd forgotten you were coming.' Still not daring to turn over, he guiltily shook Patrick's hand, wincing a little at Patrick's perhaps-firmer-than-it-needed-to-be grip, and glanced across at Izzy. 'Sorry. I didn't put two and two together.' *Or rather, you and you together*, he thought.

'Sweetheart?' said Patrick, bending down to kiss Izzy on the lips, and Liam wondered whether he was marking his territory.

'Hey, baby,' said Izzy, and Liam hid a smile. Patrick was the last person anyone would refer to as 'baby', and by the look that flashed across his face, he knew it.

'We're all checked in, but I just need to go and sort something out. Back in fifteen.'

'Take your time,' said Izzy, stretching out languorously on her sun lounger. 'I've got Liam to keep me company.'

'Okay.' Patrick hesitated for a moment, then he leant down and kissed her again. 'Careful you don't get burnt,' he said.

Though it wasn't until he'd gone that Liam realised Patrick might not have been referring to the sun.

'Have you left anything for the other guests?'

Livia was smiling at the piled-high plate a freshly showered Jed had brought back from the breakfast buffet, so he made a show of how heavy it was, then looked pointedly at the pile of used crockery in front of her. 'And how many visits have *you* made to the buffet table already this morning?'

'That's not the point.' Livia reached over and helped herself to a piece of one of his pastries. 'You look like a condemned man who couldn't decide what to have for his last meal, so he chose one of everything.'

'Condemned man, eh?' Jed gave her a look as he sat down at the table, and Livia narrowed her eyes at him.

'Not funny,' she said, unable to stop her mouth turning up at the corners.

'I've been for a run. A long one.'

'Don't I know it?'

'Plus, in the spirit of equality . . .' He leant over and kissed her stomach, and decided to try a variation of last night's joke excuse. 'I'm eating for two.'

'Well, you both need to hurry up. We've got things to do.'

He indicated his plate again. 'So have I.'

'Have you even said hello to anyone yet?'

'I have. Though they're lucky I'm still speaking to them, after this little stunt.'

'If by "this little stunt", you're referring to our wedding, then . . .'

Livia looked hurt, and Jed immediately felt awful. 'You know what I mean,' he said, quickly and through a mouthful of croissant. He reached over and took her hand, then let it go when he realised that would only slow his eating down. 'How on earth did you convince them to keep it from me?'

'Liam's good at keeping secrets. You have to be, when your love life's as complicated as his is.' Livia nodded towards the pool area, where Jed's brother, his tongue almost hanging out, was trying his best to engage a sunbathing Izzy in conversation. 'Though it seems I could say the same about Patrick.'

'I know! She's gor—' Jed caught himself. Livia was already sensitive enough about her appearance without him making her think he was lusting after Patrick's admittedly very lithe twenty-something girlfriend. 'Got to be, what, half his age?'

'And IQ.'

'I take it you don't approve?'

'It's not really for me to approve or not, is it?' said Livia, and Jed was about to reply with a 'quite' until he suddenly realised she hadn't finished. 'Although I don't know what on earth he's thinking,' she added.

'Maybe he isn't?'

'Isn't what?'

'Thinking.' Jed drained the remainder of his orange juice. 'He probably just wants a bit of fun.'

'A woman his age wouldn't be?'

Jed paused, half out of his seat on his way to refill his glass. 'Wouldn't be . . . ?' he said, sitting back down again reluctantly.

'Fun.'

'Well . . .' Jed stared at his plate. He could speak, or he could eat, and Livia's tone was telling him the second option was the sensible one, especially if they did have, as she'd said, *things to do*.

'Well what?'

'I think . . .' He changed tack quickly. 'I mean, I'd imagine Patrick thinks that someone his age might make a few more . . . demands.'

'Demands?'

Jed swallowed hard. Livia had that amused look on her face that usually preceded a lecture, and while that might give him the time he needed to clear his plate, it wouldn't perhaps be the best way to start their wedding day. 'You know,' he said, as casually as he could, filling his cup from the pot of coffee the waiter had just deposited on their table.

'He might be thinking that he doesn't want to get married. Again. At least not yet. And that someone his age might be desperate to . . . well, desperate to. Get married. Before, you know, it's, um . . .'

'Too late?'

Livia had raised both eyebrows, and they'd stayed up, which made her look like she was a victim of a bad Botox session. It also meant he was expected to explain himself, so he took another bite of croissant and chewed slowly, as if to indicate he was thinking. 'Yeah,' he said, washing the croissant down with a mouthful of coffee, though he feared he'd made a mistake almost as soon as the word had left his mouth. He hadn't wanted Livia to make any comparisons to their situation, but he remembered that was always going to happen. As a man, you could comment on the simplest of things and get caught out: yesterday he'd remarked, offhandedly, that Livia seemed to be enjoying her lunch – a throwaway line, really – and she'd funnelled that into asking him whether he was implying that she looked fat. Though, in retrospect, his 'You *are* fat' in reply – meant as a get-out-of-jail-free card for Livia to be able to eat as much as she wanted while pregnant – perhaps hadn't been the smartest of responses. 'Because they might be worried that they're, er, in danger of, um, being left on the, you know, *shelf* . . .'

'Right,' said Livia, in a way that suggested he wasn't.

'Plus Patrick's quite a catch, isn't he?' he continued, quickly. 'I mean, he doesn't look like he's nudging fifty. And he's loaded.'

'Maybe I should be marrying him, then?'

'Maybe you should!' suggested Jed, though he quickly added: 'Put yourself in their shoes before you judge people. Everyone's relationship works differently, remember. Look at Rachel and Rich.'

'Bad example.'

'Why?' said Jed.

'They've split up.'

'Ah.' Jed peered around the courtyard, checking Rachel wasn't in earshot. 'And was that a mutual decision, or . . . ?'

'When is it ever?'

'Poor Rachel. And, um, where *is* she?' he asked, grateful for the opportunity to steer the subject away from himself. 'I didn't see her in the cab with Patrick and Izzy. Then again, she might have been hidden underneath Izzy's shopping bag.'

Livia smiled both briefly and politely, as if to both acknowledge and dismiss his attempt at humour. 'Sightseeing.'

Jed glanced back out through the doors, to where Liam appeared to be blatantly staring at Izzy. 'As Liam appears to be.'

'I hope it doesn't run in the family.'

'She's hardly my . . . I mean, I wouldn't . . .' Jed stopped talking, realising there wasn't much he could say that wouldn't get him into trouble, and he suspected he'd already had a lucky escape. Besides, Livia looked like she'd been joking. He hoped.

He began buttering his second croissant, wondering whether now was the time to try to talk to her about his feelings regarding their upcoming nuptials, but he hadn't even got as far as the first *L* of 'Listen, Liv . . .' when a blood-curdling scream coming from the direction of the hotel's reception made her expression quickly morph into a look of terror. Jed feared some mad person had just run into the hotel, so he instinctively grabbed the nearest item of cutlery to defend her with – though in retrospect, when he glanced down, he realised he probably wouldn't have much success with a dessertspoon.

'Oh *no!*' said Livia, under her breath, so Jed took her hand.

'What is it?'

'Sally!'

He followed Livia's gaze through the open glass doors and towards the reception desk, where a woman Livia's age was holding the source of the noise – a very boisterous, violently wriggling blond child, perhaps around two years old (Jed's lack of experience of all things paternal made it difficult for him to tell). Behind them, an extremely stressed-looking man who Jed recognised as Sally's husband Oliver was struggling with what looked like enough luggage for a rock band on a round-the-world tour.

'You didn't tell me they were coming too!'

'They're not! At least, *I* didn't invite them.'

'Well, *I* certainly didn't.'

'I didn't say you did.'

'On account of me not knowing what was—'

'Jed! Just . . .' Livia was giving him one of her looks again. 'Don't say anything!'

'But . . .' Jed stopped talking altogether, deciding to follow her advice. At least that way, he probably wouldn't get into trouble. Besides, Livia was already waving at Sally, so any window of opportunity he'd had to try to talk about what was happening later looked like it had been rapidly slammed shut.

He sighed, reluctantly slid his breakfast plate away, swivelled round in his chair and fixed a smile on his face, while over at reception, Sally made the 'oh my god!' face, nudged her husband, and the three of them made their way through the doors towards their table. As the two women embraced and Livia planted a kiss on the child's face – something Jed wouldn't have dared to do, given the river of snot running from its nostrils – he reluctantly stood up.

'Well, this is a surprise,' said Oliver, vigorously shaking Jed's hand.

'Isn't it?' said Livia, and Sally nodded.

'What are you two doing here?'

Jed looked longingly down at his plate. 'Having breakfast?' he ventured.

'No, I meant . . .'

'Oh, *here* here?' He looked at Livia, but when she didn't prompt him, he just shrugged. 'Oh, you know . . .'

'Getting a weekend away in while you still can, before it all changes?' suggested Sally.

'Something like that,' said Livia, shooting Jed a look at the sound of his audible swallow.

'Lucky buggers,' said Oliver, and Sally made a face, so Jed nodded at the pile of luggage Oliver had just deposited on the floor. 'You guys staying a while?'

'Just tonight.'

When Oliver didn't continue, Jed frowned. 'But you look like you've packed for a *month*.'

'You have so much to learn!' Oliver laughed, and patted the large canvas case by his feet. 'Travel cot – Barney won't sleep in any other bed apart from that, and if Barney doesn't sleep, then neither do we! Then there are clothes, of course, plus spares for all of us in case of any accidents, plus nappies for the little one, even though we're potty training him at the moment. Oh, and his travel potty. And his stroller. Bloody ironic name, because he just wants to run everywhere at the mo . . . Hold on.'

Sally had put Barney down on the floor, and as if on cue, he'd sprinted unsteadily off towards the buffet, so Oliver set off after him, returning after a moment holding the red-faced child upside down. 'Now Barney,' he said, patiently. 'What have we told you about running . . . *Ow!*'

'Barney,' said Sally, in a less-understanding tone – and one Jed recognised from whenever Livia addressed Liam. 'What have we told you about biting?'

Oliver was rubbing a spot on his thigh – Jed could see the outline of tiny teeth on the fabric of his trousers, accentuated by a double snot-smear – while Barney stared demonically up at him.

'Say sorry to Daddy,' ordered Sally, as Oliver lowered him to the floor.

'No!' shouted Barney.

'Barney?'

'No!'

'Barney!'

'No!'

'Say sorry, or you'll go in the naughty corner!'

'No!' shouted Barney, even louder than before.

'Right,' said Sally, reaching down to grab him, but Barney was too quick for her, darting off in the opposite direction towards the pool, and as she set off in pursuit, Oliver gave Jed an earnest look.

'In a few months, he'll be just tall enough that his teeth will be level with the old chap,' he said, pointing down at his privates. 'I'm not looking forward to that day, I can tell you.'

Jed glanced out to the pool, where Sally had managed to catch Barney and seemed to be having some stern words with him. To her credit, Livia seemed a bit shocked by the whole series of events, though Jed knew he could hardly bring this up in conversation later. It was a little too late, after all. About six months too late, in fact.

'I'm sure it's just a phase,' suggested Livia, and Oliver nodded.

'As long as it doesn't last the full eighteen years.' Then he leant across to Jed. 'Three words: Never. Have. Kids,' he said, under his breath, and glanced theatrically at Livia's stomach. 'Oh, sorry. Too late.' He burst out in maniacal laughter, and Jed nervously joined in. 'Hey, don't mind me. I'm sure yours will be different . . .'

Sally was bringing the slightly calmer child back, and as she set him down on the floor between them all, Jed felt a tugging on his trouser leg. 'Hello, Barney,' he said, crouching to Barney's level, trying not to think about whatever the substance was that had left visible fingerprints on his chinos. 'How are you . . . ?'

'Cock-up!'

Jed stood up quickly and instinctively covered his groin with his hands, and Oliver rolled his eyes. 'He means "yoghurt". He can't get enough of the stuff. Apparently, it's like crack cocaine, but for kids. Though I'll tell you, the amount that comes back out again, it'd be cheaper to scoop it up and just repackage it. And as for the amount of wet wipes we get through as a result . . .' He sighed. 'I wish I had shares in Andrex. Could afford a bloody nanny then. Spare ourselves all this . . .'

'We better feed him,' said Sally, ominously, and Jed frowned.

'Or?'

He'd asked the question automatically, partly interested in case the answer might come in useful in the future, but Oliver's horrified expression made him instantly regret it.

'You don't want to know. May I?' he said, pointing at Jed's unopened pot of yoghurt on the table.

'Be my guest.'

Oliver picked up the yoghurt in one hand and Barney in the other, and to another full-volume cry of 'Cock-up!' sat the child down to feed him.

'So!' Sally smiled at the two of them, as if what they'd just witnessed was what passed for normal in her world, though to Jed's horror, he realised it probably was. 'What are you guys up to today? Anything special?'

'Not really,' said Livia, quickly. 'You?'

'Oliver's taking Barney to the aquarium.'

'He likes fish?'

'He likes *a* fish. *N-E-M-O*, to be precise' said Oliver. 'He's watched it enough times. And someone' – he gave Sally a look – 'promised him the aquarium was where *N-E-M-O* lived.'

'So you're taking Barney to "find" him?' Livia broke into a broad grin. 'How lovely!'

'I bloody hope so,' said Oliver. 'Otherwise that little meltdown will be nothing compared to what will happen.'

'You not going?' Livia asked Sally.

She shook her head frantically. 'I've got one thing on my mind, and that's sleep,' she said, with the same relish a drug user might exhibit when talking about an upcoming fix. 'Hey, maybe we could meet up later, if you're not . . . ?'

'Well, we're . . .' Livia was looking at him, her mouth flapping like the aforementioned fish, and Jed let her suffer for a second or two, then he nodded.

'It's kind of our . . .'

'Yes, our . . .'

'Anniversary,' said Jed, quickly, slipping an arm around Livia's shoulders. 'So we've got, you know . . .'

'Plans,' said Livia.

'Yes. Plans,' confirmed Jed.

'Later,' said Livia.

Sally was looking from one of them to the other, as if sitting by the net at a tennis match. 'Right,' she said, followed by: 'Ri-ight. Say no more.' She winked at Livia, who took it as a cue to snake an arm around Jed's waist. A little too tightly for his liking. 'I'd be doing the same if I were you,' she said, then she leaned in close and lowered her voice. 'Though that kind of thing's a distant memory for the two of us.'

''Specially when you're worried you might end up with another one of these,' interrupted Oliver from the table, where he seemed to be wearing the best part of the pot of yoghurt. 'Isn't that right, Barney?'

'Cock-up!' said Barney, hammering delightedly on the table with his spoon.

'Right. Well, we'd better leave you two lovebirds . . .' Oliver stood up, lifted Barney onto his shoulders and stared pointedly at Sally. 'Shall we?'

Sally smiled. 'You don't want to borrow a child for the day?'

'I've already got one, thanks,' said Livia, squeezing Jed even tighter, though it took him a second to realise she perhaps wasn't referring to the baby in her belly.

'Oh well. Worth a try!' Sally hoisted up as many of their bags as she could manage, leaving Oliver to struggle with Barney and the rest. 'Well, have fun!'

'While you still can . . .' said Oliver with a wink, before leading his wife and son away.

Jed checked his chair for yoghurt, then sat back down and watched the three of them stride into the nearest lift. As the shell-shocked occupants hurried out, quite possibly due to the piercing scream Barney had just emitted, Livia sighed. 'Well, we seem to have got away with it.'

'Don't you think they might be a bit suspicious when they see us getting *married* later?'

'Jed, the ceremony's at six. Barney will be in bed by then. By the looks of things, Oliver and Sally probably will be too. And they certainly won't be able to leave the room.'

'What on earth did they come away for then?' he asked, but Livia was too busy pointedly checking the time, so instead he poured himself another coffee, then looked up sharply at Livia's harrumph. 'What?'

She tapped the face of her watch impatiently. 'Could you just get a move on, please?'

'What for?'

'I told you. We've got something to do. In town.'

'Something to do?'

'It's a surprise.'

Jed raised both eyebrows. 'Another one?' he said. 'Haven't I even got time to enjoy my breakfast?'

'You're the one who took ages out on your run this morning. I was beginning to think you weren't coming back.'

Jed did his best to keep his expression as impassive as possible, sure Livia could tell that the thought had crossed his mind *and* that seeing Oliver and Sally had brought it front and centre again.

'I got lost.'

Livia reached across the table and took his hand. 'Well, don't make a habit of it.'

Jed opened his mouth to protest, then he bit off his reply. Something he suspected he might be doing a lot more of as the day went on.

Patrick grimaced at a loudly snoring Liam, who'd fallen asleep, face down, in the direct sun. 'I hope he's got some sunblock on?'

'Oh yes.' Izzy shielded her eyes as she looked up at him. 'I made sure of it.'

'Good,' said Patrick, though he wasn't quite sure how to take that. 'Well, have I got a surprise for you . . .'

'A surprise?'

Patrick couldn't keep the grin from his face, though Izzy didn't appear to be particularly enthusiastic about being disturbed from her sunbathing.

'Uh-huh.'

'A Livia-type surprise?'

'Well, no . . .' spluttered Patrick, and Izzy laughed.

'And that surprise is?'

'We're going on a tour.'

'Of Barcelona?'

'No, the lost city of Atlantis. Of course Barcelona.'

'Oh.'

'Come on. You can't come all the way to somewhere like this and not see the sights.'

'I saw the sights,' said Izzy, flatly. 'From the plane.'

'I mean *actually* see them. The architecture. Some street life. Take in a bit of the atmosphere.'

Izzy adjusted the straps of her bikini, careful to avoid tan lines. 'I've *been* taking in the atmosphere.'

'Not just the *sun*. Barcelona has a really cool vibe to it. El Born, El Raval, the Gótico, Barceloneta . . .' Patrick counted off the districts on his fingers. 'Then there's Gaudí's Park Güell, and of course the Sagrada Família. Which I'm pretty *família* with . . .' He leant over and nudged Izzy, though if she got his joke, she didn't let on. 'There's an exhibition on at the Picasso Museum. His Blue Period. Or we could stop for some lunch at this restaurant I know on the beach . . .' At the mention of the word 'beach', Izzy perked up a little, so Patrick decided to seize the momentum. 'It'll be fun,' he said, taking her by the hand and helping – well, almost *dragging* – her up off the sun lounger.

Izzy gave him a look that suggested she doubted it. 'Okay, okay.'

She slipped her dress on over her bikini, and Patrick had to stop himself from clapping his hands in anticipation. 'Great!'

'We don't have to walk, do we?' she said, wriggling her feet into her sandals.

'Chauffeur-driven.'

'*Chauffeur-driven?*'

Izzy had widened her eyes, though they narrowed rapidly once Patrick led her outside and across to the other side of the street, where a small, bright yellow, open-topped three-wheeler was parked in front of the hotel.

'Ta-da!' he said.

'What's *that?*'

'It's called a GoCar.'

'It's hardly the Porsche, is it?'

'No, but it's the best way to see the city.'

'If you're five years old, perhaps,' she huffed. 'It looks ridiculous. And so will I.'

'You're much too beautiful to look ridiculous. Besides, nobody will care what you look like.'

He handed her a crash helmet in a matching yellow, and Izzy regarded it suspiciously. 'I'm not wearing that.'

'Why not?'

'My *hair*?'

'It'll get even more messed up if you don't. Especially if we hit something.'

Izzy gave him a look, as if that was exactly what she was considering doing, then with an exaggerated sigh she strapped the helmet on and climbed reluctantly into the passenger seat.

'Thank you,' said Patrick, jumping in next to her. 'Ready?'

'As I'll ever be.'

'Great,' he said again, although slightly less confidently than before.

He hit the start button, and they set off along the road in the buzzy little vehicle, heading through the Gótico, along cobbled lanes and dark passageways that just oozed history. Patrick felt in his element, enjoying the sensation of whizzing along the city's narrow streets, though when he grinned across at Izzy, she seemed to be more interested in examining her nails. He shook his head as he steered them towards the port, then he reached down and pressed a button on the dashboard.

'On your right' – a tinny, robotic female voice had begun blaring out of the satnav, making Izzy jump – 'you'll see the famous statue of Christopher Columbus. It stands at the bottom of Las Ramblas, Barcelona's most famous thoroughfare, lined with flower stalls, restaurants and street performers, which – rather than being just one street, as most visitors think – is actually a series of roads . . .'

'Can't we turn that off?' she huffed.

'Would you rather I told you what everything . . . ?' Izzy silenced him with a look, and Patrick sighed as he hit the mute button. 'That's the whole point of this thing. We drive around, the GPS tells it where we are, and it tells *us* what we're looking at.'

'It's bad enough that I've had you doing that since we got here.'

Izzy had stretched out in her seat, lifting her dress to her thighs to expose as much flesh as possible to the sun, and while he'd normally enjoy such a sight, Patrick felt his anger rise.

'You could show some enthusiasm for one of my favourite places, rather than simply treating this as some mobile tanning opportunity.'

He'd snapped at her, and Izzy jerked back upright, as if she'd been told off by a teacher at school, and Patrick wondered whether he'd pay for that later. But then he thought, *What the hell.* He was paying for everything else.

He reached down and reactivated the navigation, then steered the GoCar towards the west of the city, Izzy doing her best to appear interested in what she evidently thought were just lumps of concrete rather than some of the world's most influential architecture. After an uncomfortable few minutes, they pulled up at a red traffic light in front of a huge, intricately decorated, circular building.

'In front of you, you'll see Barcelona's old bullring,' the satnav informed them. 'This used to be a hub of entertainment until bullfighting was banned in Catalonia. Today it's a shopping centre, where some of the world's premier brands have outlets . . .'

Too late, Patrick reached for the mute button again, but despite them being in the middle lane, Izzy was already climbing out of the GoCar's cockpit. As she pulled her helmet off and shook her hair free, he frowned up at her.

'What are you doing?'

'I'm sorry, baby, but I didn't come to Barcelona to be ferried around in something that sounds like a broken lawnmower, and with a bad *Doctor Who* villain blaring in my ear, just to look at a succession of stuffy old buildings.'

What did you come here for, then? Patrick wanted to ask. Though he suspected he might not like the answer if he did. 'Izzy, they're hardly stuffy . . .'

'They're *buildings*, Patrick. Old ones too. We should be *doing* stuff. Not just seeing stuff.'

'Seeing stuff *is* doing stuff.'

'Maybe.' Izzy looked at him for a moment. 'Here,' she said, passing him her helmet, then she nodded towards the satnav. 'Sounds like you and her have a lot more in common.'

'Izzy, wait . . .'

'No, honestly . . .' she said, as if she was doing *him* a favour. 'I'll see you back at the hotel.'

'Izzy!' he shouted, but the lights had changed and she was already skipping through the slowly moving line of cars to their right. 'How will you find your way . . . ?' Patrick stopped talking. It was doubtful she could hear him above the noise of the traffic – doubtful Izzy was even listening, in fact.

As she strode purposefully off towards the shopping centre, he sat there, dumbfounded, until an impatient beeping from the car behind snapped him out of his mood. He peered around anxiously for a parking spot, intending to abandon the GoCar and chase after her, but he was too late. Izzy had already disappeared into the crowds thronging towards the bullring.

'Women!' he said, to no one in particular, then he gritted his teeth, put the vehicle in gear and drove angrily back to the hotel.

Rachel climbed down from the open-topped bus and gazed up at the stadium. She hadn't planned to get off here, wasn't at all a football fan herself, but given the excited way everyone else on the bus seemed to be chattering in anticipation at seeing the Nou Camp, Barcelona's famous football ground and the first stop on the tour, she'd thought she should at least take a quick peek.

Rich wouldn't have wanted to do this, of course; the idea of going to see anything related to the team that had so humiliated his beloved Gunners would probably have sent him scurrying to the nearest bar (if he hadn't been in it already), though he'd probably even turn his nose up at the local *cerveza*, Estrella, seeing as it was the club's official beer. Then again, Rich probably wouldn't have wanted to come on an open-top bus tour in the first place. It would have cut into his 'valuable drinking time', as he was fond of describing any weekend lunchtime before a game. But now, as Rachel took in the huge structure towering over her, a thought occurred to her: they'd been at a party recently where – not knowing she was with someone – some guy had tried to chat Rachel up, and while she hadn't responded in kind, Rich had seen what was going on and . . . well, suffice to say, once they'd got back to her place he'd been more attentive than she'd experienced in a long while. And though it perhaps wasn't quite the same thing, being here might just have the same effect – if not, it'd be a great way to stick two fingers up to Rich in the most effective way possible. To kick him where it would *really* hurt – right up the Arsenal. And make him see she wasn't the walkover his football team had been.

She hurried round the outside of the building, past the dozens of souvenir stands selling breathtakingly expensive commemorative shirts, 'official' calendars, postcards and even (despite the midday heat) thick woollen red-and-blue scarves, until she saw what she was looking for – a huge photo of the team's stars, emblazoned on the stadium wall next to a large 'FCB' logo. It was *perfect*, Rachel thought, pulling her phone from her pocket and taking a succession of photos.

She reviewed the images, then frowned at the screen. Something was missing. Despite having lots of shots of the stadium, she only had one shot at this. And she needed it to really hit home.

Rachel peered at the crowds thronging around outside the stadium, searching for inspiration. Behind her, a group of teenagers were gathered at one of the souvenir stands, excitedly trying on all manner of FC Barcelona paraphernalia, from tracksuit tops to caps, hoodies and bags, and even cardboard masks of the players. Now that was an idea – maybe not a mask, but she could certainly use a couple of props.

She strolled casually across to the stand and idly picked up one of the shirts, the name 'Messi' emblazoned across the back in bright yellow letters above a large number 10. It couldn't be more perfect, she thought. Well, unless the player's name ended in a *Y*, because that's how it might get once Rich saw her wearing it.

'Can I try?' she said to the man behind the counter, miming pulling it over her head in case he didn't understand her, and when he nodded, Rachel slipped it on. It was a little tight, perhaps, but at least that would accentuate her figure. After all, she also wanted to show Rich what he was missing. If not that she'd been missing *him*.

Scanning the rack in front of her, she picked up a scarf and – doing her best to ignore the sweltering temperature – draped it round her neck, then located a cap with the club's logo on the front and tried that on too. There was a mirror to her left, so she stepped over and checked her reflection, then had to stifle a laugh. Rich had raged at the TV when Barcelona had thrashed Arsenal. Now he'd be raging at his phone when he saw the picture she was about to send him!

She glanced up at the stallholder, but he was too busy checking the group of teenagers weren't trying to steal anything to be watching her, so she took a step back from the mirror, as if actually considering buying the whole, lurid combination, then turned around so the rear of the shirt was visible, looked back coquettishly over her shoulder, quickly raised her phone and snapped a selfie, careful to get the stadium and the photo of the players behind her in the shot. It was a little difficult, given the length of her arm and the amount of references she was trying to get in, but Rachel had always hated those ridiculous selfie sticks everyone seemed to be using now (and that had nearly taken her eye out on a number of occasions already today), and besides, she hadn't thought she'd be needing one. Normally, when there were two of you travelling, there'd always be one to take the photo while one was *in* the photo, and any selfies would be more of the close-up, just-the-two-of-you, intimate variety.

She checked her phone, and to her amazement she'd got the shot she wanted first time. As she admired the photo, she heard a gruff Spanish voice behind her.

'Is good?'

Rachel wheeled round to find the stallholder looking at her with raised eyebrows. 'Oh yes, perfect,' she said, before realising he was referring to the items she was wearing. 'I mean, no. Sorry.'

As he scowled at her, she quickly put the cap and scarf back where she'd found them, then tugged the shirt off and handed it back to him. The day was getting hotter, so she walked over to where the stadium could provide some shade, and double-checked the photo. Then she took a deep breath, hit 'Share', tapped the WhatsApp icon and scrolled through to Rich's number.

Wish you were here, she typed, followed by a series of question marks, and hurriedly pressed send before she lost her nerve. Then – to ensure she wouldn't spend the rest of the day obsessing about whether he'd seen it and (more importantly) whether he'd replied – she blocked his number, slipped her phone back into her pocket and – with a huge smile on her face – made her way back towards the bus stop.

Chapter 4

Patrick was marching crossly back through the hotel's reception when Livia's 'On your own?' took him by surprise. She was sitting on the sofa opposite the lift, and when she patted the cushion next to her, he fixed a smile on his face and made his way across the lobby.

'It would seem so. Izzy's gone—'

'Shopping?'

'How did you know?'

'Lucky guess.'

'I fear my attempt to play tour guide was . . . unappreciated,' he said, sitting down next to her, and Livia sighed.

'I'm hoping that's not how Jed feels about all of this.'

'What do you mean?'

'Nothing. I'm sure I'm just being silly. You'd be flattered, wouldn't you, Patrick, if Izzy . . . ?'

'Steady on! I'm very fond of her and everything, but it's a little too early to—' Patrick caught himself. Livia seemed a little on edge, and he reminded himself that her comment wasn't really about him. 'Of course I would. And I'm sure he is.' He patted the back of her hand supportively. 'What are you doing down here on your own?'

'Just waiting for Jed,' said Livia, glancing towards the lift. 'I'm taking him into town to get the rings.'

'Convinced him to get you an engagement ring, have you? Because it's possibly the shortest engagement I've ever—'

'Nope. The ones we're exchanging later.'

'Exchanging?'

'That's right.'

'Um . . .'

'What?'

'The watch incident?'

'What about it?'

'Jed hates jewellery.'

'This is a *wedding* ring.'

'Right.'

'Besides, he doesn't have to wear it on his finger.'

'Through his nose?' Patrick had been joking, but Livia's expression suggested it wasn't his best attempt at humour. 'Oh. Right. Well, if you happen to bump into a lost-looking Izzy when you're in town . . .'

'Midlife crisis going well, then?'

Patrick gave her a look. 'Some days, I wish I'd stopped at the Porsche.'

'Turning out to be rather high-maintenance?'

'The Porsche, no. Izzy . . .' He sighed. 'There are times I think she's the best thing that's ever happened to me. But there are also times when I look at her and wonder what on earth she's doing with me. And who I'm trying to kid.'

'"Kid" being the appropriate word?'

He rolled his eyes. 'I always used to laugh at those older men who paraded around with these much younger women, but now I'm one of them.'

Livia smiled sympathetically. 'And you're worried people are laughing at you?'

Patrick thought for a moment. 'I wasn't. Though I am now!' He forced a grin. 'No, it's not that.'

'Thinking you're a perv, then?'

'No! Well, perhaps a little. But surely I deserve a little fun? After—'

'Of course you do!' Livia gave his hand a squeeze. 'Only . . .'

'What?'

'This is fun, is it?'

'Yes, it is. Most of the time.'

'So, what are you going to do?'

Patrick shrugged. 'Why do I need to *do* anything?'

'Because, right now, you don't seem particularly happy.'

'That's because we've just had an argument. And I know I'd be even more unhappy without her.'

'You sure you're not just trying to rub Sarah's face in it?'

Patrick laughed. 'This would be a pretty extreme way of doing that, wouldn't it?' He shook his head. 'No, this isn't about revenge, Liv. It's more . . . I don't know what it's more of, to be honest. Sarah left me. Had an affair, remember? And because of that, she got to keep the house, and look after my daughter . . . It was almost as if she got rewarded for the shitty way she behaved. And that makes *me* feel pretty shitty, you know? Izzy . . . doesn't. Quite the opposite, in fact. We have – what is it the youth say? – lots of LOLs. It's fun. There's no pressure. We're both having a good time. And it turns out we've actually got a lot more in common than I first thought.'

'I don't dare ask what that is!'

'Plus my ego needed a boost.'

'And is it getting one?'

'You bet it is!' he said. Walking round with someone who looked like Izzy on his arm, incidents like the man in Stella McCartney, and then Liam by the pool . . . Men were always flirting with – or, at least, leering at – Izzy. He felt the same sense of pride when people admired the Porsche. Though, admittedly, that didn't come with a helping of jealousy. Or was it insecurity? 'Besides,' he continued, 'what's the alternative? I try to find someone my own age, someone who doesn't have all the baggage you accumulate when you get to this stage in life, all the bitterness and mistrust that going through betrayal and a divorce can give you . . . ?'

'Good luck with that!'

'Or I spend my time with someone a bit less . . . cynical.'

Livia shifted her position on the sofa so she could look at him directly. 'Did it ever occur to you that the reason she's with you is because she *is* cynical?'

'Huh?'

'Why isn't Izzy with someone her own age?'

'Thanks very much!'

'No, I mean . . . what issues does she have that you help her with?'

Patrick thought for a moment. 'Cash flow, perhaps?'

'I'm sure that's not all . . .'

'Come on, Liv. I'd love to think she was with me for my looks and sparkling personality . . .' He paused. 'In fact, that's what I *am* going to think.'

'Patrick . . .'

'Hey – not everyone's lucky enough to have what you and Jed have. Some of us . . . we just go with what's in front of us. I tried the road you went down, and for whatever reason, it didn't work out for me. So can you blame me for wanting to take the path less travelled?'

Livia made a face as if to suggest that Izzy was hardly 'less travelled', and Patrick laughed, despite himself. 'There's a reason that route doesn't get a lot of traffic, Patrick. And it's usually because the people who take it end up getting lost.' She hesitated for a moment. 'And, you know, the money thing . . .'

Patrick shrugged. 'Everything costs. My divorce certainly did, and that wasn't even my fault! So if you're going to be paying, you might as well get what you want.'

Livia nodded contemplatively. 'Is Izzy what you want?'

He thought for a moment. 'Maybe.'

'And is Izzy getting what *she* wants?'

'She wouldn't be here if she wasn't. She's a grown woman.'

'Only just!'

'Even so. She can make her own choices.'

'What if her own choices include wanting to get married? Having kids?'

'Well, I'm afraid where I'm concerned, that's not on the table. Besides, she's much too young.'

'You might think that. She might not.'

'Why? What's she been saying?' Patrick gave her a look of mock horror, then he shook his head. 'Does she really look like the kind of person who's ready for the school run?'

Livia laughed. 'Only if she's the one being dropped off!'

'Ha ha. Besides, she knows the score.'

'Does she? Have you actually told her?'

Patrick looked over his shoulder towards the lift, willing Jed to appear like he had earlier and bring this uncomfortable conversation to a close. 'As I'm sure you can imagine, we don't tend to have a lot of deep and meaningful conversations.'

'That's because you're too busy having—'

'Fun! And no, it's because we don't need to.'

'Hey!' Livia reached over and patted him on the knee. 'As long as you're happy.'

'Who *is* happy, Liv? Look around you. Rachel's got a face on her like it's the end of the world. Rich obviously wasn't happy, or he'd be here today. And Liam . . . to be honest, it's hard to tell how he feels about anything, but that smile on his face quite often seems to be as fake as whatever lines he uses on those women of his. Besides, even if you think you're happy, it's only a temporary thing. No, as long as you're not *un*happy – I think that's as much as you can ask for.' He stopped talking abruptly when he saw Livia's face had fallen. 'But hey.

Don't listen to me. We're here for your wedding. And that's a happy thing, yes?'

'It is.' Livia looked exasperatedly at her watch. 'Assuming Jed gets his backside in gear.'

Patrick nodded, then his expression changed, as if a thought had just occurred to him. 'Speaking of knowing the score, Liv, tell me something . . .' he said, his voice a few decibels quieter than normal. 'Jed's aware this whole thing isn't legal, right?'

'What? Me press-ganging him into marrying me? Like when you beat a confession out of a prisoner?'

'No, the actual marriage. In England, I mean. The first thing Jed knew about this was when you popped the question yesterday, so I'm assuming you haven't given notice or anything?'

Livia looked at him guiltily. 'Um . . . no. We'd have had to do that twenty-eight days before this. Which would have meant him knowing what was going on, obviously.'

'So he has no idea that what he's going to be doing later doesn't mean anything.'

'It means something to me!'

'That's not what I meant, and you know it.'

Livia glanced towards the lift again, a little anxiously this time, in case Jed might suddenly appear and overhear them. 'It's symbolic, though, isn't it? As far as Jed's concerned, he's marrying me. The fact we'll have to get *actually* married back in England to rubber-stamp it is neither here nor there.' She let out a nervous laugh. 'Well, it's here *and* there, of course.'

Patrick harrumphed, provoking a 'What?' from Livia.

He held his hands up. 'Okay. Tricking him into marrying you is one thing, but tricking him into thinking he's marrying you when actually he isn't is something completely different.'

'Why? Perception is reality and all that.'

'Except it's not in this case, is it?'

'Well . . .'

'How do you think he's going to feel when he finds out?'

'If he finds out.'

'*When* he finds out. People always do, Liv. And trust me, there's nothing worse than secrets to wreck a marriage. Even when it's not a legal one.'

'So you think what I'm doing is wrong?'

Patrick reached over and patted the back of her hand. 'Not necessarily. I just think you might be going about it in slightly the wrong way.'

'But I'm doing it because I love him, Patrick. Because we love each other. Even if I am tricking him into it, surely that justifies . . .'

Livia's voice had trailed off, so Patrick folded his arms. 'There's tricking, and there's presenting someone with a fait accompli . . .'

'That's just how we *are*, though! When we're back in England, I'll tell him we simply have to get it "ratified".' Livia made air quotes around the last word, then she sat back on the sofa and nodded, as if pleased with her plan *and* her explanation. 'And besides, who's going to tell him?'

Patrick pursed his lips. That sounded too much like a warning.

'Liv . . .'

'*Please*, Patrick. I asked you here to give *me* away. Not the game.'

'Take it from me, Liv, men don't like to be made fools of, especially in public. Jed might already feel like an idiot because you've done this to him, and in front of everyone . . .'

'But it was supposed to be a surprise. Jed likes surprises. Tonight's going to be *fun*.'

'He needs to know. Because if he ever finds out that he's stood up in front of us all this evening and gone through with something, when everyone except for him knew it didn't amount to anything . . . can you blame him if he reacts badly to that?'

'If you tell him, I'll never forgive you.'

Livia was looking at him imploringly, suddenly vulnerable, so Patrick let out a long sigh. 'Of course I won't,' he said. 'But if *you* don't, he might never forgive *you*. Have you thought about that?'

After the third person had spotted him and burst out laughing, Liam had peeled himself up off his sun lounger and hurried into the poolside toilets – and now, standing in front of the full-length mirror, he could see what the source of the amusement was. Thanks to Izzy's 'artful' application of sunblock, his back was now an angry red, apart from . . . a pretty anatomically accurate, white-outlined representation of a certain part of the male anatomy stretching from just above his buttocks all the way up between his shoulder blades. He'd assumed the people walking past and pointing had been doing so because they'd recognised him – but now he knew differently.

Frantically, he grabbed a hand towel from the pile next to the sink and scrubbed at any part of the 'design' he could reach, hoping it might come off, but to no avail – Izzy's factor 50 had done its job. Mouthing a silent 'Fuck!', he stalked back outside, keeping his back to the wall as best he could, though when he reached his sun lounger, a gruff voice from behind him made him jump.

'Look at that prick!'

Angrily he wheeled round, to see a huge, muscled man dressed in a tiny pair of Speedos staring at him, a gorgeous woman on his arm, and before Liam could help himself, his 'What did you say?' made the pair stop in their tracks.

'I said, look at that prick.' The man pointed at him. 'The one someone's drawn on your back, I mean.'

Liam glared at him. This happened a lot. Someone – or more accurately, usually someone's girlfriend – would notice him and point him out to their partner, which for some reason would turn them into

Mister Aggressive. And while Liam knew it normally came from insecurity, worried the reality star might give *their* relationship a dose of reality – it didn't stop it being incredibly annoying. He'd normally laugh it off, and try and diffuse the situation with a joke. But there were some times he just didn't find it funny.

'What's it to you?'

The meathead opened his mouth, then closed it again. He obviously hadn't thought this through any further than the first insult. 'There's a huge prick. On your back,' he repeated after a moment, just in case Liam wasn't aware of it.

The way the man's girlfriend was smiling, Liam suspected the balance had swung in his favour. He winked at the woman and – perhaps not thinking things through himself – said, 'I'd be more worried about the one in front of me, if I were you!' And while he'd meant it as a reflection of his own physical attributes, by the way the man's expression had darkened Liam could see how his comment had perhaps been open to misinterpretation.

'*What did you say?*'

'Here!' said Liam, quickly, glancing down at the front of his shorts. 'As opposed to . . .' He nodded at the man, then realised to his horror he'd possibly just accused him of being somewhat underdeveloped in the manhood area. Though given the fit of his budgie smugglers, he guessed that accusation wouldn't have been wrong.

The man took a menacing step towards him, so Liam held both hands up. 'Hey,' he said, 'you started it!'

'And I'll finish it, if you're not careful.'

'Leave it, Darren!' The man's girlfriend was grabbing on to his arm, holding him back in an almost comical way, and Liam half-expected her to add 'He's not worth it' – though judging by the way she seemed to be sizing him up, he suspected she possibly thought he *was*.

The man – Darren – mumbled something to himself as he allowed himself to be led away, and Liam breathed a sigh of relief. He found his

T-shirt and hurriedly pulled it on, though as he grabbed his bag and marched back into reception – surely his room was ready now? – the hotel manager beckoned him over.

'Excuse me, *señor?*'

'It wasn't my fault,' Liam protested. 'The girl who was next to me earlier drew something on my back with sunscreen, and he just . . . well, I don't know what he just. Some people . . .'

'I don't understand,' said the manager.

'Nor do I. It's as if they're jealous because I'm a celebrity, and for some reason they think I'm going to steal their girlfriend. Obviously I could if I wanted to, but . . .'

The manager gave a quick shake of his head, as if trying to clear it. 'Let me start again. You are Liam Woodward, yes?'

Finally, thought Liam. 'Yes!'

'You are . . .' The manager narrowed his eyes. *'El mejor hombre?'*

Liam hesitated. Maybe that was what *Big Brother* was called here in Spain. Though he didn't want to take any chances. 'What?'

'Sorry. I am trying to remember how to translate. The . . . best man? For the wedding of Jed and Livia?'

'Oh. Yeah, that's me,' said Liam, a little deflated.

'You maybe have a small problem.'

'Nah. I'll keep my shirt on, and—'

'It is not your shirt.'

'Huh?'

'You are in charge of the wedding?'

'I suppose so . . .' said Liam, suspiciously, hoping the man wasn't going to ask for any money. That kind of thing was Livia's department. Plus, his royalty cheques (rather than reality cheques, which Jed kept telling him were something he needed) had starting getting scarcer, and in terms of other employment . . . he had to admit that 'being famous' hadn't turned out to be the best career option so far, didn't quite get you that many enquiries via LinkedIn, and Liam wasn't sure exactly what else he was qualified to do.

'Because the DJ is here. For tonight.'

'And that's a problem because . . . ?'

'See for yourself.'

Liam followed the manager through a door and down the stairs to the hotel's car park, where a man in a baggy Hawaiian shirt was unloading a pair of gigantic loudspeakers from the back of a battered old Volvo.

'I don't understand.'

'Perhaps I should have said "hear for yourself".' The hotel manager placed a finger on his lips. 'Listen,' he said.

Liam did as instructed for a moment, then he frowned. 'Is that . . . sobbing?'

The manager nodded. 'His wife left him.'

'What? When?'

'A long time ago.'

'So why is he crying?'

'Because I have just told him that tonight there will be a wedding. And today is his wedding anniversary.'

'Ah.' Liam made a face. 'Can we find a replacement?'

'No. And neither can he,' said the manager as they walked across to where the man was struggling with an armful of cables. 'Which is part of his problem.'

Liam stood there for a moment, wondering what to do. He'd been the cause of more than a few tears in his time, but the people crying had always been women, and while he'd usually been able to get them to stop, his tried-and-tested method had never been – and wasn't ever going to be – tried or tested on a man. Thinking that perhaps a brush with celebrity might lighten the mood a bit, he cleared his throat, put his smile on full beam and tapped the man on the shoulder.

'*Hola!*' he said, cheerily, adding a begrudging 'I'm Liam' when the man failed to recognise him. 'From *Big Brother*?'

'Roberto,' said the DJ, miserably. 'From Barcelona.'

'No, I meant . . . Never mind. Can I help you with that?'

'If you like.'

Liam hefted one of the speakers, then followed Roberto back up the stairs and into the hotel. 'Where do you want this?'

Roberto shrugged indifferently. 'I don't care.'

'Right.' The manager indicated that Liam should put it in a small room behind reception, and he did as he was told before following Roberto back downstairs. 'So listen, *amigo*. Are you going to be okay to DJ this evening?'

Roberto shrugged again, and showed Liam the playlist on his iPad. 'I press play, everyone dances. It's not, how do you say . . . ?'

'Rocket science.'

'A rocking séance.'

'Close enough,' said Liam.

He peered at the tablet's screen, and swiped up and down the selection – mainly bands from the '60s and '70s that you possibly had to be *in* your 60s or 70s to appreciate. From what he could see, Roberto's choice of songs wasn't going to lead to a rocking anything.

'Is okay? The music?'

'Not my taste, to be honest, but I'm sure the olds will like it.' Liam carried on scrolling, pausing when he saw a group called 'Three Dog Night'. He'd had a few of those in his time. 'You've not got anything a bit more . . . modern?'

Roberto looked offended. 'I have some Dire Straits.'

'Which is exactly what this playlist is. You do know there's going to be a wedding?'

Roberto had visibly flinched at the word. 'Ha!' he said, contemptuously, and Liam and the hotel manager exchanged glances.

'Is your wedding?'

'No!' Liam let out a short laugh. 'I'm the best man.'

'*Qué?*'

'The best man. *El* . . .' Liam hesitated – what was the rest of it? But before he could go with '*besto mano*', Roberto glared at him, burst into tears again and stomped off towards his car. 'What the . . . ?'

The hotel manager made a face. 'His wife. She ran off with *his* best man.'

'Great.' Liam winced at the screech of tyres, then peered after the rapidly disappearing Volvo. 'He is coming back, I take it?'

The manager shrugged. 'I think perhaps no.'

Liam recalled Roberto's playlist, and found himself hoping exactly that. Maybe this was a blessing in disguise. After all, women loved a DJ, didn't they? Up in front of everyone, looking cool (if a little sweaty), throwing down some bangin' choonz, MC-ing the evening, responding to 'Do you do requests?' with 'I'll do whatever you like, love' . . . He'd been to Ibiza a few times, and while this was hardly Pacha, all he had to do was stand up there, nodding his head in time to the music, a set of earphones held casually to one ear, his shirt open . . . Or maybe he'd forego the 'open shirt' bit in case it fell off and exposed his back, thus exposing Patrick's crazy girlfriend's handiwork. Even so, once he'd smashed it as the DJ, he'd have his pick of the female guests. Which meant he could relax for the rest of the afternoon, perhaps try and get his tan evened out.

With a smile, he headed upstairs to the bar, ordered himself a cold beer, pulled his phone out of his pocket and navigated to Spotify.

'Beautiful, isn't it?' Jed was flicking through the photos he'd just taken on his phone, before noticing that the last one of Livia in front of what the guidebook had reliably informed him was another of Gaudí's masterpieces – not that he could pronounce the building's name – seemed to show her frowning at her watch.

'I suppose.'

'Something wrong?' he said, though he really hoped there wasn't. For the last half an hour, they'd enjoyed a pleasant stroll down Passeig de Gràcia, Barcelona's grandest street, alternately admiring the boulevard's incredible architecture and popping inside the various shops to make the most of their air conditioning – and so far, Livia hadn't mentioned the word 'wedding' once.

'We're going to be late.'

'You still haven't told me what for.'

Livia gave him a look. 'Plus we're just a little far from a toilet for my liking.'

'Can't you hold it?'

'That's easy for you to say. You haven't got *your* baby putting all its weight directly onto your bladder whenever you take a step.'

Jed returned Livia's smirk. It was a running joke between them that their baby always became 'his' baby whenever it was causing some problem. He made a mental note to remind her of that when – *if* – the child ever did something good, then smiled supportively.

'Well, department stores always have toilets, and we're not that far from the El Corte Inglés in Plaça Catalunya . . .'

'We are if you're six months pregnant and wearing heels.'

'Well, if you hadn't insisted on . . .' Jed swallowed the rest of the sentence, deciding it might be in his interest to change tack. He knew Livia felt the size of a small planet, and any occasion she had a chance to dress up and remind herself she was actually a woman was a good thing. 'They're renovating that building over there. Maybe there's a Portaloo?'

'Hardly, Jed.'

'Do you actually need to go now?'

'No.'

'So, what's the . . . ?'

'I don't always get a lot of notice.'

'Oh-kay . . .' Jed peered up and down the street. 'There's always behind a tree.'

'That's helpful. Thank you.'

She took the arm he was offering her, and they walked on in comfortable silence for a while, Jed trying to work out where this mystery tour was taking them, Livia making a selection of faces at her side-on reflection in the various shop windows, until she suddenly stopped in her tracks.

'This is the place,' she said, pointing excitedly at the jeweller's on the corner in front of them, and Jed grunted in acknowledgement as he squinted at the building. He'd begun perspiring heavily the moment they'd exited the cool confines of the hotel, and while he longed to set foot in what was sure to be the shop's air-conditioned interior, he knew what was inside might make him sweat even more.

'What place?'

'Hello?' Livia was pointing at a display of extremely sparkly rings in the window, and he almost wanted to facepalm. *Of course* she'd need a ring. He guessed she hadn't brought one with her, just in case he'd said no yesterday – that would be a refund no one would want to go in and ask for – and the idea that she'd considered he might have refused her proposal made him feel terrible.

'Looks expensive,' he said, taking in the security-locked door, armed guard and – always the telltale sign – the lack of prices in the window.

'Is that all you've got to contribute?'

'It does. Just saying.'

'I'm sorry. Would you rather we had a look on eBay? Or maybe waited until we got home and then went to Argos?'

Jed kept quiet, suspecting 'yes' wouldn't be the most diplomatic answer. And nor would 'I'd rather we didn't go *anywhere*'.

Livia mock-glared at him, then pressed the door buzzer, and as the security guard hauled the heavy glass door open for them and ushered them inside, Jed nudged her. 'You realise he probably adds about twenty per cent to the price of everything in here?'

'Will you stop moaning? It's not as if you're paying, is it?'

For a moment, Jed wanted to point out that seeing as he and Livia had a joint bank account, then technically he was, but he decided to do as instructed. 'Okay,' he said. 'But let me do the talking.'

'Whatever for?'

'Well, they might see that you're, you know . . .' Jed glanced at her stomach. 'First rule of sales – if you know the prospect's desperate for what you're selling, you can inflate the price by quite a—' He stopped talking again, though this time because Livia's look suggested it might be good for his continued well-being.

As she marched up to the counter, he trailed unenthusiastically behind, hanging back like a reluctant child at the dentist's as she smiled at the assistant.

'Do you speak English?' she said, brightly.

'Of course,' said the man, with a more refined accent than Jed had. 'How can I help?'

'Olivia Wilson? I phoned ahead?'

Livia mimed putting a phone to her ear, and Jed sniggered. 'He's already said he speaks English, Liv. You don't have to mime everything.'

'Maybe *you* could make like a mime and keep quiet?'

The assistant smiled politely through their exchange. 'Oh yes,' he said, once he was sure they'd finished. 'From England. You're here for the rings.'

At the mention of the plural, Jed looked up suddenly. '*Rings?*'

'That's right,' said Livia, and he frowned.

'How many were you planning on wearing?'

'One.'

'So . . . ?'

'So we need to get you one too.'

Jed's jaw dropped. 'Hold on. You didn't say anything about me wearing a wedding ring.'

'What did you think you'd be doing?'

Jed frowned at her. He hadn't thought he'd be 'doing' *any* of this, so it wasn't really a fair question. 'Well, I thought I might just get a tattoo saying "Property of Livia" . . .'

'That's not funny.'

'Well, that's what it feels like to me. I don't want to wear a ring.'

Livia placed a hand on his arm. 'Why ever not?'

'Because . . .' Jed thought for a moment. The real reason – that what a wedding ring represented was so abhorrent to him – possibly wasn't the best of arguments right now. Nor perhaps was he saying he'd always thought jewellery on men was naff, though Livia knew he'd never been a fan: she'd tried to buy him an expensive watch for his thirtieth birthday but he'd rejected it in favour of the cheap Casio digital model that Liam had given him years ago. In the end 'I don't wear jewellery' was the best he could come up with. And, perhaps not surprisingly, Livia had an answer for that.

'But this is a *wedding ring*.'

'It's still a ring,' he said, petulantly. 'From a jeweller's. So it's jewellery.'

'Yes, but . . .' Livia was already sounding exasperated, and Jed suspected this was an argument he wasn't going to win, even though he might be within his rights. 'It's symbolic, isn't it?'

'Symbolic,' said Jed, though he didn't want to ask, 'of what?'

'Of our commitment.'

'We're already committed, Liv.'

'I know, but . . .' The assistant was watching them interestedly, so Livia took Jed by the arm – rather firmly, he felt – and steered him away from the counter. 'They make some really nice rings for men nowadays. And the one I've picked out for you is . . .'

'You've *already chosen one*?' Jed found himself struggling to keep his voice down. How could Livia have forgotten the watch incident? 'Christ, Liv. I wouldn't buy *you* anything like this without you seeing it first, without at least discussing it, and now you feel you can just choose me a ring and expect me to wear it every day of my life without me even having a say in terms of what it looks like?'

'Jed . . .'

'What's happening to you? I get that you usually know best, but this is like you don't even know *me*.'

'That's not—'

'I don't want one!' he said, realising he was a foot stamp away from doing a pretty good impression of Barney's earlier tantrum. 'I'll lose it. Or I'll scratch it. And I don't want to go through the hassle of taking it off every time I want to do anything.'

'Like what?'

'Like . . .' Jed's mind went blank. He supposed he could possibly say DIY, but Livia already complained he didn't pull his weight around the house, so that was a whole can of worms he didn't want to open. 'Everything!'

'You could wear it round your neck.'

'What, like those African tribeswomen? How big a ring were you planning on—'

'Not like *that*. On a thong.' She caught sight of his expression. 'A piece of leather. Not a pair of my *pants*. Though it's a free country.'

Jed pursed his lips. Under normal circumstances, Livia's comment would have made him smile, but this was a million miles from normal circumstances.

He peered round the shop's luxurious interior. It was full of couples, choosing presents for each other, perhaps, or gifts for family members, or maybe doing exactly what he and Livia were doing. Though, tellingly, none of them were having an argument.

101

'Well, it's a no from me, I'm afraid. Which should be good news for you, because it means you can spend double on yours.'

'But what are we going to exchange?'

Jed threw his hands up in the air, perhaps a bit too vigorously given how Livia's face had fallen. 'Vows?'

Livia put a hand on her stomach, and looked around for the nearest chair, though she shrugged off Jed's attempt to help her towards it. 'Why wouldn't you want to wear a wedding ring?' she said, lowering herself onto the plush leather sofa in the corner of the shop. 'Are you ashamed of being married to me?'

'Not at all. It's just . . .' Jed took a deep breath, but Livia leapt in before he could collect his thoughts.

'Or are you worried it'll cramp your style when you go out on the pull?'

'Liv, don't be like that.' Jed looked at her imploringly. They didn't argue much, but whenever they did, this was Livia's sure-fire way of winning. Not by shouting the loudest, but by making him feel bad. And even after ten years, he hadn't developed a strategy to deal with it.

'Why are *you* being like that?'

'I'm going through with the wedding, aren't I?'

Almost as soon as the words had left his lips, Jed knew he'd made a mistake, particularly given how Livia's eyes had widened. And while she was never normally that emotional, the way the pregnancy had stirred up her hormones meant he'd probably just lit a fire it would take a good while for him to extinguish. If he even could.

'*Going through* with the wedding?' she said softly, her voice cracking a little.

'Well, yes.' He sat down gingerly next to her on the sofa, hating the fact that he'd hurt her, desperate to make things right, to explain – not that he had the faintest idea how. 'Seeing as you rather painted me into a corner with this whole Barcelona business . . .'

'Is that how you feel?' she said, sounding like she was on the verge of tears, and he frowned. Surely Livia could see that was what she'd done. Possibly what she'd even relied on to get him to say yes.

'Haven't you?'

Jed was arguing, though he understood it was pointless, knew how this was bound to go: Livia would pick on something he'd said – a word out of place or a thoughtless utterance – grab on to it with both hands, then beat him into guilty submission with it until he'd lost the will to resist. But how could he possibly explain the real reason – that he was afraid of letting her down as her husband? Because if he wasn't confident he could fulfil that role, how on earth could she rely on him to be a good father?

'Okay, Jed.' She sniffed loudly. 'Maybe I did – what was it? – "paint you into a corner".'

'Thank you,' said Jed, before realising from Livia's tone that this wasn't exactly going to be an admission of guilt. And certainly not an apology.

'And do you want to know *why* I "painted you into a corner"?'

Jed had to stop himself from flinching at Livia's aggressive use of air quotes. 'That wasn't what I—'

'Why I *had* to paint you into a corner? To *force* you to marry me?'

'That's not—'

'Because we've been together ten years, Jed. *Ten years*. And not *once* have you thought that I might like to make things a bit more permanent. Not for *one moment* did you consider that I might not want to be the world's oldest girlfriend . . .'

'You're hardly—'

' . . . or unmarried mother.'

'*Liv*—'

'But no, despite all our friends tying the knot, and me dropping the kinds of hints that even Stevie Wonder could see, you never once thought to ask me. Even after you got me pregnant.'

Jed bit his tongue. The baby had been Livia's idea too – and while he'd been more than happy to go along with it, right now he knew better than to remind her of that.

'And this is typical of you,' she continued. 'Not thinking about anyone else. Happy to just keep bumbling along while it suits you. As long as good old Jed's life isn't being interrupted or inconvenienced in any way; as long as you can go down to the pub every Wednesday night with that idiotic brother of yours . . .'

Jed opened his mouth to object, but to be fair, Livia could have chosen a number of much worse adjectives than 'idiotic' to describe Liam, and they'd all have been appropriate. Besides, he was pretty sure she hadn't finished.

'Well, I've got news for you.' Livia had folded her arms. 'Things are going to change. Things have to change. Because in a few months you're not going to know what's hit you. And if you – if *we* – don't have all our ducks in a row by then . . .'

Jed was nodding furiously. Why couldn't Livia see that this was his problem? As they'd witnessed all too vividly with Oliver and Sally, having a child changed your relationship, exposed the cracks, put you under pressure. Jed was already worried he wouldn't measure up when the baby arrived. Factor in that marriage was bound to change them too, change *him* – and not for the better – and they might as well say their goodbyes now.

He glanced anxiously around the shop; although they were still talking in whispers, they'd become stage ones, and several disapproving glances were coming his way. Even though the other customers might not speak English, given that an extremely agitated, upset-looking, heavily pregnant woman was sitting next to him – and becoming more agitated and upset by the second – Jed could see why they might be glaring daggers at him.

'Liv, *please*. Let's not do this here.'

'One thing I wanted. *One thing*. To be your wife,' she said, too upset to pay attention to him. 'And you didn't – or wouldn't – do anything about that. Couldn't even tell. So I was the one who had to get down on one knee – *and* in my condition – and do you know how many of my friends have had to do that? None,' she added, before giving him a chance to answer. 'So I'm sorry if you showing the world that you're my husband is such a horrendous thing that you can't even bring yourself to wear one small piece of jewellery . . . No, hang on, why should I be surprised? You didn't want to get married in the first place, so why on earth would you want to broadcast the fact?'

'Liv . . .' Jed imagined that was probably a rhetorical question, and even if it wasn't, he couldn't think what an appropriate answer might be. 'It's not that,' he said eventually, after a pause so long he'd started to doubt his initial assessment.

'Well, what is it, Jed?' she snapped, all attempts to keep her voice low long-forgotten. 'Why on earth do you find the idea of marrying me so . . . horrible?'

'I don't. I just . . .' He reached out to take her hand, to hold her close, trying to find the right words to soothe her, but Livia was already shaking him off angrily.

'Just leave me alone!' she shouted.

And as she hauled herself up and stomped out of the shop, Jed knew better than to follow her.

Livia was striding purposefully down Passeig de Gràcia, though with no idea where she was headed. Surprised to find herself on the verge of tears – Livia had never been a crier – she made herself do some of those breathing exercises she'd learned at her antenatal classes, until the urge had disappeared. So much for her brilliant plan to surprise him like this, and for this weekend to be one last big hurrah before the baby arrived.

Had she got him all wrong, thinking he'd appreciate all of this, just like he used to appreciate all the other times they'd been crazy and spontaneous? How could anyone not love the idea of a small, intimate ceremony followed by dinner with their closest friends, at a lovely old hotel in a city you couldn't fail to have a good time in, where the sun shone, the beer was cheap and cold (even the non-alcoholic version, in her case), and – to add a drop or two of poignancy to the mix – the city where they'd met . . . *and* on their tenth anniversary? Why it was all going so wrong was beyond her.

While her earlier conversation with Patrick had made her feel a little guilty, Livia hadn't felt guilty enough to tell Jed the truth – not that at the jeweller's had been the appropriate time. Nor would *any* time this weekend, she suspected. No – they'd go through with tonight's 'ceremony' as planned, then later, perhaps *much* later, certainly not today, she'd 'fess up and they'd have a laugh about it like they always did, and make plans together to go and do it all over again, but for real this time.

She hoped.

A woman pushing a pram was heading towards her, and Livia couldn't help but take a peek inside. There, peacefully sleeping, dressed up in the cutest of white outfits, was the most beautiful baby she'd ever seen. She felt her stomach lurch – her child, maybe sensing another nearby, perhaps wanting to say hello – and found herself surprised to feel quite emotional. In three months she'd be a *mother*. Though hopefully not a single one, after her and Jed's little bust-up.

The woman looked at her stomach, smiling broadly before heading off along the street, and Livia felt a weird mix of contentment and nervousness envelop her. Soon she'd be a member of a club that, a year or so ago, she'd suddenly found herself so desperate to join. And while Jed had assured her she'd be a good mother, that she was good at everything she set her mind to, Livia had her doubts. Knew she'd be calling on Jed a *lot*. Was convinced she'd be needing him more than ever if she wanted to avoid bringing another Barney into the world. Which was why she was so keen to get married. To (hopefully) guarantee that Jed would be there for her. And to convince her that everything would be okay.

She shuddered briefly. She'd known Sally and Oliver back when they weren't even 'trying' – though they'd admitted they weren't trying not to – and they'd been totally different people. The life and soul of any party, able to start one almost out of nothing, always the last man and woman standing – yet now? This morning was the first time Livia had seen either of them for the best part of a year. Though by the looks of them, they'd aged about five times that much.

She'd managed to keep a straight face in front of them, in front of *Jed*, but secretly she suspected she'd been just as appalled as he'd looked. Because parenthood was like when you were facing a wild animal, wasn't it? Show the first sniff of fear and you were in trouble. So Livia had put up with the tantrum, ignored the snot, not screwed her face up at the screaming, and reminded herself theirs would be different. In a mantra. Over and over and over.

She slowed her pace and looked back over her shoulder, a little surprised not to see Jed hurrying after her, especially since given her current size, she wasn't that difficult to catch. Although maybe he'd come out of the jeweller's and simply headed in the wrong direction. It wouldn't be the first time. Jed was one of those rare beasts – a man who'd actually admit he had a poor sense of direction. Luckily for the both of them, Livia was a dab hand with a map.

A bridal boutique on the opposite side of the street caught her eye, so she crossed the road, intending to admire the stick-thin, faceless mannequins in the window. And though the figures themselves were perhaps a little scary, the dresses on display were . . . 'amazing' didn't quite do them justice: intricate, ornate creations in the whitest of whites, beautifully sculpted at the waist – though obviously not designed for someone whose current favourite T-shirt (a present from Jed) had a caption on the front which read *Does My Mum Look Big In This?*

The shop was busy, and as Livia peered into the expensively dec-orated interior she was surprised to find herself feeling a little jeal-ous. To the left, a young woman was trying on a dress in front of a huge mirror, her girlfriends snapping away excitedly on their phones, occasionally stopping to sip from glasses of cava, all of them with the broadest of smiles on their faces. In the far corner, an older lady and a girl Livia assumed must be her daughter were sitting at a desk leaf-ing through a catalogue, the looks of delight on both of their faces something to behold. At the back, a strikingly beautiful woman was standing, motionless, in an equally stunning creation, while an assistant fussed around her, pinning and clipping parts of her dress – a first fit-ting, Livia guessed – and as she watched them, she was surprised to find her jealousy being replaced by anger. This was what she was forgoing, thanks to Jed's thoughtlessness. What she was missing out on, because her boyfriend hadn't even thought she might want *just one day* where she was a little bit more special than everyone else.

Okay, so parading around looking like a meringue, paranoid some-one was going to spill something on a dress that probably cost more than their car *and* that she'd only ever wear the once probably wouldn't be top of her bucket list, but even so, there was a principle at stake here. If you thought about it (and Livia had thought about it), all she was asking of him was that he wear one *tiny* piece of jewellery – and under his shirt on a piece of bloody *string*, if he wanted – so why was *she* the bad guy all of a sudden?

Suddenly feeling a little light-headed in the afternoon heat, Livia lowered herself onto a nearby shady bench, looked at her watch, then caught herself. *Keep your eye on the prize*, Patrick had always told her – and right now, she was almost in danger of forgetting that. If Jed didn't want to wear a ring . . . he was right, she could spend the money on herself! So she'd calm down, go back to the jeweller's, collect *her* ring, then head back to the hotel and get on with the day as planned. In a few hours, she'd be married. How they did it . . . well, surely the important thing was *that* they did it. And they would.

Assuming Jed wasn't in a taxi right now, heading for the airport.

'I take?'

The man had spoken in heavily accented English, and Rachel looked up with a start. He was a little older than she was, she guessed, well built, olive-skinned, dressed in a shiny black tracksuit and matching baseball cap, and more than a little sweaty. Although the sun *was* hot – and after several hours of sightseeing, Rachel was sure she wasn't smelling like a rose herself.

'I'm okay, thank you,' she said, politely but curtly, then she repositioned herself, trying desperately to get the whole of the stunning cathedral in the background, though as she'd found out at the stadium earlier, selfies weren't always that easy to take, especially when you were trying to include something as impressively large as Barcelona's most famous building, the Sagrada Família. But this was the last stop on her bus tour before she headed back to the hotel, and Rachel was determined to have at least one other photo that included her, to prove she'd actually been here and not just uploaded a random selection from Google Images to her Facebook page.

'I take,' insisted the man, maintaining eye contact as he knelt down to tighten the laces on his pristine Nike trainers. 'Then it will be a photo of two beautiful things. Not half of one.'

Rachel blushed. As cheesy as it was, the compliment was welcome after what had been a harrowing dumping (assuming it *was* a compliment, and not just something lost in translation).

'Well . . . yes, then. Thank you.' She handed the man her iPhone and pointed to the camera button on the screen. 'Here. You just have to—'

'Is okay,' said the man. 'I know where to touch.'

I'll bet you do, thought Rachel, noticing the glint in his eye. But, she reminded herself, she was only here for the weekend, and a holiday fling was the last thing she was after – especially with someone whose everyday wardrobe evidently came from whatever the Spanish equivalent of JD Sports was.

'Is new iPhone, *sí?*' he continued, examining her mobile, and Rachel smiled politely. She'd only got it yesterday from the Apple store round the corner from her office – to cheer herself up, though she'd hesitated when she realised it cost more than the whole of her forthcoming weekend in Barcelona would.

'Right. I mean, *sí*,' Rachel said, wishing he'd just get on with taking the photo, then she felt a little ungrateful. The man was doing her a favour, after all, and besides, if you counted her row-mate on the flight this morning, two men had begun talking to her out of the blue so far today, and although neither of them were her type (and actually, she wondered if the man on the plane was *anyone's* type), she supposed it was better than nothing.

'Okay,' said the man, holding her phone up at arm's length and squinting at the screen. 'You go back a little . . .'

'Here?' asked Rachel, taking a step closer to the cathedral.

'More,' said the man, moving a yard backwards himself, so she did as she was told.

'*Here?*'

'More,' he said, checking the traffic, then stepping backwards off the kerb.

Rachel frowned. 'I just want me and the building, not me and the whole city,' she said, wondering why the man seemed to be edging further away from her.

And slipping her phone into the pocket of his tracksuit top.

Before turning round and making a run for it . . .

'Stop!' she shouted at his rapidly disappearing back, already fearing she was too late. 'Thief!'

A nearby group of Japanese tourists began babbling excitedly (a few of them even taking photos of her) as she scrabbled for the *Lonely Planet* guidebook in her bag, flicking quickly through to the phrase-book section at the back to try and locate the Spanish word for 'thief', hoping that shouting *that* might provoke more of a response from the assembled crowds. Then she cursed her stupidity. They were tourists – they probably didn't *speak* Spanish.

Desperately, Rachel began to give chase, though she gave up after little more than a yard or two. She'd never catch him, especially wearing the powder-blue Menorcan sandals she'd treated herself to from a shop earlier, which were starting to chafe quite painfully.

She stood helplessly on the kerb as – from the other side of the road – the thief glanced back over his shoulder to check whether she was chasing him, then he gave her a disdainful sneer, tapped the pocket where her phone was and slowed down to an arrogant strut.

Rachel couldn't believe it. How could she have just given a complete stranger her phone like that? She'd always been too trusting. Too naive. Though perhaps this was karma for sending that photo to Rich. She wasn't a nasty person. And the one time she'd done something like that, something so out of character . . . clearly it had come back to bite her on the backside.

Then, suddenly, someone flashed past her, a blur of pumping arms and heavily muscled legs, and within moments the man – she'd caught a whiff of his Lynx body spray as he'd passed, the same one Rich wore but smelling a *lot* sexier right now – had caught the thief up, grabbing him by his tracksuit collar just as he climbed onto the back of a waiting moped.

Rachel hurried across the road, narrowly avoiding a funny-looking, bright yellow three-wheeler, but by the time she reached the opposite pavement the moped had sped off and the thief was nowhere to be seen. 'My *phone!*' she wailed, and the man turned to acknowledge her, his face a little flushed from the chase. He was good-looking, a foot taller than she was, athletically built and with the bluest eyes Rachel had ever seen. And (she realised, once she'd finally stopped checking him out) he appeared to be holding the thief's tracksuit top.

'Ta-da!' he said, slightly out of breath, then to her amazement he reached into the tracksuit's pocket and retrieved her phone. 'Is anything else missing?'

'No, I . . . I mean, he . . .' Rachel stopped talking and pretended to check her bag, not wanting to admit she'd handed her phone over willingly, or that answering yes to the thief's 'I take?' had virtually been giving him permission to steal it. 'That was amazing. And brave!'

'Hey – I'm hardly Sherlock Holmes. I was . . . I was watching you.' He grinned sheepishly. 'Anyway, then I heard you shout, saw him running, and put two and two together.' He handed the phone back to her and threw the tracksuit top into a nearby bin. 'And it was hardly brave. Unless you count running across the street without looking. Which, given how the Spanish don't often stop at zebra crossings, was probably more reckless.'

'Even so. How can I ever thank you?'

'No need.'

'I feel so . . .' Rachel hesitated. When she thought about it, she was feeling a number of things right now.

'Stupid?'

'Well, yes. And thank you for pointing that out.'

'Don't. These people are professionals. They know tourists get distracted by the beauty of the buildings, so they . . . Are you okay?'

Rachel realised she'd grabbed the man's arm – her knees had suddenly gone weak as the adrenaline wore off. Either that or it was the effect of standing so close to him. 'Yes. I'm just a little . . . I think I need to sit down.'

'Come on.' He steered her to a nearby bench and nodded at the café across the pavement. 'Can I get you some water? A coffee?'

'I don't like coffee. I'm more of a tea girl.' Rachel shook her head, though more because she didn't know why she'd blurted that out. 'I've got some. Water. Not tea. In my bag.'

'Right. Good to know. My name's Jay, by the way.'

'Rachel.'

'It's definitely Jay. I've seen my birth certificate.'

'No, *I'm* Rachel . . .'

She realised he was joking, then felt her lower lip begin to tremble – and to her surprise, Rachel burst into tears.

'Hey,' Jay said. 'My joke wasn't that bad, surely?'

'No,' she sobbed. 'Sorry. I'm being silly.'

'I understand.' He smiled sympathetically. 'You've just been robbed. It must have been quite a shock.'

Rachel nodded, though in actual fact she wasn't crying about being robbed. She was crying about how she *wouldn't* have been robbed if her original plan had worked out and she'd been here with her boyfriend (or rather, *ex*-boyfriend), because then *he'd* have been the one taking the photo so she wouldn't have had to hand her phone to someone dressed (now she thought about it) for running away rather than just running. And while up until about two minutes ago she'd surprised herself by having a good time, had even thought she might like to do more of this solo-travelling lark, yet again her inability to pick men had even brought that to an end.

'Hold on . . .' Jay hauled himself up from the bench and walked across to the café, helping himself to a handful of serviettes from the dispenser on a vacant table. 'Here,' he said, handing them to her as he sat back down.

Rachel blew her nose loudly, then took a few breaths to calm herself. 'Thanks.'

'You sure you're okay?'

'I think so. Yes. Now, at least.'

'Great.'

They sat, staring at the cathedral for a moment or two, and then, as if reading her mind, Jay said, 'Stunning, isn't it?'

'It is,' said Rachel, though she was torn between gawping at the intricate carvings on the towering spires, the ornate stonework above the doorway, the religious sculptures – each a work of art in its own right . . . and the well-put-together figure next to her. 'And the statues . . .' She pointed to the space in front of the cathedral where a crowd was gathered, admiring an incredibly lifelike carving of a man dressed in robes. 'They almost seem *alive*.'

'Um, that one is.'

'Huh?'

'It's a guy with his face painted stone grey. He's a street performer.'

'Ah.' Rachel narrowed her eyes and realised – to her embarrassment – Jay was right, so she turned her attention back to the magnificent building. 'Gaudy,' she said, reaching for her guidebook. 'Isn't it?'

'Well, it's perhaps a little OTT for some people,' said Jay, then he laughed and facepalmed exaggeratedly. 'Oh, you mean the *architect*. His name's Gaudí. Rhymes with "rowdy".'

'Oh. Sorry about my accent. I can't pronounce any of these words. My Spanish is . . . well, non-existent, really.'

'Don't worry,' said Jay. 'Though we're actually in Catalonia. So technically we should be speaking Catalan.'

'Do you? Speak Catalan, I mean?'

'No. But I speak a little Spanish and there are some similarities, so I understand a bit.' He nodded towards the cathedral. 'Though when something's as breathtaking as that masterpiece, words can't really do it justice, whatever language you use.'

'Shame about all the cranes, though,' said Rachel. 'Are they repairing something?'

Jay smiled. 'Still building it, would you believe? Started in 1882, or thereabouts, and it's due to be completed in 2026. Or 2028. They're not sure. Even after a hundred and thirty years, they're reluctant to give a finish date.'

Rachel frowned. 'Sounds like they're using the same builders who did my bathroom,' she said, and Jay laughed.

'They're just taking their time. When something's worth doing and all that, I suppose . . .' He sat back on the bench, stretched out his legs, and laced his fingers behind his head. 'You know, I walk past this thing pretty much every day, and I've never actually just sat and looked at it?'

Rachel hoped Jay couldn't see her doing the same where he was concerned out of the corner of her eye. 'That's usually the way. Sometimes you just don't appreciate what's right in front of . . .' She stopped talking. That had been the line Rich had used when he'd finished with her, possibly to try to make her feel better, but it had had the opposite effect, and now, just as she had then, she swallowed so hard it made a sound.

'Are you *sure* you're okay?'

'Sorry. I'm just feeling a little weak. I . . .' Then, to her horror, and for the second time since arriving in Barcelona, her stomach started rumbling, so loudly that for a moment she hoped the noise was coming from the Metro line which passed underneath. 'I haven't eaten any lunch,' Rachel said quickly, though the truth was she hadn't had much breakfast either – all the cafés at Gatwick had been full of couples, and when she'd realised she'd be the only single (in both senses of the word) diner, she'd decided to skip what every diet she'd ever been on had insisted was the most important meal of the day. Then at the hotel, despite Livia's insistence, all she'd managed was a cup of coffee and half a croissant, and since then she'd been too busy taking in the Catalan capital's beautiful old streets to think about stopping for food.

She caught sight of a clock on the front of a nearby pharmacy, and realised it was well past one o'clock. 'So, I'm guessing you live here?'

'Yeah. Coming up to two years now.'

'You lucky thing,' said Rachel, genuinely. She'd only been here a matter of hours and she already loved the city.

'Aren't I? I mean, it was a bit of a wrench leaving England, but this job came up by chance, and sometimes in life you find yourself standing in front of a door, and unless you go through it, you'll never know where it leads.'

'That's good advice,' said Rachel, though the only door she'd seen recently was the one Rich had shown her. 'What do you do, if you don't mind me asking?'

'I'm a teacher. At the international school just round the corner.'

'What do you teach?'

'Kids.'

'No, I mean what sub— All right. You got me again.'

'D'you need me to fetch you more tissues?'

'Ha ha!'

'Maths.'

'Wow! That's . . .' Her voice trailed off, and Jay grinned.

'I know. Numbers aren't exactly exciting.'

Rachel had to bite her lip. She suspected getting *Jay's* number might be. 'Actually, I've got a degree in maths, so . . . No, you're right. They're not.' She blew her nose again. 'What brought you here in the first place? And please don't say EasyJet.'

Jay made a wistful face. '*Amor.*'

'A what?'

'*Amor,*' he said, enunciating carefully, elongating the *o*, then rolling the *r* like an ecstatic cat. 'Love.'

'Love?' Rachel felt a sensation she was surprised to recognise as disappointment.

'But as of . . .' He looked at his watch. 'A month ago, me and her are *no more.*'

He'd pronounced those last two words in the same way as his earlier '*amor*', and Rachel laughed. 'Very good. As is your accent.'

Jay shrugged. 'I sound better than I am – especially to someone who doesn't speak it.'

'Are you fluent?'

'Restaurant-fluent, maybe. But get me onto something that's unfamiliar territory . . .'

'Like?'

He smiled. 'Anything apart from restaurants, really.'

At the thought of food, Rachel felt her stomach rumble again, and hoped Jay hadn't heard it this time. 'Well, seeing as you're the restaurant expert, can you recommend somewhere good where I can try some tapas?'

'Not around here,' Jay said, with a quick gesture at the many bars that lined the streets around the cathedral. 'These are more for tourists who don't know any better.'

'Like me, you mean?'

'Touché,' said Jay. 'But for good tapas, you really need to go where the locals . . . Ah. You don't speak any Spanish.'

'Er . . . what's the opposite of *sí*?' asked Rachel.

'*No*,' said Jay.

'In that case, *no*.'

'Shame, because there's this place I know in my 'hood – it's my favourite, actually, but unless you know what you're ordering, it can be a bit daunting.' He thought for a moment. 'There are a couple of others that I can point you towards . . . They've got pictures of the dishes on the menu, so . . .'

Rachel pulled the free tourist map she'd collected from the hotel earlier out of her handbag and unfolded it. 'Where's that first place? Your favourite?'

'It's on Plaça Sant Agusti Vell.'

'Okay. So, that was Plaça . . .' Rachel stared blankly at the map, unable to decipher the maze of exotically named streets, then realised she'd been holding it upside down. What she *also* realised was that she was standing in front of one of those 'doors' that Jay had mentioned earlier, and to her surprise – though it was possibly the most impulsive whim she'd ever had – she decided to follow his advice. 'Listen, I'd love to try somewhere good, but I don't speak Spanish. You do – and I'd like to say thank you . . .'

'*Gracias*.'

'*Grassy*, um, *arse* – for you being so brave and rescuing my phone, so perhaps I could, you know, buy you lunch? That's if you haven't eaten yet. I mean, if you have plans, I'll understand, and you might not want to have lunch with some silly tourist who . . .' Rachel's voice began to trail off. What was she doing? The ink was hardly dry on her dumping, and here she was, asking a complete stranger out for lunch – and a gorgeous one, at that. 'No, what am I thinking? I've already taken up too much of your time . . .' She stood up, embarrassed, and began to fold her map up, cursing under her breath when it didn't seem to want to follow what she was sure were the right creases, then she noticed Jay was grinning up at her.

'I'd love to have lunch with you,' he said. 'Though we'll go Dutch.'

'I'd prefer something . . . local?'

Jay laughed. 'I see what you did there,' he said, with a smile that melted her inside.

Chapter 5

Jay had flagged down a taxi, and soon Rachel found herself whizzing down wide, tree-lined boulevards, past grand fountains, then through narrower, almost medieval streets, eventually arriving in a small, sun-drenched plaza.

'You live on this square?' she said, marvelling at the gothic archi-tecture, and Jay grinned.

'Well, not actually *on* this square. Though there are a couple of drunks who do . . .'

He passed the driver a five-euro note, waved away Rachel's attempt to pay, then led her into a tiny, almost nondescript restaurant on one corner, the kind of place she'd have walked right past if she'd been on her own, and suddenly she felt she'd stepped back a hundred years in time. The interior was quite dark, but once her eyes became accustomed to the gloom, she made out the old, brick-vaulted ceilings, the curled-edged, brightly coloured posters advertising old bullfights, a framed, autographed old-style Barcelona football shirt above the door (which she made a mental note to photograph for Rich's benefit) and a row of antique wooden barrels lining the far wall. As Jay shook hands with an old man behind the bar (and said something to him that could have been in Chinese, for all she knew), she clambered up onto the nearest stool.

'So, what's good here?'

'Everything.' Jay grinned as he took the seat next to her. 'Is there anything you don't like?'

Not so far, Rachel thought, looking him up and down surreptitiously. 'Nope. I'm completely in your hands,' she said, colouring slightly. 'I mean, whatever you recommend.'

'Right.' Jay cracked his knuckles theatrically. '*Para empezar, una botella de cava de la casa,*' he said to the old man – the owner, Rachel guessed, by the way he was directing the waiters – before rattling off their order. Rachel watched him, impressed.

He turned to her and smiled *that* smile again, and for a moment that lasted an embarrassingly long time, she couldn't tear her gaze away from Jay's eyes, but fortunately the owner chose that instant to deposit a bottle of something ice cold down on the bar in front of them, along with a pair of what looked suspiciously like champagne flutes.

'What's this?' said Rachel, hoping she had enough euros left in her purse.

'Don't worry, it's not champagne,' Jay said, as if reading her mind. 'It's cava. They produce it near here.' He extracted the cork expertly with a muted pop, filled up their glasses and handed her one. 'Try it.'

Rachel clinked her glass against his. 'Here's to Good Samaritans. Or knights in shining armour,' she said, taking a sip.

'And to not being alone in Catalonia – for one afternoon, at least,' said Jay, holding her gaze again, as if daring her to look away. He downed a third of his glass, then raised both eyebrows. 'Well?'

'It's *lovely*.' Rachel took another sip, just to make sure – and because sitting so close to Jay, their knees nearly touching, she'd suddenly felt like she needed a drink. 'And the difference between this and champagne is?'

'About twenty euros a bottle,' he said. 'Seriously, you'd have to ask the French. I've never been able to tell the difference. And I bet most of them couldn't either.'

The food began to arrive, each dish announced by the owner as if he was giving away a family secret: *croquetas, chorizo, berenjenas con miel y queso de cabra* (which Rachel decided was possibly the most heavenly thing she'd ever eaten), *jamón*, a plate of *patatas bravas* so spicy they made the top of her head prickle, and some sort of fish she didn't really care for and that Jay explained was pickled (which, after much more of this cava, Rachel thought, might be a good description of her). As they ate and ate, they talked and talked, and although Jay had to explain his joke about 'Spanish Tortilla' being a good name for a language school *twice*, by the time they'd finished the bottle, Rachel felt as if they'd known each other for years.

The owner reappeared, and with a friendly smile and a wink at Jay, began to clear their plates, and Rachel patted her stomach, pleased to feel it wasn't – as she'd begun to fear – currently the same size as Livia's. 'Delicious,' she said.

'What was your least favourite?'

'The fish.'

Jay speared the last piece with his fork and popped it into his mouth. 'That's the beauty of tapas. You can order loads of different things, and if there's something you don't like, there's still plenty more to eat. Whereas in a normal restaurant, you only get the one main course, so if you don't like what you've ordered, you're stuffed.'

'Or not,' suggested Rachel, and Jay laughed, though when he climbed down from his stool, her face fell. 'Do you have to go?'

Jay nodded. 'This may fall under the category of too much information, but yes – to the toilet.'

'Ah. Okay. Good. Well, not *good*, obviously, in that you have to go because your bladder . . .' Rachel mimed shooting herself in the temple, then picked up the empty cava bottle. 'How strong *is* this stuff?'

As Jay pretend-stumbled his way to the gents, she sneakily paid the bill (asking for it using the universal 'write something in the sky' gesture), then smiled at Jay's indignant expression when he returned and saw what she'd done.

'That was naughty,' he said, leading her out into the balmy afternoon.

Rachel bit her tongue as they made their way through the square. *You ain't seen nothin' yet* had been the first response that popped into her head, and she was pretty sure it wasn't the cava talking. 'Like I said – my treat. For what you did earlier.'

'Well, thank you.'

'No – thank *you*.'

'So . . .'

'So?'

'This is me.'

'What?'

Jay nodded at the graffiti-covered door he'd stopped in front of. 'My flat.'

'Oh. Right.'

'I'd invite you in for a coffee, but . . .'

'I don't like coffee.'

'Exactly. And I don't have any tea.'

'Well, I'd hate this to be the end of a beautiful friendship, simply because we're incompatible in terms of hot beverages . . .' Rachel said, suggestively, then she blushed. She didn't know what had come over her. Perhaps it *was* the cava. But whatever it was seemed to have done the trick, given the look of surprise – mixed with pleasure – on Jay's face.

'So . . . did you want to come in anyway?' he said, then he laughed.

'What's so funny?'

'You just looked at your watch. Will you be timing me? Or have you only got a short window of—'

'No, it's not that. I've got a wedding to go to, and . . .'

'Not yours, I hope?' Jay said, mock-horrified.

'God no! Not that I'm anti-marriage or anything. It's my friend's. Her name's Livia. It's at our hotel. The . . .' Rachel struggled to remember the name of where she was staying. 'Catalonia. Or something Catalonia. I forget. Anyway, it's there. This evening. It's why I'm here. For that. I'm flying back home tomorrow. And I'm rambling.'

Jay smiled again, and Rachel almost wished he'd stop. It was making him all the more irresistible. 'What time does it . . . ?'

'Sex,' said Rachel, then she slapped a hand over her open mouth. 'Oh my god! I'm so sorry! *Six*, I meant to say. Not . . .'

Jay tried – and failed – to swallow a laugh. 'Don't worry. Well, in that case . . .'

He'd pulled his keys out from his pocket, and Rachel stared at him for a moment. Those 'doors' were coming thick and fast today – both physically *and* metaphorically. This particular one was very tempting. And, it occurred to her, going through it – or rather, going through *with* it – would be an *excellent* way to get over Rich. Especially since she hadn't heard a thing from him all day.

'In that case, I'd love to,' she said, taking Jay's hand and following him inside.

Jed had sat awkwardly in the jeweller's, alternately glancing down at his phone and up at the door, for about ten minutes – Livia's usual cooling-off time – but when there was no sign of her after that, he'd mumbled his apologies and headed out of the shop. The staff had been giving him funny looks anyway, so he was glad to go. Even though he had no idea *where* to go.

He could head back to the hotel, he supposed. Find Livia and try to talk things through, like adults, even apologise for his outburst . . . But then again, he didn't feel like apologising. Because none of this was his fault.

How had it come to this, he wondered. He'd been so looking forward to it – just the two of them, here to celebrate their anniversary, in the place they'd first met – and yet Livia's proposal had hijacked the whole thing. So instead of them having the wonderful weekend he'd been hoping for – the last weekend away they'd probably be having on their own, perhaps the last weekend away for years that wouldn't involve staying at some child-friendly hotel, eating dinner at six on the dot in some awful tourist joint that sold whatever that country's version of fish fingers and baked beans was, or heading for some sort of family-friendly attraction that would probably give him a headache within five minutes of getting there – now he and Livia probably weren't speaking. Not that he'd know what to say anyway.

Anxious to get out of the heat, he crossed the road and found himself on the corner of Plaça Catalunya, the city's main square. On one side, occupying a large, ocean-liner-shaped building, was the El Corte Inglés department store. Livia might be in there, having gone in search of a toilet, so Jed headed inside, grateful for the blast of air conditioning that almost knocked him over as he pushed open the heavy swing doors.

'*Servicios, por favor?*' he said to the red-jacketed security guard, though his blank-faced reaction to the man's '*Abajo*' meant it was followed by a gruff 'Downstairs.' He nodded his thanks, made his way towards the escalator and headed down to the basement, though after he'd found the toilets, he soon realised there was no way Livia would have waited in the dozen-or-so person queue. Besides, the store's food floor was hardly the most relaxing place to be, full as it was of tourists cramming their baskets full of shrink-wrapped packets of *jamón* that came from those weirdly preserved pig legs you saw hanging in most tapas bars, or *turrones*, strange, nougat-like confectionary items that he'd once had an argument with Livia about when she'd informed him they were a Spanish Christmas tradition, whereas he'd insisted that 'Two Ronnies' was very much an English thing. How Livia had laughed when they'd realised their confusion. Though she probably wasn't laughing now.

Jed allowed himself the briefest of smiles at the memory as he rode the escalator back up to the ground floor, doing his best to hang on to the rubber-belted handrail, which seemed to be moving faster than the stairs were, then had a sudden realisation. *This* was exactly how he was feeling. He might have had both feet anchored steadily to the ground, but everything else was moving just that little bit too fast. Jed knew the only way to avoid falling was either to let go or take a step up. And right now, letting go was the more appealing option.

He stumbled off at the top, still lost in thought, and almost tripped over a stroller containing a wild-eyed but well-strapped-in Barney, with a harassed-looking Oliver standing behind it.

'Sorry. Miles away.' Jed glanced around the shop's brightly lit interior. 'On your own?'

Oliver nodded down at the stroller, where Barney seemed to be trying to chew through his retaining belts. 'Sadly not,' he said, then he did an eye roll. 'Oh, you mean Sally?'

'Yeah.'

'At the hotel, catching up on some long-overdue sleep by the pool. Which I'm under strict instructions not to interrupt for at least the next two hours.'

'Ah. Right.' Jed squatted down in front of the stroller, though Barney's yoghurt, snot and god-knows-what-else encrusted face made him stand quickly back up again. 'How was the aquarium?'

'Didn't even make it that far. His lordship here decided to throw a tantrum on the Metro, so we thought we'd walk, which meant he needed to wear sunscreen, and if you've ever tried to apply factor fifty to a child who's hard enough to keep a hold of when he's not covered in a slippery substance . . .' Oliver shook his head.

'So you took him to a department store instead?'

'He's two. He likes the lights on the displays, and riding up and down the escalators. Plus the aquarium's twenty euros to get in, he'll hardly know the difference, and even if he does, it's unlikely he's going to remember anything. I tell you, all they're interested in at this age is where their next meal is coming from, and then how they can eject that from either end in the way that causes you the most inconvenience possible.'

'Right,' said Jed again, waiting for Oliver to enlighten him as to what the positives were, though when none came, he cleared his throat. 'So, tell me. Is it, you know, what you expected?'

'Fatherhood?' Oliver let out a slightly manic laugh that Jed didn't particularly like the sound of. 'Want to take him for a turn round the block and find out?'

He'd pushed the stroller forwards and let go of the handles, and when Jed hesitated, Oliver laughed again. 'Only kidding. Yeah, it's . . . full on, obviously. And tiring. And expensive. And at times, mind-numbingly boring. But that's what you sign up for, isn't it?'

Jed tried to keep his expression as neutral as possible. 'I'm not hearing much of an upside.'

'Aha. But that doesn't come yet, does it?'

'When does it come?' asked Jed, after a longer-than-he-was-comfortable-with pause, and Oliver reached down and covered Barney's ears with his hands.

'Once we send the little bugger off to boarding school, I guess.'

Jed shuddered. Livia wasn't the sending-off-to-boarding-school type, plus he hardly earned a sending-off-to-boarding-school salary. And in any case, what was the point of having a baby, of creating another person, a smaller version of him and Livia, if all they were going to do was pay someone else to take responsibility for its travels out into the big wide world? Surely the whole reason was that you shaped them when they were malleable, instilled some of your sensibilities into them while you could, rather than paying a price he imagined would be similar to a stay in a five-star hotel for the best part of twelve years, in the vain hope that your child might turn out to be the next prime minister? No – Jed knew he wanted the child to be there. To be there for the child. Unlike his dad had been when he and Liam were growing up.

'You're serious?'

'Deathly,' said Oliver. 'I married Sally so she and I could have a relationship, have some fun together, maybe even on the odd occasion have sex. Not so I could play second fiddle to this ungrateful bundle of shit and snot.'

'Speaking of which . . .' Jed nodded down at Barney, who seemed intent on wiping whatever it was that was emerging from his nostrils on the corner of a nearby display, though Jed doubted it was snot. If it was, it was a different colour to any snot he had ever seen.

'Oh, goody.' Oliver reached into the huge rucksack hanging from the back of the stroller, found a packet of wet wipes, removed one with the flourish of a waiter with a serviette in a high-end restaurant, then knelt down in front of his son. 'Now, hold still, Barney, while Daddy tries to make you look at least half respectable . . .'

Barney struggled against the straps holding him into the stroller, trying to avoid Oliver's frantic attempts with the wipes, then he suddenly sat dead still, and his face contorted into a frown as if concentrating on some major problem.

'Good boy?' suggested Jed, though Oliver was looking as if Barney was anything but.

'Oh no . . . !'

'What's wrong?'

Oliver sniffed the air suspiciously. 'I won't go into detail, but that face generally means someone might be filling their nappy.' He stood back up and nudged Jed in the ribs. 'His, I mean. He's supposed to be potty training. Though I suspect it's called that because it's driving *us* potty. Which is why he's back in nappies this weekend.' He glanced around the shop. 'Listen, I'd better find a place to change him.' Oliver patted his pockets. 'Now where did I put the receipt?'

As Jed let out a nervous laugh, Oliver narrowed his eyes at the nearby information sign. 'Any idea where the toilets might be?'

'Downstairs,' said Jed, pleased he could finally help in some way.

'Thanks!' Oliver was already pushing the stroller at speed towards the down escalator. 'Might see you later,' he called, over his shoulder. 'We should grab a drink or six!' And Jed nodded. A drink – or six – sounded like a very good idea.

He watched them go, then realised to his embarrassment he was standing in the middle of the hosiery department, so – at a loss as to what else to do – Jed strolled around the ground floor, making the most of the store's air conditioning. Maybe Livia was in here, doing the same. Perhaps she was having second thoughts too – not about the wedding, but maybe about the way in which she'd gone about things. Surely she could see she'd forced him into it? And if that were the case, then she had to understand why he was feeling the way he was . . . Though as he thought about it, Jed realised Livia didn't know how he was feeling. Because he hadn't told her. As far as she knew, his strop had been all about the ring. But how to tell her that it was the least of his worries?

All of a sudden, Jed decided Oliver's suggestion was spot on. A drink might make things clearer – or it might not. But right now, either of those things was appealing. He checked his watch – just gone two – then made his way towards the exit, past stand after brightly lit stand selling cosmetics, and in between the garish perfume counters, doing his best to avoid being sprayed in the eye by the demonstrator girls, who seemed determined to douse everyone who walked past with whatever fragrance they were selling, as if there was some sort of competition between them. As he reached the door, an extremely pretty girl dressed all in black stepped in front of him.

'Escape for Men?' she said, holding a bottle of aftershave out towards him.

'If only,' said Jed, as he stepped smartly around her and hurried back outside.

Livia retraced her steps and peered in through the jeweller's window, but there was no sign of Jed. Nor was he in either of the two bars round the corner, or answering his mobile, and so she harrumphed in frustration. Maybe she *had* pushed him a little too far. After all, she'd known he wasn't a jewellery man – the one time she'd tried to buy him a decent watch to replace the crappy Casio he wore, he'd begrudgingly tried it on, made a sarcastic comment about not being Liberace and asked her if she'd kept the receipt.

She swallowed hard, trying to force back down the growing fear that his response to the ring was symptomatic of something bigger. She'd buried her disappointment at Jed's reaction to her popping the question yesterday, telling herself it was simply because of her putting him on the spot, but now it was nagging annoyingly at her. As she thought about it, since then his mood had been . . . Livia struggled to find the appropriate word, but it certainly wasn't 'enthusiastic'. Not that she was worried he might not turn up this evening – she knew he'd never do that to her – but if she *had* read him wrong, she might have driven a wedge between them that she'd find difficult to remove.

Maybe she was overreacting, and it was simply the jewellery thing. Perhaps she should be the bigger person, apologise for losing it earlier, blame it on her hormones, come clean about everything, then they'd kiss and make up and everything would be back to – well, if not normal, some sense of normality, at least.

She pulled her phone out of her bag and considered texting him, then put it away again. Whatever she decided to do, it was probably best to give him a while to calm down. *Then* she'd try to talk him round.

And if Jed still didn't want to wear a ring then she supposed she could let him have that one.

She called back in at the jeweller's to pick her ring up, relieved that a different assistant was helping her, then grabbed a taxi for the short journey to the hotel. Maybe Jed was back in the room – or more likely, Livia thought, sinking a cold beer or three by the pool with his brother. But when she spotted Liam sitting outside at the bar, talking to some woman she didn't recognise with what Livia suspected wasn't his first beer (or his first chat-up attempt) of the day, she began to worry a little. She stopped off at reception to phone her room, and when no one answered, she made her way over to where Liam was sitting, fixed a smile on her face and cleared her throat.

'Sweetheart?' she said, mischievously slipping an arm around his shoulders. 'Who's your new friend?' And before he could protest, the woman took one look at Livia's stomach, shot Liam an angry glance, then got up and left.

'Liv!' he said, glaring at her.

'Sorry. Couldn't resist it.' She clambered up onto the adjacent stool, slapping away the 'helping' hand Liam placed on her backside. 'Another one bites the dust, eh?'

'Thanks to you!'

'I thought you needed rescuing.'

'From what?'

'Yourself!'

Liam made the 'does not compute' face for a moment or two, then he grinned. 'Oh. *Her*. No. We were just talking.'

'About?'

Liam shrugged. 'Dunno. Don't speak Spanish, do I?'

Livia shook her head and decided not to ask the obvious question. 'Tell me something. When are you going to start thinking about settling down?'

'Me?' Liam looked as if she'd just asked him to donate a kidney on the spot. 'What for?'

'Well, because . . .'

Livia paused, wondering where to start, but before she could, Liam grinned. 'See?'

'See what?'

'You couldn't think of a reason.'

'No – I could think of too many. Especially where you're concerned.'

'Nah, you're all right.' Liam gestured towards her with his beer bottle. 'Besides, look at Patrick.'

'How do you mean?'

'He settled down once and look how that turned out. Actually, maybe you're right, and it is a good idea, because now he's going out with a girl younger than *me*.'

'Huh?'

'So maybe I should settle down, get divorced, then I can meet—'

'Liam!' Livia stared at him for a moment, wondering whether he was trying to be clever, then realised he didn't really have it in him. 'That's not usually how it works. And in any case, Patrick's quite a catch.'

'And I'm not?'

'Not unless there's something Jed hasn't told me, and you're a secret dot-com millionaire, or you've got a dying aunt with a house in Mayfair and you're her favourite nephew . . .' She rested a hand affectionately on his cheek. 'Still, I suppose your face is your fortune. Luckily for you.'

'Cheers. I think.' Liam sipped his beer. 'In any case, marriage . . .'

He gave a theatrical shudder, and Livia glared at him. 'What is it about you men that you see marriage as some sort of prison sentence? It's not a punishment, Liam. It's a . . .' Livia searched for the right word. 'Reward.'

'*Reward?*'

'That's right. You meet someone, you put in the time to develop that relationship, do right by each other, decide what compromises, if any, you're prepared to make, and if you get that all right, marriage is the prize you get at the end of it. You've *won*.'

'Won? At what?'

'This.' Livia waved her arms around. 'Life. That's what it's all about. Trying to meet someone you can make a future with. And actually *doing* that. As opposed to running from one conquest to another, collecting notches on your bedpost.'

'What if that *is* my life?'

'Huh?'

Liam nodded towards Livia's stomach. 'There's more than one way, you know? Not everyone wants to settle down and do the kids thing. And if you ask me, there's more than enough children in this world already.'

'Cross Liam off the godfather list.' Livia was miming writing in an imaginary notebook, and Liam laughed.

'Besides,' he continued, 'like I said, look at Patrick. He's a nice guy, right? Successful. Smart. And yet, when he decided to go down the traditional route, look how that worked out for him. And you and Jed have been bumping along, no pun intended' – he poked her gently in the stomach – 'pretty well for all this time. Why on earth change it, just because "that's what people do"? Maybe they shouldn't be doing it. We're here for a good time, not a long time. You've got to enjoy the moment. Stop and smell the coffee. We're human *beings*, not *doings*.'

'Have you finished?'

'I think so, yes.'

'Well, all I can say is that it's a good idea that not everyone feels the same way you do.'

'You'd be surprised.'

'Surprise me, then.'

'Jed, for one. At least, he did,' added Liam, quickly.

'What?'

'Until you ambushed him this weekend.'

'What?' said Livia again, and a shadow crossed Liam's face, as if he'd quickly realised he'd misspoken.

'Calm down, Liv. I'm not saying he doesn't love you or anything like that. But did you ever ask him why he never asked you to marry him? Or why he wasn't pushing you to start a family?'

'Um . . .'

Liam shifted guiltily on his stool. 'I mean, he's really excited about it now. But I didn't see him hurrying along to Mothercare the minute you two decided you were going to . . .' Liam's eyes flicked down to Livia's belly. 'Go for it.'

'Well, no. I just assumed he was a man, you know?'

'And that's your problem! You women always think you have all the answers. That you know best. Us men . . . we're not like this because we're all bastards . . .' Liam sighed, and took another mouthful of beer. 'Liv, you never met our dad, did you?'

'No.'

'Well, there are times our mum wishes she hadn't either. We didn't have the greatest of childhoods. He wasn't around a lot. Especially overnight, if you know what I mean?'

'Oh, Liam, I'm so—'

'Because he was out shagging other women.'

'I get it, Liam.'

'And when he *was* there . . . He got angry. A lot. Said our mum had tricked him into marrying her by letting him get her up the duff. And he'd take it out on her too, and not just verbally. Right until Jed was old enough to stop him.'

'He's never said—'

''Course he hasn't. He was too worried you'd think he was exactly the same.'

'But Jed's nothing like that.'

133

'I know that, and you know that. Doesn't mean he does.' Liam nodded sagely. 'Suffice to say the atmosphere at home wasn't always the best. And that's why me and Jed grew up thinking there must be another way. It's why I don't make commitments I can't keep. And probably why Jed's been faithful to you for all this time. *Despite* you not being married.'

Livia stared at him, gobsmacked at Liam's revelation, her heart swelling with love for her fiancé. While she'd have preferred to have heard all of this from Jed, she was beginning to understand why she never had.

'I . . . I'm sorry. I had no idea.'

'You know, Jed used to be like me. Worse than me, in fact . . . There was this one time—'

Livia silenced him with a look. This was information she didn't particularly want to hear, especially a few hours before she got married. 'And what happened to make him change?'

Liam shifted uncomfortably in his seat. 'Well, he won the lottery, didn't he?'

'Huh? I don't—'

'He met you.'

Livia's jaw dropped open. She was unaccustomed to sincerity from Liam. Assuming that was what it was. 'So . . . ?'

'So that's the reason Jed never asked you to marry him. Never came out and said he wanted kids. Because his experience of those two things is, quite frankly, shit.' Liam shook his head. 'You know how they say your parents can either be a role model or a warning? Well, our dad was definitely the latter. And you're a part of your mum and dad, aren't you? Even though you might be determined not to be. And that's why Jed was as he was. He thought if he didn't go down the same roads, make the same decisions, he might be able to stop destiny repeating itself.' Liam folded his arms. 'And now he finds himself in the exact situation he swore he was going to avoid.'

'Jesus, Liam! Why didn't he tell me?'

'And risk scaring you off?' Liam grinned, then his expression changed. 'I thought you two had decided you didn't want to do the traditional thing?'

'This is hardly traditional.'

Liam raised both eyebrows at her, and Livia was suddenly struck by his implication. 'Believe it or not, you two were my role models,' he said with a shake of his head. 'Showed me there was another way. So – what happened?'

'Maybe I changed,' she said defiantly, and Liam let out a short laugh. 'What's so funny?'

'How can you be sure that Jed has? Or will?'

Livia looked at him for a moment. 'Because he needs to.'

'Why?'

'Because he loves me, and I love him. Not that you'd know what that feels like.'

'You'd be surprised.'

'Yes. I would.' Liam's gaze was making her feel uncomfortable, so she looked away. Right now, all she wanted to do was find Jed, hold him close, tell him she understood.

'Anyway, let's hope that's enough of a reason,' Liam said, then he peered over Livia's shoulder towards the hotel's reception desk. 'Where is that brother of mine at, out of interest? I haven't seen him since this morning.'

Livia shrugged as nonchalantly as she could, which, right now, wasn't very nonchalantly at all, then she checked the time, conscious she'd agreed to meet Rachel by the pool in fifteen minutes. 'Actually, I've got no idea where Jed's "at",' she said, slipping down from her stool.

And as she headed back to her room, she realised that was worryingly true.

Liam waited until he was sure Livia had gone, then he pulled his phone out and dialled Jed's number, but when there was no answer, he anxiously slipped it back in his pocket. Where *was* Jed? Going AWOL was very unlike him. But his brother had never enjoyed surprises. And given the look on his face this morning, he seemed to have particularly resented this one.

Maybe Liam shouldn't have laughed. Perhaps teasing him like that had been a step too far. But that was what brothers did, wasn't it? Took the piss out of each other. After all, Jed had been doing it to him for as long as Liam could remember – though admittedly, the way Liam's life had gone, Jed had been supplied with an abundance of material – so it was only fair he got a bit of payback at his brother's expense. And seeing as there hadn't been the chance for a stag do, with all the associated mickey-taking, getting plastered, stripping-the-groom-naked-and-duct-taping-him-to-a-lamp-post, lap dancing and so on that Liam couldn't wait for if – god forbid – he ever got drunk enough to get engaged, taking Livia's side in this particularly stunning prank had been his best alternative.

Liam began to worry that – for the first time in his life – Jed might actually be preparing to let Livia down. To not go through with the wedding, by just not turning up. And Liam couldn't imagine how *that* particular scenario would play out.

But then again, Livia hadn't seemed worried, so maybe he shouldn't be either. After all, he knew how much his brother loved her, so surely there was no way he'd let her down on a day as important to her as today evidently was. Trouble was, he also knew how Jed felt about marriage. And right now, he wouldn't bet as to which emotion was the strongest.

Liam smiled grimly. This was why he didn't do relationships – or rather, why he preferred to chase women who were already in one. Sex was just a physical act, after all – like the spinning classes he regularly went to at his local gym, only marginally less sweaty (plus Liam couldn't usually last more than forty-five minutes in the saddle). It was only when emotions were involved that things started to get complicated.

He'd been seeing someone recently. A girl who'd worked at a café round the corner from his flat in Elephant and Castle. Trouble was, her boyfriend was a lot bigger than Liam was, and when he'd found that out, Liam had told her they ought to break it off. When her boyfriend found out about them, he'd threatened to do the same to a certain part of Liam's anatomy, so he'd got out of there as quickly as he could. Which proved his theory.

And double standards, he knew, but who wanted to have a relationship with someone who was prepared to see someone else – someone like *him* – when they were already *in* a relationship? They had form. Couldn't be trusted. And were bound to do it again. And in Liam's (little black) book, that was a no-no.

Besides, he still felt a little guilty about lying to Livia, or if not *lying* exactly, then not coming clean when she'd told him he didn't know what it was like to be in love. Of course he did. He'd known it for almost ten years. Since Jed had first marched up to him with a girl on his arm and said, 'Liam, meet Livia.'

He'd always been surprised she wasn't able to tell. But then again, Liam had always done his best to hide it – after all, being in love with your brother's girlfriend was a whole world of nope – and what better way to hide the fact that you loved someone than by pretending you couldn't love anyone? No, he had to accept that, just like arriving on this planet, Jed had got there first. And there wasn't anything Liam could do about it. Except try not to let it get him down.

Besides, he knew he wasn't right for her. He'd worked that out pretty quickly, and mainly because he'd realised that Jed was. So now, all he could hope for was that, one day, he'd meet someone who made him feel like Livia made Jed feel. Then, perhaps, all this playing the field could stop.

Jed had told him once that there'd been a woman at work, some-one he'd felt a spark with. 'Why didn't you act on it?' Liam had asked, incredulously, but Jed had just smiled. 'Because she wasn't Livia,' he'd said. And though it went against everything *he* stood for, Liam had known exactly what his brother meant.

He thought back to one of his favourite films, *Jurassic Park*. He'd seen it countless times as a kid, and several more as an adult. There was a line in there, when Jeff Goldblum was talking about the ethics of breed-ing the dinosaurs – something about being too busy thinking about if they could, to wonder whether they should. Liam often thought that applied to his various conquests.

But Jed and Livia . . . they were his touchstone. The opposite of his and Jed's parents. Which was why Liam needed this wedding to go ahead. It would be proof that happy endings did exist. And if Jed couldn't see it was the right thing to do, then someone – perhaps even Liam – would have to change his mind. And fast.

He pulled his phone out again, dialled Jed's number, cancelled the call almost as quickly, then swiftly hit redial. But when there was no answer, he did the only thing he could think of, and ran upstairs to get help.

Patrick smiled at the desperate knocking coming from his hotel room door, impressed Izzy had managed to find her way back to the hotel by herself, and so quickly. He'd been expecting a 'come and get me' phone call, or to see her accompanied by an angry taxi driver because she hadn't any money, but when he threw the door open, instead of a contrite-looking twenty-two-year-old, an anxious-looking Liam was hopping from one foot to the other in the hallway.

'Don't tell me. Too many beers, and the toilet's occupied. Or the woman you've just slept with's husband has come back, found you, kicked you out and your key's still—'

'It's Jed.'

'What's wrong with him?' said Patrick, suddenly concerned.

'Hard to say.'

'Sorry, Liam. I don't quite follow.'

Liam pushed past Patrick, checked no one else was in the room and motioned for him to shut the door. 'It's hard to say what's wrong with Jed, because no one knows where he is.'

'Have you asked Livia?'

'Of course!'

'I hope you didn't alarm her?'

'Yeah, sure. I said, "Hey, Liv. Any idea where your husband-to-be is, because it's . . ."' – he checked his watch – '". . . four hours until you get married, and I think he's done a runner?" I can just see that going down a treat.' He shook his head exasperatedly. 'In any case, she's the one who told me he was missing.'

'She said that?'

'In so many words . . .'

'How many words?'

Liam thought for a moment, then he mouthed something to himself while counting off on his fingers. 'Eight. I think.'

'And they were?'

Liam's brow scrunched up in concentration again. 'Um – "actually", "I've", "got", "no", "idea", "where", "Jed's", and "at".'

'You're sure that's what she said?'

'Yes, I'm sure.'

'She didn't actually use the word "missing"?'

'Nope.'

Patrick thought for a moment, hoping *he* wasn't the cause of Jed's disappearance. Why had he told Livia to be honest with him? As he well knew, sometimes secrets were secrets for a reason. 'When was the last time you saw him?'

'This morning.'

'Did you try calling his . . .' Patrick stopped talking. Liam was making the 'do you think I'm stupid?' face. 'Okay. Fair point. Have you checked around the hotel?'

Liam nodded. 'Yeah. And there's no sign. His passport's still here, though.'

'How do you know?'

'I got it from reception earlier. He'd forgotten to pick it up after he'd checked in. I said I'd give it to him.' He reached into his pocket and retrieved Jed's passport, although Patrick didn't want to ask why Liam had kept it, but if it *was* to prevent an escape, finally Liam had done something right. 'Livia's going to be so pissed with me.'

'With *you*?'

'Yeah. I'm the best man, and I've lost the groom. I should have stuck with him all day. Not . . . well, it's not important what I was doing. But she is going to kill me.'

'Right, Liam, because this is all about you.' Patrick folded his arms. 'Who saw him last?'

Liam shrugged. 'Livia, I guess.'

'Any idea where?'

'She'd just come back from town, so . . .'

'Right.' Patrick narrowed his eyes as he thought. 'As far as I know, they'd gone into the city centre to get the rings. So if he's not here at the hotel, and he hasn't gone to the airport . . .'

Liam waved Jed's passport in the air. 'I'm guessing not.'

'Then he must be . . .'

'Yeah?'

'I'm thinking.'

'You couldn't think a bit quicker, could you?'

'Could *you*?'

Liam sat down on the corner of the bed, then he got up again and started pacing round the room. 'Where's the last place you'd think of looking for him?'

'Huh?'

'Things are always in the last place you look, aren't they? So if we can work out where the last place he'd be is, then . . .'

'Liam, that's . . .' Patrick thought for a moment, then he fished around in his pocket for the GoCar's keys. 'You stay here at the hotel and think about that, and call me when it occurs to you. And, of course, call me if he comes back.'

'Duh!' said Liam.

'And make sure Livia doesn't . . . or just make sure she's okay. And whatever you do, don't tell her he's missing.'

As Patrick hurriedly collected his key card and wallet from the table by the door, Liam stuck his hands into his pockets. 'Where are you going?'

Patrick tapped a finger against the side of his nose. 'To the only place I can think of that he might actually be.'

He led Liam out of his room, then rushed downstairs and headed back outside, grateful he hadn't returned the GoCar yet. While he still didn't know where Izzy was, any problems the two of them were having would just have to wait. Besides, she was a big girl. She could take care of herself. And, thankfully, she didn't have his credit card.

Patrick thought back to his earlier 'cold feet' comment. He'd meant it as a joke. But as he knew from his own situation, sometimes all it took was the tiniest thing to push people overboard: Liam taking the mickey – or even the ring – might have been the last straw that broke the camel's back, if you excused the mixed metaphor. Not that he'd thought Jed had been anywhere near breaking point, but appearances could be deceptive. He'd learned that from his wife.

He remembered his own wedding, all those years ago, when he was full of hope – or naivety, as he now thought of it. He'd been nervous enough then, even had second thoughts himself, and that was when he'd *wanted* to get married, when he'd been planning it for months, when he'd been looking forward to finally getting a ring on Sarah's finger. Whereas Jed . . . he'd had this sprung on him. Probably thought he didn't have any choice. Didn't want to let Livia down – especially given the fact she was pregnant. The fact that they'd all flown out for the event probably just added to the pressure. And sometimes, people just . . . snapped.

Of course, this might all be his fault. Say Livia had come clean, as per his advice. Told Jed it was all just a show. He might have interpreted that to mean it was a farce, and if that was the case, then he wouldn't feel so bad about standing her up. Missing it. Letting her down. Because actually, it wouldn't be letting her down at all. He might even see it as serving her right.

Patrick pulled his phone out and dialled Jed's number, but the call went straight to voicemail, so instead he jumped into the GoCar, switched on the navigation screen, typed in Jed's possible location and pressed 'Go'. Patrick had never been a betting man, but if all this had happened to him, he knew where he'd probably be right now.

So that was where he headed.

Chapter 6

Rachel almost skipped towards the Metro, trying – and failing – to prevent the Cheshire-cat grin from creeping back onto her face, something that people had been noticing, and that one or two had even given her a wide berth because of. She'd just slept with Jay. Who she'd just met. And in the *afternoon*. What had she been thinking?

In actual fact, she *hadn't* been thinking. Not with her head, at least. If nothing else, she'd proved that Rich's comment about her not being impulsive was rubbish: asking Jay to lunch had been impulsive. Going up to his flat afterwards had been impulsive too. The couple of times she'd been impulsive while she'd been up there had made four. And then, as she'd left, she'd even thought about asking Jay to the wedding later. Though Rachel wasn't *that* impulsive. Unfortunately.

So, instead, she'd left him sleeping peacefully in his bed, retrieved her clothes from the various parts of his flat she'd been shocked to find them in and dressed herself as silently as she could. Then – careful not to wake him – she'd snuck out of his flat and out of his life.

She knew Jay was possibly as embarrassed as she was, and probably wouldn't have come this evening anyway, but that was okay. He lived in Barcelona, she lived in Brighton, and EasyJet wasn't *that* easy – even though *she* had been. No, all it had been was a holiday romance. Or not even that – a fling. Which, Rachel suspected, was precisely what she'd needed after being chucked.

Maybe she shouldn't tell Livia. As her maid of honour, what she'd just done hadn't quite lived up to the title. But Livia would want to know how her sightseeing had gone, and Rachel doubted she could lie about it, or pretend to have been on the open-top bus for all this time. In any case, the fact that her smile would have to be removed surgically would probably give the real story away.

Funnily enough, she felt like crying too, her emotions (like her clothes) all over the place. She'd never had a one-night stand before (although technically it had been a one-afternoon stand, and they hadn't actually *been* standing, except for that bit against the bathroom door en route to the bedroom). Never slept with anyone on the first date. It had taken her a month to finally sleep with Rich (and now she thought about it, it hadn't been worth the wait), so this afternoon had been completely out of character. Maybe it had been the emotion of being robbed, or the half a bottle of cava, but Rachel hadn't been able to help herself.

Twice.

Although why shouldn't she have? She was (technically) single; Jay was too (or so he'd said, and she believed him: she'd used the opportunity while retrieving her clothes to do a quick recce of his flat, and it was definitely a single man's apartment – a girl could tell these things, usually from the lack of dusting or the unhealthy contents of the fridge). In any case, there was no law against that sort of thing, otherwise (according to Livia) Jed's brother would already have been sent down for a long, long time. Besides, it was never too late to change. And god knows, Rachel felt she could do with a little excitement in her life.

Suddenly, she felt upset for a different reason, wishing she *had* invited Jay to the wedding. Then again, Livia might have been mad at her – and how would she have explained who on earth he was to Jed, or Liam, or Patrick, or even Izzy, without embarrassing the both of them? Also, how did she know it was really over between her and Rich? Yes, they'd had a big row over coming here, which had ended with him telling her it was probably best they split up, but he might have meant temporarily, simply to get out of having to come here. Perhaps, like Livia had suggested, he *would* be waiting for her at the airport tomorrow, a huge bunch of flowers in one hand, that cheekily winning smile on his face, begging her to forgive him, and if that were the case . . . Rachel had watched the 'we were on a break' storyline from *Friends* often enough to know that argument rarely stood up.

The thought of Rich finding out made her feel even more guilty. Sleeping with someone else on what was supposed to have been a weekend away with your (admittedly ex-) partner? That, apparently, was what people like Liam did (though – also apparently – not necessarily with the 'ex' part). And no one thought very highly of them, did they?

The more she thought about it, the more Rachel felt ashamed *and* stupid. And while asking Jay to the wedding might have given some sort of validity to what they'd just done, she didn't have his contact details, and even if she *did* go back and ask him, surely it would seem a little false? No, she should have said something earlier, woken him up with the briefest of goodbye kisses, invited the kind of throwaway comment you made at the end of embarrassing situations like that – a way to part without any awkwardness. A 'see you around' when you knew you probably wouldn't ever see the other person again, mainly because you'd never seen them around before.

Not that she'd mind going looking, though Rachel doubted she'd be able to find his flat again – it was taking her long enough to find the Metro station. No, in her heart, she knew that was that. It had been fun, but that was all it was. And all it ever would be.

Finally, gratefully, Rachel spotted the red-and-white 'Metro' sign and headed down the steps. She bought herself a ticket, swiping through the barrier just as her train arrived – so she hurried over and leapt into the carriage before the doors could close.

As the train sped away, she sighed, then let out a giggle and had to put her hand over her mouth. The sex had been *good*. Much better than it had ever been with Rich. And while maybe that had partly been due to the excitement of the nature of their liaison, Jay had also known which buttons to press. Whereas Rich? There were times he'd miss the entire keyboard. He'd asked her once what her favourite position in bed was, and Rachel had had to stop herself from saying, 'You on your side, so you don't snore.'

A nearby seat became available, so Rachel sank onto it gratefully and – embarrassed – peered furtively up and down the carriage, sure that everyone could tell she'd just had sex. People had a look, didn't they? And though that look was sometimes hard to define, it was exactly the same as the one on her face, the one she could see oh-so-clearly in her reflection in the train window.

She glanced up again in time to see a pair of large men, dressed in street clothes but with tennis-racquet holders slung over their shoulders, making their way along the packed carriage towards her, and instinctively she clutched her bag a little more tightly. Jay had warned her about the thieves on the Barcelona Metro system – they'd been bad enough on the street – and he wasn't here to save her this time. But instead of trying to snatch her belongings, the men stopped in the space in front of the doors, opened their bags and, to her surprise – though Rachel hadn't really expected them to start rallying – produced a pair of violins.

'*Buenos tardes, señores y señoras,*' said the larger of the two. '*Un poco de música para todos . . .*'

Rachel's Spanish hadn't improved, despite her liaison with Jay, though she recognised the word for 'music'. The men were buskers, and as they launched into an almost comically poor violin-duet version of 'Gangnam Style', she relaxed a little. The two of them made a funny pair – the fatter one playing animatedly, adding the odd musical embellishment, tapping his feet to the rhythm, even singing along with the chorus, whereas the other one seemed simply to be going automatically through the motions, as if he'd rather be anywhere but here . . .

Rachel suddenly sat up straight. *This* had been her and Rich: she'd been the fatter one, as it were, always putting in the extra effort, trying to make the relationship something it wasn't, while next to her, Rich had been simply turning up (unless the football was on), not expecting much, taking what he could get, relying on his charm, the same expression on his face, the same boredom in his eyes.

Rachel didn't know whether to laugh or cry. Rich had simply been going through the motions. So why had she been experiencing all the emotions? All at once, she felt dirty. But not about what she'd done with Jay – rather what she'd been doing with Rich. Why had she put up with a situation like that for so long, when being on her own would at least have given her self-respect?

She retrieved her mobile from her bag and saw a message from Livia, who was trying to track her down. *Just heading back now*, she texted back, then she put her phone away, remembering she wouldn't even have it if weren't for Jay's athletic chasing-down of the robber, and a wave of excitement rippled through her at the memory. Almost immediately, it pinged again – Livia's reply, she assumed, though when she checked it, she saw a series of texts from Rich, and Rachel stared at the screen for a second or two before deleting them unread. Probably just some rude response to her football stadium picture earlier, especially since she'd blocked him on WhatsApp, and she'd hate for some sarcastic comment from him to interfere with the buzz she was experiencing.

The buskers finished playing, and with a loud '*Gracias!*' made their way up and down the carriage, each brandishing a Starbucks paper cup for collecting money, but when they appeared in front of her, Rachel could only dismiss them with a shy smile. Neither of them seemed that bothered, and Rachel tried not to draw too many parallels. Thinking about Rich was the last thing she wanted to do right now.

The train arrived at her stop, so she got off and hurried back to the hotel, deciding she *would* tell Livia her news. Her face was flushed, but she could blame that on the sun. As for the broad smile on her face . . .

she had no one to blame for that but herself. And a certain someone called Jay.

And the realisation made her smile even broader still.

'Looks like my sightseeing suggestion did the trick?' said Livia. She and Rachel were stretched out on adjacent sun loungers, under an umbrella at the far end of the pool, watching a group of excited Spanish children playing some sort of piggy-in-the-middle game in the water with a small rubber ball. At least, Livia was watching the children. Rachel seemed miles away. And had a huge grin on her face.

'Sorry?' said Rachel.

'You seem a *lot* happier than when you arrived. I'm guessing you had a good time.'

'Oh yes,' said Rachel, with a giggle.

'What's so funny?'

'Oh, nothing.'

Livia regarded her friend pointedly over the top of her sunglasses, then repositioned them on her nose. 'Men, eh?' she said; then, when Rachel didn't take the bait, added, 'Did you really have no idea?'

'About?'

'Rich.'

'Can we not talk about him, please?'

'Sorry.' Livia paused as the ball suddenly landed by their feet, and Rachel picked it up and lobbed it back into the water, to a chorus of *gracias*.

'Seriously, though. I thought things were going okay?'

'"Okay" would be putting a bit too much of a positive spin on it. And if you think about it, even "okay" isn't that great, is it?' Rachel grinned. 'Maybe he just didn't want to come to your wedding.'

'Thanks very much!'

'I didn't mean it like that. I mean weddings in general. They can make people think about their own relationships a bit, can't they?'

'Maybe he worried it would give you some ideas.' Rachel mimed sticking her fingers down her throat, and Livia laughed. 'All I meant was . . . weddings can be hard for couples, can't they? Especially if they've been together for a while. And especially if they're not on the same page, relationship-wise.'

'I'm not sure Rich and I were even reading the same book.' Rachel stuck a leg out into the direct sunlight, then hastily pulled it back in again. 'The truth is, things *had* been a bit rocky recently, but I just thought that was how it was. Sure, Rich has his faults – everyone does. And I'm hardly perfect. But by the time you get to my age, life has kind of taught you perfection doesn't exist. Therefore, what's the point in going after it? You might as well just find someone whose faults don't annoy you that much, and stick with them.'

'Thanks!' Livia made a face. 'I can't *wait* to be married now.'

'Sorry!' They lay there in silence for a moment, then Rachel sat up. 'Liv, can I ask you something?' she said, adjusting the height of her sun lounger.

'Sure.'

'When did you know?'

'Know what?'

'That Jed was the one.'

Livia hauled herself up into a sitting position. 'The moment I saw him.'

'How could you tell?'

'You just . . . feel it, I suppose. And when that happens with someone, there's not a lot you can do about it. Except hope they fall in love with you.'

'What if they don't?'

Livia rubbed her stomach, then rolled her eyes at Rachel's horrified expression. 'Not like this. God no! That's the worst thing you can do to anyone, *including* your baby. No, falling in love and falling pregnant . . . it's a different *kind* of fall. Plus there's something you can do to prevent the second one. But nothing you can do about the first.' She smiled. 'Did you love Rich?'

Rachel thought about it. Then thought some more, and Livia let out a short laugh.

'I'll take that as a no.'

'It's just . . . I mean, "love" – that's a pretty strong word, isn't it?'

'It is.'

'There were things about him I . . . not *loved*, exactly. But like I said earlier, didn't piss me off. Too much.'

Livia laughed again. 'But there were things about him that did?'

'Yeah. Like his devotion to a bunch of men in shorts running around a football pitch for ninety minutes every week. The fact that he's the only man in the world who irons his underwear, and they're briefs. Or how his answer to me complaining he always left my toilet seat up was to pee with it down, which – trust me – is a *lot* worse. Blaming the fact that I was shouting at him on my period, even though it was always because *he* was being a twat. Not listening to me, then swearing I hadn't told him the thing he hadn't listened to. Always assuming I'd be the designated driver because, and I quote, I "need the practice". Mansplaining all the time, even when it was something I know a lot more about than he does. Forgetting my birthday, then sulking because I didn't make a big enough deal about his. Thinking that a bunch of flowers from the petrol station would do for Valentine's Day, or buying one from the supermarket but forgetting to remove the "Reduced" sticker from the cellophane. Snoring. Stealing the duvet. Expecting a medal for making me a cup of tea, even though he'd always forget I don't take sugar. Eating with his mouth open. Talking while he was eating. Spending his evenings on his phone, instead of me. And don't get me started on his internet browsing history.' Rachel paused for breath, then smiled grimly. 'So yes, I suppose there were. Are.'

'Well, in that case, you should be pleased you've split up.'

'I'm . . .' Rachel looked like she was thinking about it. 'Not *dis*-pleased. Just a bit disappointed. And hoping there is, in fact, more to life than marriage and kids – no offence – while a little worried that I'm one failed relationship closer to becoming that single old cat lady that people avoid in the street.'

'You don't have a cat.'

'For precisely that reason,' laughed Rachel. 'And I *love* cats.'

Livia glanced across at her, relieved her friend was back to making jokes. 'Why did you stay with him for so long, if things weren't great?'

'Because there were times when they were. He could be charming, and sweet – when he could be bothered – and funny, and daft, and a gentleman, and not that demanding – which sometimes is a real bonus – and he had a good job, and a nice car, and his mates all seemed decent . . .' Rachel shrugged her shoulders exaggeratedly. 'I guess it was like when you binge-watch a box set, and halfway through Season Two you realise that while it's not actually the best thing you've ever watched, and you're not, you know . . .'

'Engaged?'

'Exactly.' Rachel gave her a brief smile. 'You've invested all this time in it, so you kind of feel duty-bound to keep going. To see what the ending's like. Or if it gets better.'

Livia gave her a look. 'Rachel, you're a beautiful girl. You shouldn't feel like that. Any man would be lucky to have you.'

'Maybe.' Rachel wasn't sounding convinced, though Livia suspected that was just the post-dumping blues talking. 'I've just never felt it, you know?'

'Felt what?'

'Love.'

'You're kidding?'

Rachel shook her head. 'Unless I've just missed the signs. Though I'm not sure I know what they are any more.'

'You've *never been in love*.'

'I don't think so.'

Livia laughed again. 'You'd know if you had. Believe me.'

'I mean, I've had relationships that, when they've ended . . . I've kind of missed the relationship rather than the person themselves. I just hope I never get to the point where I really can't be bothered to do the whole thing again.'

'Maybe you're trying too hard.'

'Huh?'

'Maybe you should just . . . let it happen.'

'Just like that?'

Livia nodded. 'Hey – I realise I was lucky with Jed, even though I had to come all the way to Barcelona to meet him, and yes, I was thinking I was the one who was in danger of being left on the shelf, even all those years ago. He was here for the football. Barcelona were playing . . .' Livia frowned. 'Well, I can't remember who it was. But he'd stupidly assumed he could come here and buy tickets *just like that*, and when he found out they were all sold out, he ended up watching the game in the bar we were in and . . . it's a long story, and it involves a lot of cocktails, and . . .'

'You dancing on a table?'

'I've told you?'

'Once or twice. Usually when you're drunk.'

Livia smiled wistfully. 'Anyway, my point is, sometimes you find love in the strangest of places. Especially when you're not looking for it.'

'But I'm always looking for it. And then, even when I do bump into someone who maybe I could, conceivably, fall in love with . . .'

Livia stared at her. Rachel was pretending to be fascinated by the poolside bar's laminated drinks menu. 'What?'

'Nothing.'

'Come on. Spill.'

'This afternoon. When I was out sightseeing. I . . . met someone.'

'Met someone?'

'Well, I got robbed and . . .'

'You fancied your robber? I know they say that bad boys—'

'No! He – *Jay* – rescued me. Got my phone back. So I bought him lunch to say thank you. And one thing led to another.'

Livia narrowed her eyes. 'So, by "met", you mean . . . ?'

Rachel nodded, and made a guilty face. 'Twice,' she said, and Livia couldn't prevent her jaw from gaping open.

'Rach!'

'I know. I didn't know I had it in me.'

'If you'll excuse the phrase! Where?'

'At his flat.'

Livia widened her eyes in admiration. 'And?'

'There is no *and*. He lives here, I live in England. Long-distance relationships don't work.'

'Out of interest, have you ever had one?'

'Well, no, but—'

'So how do you know they don't?' Livia leant in conspiratorially. 'Tell me more.'

'There's nothing more to tell. It was a fling, that's all. Though between you and me, I did consider asking him if he wanted to come tonight.'

'That's . . . Rich.'

Rachel laughed. 'I know. I'm sorry. I didn't think it was appropriate either, so I didn't in the end, although to be honest, right now, I'm rather regretting—'

'No.' Livia put a hand on the top of her friend's head, and swivelled it round so Rachel could see who had just appeared at the other end of the pool and was now grinning sheepishly at the two of them. 'Over there. That's *Rich*!'

Surprised by the sound of what he assumed must be a lawnmower out-side – an odd thing to hear on a pedestrian street in the middle of the city – Jed turned and peered out of the bar's window, just in time to see Patrick manoeuvring a small, yellow three-wheeler into the nearest parking space. For a moment he considered hiding, but that would be childish, and besides, if Patrick had managed to find the bar he was in in a city with this many bars, then finding him *in* the bar probably wouldn't be that hard.

In any case, he could do with someone to talk to. He'd been sit-ting here for what seemed like an age, and he still hadn't come to any conclusions as to what on earth he was going to do. Or managed to get through more than half a glass of Estrella – though that was possibly a good thing. He raised his eyebrows in a silent greeting as Patrick made his way inside and climbed up onto the adjacent stool, then resumed staring miserably into his beer.

'Aha.' Patrick smiled wistfully. 'The eternal question.'

'Huh?'

He tapped his index finger on the bar in front of Jed's glass. 'Is it half full, or half empty?'

'That's what I'm trying to decide.'

'And?'

'Jury's still out, I'm afraid.'

Patrick glanced at his watch, not so subtly that Jed didn't get the message, then he gazed around the bar's interior. 'Well, this place hasn't changed much in ten years.'

'I just wish it wasn't the only thing.'

'*Tempus fugit?*'

'I don't think that's what it's called.'

'No, that's Latin for "time flies" . . .' Patrick spotted the look Jed was giving him, and laughed. 'Ha. Yes. Very good. Well, at least you've still got your sense of humour.'

'Only just.'

'Even so.' He clapped Jed on the shoulder. 'Thought I might find you here.'

Jed sighed. 'Sent you to get me, has she?'

Patrick nodded at the barman to get his attention. 'No, actually. Livia doesn't know you've gone AWOL. We – Liam and I – were getting a bit worried. So I just thought I'd come and see if you were okay.'

'Right.'

'So at the risk of asking a question I can probably guess the answer to, *are* you?'

Jed had picked up his beer bottle and started to top up his glass, then – seeing how much his hands were shaking – put it straight back down again. 'I don't think I can go through with it, Patrick.'

'Why not?'

'It's just . . .' Jed slumped down onto the bar. 'Not how I expected things to go,' he said, miserably.

The barman had just appeared in front of them, so Patrick pointed at Jed's beer and made the 'two' sign. 'Isn't that the whole point of a surprise wedding?'

'I don't mean the ceremony part. That's *exactly* what I'd expect – Livia's organised the whole thing with military precision. It's the assumption that I'll just go along with it all.' Jed drained the rest of his beer in one, grimacing at the fact it was now room temperature. 'She packed me a tie, you know. I haven't worn a tie for ten years. Why should I suddenly put one on now?'

'I'm sure you don't have to—'

'I don't just mean the *tie*. It's symbolic. Not *one part* of this have I had any say in.' He hauled himself upright, stared helplessly at his reflection in the mirror behind the bar, then looked away, unable even to meet his own gaze. 'It's just not right.'

'Have you said anything to her? Told her how you feel?'

Jed gave him a look. 'Oh, sure. A couple of hours before a wedding she's spent I don't know how long planning behind my back, I march up to her and say, "Hey, Liv, I've got a few thoughts about how today should go, the main one being – it shouldn't." I can really see *that* going down well!' He reached up and scratched the top of his head agitatedly. 'I get that being married is important to her, but doing it like *this*?'

'Maybe she thought you might *like* a surprise.'

'A surprise is giving someone what they want when they're not expecting it. This? It's been an ambush, from start to finish. And you shouldn't have to do that to get the person you love to marry you.'

'No,' said Patrick, nodding his thanks to the barman, who'd just deposited two bottles of Estrella in front of them. 'You shouldn't.'

'Thank you!'

'By which I mean, why did she have to?'

'What?'

'Why did Livia have to go to these lengths?'

'You're saying it's *my* fault?'

'Well, "fault" is a strong word . . .' Patrick grinned. 'You've been together for what? Ten years?'

'To the day.'

'And seeing as you never proposed, can you blame her for taking matters into her own—'

'Hers wasn't a proposal. It was an ultimatum.'

'It's still her right, though.'

'Why? It's not a leap year.'

'No, but it is 2018. It may have passed people like your brother by, but women have the vote now. And what are you so put out about anyway? That she beat you to it? That she put you on the spot? That she picked your *clothes*?'

'No, it's just . . .' Jed waved his hands around again. 'Everything. Doing it here.' He thought for a moment. 'No stag do.'

'Hang on. You didn't care about getting married but Livia does, and now you're finding fault with her arrangements?'

'Yeah, I know how that sounds, but . . . remember last year, when she bought me that watch for my birthday?'

'The one you made her take back?'

'It was a Rolex. Gold. Really quite something. If you like that kind of thing.'

'Which you evidently don't?'

'That's not the point. It's just . . . a watch like that, it's going to last you the rest of your life, isn't it? You're going to be wearing it a lot. Looking at it all the time. And if that's the case . . . I'd just have liked to have been involved in choosing it, that's all.'

Patrick frowned. 'So, I'm confused. Is it the fact that you're getting married, the fact that you're getting married *here*, the fact that you're only getting married because Livia asked you, or the fact that you're getting married the way Livia's choosing?'

'*All* of it.' Jed sighed, conscious he probably sounded like he was inventing excuses. But the alternative would be to admit to Patrick the one thing he couldn't do anything about. 'You know what I'm like.'

'And so does Livia. Which is probably why she thought you needed a nudge.'

'But that's my point. This isn't a nudge. It's a full-on, both-hands shove. And into the back of a waiting kidnapper's van, with its engine running, "Married Life" written on the side and a full tank of petrol . . .'

'Okay, okay!' Patrick smiled. 'So, were you thinking of splitting up? Leaving her? Finding someone else?'

'What is this? The Spanish Inquisition? Of course not!'

'So what's going to change?'

'Huh?'

'Once you're married. What difference will it make?'

'To me? Or to Livia?'

'To you, dummy.'

Jed thought for a moment. Then a moment longer.

'Exactly. Bugger all. You don't have to change your surname. You won't be going from a Ms to a Mrs. Fundamentally, all this means is that you and your friends are going to have a great party here in this wonderful city, you'll make the woman you love incredibly happy, you won't start feeling awkward at describing her as your partner or even girlfriend – which, trust me, starts to sound pretty weird the older you get – and your child won't have to face any awkward questions at school as to why Mummy and Daddy have different surnames. *And*, despite all of that, you won't feel any different afterwards. So, I'll ask again – what's going to change?'

'I might,' said Jed, softly.

'Huh?'

'My dad . . . He always told me my mum tricked him into getting married, by getting pregnant with me. And he resented the hell out of her for it. Got his own back by cheating on her. A lot. And rubbing her face in it.'

'So?'

'So what if that's *me*?'

'Why is it likely to be?'

'I don't know. He was – is – a real . . .' Jed struggled to find the right word. 'Loser, Patrick. And I've spent my whole life trying not to be like him, but sometimes . . . history repeats itself, doesn't it?'

Patrick swallowed a mouthful of beer and regarded Jed levelly. 'You know Sarah cheated on me, right?'

'Right.'

'Everyone knew. Except for me. Until it was too late. If I'd realised how unhappy she was, I could have prevented . . .' He stopped talking, and gulped down another mouthful. 'Anyway, the point is, forewarned is forearmed. You two are in *love*. Livia really wanted you to marry her, probably would have loved for you to ask her, and for some reason you missed that. And if you ask me, you're lucky that this is the way she's dealing with it.'

Jed stared at him. On some level he knew Patrick probably had a point, but he didn't want to admit it – and besides, it didn't make what she'd done right. 'Maybe,' he said, then he sat up straighter and patted the bar affectionately. 'This is where we met, you know?'

'I'm flattered you remember.'

'Me and *Livia*,' said Jed, then he realised Patrick had been joking. 'Yes, very good.'

Patrick raised and lowered his eyebrows in a 'gotcha!' kind of way. 'We were here on a work trip. Team-bonding session. Who'd have thought she'd have ended up bonding with you?'

Jed ignored the insult. 'She was dancing on one of the tables.'

Patrick smiled fondly at the memory. 'I still have the photos. She was very drunk. Probably why she agreed to go out with you in the first place.'

'Ha bloody ha!' Jed picked his beer up, then he put it back down again. 'It was all going along just fine, then we decided we'd start a family, and almost straight away she got, you know . . .' He mimed a pregnant stomach. 'And don't get me wrong, I'm really happy about that, but I'd just about got used to the idea, then all of a sudden *this* happens . . .' Jed put his head in his hands. 'Patrick, you've been married.'

'"Been" being the operative word.'

'And that's exactly my point. Married people . . . you've always got that divorce thing looming on the horizon, haven't you? Whereas couples who aren't married stay together because they want to be together. Not because they've signed a contract.'

'It's not exactly a contract.'

'Well, that's how it feels. Like I'm signing my life away. Betting half of everything I own that Liv and I are going to stay together.'

'It's Livia's place you live in, right?'

'That's not what I meant,' said Jed, exasperatedly. 'I just always thought Livia was different. That *we'd* be different. That people who got married only did it because they'd run out of ideas.'

'Hey!'

'Present company excepted. We were full of ideas. No children. No ties. We could just please ourselves. Go where we wanted. Do what we wanted. Live how we wanted. And I thought Livia wanted that too. But it turns out she's just as conventional as the rest of them.'

'Doesn't look like that to me.'

'Whatever,' said Jed. 'But marriage, motherhood . . . it changes people, doesn't it.'

'People change anyway. It's called getting older. It comes with the territory. And that's not necessarily down to being married. And the way I see it, you've got two options.'

'And they are?'

'Just go with it . . .'

'Or?'

'Same answer, except remove the "with it".' Patrick smiled. 'When was the last time Livia danced on a table, do you think?'

Jed let out a short laugh. 'A long time ago.'

'And do you think she'd still like to?'

'She'd be worried she'd fall off! And don't get me wrong – I love her to bits. But I never thought I'd end up with someone who'd worry about things like that.'

'Okay. Well, tell me something. When was the last time *you* got up and danced on a table?'

Jed stared at him for a moment, then returned his gaze to his beer. 'You're too good at this, you know?'

'Only because I already have the scars.' Patrick folded his arms and leant heavily on the bar. 'Listen, Jed. I'm the last person to be a cheerleader for marriage after how mine ended up. But I'm a huge fan of Livia. And like it or not, there comes a time when we have to save dancing on tables just for special occasions. It might not be nice to hear, but it's a fact. And if marrying Livia is what it takes to keep her – even just to make her happy – then if I were in your shoes, I know what I'd do.'

'But marriage just doesn't mean that much to me.'

'Then what's the big deal?'

Jed frowned at him. 'I can kind of see the logic in that statement, but it doesn't stop it from being wrong.'

'Okay, think of it another way. It might not be a big deal to you, but it's obviously a big deal to Livia, and just look at the lengths she's gone to try to make it one for you. I mean, how many of your other friends' partners have hijacked an anniversary weekend in their favourite city, proposed to them and arranged a surprise wedding, all without you having to lift a finger, or get involved in the arrangements, or spend weekend after weekend choosing venues and menus . . . ? In my mind, that still makes you the different ones. And it's a hell of a story for the grandkids . . .' Patrick laughed. 'Your *face*!' he said, nudging Jed playfully. 'You might worry you're doing the same as everyone else, but it doesn't mean you can't do it differently, does it?'

'How?'

Patrick motioned for Jed to drink up. 'Seems to me you've already started,' he said.

'Well, when you put it like that . . .' Jed shook his head slowly. 'The problem is, I *want* it to mean something.'

'It does. To Livia. Otherwise she wouldn't have gone to all this trouble. And after ten years, the fact that it means something to her should mean something to you. And in fact, the fact that it means so much to her that she's gone to all this trouble, risked being publicly humiliated in front of all her friends, just to get you to stand next to her for five minutes and grunt "I do" . . .' Patrick grinned. 'She's a smart cookie. She's not going to – how did you put it earlier? – "bet half of everything" on you if she thinks you're a loser.'

'Maybe.'

Patrick put his arm around Jed's shoulders and gave him a squeeze. 'Jed, you've got a lot of stuff swirling around in that head of yours right now, but really this all comes down to one thing. Do you want to spend the rest of your life with Livia?'

'Of course I do!'

'In that case . . .' Patrick tossed a ten-euro note onto the bar, then hauled himself up off his stool. 'Let's go and get married.'

'You mean me and Livia, right?'

'Right,' said Patrick, adding, 'Or not,' when he saw Jed had stayed put. 'But whichever, you need to make a decision. Tell Livia how you feel. And soon.'

'Okay,' said Jed, resignedly.

Wearily, he stood up and followed Patrick outside to where the GoCar was parked. 'But I think I'll walk, if it's all the same to you?'

'Don't worry. This thing's pretty safe . . .'

'It's not that. I've got a big conversation I need to have, so I just need to work out what to say when I get back to the hotel. And how to say it.'

'Sure.' Patrick slipped on his crash helmet. 'Me too, funnily enough.'

'You?'

'Izzy.'

'Hence the crash helmet?'

'Ha. Maybe that's not a bad idea.'

'Things not working out?'

'Surprised?' Patrick said, and Jed shuddered at the word. He'd already had enough surprises for one weekend.

Liam was getting desperate. Not about Jed's whereabouts – Patrick had just texted him with *found him, heading back* and a smiley face, so he knew he could relax on that front – but about his prospects for this evening. So far today he'd tried to make conversation with at least half a dozen women, with little success – no thanks to Livia – and had even considered the girl working at the hotel bar, though he suspected the only reason she'd been so friendly was because he'd miscalculated the exchange rate and left her a much larger tip than he'd intended. Flirting with someone round the pool was out of bounds – though only because he couldn't take his T-shirt off thanks to Izzy's 'artistic' application of sunblock on his back, and it was too hot to sit out there with it on. Eventually, reluctantly, he'd slipped his phone from his pocket and launched Tinder, although then he remembered what had happened the previous evening and killed the app just as quickly as last night's date had killed his desire.

Maybe he was doing this all wrong. Trying too hard. Perhaps he should wait and let them come to him. After all, as best man he'd be the centre of attention this evening, apart from Livia and Jed. He had a sharp suit with him, and would be knocking them dead with his speech (although he still hadn't written a word of it), plus he'd be the one dictating the tunes later. Women liked a man in a suit, they loved a sense of humour, and how many DJs did you see going home on their own? No, tonight was going to be his night. As well as Jed and Livia's, of course.

And if the worst came to the worst, that Rachel girl was apparently pretty fit. And desperate – Livia had texted him earlier to tell him Rachel had just been dumped (in a 'stay away/tread carefully' way rather than encouraging him to 'comfort' her), which meant she was odds-on to be that perfect combination of vulnerable and drunk. Liam had been told he was a good listener – which was just as well, given how much most of the women he'd dated loved to talk. He'd probably be sitting next to her, or at least could sit himself down in the empty seat next to her, so all he'd need to do was keep topping up her glass . . .

Liam caught himself. What was he thinking? This was his brother's wedding, and here he was, wondering how best to guarantee he got a shag this evening – even considering that an emotionally traumatised woman might be his best bet – plus he'd already tried to chat up Patrick's girlfriend. He hadn't known who she was, but still . . . Maybe the sunburn tattoo on his back just about summed him up. Besides, even if he did get lucky, the moment he took his shirt off (unless he kept the lights off), the game would surely be up.

What was worse, his brother's apparent cold feet might actually be his fault. Taking the piss when he'd known what Jed already felt about the situation, then pretty much spelling out to Livia why Jed had never asked her to marry him in the first place . . . Perhaps not the most sensible approach, given the circumstances. Or the best timing. No, he decided, on second thoughts, a night off wouldn't kill him. He'd do his best to smooth things over between Jed and Livia, then he'd give a textbook speech and DJ the night to perfection. If anything happened – well, that would be a bonus.

He glanced at his watch, wondering what the strange feeling he was experiencing could be. And then he realised. He was feeling good about himself. And Liam hadn't felt that way for a long, long time.

Still with a few hours to kill, Liam decided spending them at the bar probably wasn't the most sensible approach, so instead he went up to his room, changed into his gym gear and headed to what the hotel's website described as their 'fitness centre'.

Gently, he cracked the door open and peered through the gap. Apart from a treadmill that had seen better days, a couple of exercise bikes and a rack of weights that his gran could probably lift in one hand, there wasn't that much to keep him occupied. Though when Liam strode into the mercifully air-conditioned room, he saw something else – or rather *someone* else – he'd rather spend time on.

'*Hola!*' he said, flashing the woman his best, recently whitened smile, though 'Oh la la!' would probably have been more appropriate. She was gorgeous: around his age, wearing a tightly fitting pair of yoga pants – were there any other type? – and a sports bra that was struggling to contain what the *Daily Mail* would describe as her 'ample assets'.

'*Hola*,' she said, looking up from some sort of yoga pose on the mat in front of the mirror, demonstrating the kind of flexibility that sent Liam's mind into a spin, and he swallowed so hard it made a sound.

He circled the room, swinging his arms vigorously, pretending to engage in some sort of warm-up, all the time making sure the woman couldn't see him staring at her in the mirror. She looked familiar, though Liam couldn't place her. Normally when that happened to him it was someone he'd slept with, and not remembering their name would get him into trouble – there were only so many times you could refer to someone as 'babe' or 'darlin' in a conversation before they realised you were doing it as a cover. But the chances of him running into an ex here in Barcelona were pretty small, surely?

He watched her covertly for a while, then picked up the heaviest dumbbells and attempted to press them overhead a few times before realising they were heavier than he'd first thought, so he turned the movement into a squat, dumped them noisily back on the rack and cleared his throat.

'Um, *habla* . . .' – what was the phrase? He pulled his phone out of his pocket, punched the words into Google Translate and did his best. '*Inglés*?' he said, rhyming it with 'singles', which was perhaps appropriate, though he'd said it in his best Spanish accent, which on reflection Liam realised wasn't very Spanish at all. Or very anything, for that matter.

'Do *you*?' said the woman.

'Ha ha. That's funny. Sorry. I just wanted to ask if you were using the running machine?'

The woman glanced over at the treadmill, then down at the mat she was sitting on, in a 'do I *look* like I'm using it?' kind of way.

'No.'

'Because I thought I might. If you weren't. Planning to.'

'Knock yourself out.'

'Thanks,' Liam said, to her chest, fearing that she might knock *herself* out if she tried anything more than a slow jog. 'Will do. Not literally, of course.'

The woman smiled. 'Sorry about earlier.'

'Earlier?'

'Darren.'

'Darren?' Liam hesitated, then remembered where he'd seen the woman before. Round the pool. When her meathead boyfriend had commented on his . . . 'Oh. Right. No harm done.'

'He can just be a bit of a . . .'

'Dick?'

The woman laughed. 'Yeah.'

'Well, like I said, no harm done.' He waited until she resumed her stretching, then cleared his throat again. 'What's that you're doing?'

'Down dog.'

'Hey!' Liam held both hands up, taking the opportunity to flex his biceps. 'I only asked.'

'No – it's the name of the pose. Though now you mention it . . .' The woman narrowed her eyes at him. 'Hang on. Do I know you from somewhere else?'

Liam had to stop himself from applauding in delight. 'That's the oldest chat-up line in the book,' he said, happy he could trot out his standard response and immediately put her on the back foot.

'It would be. If I was trying to chat you up,' said the woman, though flirtatiously, and Liam grinned.

'Hey. Just a bit of banter.'

'Banter.'

'That's right.' He moved over to one of the bikes and jumped on. 'But yes, you might.'

'Are you going to enlighten me?'

'*Big Brother?*'

'The novel?'

'Huh?'

'Orwell?'

Liam frowned. What did a green duck puppet have to do with anything? 'No, my name's Liam. Liam Woodward. I was on *Big Brother*.'

The woman peered at him. 'Don't tell me . . .'

Liam stared at her for a moment, wondering whether to point out that he already had, then she shook her head.

'No. I give up.'

'I was on Season Eleven.'

'I didn't know there'd been a Season Eleven.'

'Well, there was,' said Liam, a little disgruntled.

'Did you win?'

'Nearly.'

'I remember now. I read about you in the paper. You were the one who tried to have sex with everyone. Including that woman who hosted the after-show thing.'

'*She* was flirting with *me*.'

'I think the word you're looking for is "interviewing".'

'Whatever.'

'So you didn't shag her?'

'A gentleman never kisses and tells. And don't believe everything you read in the *Daily Mail*. Except, maybe, for that.'

The woman got up from the mat, walked over to the drinking fountain in the corner, bent over (which gave Liam a perfect view of her perfect derrière) and took a huge gulp of water. 'So, what are you doing here?' she said, dabbing at the sweat on her forehead with the towel round her neck.

'Same as you. Fancied a workout.'

'In Barcelona!'

Liam jabbed a thumb in the general direction of the hotel's reception. 'My brother's getting married. You?'

'Well, as you saw, I'm here with Darren.' The woman paused for a moment. 'He's my . . . well, husband, I suppose,' she added, strolling over and hopping up onto the adjacent bike.

'You "suppose"?'

'We have an arrangement.'

'Right,' said Liam, liking what he was hearing. 'And that is?'

'You know. Non-exclusive. So we can see other people,' she said, adding, 'If we want,' as if keen to leave Liam in no doubt of the uncertainty of her status. 'He's upstairs. Having a siesta. I was bored. So I came down to work off my . . .'

'Frustrations?'

'I was going to say lunch. But now you mention it . . .'

'He *is* a dick, isn't he?'

'What does that mean?'

'Nothing. Except that if you were my girlfriend, and we were in a fancy hotel for the weekend, I certainly wouldn't waste my afternoon asleep.'

'What *would* you be doing?'

'Well, *you.*'

The woman suddenly leaned over and slapped him lightly on the shoulder, and Liam feared he'd gone too far, though he changed his mind when she ran a finger down the tattoo on his left bicep. 'What's your room number?'

Liam swallowed hard again. 'Thirteen,' he blurted out, though he couldn't stop himself from blurting out 'Why?' immediately afterwards.

The woman glanced at her watch. 'Well, I don't have long before Darren starts to wonder where I am, but if you still fancied that workout . . . ?'

Liam glanced over at the treadmill, then back at the woman. *Finally,* he thought. That – or rather *her* – was exactly what he fancied.

Patrick waved Jed off with a promise to meet him at the hotel bar at five, deposited the GoCar back at the garage, then headed to the hotel, preparing to deal with a drama of his own. He'd always hated arguments. Couldn't understand those couples who told each other everything and saw the resulting rows as a natural part of a relationship, a way to clear the air. If you were in a healthy relationship, the air shouldn't *need* clearing. No, total openness and complete honesty were a no-no as far as Patrick was concerned, along with going to the toilet in front of each other – some things needed to remain a secret, otherwise there was no air of mystery. Though, he realised wistfully, maybe that was why he was divorced. For not doing that kind of thing.

He rode the lift up to his floor, then headed back to his room, surprised to find his hands were trembling as he slid his key card into the lock. He'd pictured this weekend as a relaxing couple of days in one of his favourite cities, a chance to share what he loved about Barcelona with Izzy, punctuated by a pleasant evening where he watched two of his best friends get married, but so far he'd spent more time in shops and bars than galleries and museums, he'd had to use all his powers of negotiation and persuasion to ensure the actual wedding went ahead, and now there was another 'problem' to deal with – and this one was something he certainly hadn't seen coming. But if he wasn't happy with the way things were going, then it was possible that Izzy wasn't either. And if that was the case then – as he'd just told Jed – he needed to confront it, and sooner rather than later.

He opened his door and stepped inside, to be greeted by the sight of his naked girlfriend drying her hair in front of the full-length mirror, and his first thought was whether this particular issue might well keep. She hadn't heard him come in, and for a moment he stood there, admiring her reflection, until he remembered that doing exactly the same thing – as he'd pretended to be considering the ridiculously expensive

Japanese jeans she'd made him try on in Selfridges – was what had got him into this situation in the first place. After another moment, he took a deep breath, then closed the door with an audible bang.

'*There* you are,' she said, switching off the dryer and tossing it on the bed.

'I could say the same to you.'

'Did you enjoy your little tour?'

Something about the way she'd phrased it made his hackles rise. 'I cut it short. Like you did with your hair, I see.'

Izzy shrugged, then turned and examined her reflection. 'There was this cool little salon down one of the side streets. The guy there told me he'd do it for nothing, as long as he could take a photo of the end result.'

Patrick opened his mouth, intending to remind Izzy that no one did anything for nothing, and wondering exactly what that photo had involved, but realised he might not like where that conversation might lead. 'Besides,' she continued, 'I just fancied a change.'

Patrick stared at her. 'Listen, Izzy . . .' he said, matter-of-factly.

'You're mad at me.' It was a statement rather than a question, and when Patrick didn't answer, she pouted at him from the other side of the bed, still making no move to get dressed – something Patrick was finding a little distracting.

Izzy padded over to where he was still standing by the door, and pressed her naked body against his. 'Want me to make it up to you?' she said, standing up on tiptoe, breathing the words into his ear then nibbling on his earlobe, and Patrick felt a familiar stirring.

'Izzy . . .' He took a deep breath. 'I'm not sure it's working.'

'Hmm.' Izzy rubbed her hand up and down the front of his trousers. 'It seems to be working just fine to me. And even if it wasn't, you can get those pills that—'

'Not that.' Patrick took half a step backwards. 'Us. This was supposed to be our weekend. To do stuff together.'

She reached for his belt buckle. 'We *can* do stuff together.'

'Apart from that.' Patrick gently removed her hands from his groin area.

'Don't be like that, baby. I'm sorry I ran out, but you know how it is.'

'Actually, I'm not sure I do.'

She broke away, and stared at him incredulously. 'You want to do this *now*? A couple of hours before we have to go and watch someone get *married*?'

'I do,' he said, 'if you'll excuse the phrase. Will you please put something on so we can talk properly?'

'Suit yourself.' Izzy retrieved a towel from the bathroom and wrapped it round her torso, though it still didn't leave much to the imagination. 'Where have *you* been?' she said, flopping onto the bed and looking at him accusingly.

'I see I don't have to ask you the same question.' He nodded at the pile of shopping bags on the chair in the corner, and Izzy rolled her eyes at him.

'It's what I do, remember?'

Patrick frowned. It was looking like it was the *only* thing she did.

'Well, while you were out indulging in yet more retail therapy, I was off trying to find Jed, because he and Livia—'

'Christ, Patrick. Change the record. It's all "Jed this", and "Livia that" . . .'

'In case you hadn't noticed, we're here for their wedding.'

'Well, *you* are. I don't seem to be included.'

'Of course you are.'

'No, I'm not. Livia's hardly said two words to me since we got here. Rachel obviously didn't even want to share a taxi from the airport this morning. Fuck knows where Jed's been all day.' She shook her head. 'None of them seem to like me very much, for some reason.'

'That's not true. They just don't know you,' said Patrick, though he wondered whether *he* did either. 'Livia was saying how . . . nice you seemed.' Izzy made a face at the word, so Patrick changed tack. 'And Liam seemed quite . . . *taken* by you.'

'That's only because he wants to fuck me,' said Izzy, and Patrick had to stop himself from flinching. 'I'm serious,' she continued. 'It's like they begrudge me for going out with you, as if I'm encroaching on their territory. Or leading you astray or something, when normally you'd think the opposite was true.'

Patrick didn't say anything. He wasn't quite sure how to take that.

'You know what I mean,' Izzy said. 'Livia and Rachel both seem jealous of me simply because I'm younger than them, as if that's something I'm doing on purpose just to rub their faces in the fact they're the other side of thirty. Jed and Liam . . . To be honest, they seem to be jealous of *you* a bit.'

'You just think that because you haven't spent that much time with them. Any of them.'

Izzy glared at him. 'Can you blame me that I'd rather be off doing something I enjoy? Everyone's just so . . . smug. Like they resent me for trying to crash this cosy little group you've all got going. As if I've got no business trying to join in. How do you think that makes me feel?'

'Maybe if you just tried—'

'How?' snapped Izzy. 'You boys . . . it's easy. A few beers, and you're all best mates. Women aren't like that. We – some of us, at least – can be real bitches. Even Livia, who's got everything anyone could ever want, seems to see me as some sort of threat, like Jed's not going to be able to take his eyes off me throughout the ceremony, perhaps because I make her look like an elephant . . .'

'I'm sure that's not—'

'That's how it seems to me!'

Izzy was shouting now, so Patrick sat down on the bed next to her and took her in his arms. He'd feared this conversation might make things worse, but now all he wanted to do was to make Izzy feel better.

'Well, I don't care what they think.'

'This isn't about you,' said Izzy, incredulously. 'You've got Liam and Jed looking at you as if you've won the lottery, and Rachel and Livia as if you've lost your mind, but good on you anyway. It's only upside for you. Whereas I have to sit there feeling like an outsider. An interloper. As if I don't belong. And quite frankly, I'm starting to believe that they might be right.'

'Izzy, I—'

'And then, when I do come back, thinking you've probably done your little tour now, so we can at least have a bit of time together before the others spend the rest of the evening freezing me out, you're off on some mercy mission.'

'That wasn't quite how . . .'

'Yes it was. Liam told me where you'd gone. Once he'd finished staring at my tits. Again.'

'Yes, well, I didn't have a lot of choice.'

'You *did* have a choice. You could have let them sort themselves out for once, and actually worried about *me*.'

'But I felt—'

'Responsible?'

'Well, yes. Seeing as I introduced the two of them. And Liam's hardly able to tie his own shoelaces, let alone—'

Izzy let out a frustrated scream. 'There you go. You spend all your time worrying about Jed and where he is, and rushing off like some knight in shining armour to sort out Livia's problems, or treating Liam like he's the black sheep of *your* family rather than Jed's . . . You're not their dad, Patrick. And you're certainly not mine.'

'I'm not trying to be anyone's dad.'

'Well why do you always make me feel so *stupid*?'

'How do I—'

'By always trying to educate me. Can't we just have some fun, instead of thinking a walk down the street means learning who designed it, or a visit to a gallery is all about finding out about the paintings. You can just *look*, you know, and enjoy things without knowing what the architectural style is or . . .' She glanced exasperatedly round the room, then grabbed a leaflet about the Picasso Museum's current exhibition from the bedside table and waved it in his face. 'Whether an artist painted something when they were depressed.'

'That's not what Picasso's Blue Period actually refers to.'

'There you go again! You can't help yourself. Not everything is an opportunity to better yourself. You don't have to be reading a book while you sit by the pool. You can just . . . sit. So enough of showing me this building, or telling me about that architect, or introducing me to some artist, or taking me to a fancy restaurant because some chef I've never heard of does something amazing . . . It's as if I don't know anything. And I know lots of things. Just different things.'

'But—'

'And do you really think I want to be reminded about the life you've had before? The things you've done with your wife? What are you trying to do? Have another "go" with me, careful not to make the mistakes you made with her, desperate to stop history from repeating itself, simply because you still can't believe she left you?'

'That's not—'

'I'm not Sarah. I'm *completely different* to her. A different model. A different generation. So don't expect me to behave in the same way. Don't try and make me do the same things. Because if you do, this just isn't going to work.'

'Right.' Patrick was stroking her hair, trying to calm her down. 'I'm . . . sorry?'

'Are you asking me or telling me?'

'Telling.'

'Right.'

Patrick hesitated. He'd been intending to have things out with her, but now he'd been painted as the bad guy. And the weird thing was, Izzy had a point. That lecture he'd given Livia this morning, the talk he'd just had with Jed – well, Izzy had effectively done the same thing to him, and as the saying went, if you can't take it, you shouldn't expect to be able to dish it out. Besides, all this trying to 'better' her was hardly giving her a chance to be herself. And Patrick was beginning to suspect that there was a lot more to Izzy than he'd first thought.

He stared at her, dumbstruck, for a moment or two, before realising it was his turn to say something, though 'I apologise, Izzy. I had no idea this was how you felt' was the best he could come up with.

Izzy pushed him down onto the bed, climbed on top of him, hooked her legs around his waist then rolled the two of them over so he was on top. 'Yes, well, that's because you didn't ask me.'

'Okay. Point taken.' He bent down to kiss her, and Izzy responded enthusiastically. 'I'll do more asking and less telling in the future.'

'Good.'

With that, she undid her towel, wriggled it out from between the two of them and reached down for his belt buckle again, and Patrick felt helpless to resist. That drink with Jed might have to wait.

Chapter 7

'*Rich?*'

'All right, Rach?'

Rachel glared at him. She knew better than to assume he was enquiring about her well-being. And anyway, her shock at seeing him – combined with the day's earlier events – meant that she'd struggle to answer that particular question truthfully.

'What are you doing here?'

'I was invited, wasn't I?'

'Well, yes, but . . . I mean, I thought you and I . . .' Rachel was struggling to find an appropriate response to Rich just showing up, still not quite believing her eyes. Though maybe Livia had been right. He *had* seen what he'd been missing. And so he'd booked a last-minute flight to come and try to win her back. 'How did you . . . ?'

'Same as you. Plane.' Rich jabbed a thumb up at the sky. 'Cost me a bloody fortune, last minute.'

'But . . .' Rachel stared at him, dumbfounded. Now wasn't the time to point out that it wouldn't have if he'd come with her that morning as originally planned. 'What was all this "I don't like where we're going" stuff?' she said, suddenly wondering whether she'd overreacted, and he *had* simply meant Barcelona. Though if that were the case, surely there was even less of a reason for him to have just turned up?

At the Wedding

He shrugged, as if that simple action would excuse all the nasty things he'd said about her. 'Oh, *that.*'

'Yes, that!'

'Don't mind me. I was just a bit . . .' Rich shrugged again. 'You know.'

Rachel narrowed her eyes at him. She didn't know.

'C'mere, babe,' he said, advancing towards her with his arms wide open, and – more because she was too stunned to resist – Rachel allowed herself to be hugged. He smelled of beer, and she couldn't help wondering whether he'd needed a drink to get through the flight, or to pluck up the courage to apologise. Not that he had apologised. Yet, at least.

To her relief, Rich let her go after the briefest of embraces – he'd never been one for public shows of affection, and while she'd always thought it a little strange, as if maybe he was embarrassed of her, right now she found herself feeling strangely grateful. 'Where's the happy couple?' he said, peering round the hotel's reception.

'Livia's. . .' She glanced back over her shoulder, but Livia had made what was probably a tactical escape. And as for Jed? Well, now she thought about it, she hadn't seen him *at all*. 'Dunno. They'll be pleased you made it, though.'

'What about you?'

'What about me?'

'You don't seem that pleased. To see me. After I've made all this effort.'

He flashed her one of what Rachel had always thought of as his getting-away-with-murder smiles, and she looked at him incredulously. Rich was the bad guy here, and yet (and yet again) he seemed to be expecting a medal simply for doing what he was originally supposed to have done.

She folded her arms and stared at him until his expression started to waver. 'Hold on. You're telling me that, after I booked *and paid for*

177

a surprise weekend away in Barcelona for the two of us to come and celebrate my best friend's wedding, which you used as an excuse to dump me, so I had to come on my own and suffer the embarrassment of being the *only single person here*, I should then be grateful to you for having an attack of conscience and actually showing up?'

'Well . . .'

'What was it? Did you miss me? Or were you just bored because there wasn't a game on today?'

'There is, actually.' Rich glanced at his watch. 'We're playing City at half three. Well, half four, Barcelona time. Should be a good match, because—'

'Rich!'

'Anyway, Rach, that's not fair.'

'Not fair?' Rachel was conscious she was close to shouting now, and a few people were looking in their direction. 'What would you know about *fair*? You abandoned me, Rich. Said some really nasty things.'

'Yeah, well, I've said I'm sorry, haven't I?'

'Actually, no, I don't think you have.'

'By coming here. Turning up.'

'And what did you think? That I'd be so happy to see you that . . .' She hesitated, trying to formulate her argument, desperate to make Rich understand, hoping against hope that he'd actually come to apologise, to convince her he could change, to admit he'd got her all wrong – though the fact that she was more angry than pleased to see him said a million times more than she could right now. 'You let me down, Rich. Hurt me. And I can't just . . . *mmph!*' She stopped talking, though only because Rich was crushing her against his chest, as if she was a child with a grazed knee, and a hug would make everything okay. 'Why *did* you come?' she said, pushing him away angrily.

'What?'

'You heard.'

'Like I said, I was invited.'

Rachel bit off her first response of 'was' being the operative word.

'So it wasn't that you missed me? Realised you couldn't live without me? And that you'd said some awful things that you were desperate to take back?'

'Um, yeah.' Rich was staring at his shoes like a scolded schoolboy. 'All of that stuff.'

'Well, why didn't you say that, then?'

'You know what I'm like.'

Rachel scowled at him. She knew exactly what he was like. And she also suspected now was the time to put her foot down if she wanted him to change. 'Well, it's not good enough!'

'Bloody hell! Someone got out of the wrong side of the bed this morning.'

And got into someone else's, Rachel thought, and the memory made her blush.

'Listen,' Rich continued. 'I'll make it up to you.'

'I'm not sure you can.'

'Right. Well, I'm going.'

'Don't,' Rachel said, suddenly worried she'd overstepped the mark, then she realised Rich had meant going to the wedding and not 'back home'.

' . . . think I'll be forgiving you any time soon,' she added, quickly.

'Suit yourself. So . . .'

Rich was holding his hand out, and Rachel stared at it. Did he expect her to just shake hands, and everything would be okay again? Besides, the trouble was, Rachel wanted more than 'okay'.

'So what?'

'The key?'

'What key?'

'To our room.'

'*Our* room?'

Rachel stared at him, open-mouthed, and Rich nodded. 'I thought I'd be staying here.'

'You are. Right here, in fact,' said Rachel, then she glared at him in a 'don't you dare follow me' way, turned around smartly and headed for the lift.

'But . . .'

She could sense him hot on her heels, but the last thing she was going to do was turn round and show weakness. 'But what?'

'Your message.'

'My . . . message?'

'That WhatsApp. This morning.'

'What about it?'

'Why else d'you think I nearly killed myself trying to get to Gatwick? And like I said, paid through the nose to get here.'

Rachel froze. Surely Rich hadn't misconstrued her revengeful *Wish you were here* as her actually wishing he was? But if he had – and it was a big 'if' – and he'd rushed to the airport and jumped on a plane to come and see if she'd take him back, then (and although Rachel knew it wasn't the longest of lists) it was quite possibly the most romantic thing he had ever done for her.

She jabbed at the lift button, her head spinning. While she knew she should still be angry at him, had every right to feel resentful that he could say those things, abandon her, then expect her to forgive him, he had gone to all this effort to be here with her *and* paid for it, and she knew he'd probably be expecting to pay for it for a while. An apologetic Rich would be a super-attentive Rich, and that was all she'd ever wanted. Besides, what was her alternative – sit at the table this evening pretending to have a good time while ignoring him?

An anxious throat-clearing from behind her made her spin round – Rich, with his most contrite expression, a bit like an adorable puppy you'd just caught chewing through your charger cable – and she felt something soften inside. Maybe it was the guilt of what she'd done earlier with Jay, or more likely the probability she'd never see him again, but Rachel suddenly found herself considering giving him another chance. And *because* it would be his last chance, she suspected she could milk it for all it was worth.

'There would be conditions.'

'Anything,' said Rich, eagerly.

'One – if you ever speak to me like that again, ever tell me that I'm . . . what was it . . . ?'

'Boring. And that you needed to get out more. And—'

'I wasn't actually looking for you to answer in such detail there, Rich.'

'Sorry. You asked, though, didn't you?'

'As I was saying . . .'

'Yeah?'

' . . . then that's it. End of. Finito.'

'Right.'

'Two – no getting drunk this evening.'

'Rach, it's a *wedding* . . .'

'What does that have to do with anything?' said Rachel, in a tone that suggested no arguing.

''K,' Rich said, begrudgingly.

'And three – you pay more attention to me than your stupid Gunners.'

'Sure.'

'And four.'

'Four?'

'Delete that photo I sent you.'

'There was a photo?' Rich pulled his phone out and began scrolling through to her message, so she snatched it from him and quickly hit delete.

'Never mind.'

'Right. So?'

Rachel paused for effect, wanting to convey that she was weighing up some momentous decision, a bit like how she'd seen Livia look at a third chocolate croissant at breakfast this morning before demolishing it in two bites. 'Fine,' she said, eventually. 'But you're sleeping on the couch.'

And immediately, just as she'd known she was making the right one the second she'd followed Jay through his front door, and especially given the smug smile that had appeared on Rich's face, Rachel feared she'd made the wrong decision.

Livia scrabbled around on the bedside table for the remote control, and hurriedly turned up the volume on the room's music system. She'd left Rachel to have it out with Rich and headed back to her room for a siesta, but the noises coming through the wall from Patrick and Izzy's room next door had made that impossible, and . . . it wasn't something she'd wanted to listen to – or picture. So she'd told herself that he was having a heart attack and Izzy was trying to revive him, or even that she was trying to murder him. Which Livia could just about have believed, if Patrick hadn't sounded like he was enjoying it so much.

She'd heard them row, then the ensuing silence when she'd assumed one of them had left, but she'd been wrong – the next set of noises had told her a full-on session of make-up sex was occurring, and Livia had smiled wistfully to herself. Make-up sex – or any sex – had been off the cards for the last few months. She just hadn't felt in the mood – or attractive enough, given the way her body had changed through the pregnancy. And if she felt that way . . . well, she couldn't imagine that

Jed would want to touch her. She had packed some special lingerie for this evening – it was her wedding night after all – but she still hadn't decided whether she was going to wear it. The top half looked okay, especially given her currently porn-star-sized breasts, but the thong . . . She'd tried it on earlier and it had all but disappeared. Which was a look in itself, she supposed.

The sound of church bells from the street outside reminded her she'd soon be getting married, and Livia supposed she could start getting ready. Jed would need to get dressed too, Liam making sure he'd knotted his tie correctly – assuming Liam even knew what a tie was. Then she remembered Jed's clothes were still in their room and she started to feel a little . . . nervous? At least, she hoped that must be what the uncomfortable feeling in her stomach was.

She pulled her phone out and called Jed's number, but when it went straight to voicemail, she hastily pressed 'End' and dialled Patrick's instead, before remembering he quite probably wasn't in a position to answer. And though her call seemed to instigate a slight pause in the 'hostilities' she could hear coming through the wall, it – perhaps unsurprisingly – went unanswered.

Where *was* Jed? He hadn't been with Liam when she'd collared him earlier; Patrick was with Izzy; and Rachel – well, she had her hands full with Rich right now. And when Livia thought back, she realised she hadn't seen her fiancé – or seen anyone who'd seen him – since their earlier altercation at the jewellers, five hours ago. And while it was possible, given his comments the previous evening, that he might have been indulging in some sort of makeshift, last-minute stag afternoon, the people he should be doing it with were all here.

Anxiously, she rifled through his suitcase, desperately looking for his passport, and when she couldn't find it she tried his jacket pocket, her handbag and even under his side of the bed, but there was no sign. Surely it wasn't possible that he'd done a runner? The Jed she knew would never do something like that to her. Then again, the Jed she knew had been having to make a lot of changes recently, so maybe this was his way of saying she'd gone too far.

Her insides lurched again and Livia took a couple of deep breaths, trying to calm herself down. Pre-wedding nerves were to be expected, surely? In any case, it never took Jed that long to get ready. No, he was probably in the bar right now, downing a glass of something in preparation for the ceremony, maybe even with Liam, then he'd come up to the room, throw his suit on, and they'd go and do what they had to.

She went to retrieve her outfit from the wardrobe, but as she strode across the room, the discomfort in her stomach turned into a stabbing pain and she collapsed onto the bed; and right then, Livia knew she was in trouble.

'Patrick!' she shouted desperately, banging her fist against the wall, though she suspected his repeated cries of 'yes' weren't in response to her. In agony, she reached for her phone again, scrolled through to Liam's number and texted one word.

Help!

Liam waited for a follow-up text from Livia, assuming she'd been making some kind of joke, but when none came – and he got no reply to his *??* – he put his phone back down on the bedside table and cleared his throat.

'Babe – I've got to go.'

The woman from the gym – Liam couldn't remember her name, though he wasn't sure she'd ever told him what it was – emerged from where she'd just been pleasuring him under the sheet, rested her head on his stomach and looked up at him incredulously. '*Now?*'

'Yeah.'

'You're kidding?'

'Sorry. Emergency.' He held up his phone to indicate he wasn't making it up, texted a quick *on my way* in reply, then leapt up out of bed, pulled on his jeans and scouted round for his T-shirt.

'Who's Livia?'

'My sister-in-law. At least she will be in an hour or so. Assuming my brother turns up.'

'What's wrong with her?'

'I, um, don't know.'

The woman sat up, clutching the sheet to her chest. 'But what about *me*?'

'Sorry. Can't be helped.'

'Huh!'

'Babe – don't be like that.'

'Don't babe me!' She glowered at him, then threw the sheet off and began collecting her gym gear from the various spots around the room they'd been thrown, and as Liam enjoyed the sight of her nakedness, he mouthed a silent curse at Livia. It was almost as if she'd known he was with someone, just like at the bar earlier.

He walked over to give the woman a kiss but she pushed him away. 'Well, Mister *Big Brother*. At least you came first this time,' she said, angrily pulling her clothes back on as he followed her out through the door.

As the woman stalked off along the corridor, he made for the stairwell and rushed up to Livia's floor, only to sprint back down to reception again to double-check her room number before taking the stairs a third time. By the time he knocked on her door and a pale-faced Livia let him in, his heart was racing, as much due to the effort as his apprehension at what he was about to find.

'You took your time,' she gasped.

'I was . . .' Liam stopped talking. He couldn't see how any explanation from him would help the situation. 'Are you okay?'

'Do I *look* okay?'

'Well, no, since you—' Livia winced, and she was clutching her belly, and Liam realised it was probably the obvious question given her pregnancy but he couldn't help himself. 'Where does it hurt?'

'My stomach.'

'What about it?'

'It *hurts*, Liam.'

'Oh. Right.' He led Livia to the bed and helped her lie down. 'Is it . . . the baby?'

'I don't know. I just . . . *Ouch!*'

Livia's features were contracted in pain, and Liam stood there, dumbfounded. 'What should I do?' he said, anxiously.

'I don't know. Maybe it'll pass, and—' Livia gasped again. 'Actually, perhaps you should see if you can find a doctor.'

'Shall I get Jed?'

'Unless he's been off taking a crash course in medicine this afternoon, then . . . *Ow!*'

'Okay. Fair point. An actual doctor. Right. So . . .'

'*Hurry up*, Liam! Please!'

'Oh. Sure. Sorry.' Liam ran for the door, stopping only to retrieve Livia's mobile from the bedside table. 'Here,' he said, pressing it into her hand. 'Just in case. It'll be fine. Just keep breathing.'

'As opposed to?'

Liam forced a smile. Livia being jokey even in this kind of situation was a good sign, surely? 'Fair point,' he said.

He hurried out of the room, ran along the corridor and punched the lift button. When the doors didn't open immediately, he took the stairs two at a time then sprinted through reception, elbowing a checking-in couple out of the way. As the receptionist gave him a look, he waved a hand in the air, as if trying to erase his rudeness.

'I need a doctor,' he said, breathlessly.

'A doctor?'

Liam nodded frantically, then it occurred to him the receptionist might not have understood him. 'Er . . . *uno* . . . *doctoro?*'

'What is wrong with you?'

'Not me,' said Liam, though in truth he'd been wondering that since he got here. 'It's Livia. My friend. She's having a baby.'

'*Now?*'

'No. Well, I don't think so. But she is pregnant, and she's having some stomach problems, so . . .'

'I'm a doctor,' said a female voice behind him, and Liam whirled round to see the woman from the couple he'd just barged past smiling sympathetically. 'Where is she?'

'In her room. Upstairs.'

'303,' said the receptionist, helpfully, and Liam nodded in agreement.

'This way . . .'

He led the woman towards the lift, almost knocking over a just-returned Jed in his haste to get there. 'Bro! Where have you been?'

'Out and about,' said Jed, then his face darkened as he noticed the woman standing next to his brother. 'Where are you going in such a hurry?'

'Upstairs . . .' panted Liam. 'We're—'

'Christ, Liam, is sex all you think about?'

Liam stared back at him for a moment, then grabbed his brother by the shoulders. 'No! Well, mostly. But not right now. It's Livia. She . . .'

'She what?'

'The baby. Her stomach . . . She's having some problems . . . This lady is a doctor and . . .' The colour had drained from Jed's face so quickly Liam worried he was about to faint. 'Just come on, will you?' he said, although Jed was already way ahead of him.

As they charged towards the lift, the doors opened and Patrick stepped out, so Liam grabbed him by the shoulders and pushed him back in.

'Hey, where's the party?' he said.

'Livia's room,' said Liam, jabbing frantically at the button for the third floor.

'Really?'

'She's not well . . .' said Jed anxiously as they made space for an older Spanish couple and their luggage, though Patrick had to step out again when the 'overloaded' alarm sounded.

'I'll take the stairs,' he said. 'Room?'

Liam opened his mouth to answer, cursing that he'd forgotten so quickly, grateful for Jed's hurried '303' as the doors slid shut.

The group stood awkwardly in the lift as it began its slow ascent, Jed tapping his foot nervously, Liam at a loss as to what to say, hoping Livia would be okay and that he hadn't taken too long. But he'd managed to find a doctor. And an English one at that. Which had to count for something.

He glanced nervously at Jed, willing the lift to hurry up, wincing at both the anxious 'Come on' his brother kept repeating through gritted teeth and the tinny rendition of some Spanish pop song playing from the loudspeaker in the ceiling – the joyful tone couldn't have been more inappropriate. Once the doors finally opened, the three of them ran along the corridor, Jed dropping his key card in his haste to get inside his room, though Liam couldn't blame him – his hands were shaking almost as much. By the time Jed eventually got the door open, Liam was almost dreading what might be awaiting them.

'Liv!' Jed had rushed into the room first, and was already kneeling next to the bed by the time Liam and the doctor caught him up. 'What's wrong?'

'I don't know!' Livia said, her eyes red-rimmed. 'My stomach. It's cramping, and feels like it's going to explode, and . . .'

'Let me take a look.' The doctor had reached the bedside. 'Hello, Livia. My name's Erica. I'm a doctor. Now, how pregnant are you?'

Livia grimaced up at her. 'Surely that's—' She gritted her teeth as another wave of discomfort passed over her. '. . . a binary question?'

'How many *months.*'

'Oh. Sorry. S-*ow!*-ix.'

Livia had grabbed Jed's hand, and was squeezing it tightly. By the pained look on his face, very tightly, so Liam took a step back out of reach, just in case.

'Jed,' she said simply, and he patted the back of her hand reassuringly. 'Don't worry, Liv. I'm here.'

'N-ow!' said Livia, her accusation morphing into a yelp of pain, then she followed it with what even to Liam's untrained eye was obviously a look of love, and he swallowed hard, feeling like an intruder. He wanted to be here for them, but this was Livia and Jed's time, and while he knew it was silly, he was suddenly jealous of the bond they shared. Why hadn't he ever been with someone who'd looked at him like that? Someone who needed him like Livia seemed to need Jed?

'It'll be okay,' said Jed, though Livia didn't answer. Instead she seemed to be whispering something to herself, and when Liam could make it out, it was 'Don't let me lose this baby' on repeat.

'Okay. I'm just going to examine you,' said Erica. 'Anyone who's not the father might not want to be here.'

'No, that's okay,' wheezed Livia. 'Liam's family. At least, he will be in an hour or so.'

Jed's eyes flicked across to Patrick, who'd just burst in through the door, a little out of breath after three flights of stairs. 'As is this one,' he said.

'Okay.' The doctor lifted Livia's top up to expose her belly, provoking a whispered 'Jesus Christ!' from Liam and a subsequent glare at him from everyone else in the room, then she rested a hand on the top of Livia's bump and pressed gently. 'Does it hurt here?'

'No.'

'Here?' the doctor said, moving her hand down slightly.

'Not really.'

'How about here?' she asked, her fingers pressing just above Livia's bikini line, and Livia gave a sharp intake of breath. 'That's it.'

'Tell me something,' said the doctor. 'Have you been eating anything particularly spicy?'

'Why?' said Livia, a horrified look on her face.

Liam grimaced. 'She's not having the baby now, is she, doc? Only I was reading up on this stuff when Jed told me Liv had got up the duff . . .'

'You read up on this?' said Jed, incredulously.

'Yeah. You surprised?'

'That you can read.'

Liam glared at his brother. 'Anyway, I heard that pregnant women can eat spicy curries to help, you know . . .'

'Induce the baby?' The doctor laughed. 'That's an old wives' tale.'

'Yeah, but Livia's going to be quite an old w— *Oof!*' He'd said it to try to lighten the mood, but a swift dig in the side from Patrick told him it perhaps wasn't the most appropriate time to be joking.

The doctor was shaking her head. 'Well, it's not true. Otherwise spicy food would be on the "avoid during mid-pregnancy" list along with alcohol and smoking.'

'Right,' said Liam, though he decided to keep his other observation – that sex, too, was supposed to help things along – to himself. It was something he'd remembered mid-shag with a pregnant woman he'd met in a club a year or so ago (and suspected it was why she'd asked him home with her) – though his subsequent fear that the baby was going to make an appearance there and then meant he couldn't, in his words, 'finish the job'.

'So, have you?' repeated the doctor, and Jed nodded.

'There were those *patatas bravas* last night.'

'Okay.' The doctor stood up, and addressed Liam and Patrick. 'You two might not want to stick around for what's about to happen.'

'Why?' said Jed, anxiously. 'What's about to happen?'

'You too,' she said.

'I'm not leaving.' Jed took Livia's hand again. 'For better, for worse, right, Liv?'

Livia looked up at him, a gratitude in her eyes that almost made Liam burst into tears. 'For better, for worse.'

'I'm not going anywhere either,' said Liam, defiantly.

Patrick looked at the three of them, then he glanced at the doctor. 'Actually, I might just, you know . . .' He nodded at Jed. 'Just outside if you need me,' he said, before disappearing hastily through the door.

'Okay.' The doctor turned to Liam. 'Could you just open the window?'

'Um . . . sure,' said Liam, hesitantly. Livia was looking scared, and Liam wasn't feeling too confident himself. And what was all this open window stuff? Did they need more space? Though they were on the third floor, so surely that was just adding to the danger? Still, he'd done a decent turn in goal at some charity five-a-side thing recently, so if the baby did come, and *quickly*, he'd be there, poised, like the best Premiership keeper, to prevent it flying out into the street.

'Okay, Livia. This might be a little uncomfortable.' The doctor placed both hands on Livia's lower stomach and smiled reassuringly. 'Now, just relax.'

'Easier said than done.'

'You'll be fine. The baby's fine too. But I'm going to count to three, then I'm going to need you to push for me.'

'To *push*?' said Jed. 'The baby's coming *now*?'

'I hope not!' The doctor smiled again. 'Ready? Like you're going to do a number two. Right. One . . .'

'I'm scared, Jed.'

'Two . . .'

'Okay . . .'

'Three!'

As Livia began pushing, the doctor began applying a gentle pressure to her stomach.

'It hurts!'

'Just a little more . . .'

Livia's face was contorted in agony, Jed had turned white and Liam was beginning to wish he'd followed Patrick outside. But he had to be strong. *Be* the best man. This was his test. The sign that he had, in fact, grown up. Forget celebrity, forget being on television, this was what it was all about. What *life* was all about. Being there for the people you loved. When it counted.

He readied himself by the window, poised, cat-like, hoping the next thing he heard would be the sound of a healthy pair of lungs from an equally healthy baby, loudly announcing its arrival to the world.

Though what he *actually* heard, following Livia's massive fart, was the sound of Patrick's relieved laughter from the hallway.

'It was just *wind*?'

Patrick was laughing again, though Jed's anxiety levels hadn't quite recovered to where he felt he could join in. 'Seems like that. Last night's tapas, apparently. It turns out that being pregnant plays havoc with your digestion.'

'Who knew?'

Jed lowered his voice as a young couple walked past them in the corridor. 'Most of the hotel guests, probably, given the sounds coming out of our window. And not to mention . . .' He screwed his face up and waved a hand in front of his nose, and Patrick grimaced.

'Well, *that's* going in my speech.'

'Don't you *dare*.'

Patrick grinned, though when Jed didn't respond in kind, he nudged him gently. 'Hey – you okay?'

'Yeah. It's just . . .' Jed leant heavily against the wall. 'That was a little scary. Funny, in the end, but scary.'

'A bit like this weekend, I'm hoping?'

Patrick was watching him carefully, as if waiting for him to say something, so Jed raised both eyebrows. 'What?'

'What are you going to tell her?'

'About?'

'Come on, Jed. I'm not a betting man, but if I was, when I left you after the bar I'd have got good odds on you coming back to tell Liv that you couldn't go through with the wedding, and if that's the case, you better do it now, because . . .' He glanced at his watch. 'You've got less than an hour before you'll embarrass her in front of everyone.'

Jed looked at him strangely. 'Why would you think I'm not going through with it?'

'Well, because . . . earlier, you said . . .' Patrick shook his head as if trying to clear it. 'I don't understand.'

'You know that phrase, "You don't know what you've got till it's gone"? Well, you also don't know what you might lose until you think you're about to lose it. Back there, for a moment, I thought I was about to lose Liv. I'd do anything to keep her. And if this is what it takes . . .'

'So you're marrying her because you don't want to lose her?'

Jed nodded. 'Isn't that what most men end up doing?'

'I'd better not put *that* in my speech.'

For the first time in a while, Jed laughed. 'Is that so bad?'

Patrick thought for a moment. 'I suppose not,' he said, though in a tone that suggested the opposite, so Jed widened his eyes.

'Hey, you said it yourself. Marriage means a lot to Livia. It doesn't mean that much to me. But she does. Therefore, if it's what it takes to keep her, to make her happy . . .' He shrugged. 'Then that's fine by me.'

'What about all this "we want to be the different ones"?'

'Like you said, we *are* the different ones.' Jed began counting off on his fingers. '*She* proposed to *me*. We're getting married in Barcelona, in a private ceremony with our closest friends. We decided to have a baby first. And – no offence – we're going to stay together not because we have to, but because we want to.'

Patrick stared at him for a moment, as if weighing up what to say in response, then he smiled. 'Well, I'll drink to that. To the bar?'

Jed shook his head. 'Get hold of Liam, and meet me there in half an hour,' he said, heading off towards the elevator.

'Where are you going?' said Patrick, suspiciously.

'Oh, don't worry, I'm coming back. I just need to go and get something first.'

'Drunk?'

Jed let out a short laugh. 'That'll be later. After we're married.'

'You mean you and Livia, right?'

Jed laughed again. 'Right,' he said.

Patrick slipped back into his room, feeling all was well with the world. Livia was fine, he'd single-handedly managed to prevent Jed from running away, and he'd also managed the best part of a couple of hours (he'd timed it on the clock on the bedside table!) of hot sex with a hot twenty-two-year-old who was currently fast asleep in the bed in front of him.

In truth, he'd been grateful when Izzy had finally climbed off him and dozed off, so – doing his utmost not to wake her – he'd gently disentangled himself from her embrace, quickly dressed and headed downstairs to meet Jed as arranged. And while she might be annoyed at him leaving like that after everything they'd talked about, at least he had Livia's 'wind' story as an excuse. Besides, he was back now. Izzy might not have even noticed that he'd been gone.

He tiptoed past her, silently got undressed and jumped in the shower, wincing when the jets of hot water hit the scratches Izzy's nails had left on his back. Still, if spending the majority of your time in bed in your hotel room was what a weekend away with Izzy entailed, Patrick decided he'd just have to get used to it. It was better than a typical Saturday afternoon when he'd been married, trudging round Sainsbury's, or heading off to the garden centre, or – towards the end of his marriage, at least – sitting on his own in his London flat, trying not to picture Sarah and her younger lover 'doing it' in every room of the house he'd paid for. No, despite what Livia had said earlier, a relationship didn't have to be serious, or 'going somewhere', and if this was Izzy's idea of fun then there was no reason it couldn't be his as well.

In truth, he hadn't thought about where they might be headed when the two of them had first hooked up, and now he found himself a little relieved that he evidently didn't have to. Sex and shopping . . . There were worse ways to spend your free time. He dried himself carefully, inspected his battle scars in the mirror, then padded back into the room to find Izzy stretching herself awake like a cat might.

'Well?'

Patrick sat down beside her on the bed. So much for his escape having gone unnoticed. 'She is now.'

'Huh?'

'Livia. She was having stomach problems. We had to find a doctor. Though, funny story . . .' Izzy reached up and put a finger on his lips. 'Save it for afterwards.'

'*Afterwards?*'

Izzy pulled the duvet to one side and indicated he should join her back in bed. 'Yeah,' she breathed, biting her lower lip provocatively.

'As tempting as that sounds, we need to get ready.'

'Spoilsport.'

'Sorry.' Patrick reached across and stroked Izzy's hair, then he stood up and headed across to the wardrobe. 'Anyway, long story short, Livia's fine,' he said, locating his suit and draping it over the back of the nearest chair. 'Which means I'm all yours now.'

'Promise?'

'Promise.' Patrick smiled. 'Well, after I've given Livia away, obviously. *Then* I'm all yours. And especially tomorrow.' He stood up and retrieved his shirt from the wardrobe, inspecting it for creases, happy it had survived the journey with a few less wrinkles than he had. 'On that note, what did you fancy doing tomorrow?'

Izzy raised both eyebrows at him. 'We don't have a carefully timed schedule?'

'No. Well, yes, we did, but I thought I'd ignore it to do what *you* want. Even if it's just shopping.'

Izzy's eyebrows went even higher, though Patrick felt a little guilty at misleading her. Spain was a heavily Catholic country, and unlike England, where what Napoleon had once described as a nation of shopkeepers had become a nation of shoppers 24/7, here the shops were closed on Sundays.

'So,' he continued, 'what might you want to do?'

Izzy hopped out of bed and disappeared into the bathroom. 'Baby, do we have to make plans?'

'Of course not. We can wake up in the morning and decide. Though our flight's at four p.m., so . . .' Patrick had a sudden vision of Izzy frowning at him. 'No, you're right. Let's just wake up, have a lazy breakfast, then see how we feel. Maybe we could even just spend the day in bed . . .'

'Now *that* sounds like fun,' said Izzy, and Patrick felt his back twinge. While walking along Las Ramblas to fetch the GoCar earlier, someone had offered to sell him some Viagra. Though ibuprofen was more what he'd need if a day in bed was Izzy's plan.

'Great,' he said, pulling his shirt on and looping his tie around his neck.

'Even though we're in your favourite city?'

'And that's what'll make it so special. Hey,' he said, popping his head round the bathroom door, relieved to see Izzy wasn't on the loo, 'I'm sorry about earlier.'

'What for?'

'For trying to show you my Barcelona. When perhaps I should have been more interested in you showing me yours.'

'Kinky!'

'Not like *that*.' He shook his head, a smile on his face, and joined her in front of the mirror. 'All I'm trying to say is . . . it's easy to moan when you don't think a relationship's working, and try to change the other person. When perhaps what you should be thinking is, "What am *I* prepared to change?"'

Izzy looked up at his reflection, then swivelled round and kissed him tenderly on the lips. 'I don't want you to change at all,' she said.

'Except for maybe *that*.' She pulled the tie from round his neck, dropped it on the floor and draped her arms where it had been. Then she suddenly pulled away.

'What's wrong?'

Izzy was frowning up at him. 'Earlier. When you said you weren't sure it was working. Were you about to break up with me?'

Patrick kept his expression as impassive as he could, and shook his head. 'Why would I want to do a thing like that?' he said, surprised to find himself hoping she wouldn't give him a reason.

'Good,' she said. 'Because we can't split up.'

'Why not?'

'Because I'm . . .' Izzy couldn't meet his eyes, and her lip started to tremble, and Patrick felt his stomach set off on a rapid descent towards the floor, conscious he probably wouldn't like her answer, *whatever* it was.

'You're what?' he said.

'In love with you.'

Chapter 8

Liam sat at the bar, staring blankly at the equally blank piece of paper in front of him. Why oh why had he left it until now to think about what he was going to say in his best man speech?

He anxiously chewed the end of the cheap plastic pen he'd found in the stationery set in his room, along with a postcard featuring the hotel, and a notepad, and even an envelope (all of which he'd made a mental note to take with him when he checked out tomorrow, along with his slippers, bathrobe, a couple of towels, and as many tiny bottles of the hotel's lovely smelling shower gel as he could steal from the maid's trolley). While he always preferred to leave things to the last minute, theorising how that way he'd only need to spend a minute on them, right now he was regretting that particular approach. Plus he always got nervous in front of an audience. *Big Brother* had been different, in that all he'd seen were the cameras, not the actual viewers (although by the time he appeared on it, viewing figures were so low that they were hardly fear-inducing), and even though the audience tonight were just friends and family, and only a handful of them at that, for some reason that made it worse.

He'd read somewhere that if you were nervous about giving a speech, all you had to do was picture the audience naked and your fear would evaporate. Trouble was, that was when you already knew what you were going to say, plus Liam had a habit of doing that with every woman he met anyway, so he didn't think it'd have much of an effect – and besides, when the audience included your brother, that possibly wasn't the best thing to do. No, much better to actually think of something funny to say . . . But what? Livia's earlier gas explosion probably wasn't appropriate. Nor was the fact that she was his ideal woman. And as for Jed's severe bout of cold feet, followed by his disappearing act? Probably best to leave that out too.

What was the old showbiz adage – always leave them wanting more? Well, that was certainly going to be working for him as things stood, because unless he pulled his finger out, they wouldn't be getting anything at all.

Liam had never been a best man before. Possibly because he didn't really have a best friend. He had male friends, of course he did, but they weren't really the marrying type, and because of that, he hadn't actually been invited to that many weddings. And while he used to joke that the last one he'd been to was his parents', that wasn't actually that far wrong. Though they hadn't been getting married to each other at the time.

He narrowed his eyes, took another sip of his beer, and then another, hoping to find inspiration in the ice-cold Estrella. 'Star', the name meant, and when he'd found that out yesterday, Liam had thought it had been particularly appropriate. He'd been drinking it ever since, hoping someone might make the connection – but so far, he'd drawn a blank. A bit like he was doing in terms of ideas right now.

All he had to do was be sincere, he knew; but then again, Liam didn't really *do* sincere. Wasn't exactly known for his depth. Though there was no reason why that couldn't change. So he'd simply say something nice about Livia – and he *loved* Livia, so that shouldn't be hard – then make some rude joke about Jed (and almost three decades as his little brother had certainly given him a fair bit of material for *that*) . . .

But what could he say about Livia? That she'd been like a big sister to him – and right now, given that she was up the duff (to use a technical term), she was an even bigger sister – so actually, today was a bit like his sister and brother getting married . . . Liam jotted the 'bigger' sister' line down, then gave a brief shudder, shook his head and crossed that line out. Then he underlined it, hoping it might give him the laugh he needed, as right now, his speech was short on laughs . . . He pulled his phone out and googled 'funny best man jokes', though when he scrolled through the results, everything was either a cliché, or too rude, or inappropriate, or just not that funny. Maybe he should just say how lucky Jed was. How lucky anyone would be to be marrying someone like Livia. But Liam knew it wasn't luck. People like Jed got people like Livia. People like him didn't. And to be honest, that was starting to worry him a little.

His 'babe-dar' suddenly fired and Liam glanced to his left, where he spotted Patrick making his way through reception, Izzy on his arm, so he waved them over.

'Looking good, you two.'

'You too!' said Patrick, and just as Liam was about to point out that he was there on his own, Izzy leant in and kissed him on the cheek.

'Sorry, Liam.'

Izzy's apology took him a little by surprise, and he reached up to touch the spot where her lips had just been. 'For the kiss?'

'For drawing a dick on your back with sunblock.'

'Hey.' Liam shrugged as nonchalantly as he could, which only reminded him how painful his sunburn actually was. 'I probably deserved it,' he said, then he paused, waiting for either Patrick or Izzy to disagree, but when neither of them said anything, he cleared his throat awkwardly. 'I need help,' he said.

'Professional?' Patrick raised an eyebrow, and Liam smiled sarcastically.

'No,' he said, pulling out the stools either side of where he was sitting and patting the cushions. 'Well, maybe. But right now, with speech-writing.'

'Speech . . .?' Patrick raised both eyebrows this time, and looked at his watch. 'You do know the ceremony starts in about half an hour?'

'I know.' Liam gave him a pained look, then nodded towards his mostly empty piece of paper. 'And I've been sitting here, waiting for inspiration to strike. But it seems to be *on* strike instead.'

'That's good,' said Patrick. 'You should start with that.'

Liam nodded, and quickly jotted the phrase down. 'That's why I need your help,' he said, clicking the end of his pen nervously. 'You're funny. I'm just . . . well, I'm not sure what I am, to be honest. And I don't want to fuck it up – excuse my French. Especially in front of Jed.'

'You'll be fine.' Patrick smiled. 'Do you know what I recall most about the speeches at my wedding?'

'No?'

'And nor do I. Trust me, Jed will be too nervous – and then too drunk – to remember anything about what you say. Plus it's not like you've got a mother-in-law to offend, or a stag do to give away any secrets about, so as long as you don't insult Livia . . .' He grinned. 'Actually, a little dig probably wouldn't hurt. Tell you what, if you really want my advice . . .' He reached over, took the biro from Liam's hand, clicked the nib away and placed it ceremonially down onto the bar. 'Don't prepare anything.'

'Anything?'

'Nope. Just stand up and say what you feel.'

'You mean . . . wing it?'

'It's an approach that's got you this far in life, isn't it?'

Liam nodded, then he frowned, unsure if Patrick was having a dig. 'You think?'

'At least it'll be honest,' chimed in Izzy. 'And spontaneous. And that's all you can ask for. All people want to hear,' she said, giving Patrick a sideways glance.

'Besides,' said Patrick, peering at a spot somewhere over Liam's left shoulder. 'It's too late now for anything else.'

Liam looked at the two of them, and nodded. 'You're right,' he said, following Patrick's gaze, then – spotting his brother approaching – he realised what Patrick had meant.

With a grin, he balled up the sheet of paper, lobbed it towards the bin behind the bar, and – trying not to read anything into the fact that he missed – swivelled round on his stool to greet Jed.

'All right, bro?'

Jed looked at the three of them suspiciously. 'I wondered why my ears were burning.'

'At least it was just your ears.' Izzy gently probed Liam's sunburn. 'Most of *him* is.'

'Shit!'

'Liam, I hardly touched—'

'No. Not that. It's just . . .' Liam ducked down behind Jed, then peered round him towards the far end of the bar. The woman from the gym had just come in, though she'd looked somewhat reluctant to enter, seeing as she was hanging on to the arm of the man Liam recognised as Darren and trying desperately to put the brakes on his determined striding through the bar.

'Which one is he?' Darren bellowed, and the woman couldn't help but make eye contact with Liam.

'Shit,' said Liam again, under his breath, to Jed's obvious confusion.

As Darren stormed over towards them, Liam tried to make himself look smaller in the hope he wouldn't be spotted, but to no avail.

'Which one of you two jokers is it, then?'

Jed had already hopped off his stool and was holding a hand out for Darren to shake, and too late, Liam realised Jed must have assumed he was asking who was getting married.

'Don't say anything,' he hissed, but Jed seemed not to have heard him.

'This is the guy, is it?' bellowed Darren.

'It's . . .' The woman was doing her best to pull him away, with little success. 'No.'

Darren glowered menacingly at the two of them. 'Who's . . .' He frowned, as if trying to remember something. '*Big Brother?*'

'That would be me,' said Jed, getting as close to the wrong end of the stick as was possible. 'And you are?'

'Married to this slag!' he said, jabbing a thumb back over his shoulder to where the woman was cowering behind him.

'Oh-kay . . .' Jed had narrowed his eyes, perhaps not sure he'd heard what everyone else in the bar had heard.

'Did you hear what I said? She's *married*. To me!'

'Right. Well, I'm looking forward to joining you both this evening.'

'What?!' Darren was turning redder than even Liam's back was, and Liam couldn't work out how on earth he was going to diffuse this situation. Though running away might be an option. And certainly a better one than referring to the 'arrangement' he'd been told about earlier. Which he was beginning to suspect was possibly a little more one-sided than he'd been led to believe.

'You know.' Jed mimed putting a ring on his finger, which hardly struck Liam as the most appropriate gesture. 'And are you friends of Livia's or . . .' Jed shook his head. 'Sorry. Silly question. You must be. Otherwise I'd know who—'

'What are you going on about?'

'You are here for the wedding?'

The woman had put her hand on Darren's arm, but he'd shaken it off angrily. 'What wedding?'

'My wedding?' said Jed, looking a little confused himself now.

'*You're* getting married?'

'I am,' said Jed, proudly. 'In about . . .' He raised his hand to check the time on his watch, but before Liam could react, Darren took a step back to avoid Jed's anticipated punch and – with a loud 'And you still shagged her?' – swung his own fist. Right into Jed's face.

As Jed staggered backwards, Liam leapt off his stool and jumped onto Darren's back. Which turned out to be a mistake when Darren threw him off onto the nearby sofa and stuck a finger in his face with a brusque 'Don't!' – an instruction Liam was happy to follow. In any case, Patrick had moved to stand in front of Jed and was doing his best to ignore Izzy's excited chanting of 'Fight! Fight! Fight!'

'What was that for?' Jed had collapsed onto a stool, one hand over his eye.

'Sleeping with my wife!' said Darren.

'*Sleeping with your wife?*'

'Her!'

'I guessed that's who you were referring to, but I can assure you I didn't . . .' With his good eye, Jed glanced over at where Liam was still horizontal on the sofa, so Liam gave a couple of barely imperceptible shakes of his head, and mouthed, 'Please.'

'I mean, didn't know that was your wife,' he said, giving Liam a side look he'd seen a hundred times before. 'So it's hardly fair to, you know . . .' He gently fingered the area around his eye, wincing as he did so.

'Yeah, well, I can't smack her in the face, can I?' Darren looked at him as if daring him to challenge his logic, so Jed shook his head.

'No,' Jed said. 'No, you can't.'

'Actually, you can't just smack *anyone* in the face . . .' suggested Patrick, and Darren glared at him.

'Unless you're a boxer,' Liam interjected.

'Did you want some too?'

'Already had some, thanks,' said Liam before he could stop himself, though fortunately Darren must have thought he was referring to their earlier tussle.

'Right. Well.' With that, he gave them all a menacing glare, grabbed his wife by the arm and marched her off out through the bar, and for a moment, Liam thought about giving chase. Avenging his brother, just like Jed had always stuck up for him when he was picked on as a child. But fighting was so . . . childish; and besides, the guy had been *very* big. Plus Liam still hadn't found a date for this evening, and while it might not matter if Jed turned up with a shiner in terms of his chances later – surely Livia was a dead cert – Liam didn't want to risk his own. No, best to let this diffuse the natural way.

He hopped up off the sofa, found a serviette, grabbed a handful of ice from the bucket behind the bar and made a cold compress. 'Here,' he said, handing it to Jed, who pressed it gratefully against his eye.

'I'd ask you what all that was about, but I don't think I need to.'

Liam shrugged guiltily. 'How was I supposed to know she'd tell her husband?'

'But you knew she had one?' said Patrick.

'Well, sort of . . .'

'The wedding ring was probably a good giveaway . . .' Jed stopped talking, as if he'd suddenly realised something, and Liam took the opportunity to slip an arm round his shoulders.

'Thanks.'

'Don't mention it.'

'Seriously. You could have dobbed me in and—'

'What kind of brother would I be then?' Jed gingerly removed the cold compress from the side of his face. 'Anyway. How do I look?'

Liam examined his brother's eye, which had begun to swell rather impressively. 'Well, as long as you present the other side in any photos . . .'

'*Liam . . .!*' Jed shook his head, then caught sight of his reflection in the mirror behind the bar, wincing at what he saw. 'Livia's going to *kill* me.'

Liam made a sympathetic face. But the truth was, Livia would probably kill *him* instead.

'How do I look?' Livia was frowning at her reflection in the mirror, so Rachel smiled encouragingly.

'Like the most beautiful bride ever.'

'And the biggest.'

'Rubbish.' Rachel took a step backwards and regarded Livia's stomach. 'As long as you manage not to stand side on in any of the photographs, you should just about get away with it.'

'Ha ha.' Livia's laugh sounded a little hollow, so Rachel leaned in to give her a hug.

'Are you okay?'

'I'm not sure.'

'Liv?'

'Because I don't know if Jed is.'

'I don't understand.'

'I thought it would be such an amazing thing to do, the two of us getting married here, with all of our best friends – that it would be fun, and something we'd remember forever, but now I feel a bit . . .'

'Deflated?'

'If only,' said Livia, miserably, glancing down at her belly. 'If this is supposed to be the happiest day of my life, then I don't hold out much hope for the future.'

'Don't be silly. It's going to be a great evening. And an even greater story for your grandchildren.'

'I'm just worried . . .'

'What about?'

'That I'm forcing Jed into doing something he doesn't really want to do. Like he's going to be going through the motions later. And I'll be standing next to him knowing . . .' Livia sighed. 'Well, that he's feeling resentful.'

'That's ridiculous.'

'Is it?'

Rachel reached up to reposition a strand of Livia's hair. 'Yes. It is. Jed loves you. And even if he is doing this for you, the fact that he is . . . doesn't that tell you something?'

'I suppose,' said Livia, unconvincingly. 'This . . . the baby . . . maybe it's all too much for him. Maybe it's all too much for *me*.' She took a deep breath and fixed a smile on her face. 'Sorry. Ignore me. I'm just being an idiot.'

'Speaking of idiots . . .' said Rachel, grateful for the opportunity to change the subject.

'You mean Rich, right?'

Rachel made a face. 'Maybe not,' she said. As the afternoon had worn on, while she'd been feeling increasingly embarrassed about what she'd done with Jay, she'd also begun to feel mortified she'd given in to Rich's request so easily. 'I told him I'd give him a second chance. But it's his last chance. So he's back on for this evening.' She smiled flatly. 'I hope that's okay?'

'Of course!' Livia had taken her hand and was giving her a supportive squeeze. 'Your plus-one can be anyone you choose. Though the whole point of the "plus" in "plus-one" is that they're supposed to *add* something, right?'

'Yes, but . . .' Rachel paused as she desperately tried to think of a justification, not wanting to admit that, just as she'd given the robber permission to take her phone earlier, she'd virtually invited Rich by WhatsApp. 'He did fly all the way out here. At the last minute. At his own expense. *And* after I as good as cheated on him . . .'

'He doesn't know that, does he? And in any case, you were on a break – or rather, a break-up.'

'Even so.'

'Don't you dare talk like that. You deserve better, remember. Much better.'

'But . . . what if I can't *get* better, Liv. Can't *find* better? It's all right for you – you're about to marry the love of your life. But what if all *my* life deserves is Rich?'

'The right person's out there for you. You just need to—'

'Find them? Maybe I already have.'

'Yes. This afternoon.'

Rachel felt herself start to colour. 'No, that was just—'

'Just what? Hot afternoon sex with your knight in shining armour?'

Rachel fanned herself with her hand at the memory. 'Who I'll probably never see again. Besides, Rich promised things would be different. That he'd change.'

'People don't change, Rach. They . . . compromise.'

'Well, Rich said he'd compromise, then.'

'It's not Rich I'm worried is compromising.'

'Well, maybe I need to. Perhaps my expectations were just a little high.'

Livia was giving her a look, and Rachel opened her mouth to argue, then changed her mind. Now wasn't the time. Besides, this evening would be a perfect opportunity for her to debut the new Rachel. The confident one. The Rachel who had Rich paying her respect. Looking out for her. Looking after her. Because that was what she was going to make sure happened.

'I just think he deserves – *we* deserve – another chance,' she said. 'And one more won't hurt him.'

'It might hurt you,' said Livia, then she sighed. 'Hey, just ignore me. After all, what do I know? I had to propose to my boyfriend to get him to marry me, so . . .' She gave Rachel's shoulder a rub. 'You do what you think's best.'

Rachel forced a smile. She didn't *know* what was best. And she was starting to suspect she never had. 'Anyway, today isn't about me,' she said, aware the knocking at the door she could hear was probably Patrick, and as he knocked again, Rachel made a 'scared' face, hoping Livia knew it was aimed at her. 'Time to go?'

Livia nodded. 'You better go and find Rich.'

'Will do.' Rachel hugged her friend, then gave her a kiss on the cheek. 'Good luck!'

'You too!'

Rachel made the 'scared' face again, though this time because it was how she was feeling, then she let Patrick in, slipped out of Livia's room and headed back to hers to find Rich, but apart from the contents of his carry-on – which were strewn around the room as if a five-year-old had been playing dress-up with Rich's clothes, then left them where they'd taken them off – there was no sign of him.

She thought for a moment. Where *was* Rich? At the bar, probably, with Liam and Jed, joining in with the Dutch courage attempt. And talking them into buying the beer, no doubt.

She hurriedly got changed, anxious to get there before Rich got too drunk *despite* his earlier promise, then made her way down to the lobby. Jed, Izzy and a man she recognised as Liam were at the bar, Liam with his arm round Jed's shoulder – though who was supporting who she wasn't sure – while Izzy, for some reason, was dabbing concealer onto Jed's face. Concerned, Rachel made her way out onto the terrace, checking the poolside bar, but Rich was nowhere to be seen so she headed back inside, walked over to where the others were sitting and cleared her throat.

'Hey, Rach!' said Jed, enveloping her in a huge hug, though careful to keep the made-up side of his face away from her.

'Jed,' she said, then she leant over and kissed Izzy on both cheeks. 'And Izzy,' she said, doing her best not to run the two words together. 'How lovely to finally meet you.'

'Likewise,' said Izzy, beaming at her.

'And you must be Liam,' said Rachel. 'I'm . . . *mmph!*'

Liam had kissed her full on the lips, and Rachel had to fight the impulse not to wipe her mouth.

'Looking *hot*!' said Liam, with a grin.

'That'll be the fact that it's twenty-six degrees out . . .' Rachel felt herself colour. 'Oh. I mean, *thanks*.'

Liam winked at her. 'Any time.'

'Lovely dress,' said Izzy, admiring Rachel's outfit.

'Very posh,' said Liam.

'Jigsaw. I wouldn't normally shop there, but it was fifty per cent off.'

'Really?' said Liam. He was staring at her as if he was imagining the dress was a hundred per cent off, and she blushed.

'You look lovely too, Izzy.'

'This old thing?'

'Who're you calling old?' said Patrick.

Jed was looking a little pale, so Rachel gave him a supportive pat on the arm, then noticed the lump on the side of his face. 'What on earth happened to you?'

'He, um . . .' stuttered Liam, but Jed silenced him with a look.

'Just a little accident. Nothing worth mentioning.'

Rachel frowned. By the look of amusement on Izzy's face, she suspected there was a lot more to it than that, so she made a mental note to quiz her later.

'You ready?'

Jed made the same face Rachel had just done in front of Livia. 'As I'll ever be! How's Liv?'

'Looking gorgeous. You're a lucky man.'

He grinned sheepishly. 'So everyone keeps telling me.'

'And he's beginning to believe it,' said Liam. 'Aren't you, bro?'

Jed rolled his eyes and Rachel laughed. 'Anyone seen . . . ?' But before she could ask about the whereabouts of her boyfriend, Rich appeared through the hotel's front door, a bottle of beer in his hand,

and by the looks of him, it wasn't his first. With a polite 'Excuse me' she headed across the lobby to meet him.

'Rich?'

'All right, Rach?'

'I'm not sure,' she said, frowning at the way he was dressed, in a pair of jeans that had seen better days and a wrinkled, untucked shirt. He'd never been the snappiest of dressers, but quite frankly, if she'd seen him looking like this on the street, she'd probably have given him some loose change. 'Where have you been?'

'Me?'

'Yes, Rich. You.'

'I, um, just popped outside.'

'What for?'

'I was hot, wasn't I? Needed to get some air.'

Rachel decided not to point out it was hotter outside, though Rich was the kind of person who'd never wear a jumper indoors, simply so when he went outside he could 'feel the benefit', so maybe this was some kind of reverse-cooling technique.

'Some air?'

'Yeah. Plus it was silly to come all the way here and not see some of the city, you know?'

'And you've done that now, have you? By "popping outside"?'

'Yeah. Anyway, you had your hands full with Livia.'

'While you had yours full with a drink?'

Rich glanced down at the bottle as if it was the first time he'd seen it. 'Thought it was time to sample some of the local brew.' He took a swig, then tried unsuccessfully to stifle a burp. 'Not quite London Pride, but it'll do.'

He offered her the bottle, and Rachel shook her head slowly, suspecting if he carried on like this, the visit she'd planned to the Picasso Museum tomorrow morning might be a solo one.

'What happened to our little chat?'

'Huh?'

'The bit about not getting drunk?'

'I'm hardly drunk. Not yet, anyway . . .' Rich winked at her, and flashed her one of his smiles – something Rachel used to think was quite charming, though right now she was about as far from charmed as anyone could get.

'Aren't you going to go and get ready?'

'I am ready, aren't I?'

Rachel took his arm and led him away from the front desk. 'You can't go to a wedding like that. Where's your jacket?'

'You're joking, aren't you?' He reached up, hooked a finger into his shirt collar and tugged it to one side to get some ventilation. 'I'm sweating like a pig already.'

'But . . . your shirt?'

'What about it?'

'You might have ironed it.'

'I did. Well, the collar and cuffs, at least. Didn't want to waste valuable drinking time, did I?'

'Why would you only—'

'That's all you see when you're wearing a jacket. No point in all that wasted effort if no one's going to see it, is there?'

Rachel sighed. Not for the first time, she was doubting her earlier decision. 'But. You're. Not. Wearing. A. Jacket.'

'Duh. Sweating? Pig?'

Rachel gave him a look. She was starting to think that might be an accurate description. 'Rich, you can't turn up to Jed and Livia's wedding looking like—'

'Hello? It's a wedding. It's going to be all about the bride. No one will give a toss what *I* look like, will they?'

Rachel gritted her teeth. Rich's habit of ending every sentence with a question bugged her at the best of times, and already this evening wasn't looking like being one of the best of times. '*I* will.'

Rich opened his mouth as if to say something, then shut it hurriedly, perhaps finally remembering their earlier conversation. 'Okay, okay,' he said, as if she'd just asked him to do something completely unreasonable. 'I'll wear a jacket. But just for the ceremony, mind.'

'And your shirt?'

He glanced down at the wrinkled garment, pulling the front taut to smooth it out, then made a face when he let go of the material and it assumed its earlier condition. 'It's so bloody hot it'll smooth itself out eventually,' he said, adding an accusatory 'Especially if I'm wearing a bloody jacket!'

He gulped down the rest of his beer, and Rachel winced as this time he didn't even try to stifle his burp. 'Anyway,' he said, peering at the now-empty bottle. 'Did you want to get a drink before they come down?'

Rachel looked at her watch. They had twenty minutes, and a drink might be good – if only to relax her around Rich.

'Sounds like a plan,' she said, and Rich smiled.

'Great. Get us another one while you're there, love?'

'Don't you think you've had enough?'

'It'll be my last one.'

'Promise?'

'Promise. I won't touch another drop. Until the champagne later. You know, just to toast the bride and groom.' He leant over and kissed her on the cheek, then glanced at his watch before moving towards the door.

'Where are you going *now*?'

'Off to sort myself out. There's an H&M round the corner. You get the drinks in; I'll be back before you know it.'

Rachel gave him a look, then with a sigh she went over to the bar and ordered a glass of wine for herself and another beer for Rich, bristling slightly when she discovered he'd charged his earlier drink to her room bill rather than paying for it himself.

She sat in the lobby, sipping her drink while she waited for him to come back, though by the time she'd finished a good half of the glass, he still hadn't appeared. Maybe he was having a problem finding a jacket. Perhaps she should have gone with him. Or maybe he'd snuck past her and was already in the bar, downing a sneaky beer while she sat here . . . But no – Rich had promised. Knew what was at stake. And he'd hardly have made the effort to come all the way out here only to fall at the first hurdle, surely?

With a frown, Rachel carried the drinks back into the bar, but there was no sign of him there either. Jed was waving her over to where he, Liam and Izzy were sitting, so she walked across to join them.

'That for me?' said Liam, staring thirstily at the bottle of Estrella.

'No, it's . . .' Rachel peered around the lobby. 'I mean, yes,' she said, handing him the bottle. 'Seen Rich, by the way?'

'He's not with you?' said Liam, and Jed rolled his eyes. 'Sorry. He's obviously not. Maybe he's still watching the f— *Oof!*'

'The foof?' Rachel frowned. Liam was rubbing the spot on his side where Jed had just elbowed him in the ribs. 'What are you talking about?'

Rachel peered at Jed, then at Liam, and as Liam looked like he was desperately thinking of something to say, Izzy piped up. 'He asked us not to say anything, Rach, but he said something about wanting to watch the match.'

Rachel glared at her. 'I take it he wasn't referring to Jed and Livia's?'

Izzy pursed her lips. 'I guess not.'

'And did he say where . . . ?'

'There's an Irish pub across from the hotel,' said Jed. 'They've got Sky Sports.'

Liam nodded. 'And do an all-day breakfast. Which, if the picture of it in the window is actually what you get, it'd take all day to—'

But Rachel didn't hear the rest of Liam's sentence, as she'd already spun round on her heel.

She strode out through reception, marched determinedly across the street and pushed her way in through the pub's heavy wooden door. Once her eyes had adjusted to the gloomy interior, she spotted Rich, sitting at the far end, a half-drunk pint of Guinness on the counter in front of him, his eyes glued to the huge TV screen in the corner, and Rachel felt her heart fall so heavily she was surprised he couldn't hear the thud. *This* was why he'd been so happy when she'd told him she had to go and help Livia get ready: it had given him a chance to watch the football. She suspected half-time had been when he'd come back to the hotel to get ready – and his sweating hadn't been because he was hot, but because he was desperate to get back to the game and she'd almost caught him.

Rachel balled her hands into fists, surprised to find she was more angry than upset. Livia had been right. People didn't change. At best, they compromised. And by the looks of Rich, he wasn't even prepared to do that. She scowled at him from across the room, hoping he could feel the daggers, then spun around, headed back to the hotel and ran up the stairs to her room. How could she have been so stupid? What was the phrase he was so fond of repeating whenever his beloved club lost in some competition and she suggested he follow one of the other teams instead? 'You can change your job, your house, your wife and your car, but never your football club.' Well, that was obviously how Rich felt about things. And the last thing Rachel wanted was to always take second place to bloody Arsenal.

Grabbing his bag, she scooped up the remainder of his clothes and stuffed them back into the wheelie, realising why he'd left them in such a mess: he'd probably been worried about missing the start of the second half. Well, things were really going to kick off between the two of them now.

Dragging his suitcase behind her, Rachel headed downstairs and – pausing only to have a quick word with the receptionist – hurried back outside, crossed the street, marched into the pub, and made her way right up to where he was sitting. She cleared her throat, and Rich glanced momentarily away from the screen, raised his eyebrows in a 'hey, Rach' kind of way, then turned his attention back to it, before double-taking so hard Rachel wouldn't have been surprised if it gave him whiplash.

'Oh. Hi. I was just . . .'

'That's okay,' said Rachel, sweetly. 'What's the score?'

Rich gave her a look as if to suggest she already knew it.

'Oh – present for you!' she said, patting the top of his suitcase as if it were an obedient puppy at her heel.

'What's that?'

'Your bag.'

'I can see that, can't I?'

'Well, why did you ask what it was, then?'

'No, I meant, what are you doing with it?'

Rich was finding it hard to stop watching the game, and this fact was only making Rachel more determined to do what she knew she had to. 'I'm not doing anything with it. Not any more, anyway.'

'Eh?'

'I've packed all your things.'

'What for? Are we moving rooms?'

'One of us is.'

Rich sighed. 'Look, if this is about me leaving my stuff everywhere, it's because you've taken all the hanging space.'

'Is that really what you think?'

Rich was giving her a look to suggest that yes, actually, it was, and Rachel wanted to scream. So – and because he'd just turned his attention back to the television – she did.

'Christ, Rach! What was that for?'

'For being stupid.'

'Eh? How was I—'

'*Me*, I mean.'

'You?' he said, looking at her blankly, and Rachel screamed again.

'For god's sake, Rich!'

'Calm down, will you?'

'Calm down?' Rachel stamped her foot angrily. As far as she knew, no one in the history of the world had ever calmed down simply by being told to calm down, and she was no exception. 'Rich, just . . . don't bother.'

'Huh?'

'Coming. To the wedding, or even back to the hotel.'

'Yes!' said Rich, doing an exaggerated fist pump, and while Rachel initially couldn't believe he could be so heartless, she soon realised it was actually because his team had just scored. 'I mean, what?'

'Because you won't be able to,' she continued, matter-of-factly. 'I've told the desk staff you're not staying there any more, so not to let you in.'

'What did you do that for?'

Rachel flicked her eyes at the TV. 'Why do you think? One weekend. That's all I wanted. Just you and me, acting like a proper couple, watching a *real* couple go and do something meaningful. One Saturday when I didn't have to play second fiddle to a group of overpaid men running around in shorts who, quite frankly, don't even seem to be that good.'

'That's not fair.'

'Not fair?'

'No. Arsenal won the Cup in—'

'For god's sake, Rich, *I don't care* about your stupid football team. Who *you* seem to care about more than you do me.'

'Rach, don't be like that.'

'Why not? Give me one good reason. You promised, Rich. No football. No getting drunk. And here you are, doing both those things! *And* trying to hide them from me.'

Rich's expression suggested he knew he didn't have a leg to stand on. 'Look,' he said, eventually. 'I don't know whether it's your time of the month or something, but let's just get through this evening. We can talk about this tomorrow. On the plane, maybe?'

An excited commentary, in Spanish, had suddenly begun from the TV, and Rachel could tell Rich was having to fight very hard not to look round at it. A fight that, perhaps unsurprisingly, he lost. And in that moment, Rachel knew this was one fight she wasn't going to.

'What plane?'

'Our plane.'

'*Our* plane?'

'You've got my return ticket.'

'You didn't book one?'

'Well, no,' said Rich, falteringly. 'On account of you already having—'

'You're seriously expecting to fly back with me tomorrow, using a ticket *I* paid for, when you've let me down, lied to me, didn't even have the decency to come out here with me in the first place, and then, when you finally got here, decided you'd rather sneak off to the pub to watch the match than spend time with me?'

'Erm . . .' Rich was looking at her as if he'd finally realised he'd overstepped the mark, whereas, to her surprise, Rachel was feeling strangely happy. Perhaps, she realised, because she finally knew she'd be better off without him. Especially since he'd just glanced round at the TV *again*.

'And you can't even tear your eyes away from the football for two seconds, to try to save a two-year relationship?'

Rich was looking at her, his mouth open, and for a moment Rachel feared he was going to try to explain that he'd had a relationship with his beloved Arsenal for much longer than that. Fortunately, he didn't. Because if he had, she'd probably have punched him.

'Well?'

'Come on, Rach.' He nodded at the TV screen. 'It's nearly over.'

'No, Rich. It *is* over.'

'Where do you expect me to go?'

'I don't care,' said Rachel. 'Home, maybe?'

'But, like I said, I don't have a return ticket.'

'No, Rich. This time, you don't.'

Then – with an exaggerated fist pump of her own – Rachel swivelled smartly around, marched out of the bar and made her way back to the wedding.

'You ready?'

Patrick smiled, and Livia looked up at him nervously. 'As I'll ever be.' She held up her crossed fingers, then made a face. 'I didn't tell him, Patrick. That the wedding isn't strictly legal. I couldn't.'

'I don't think that matters.'

'Why? What's he said? Or isn't he going to turn up?' She grabbed both arms of her chair to steady herself, and Patrick moved quickly to her side.

'Oh no,' he said, helping her up. 'He'll be there.'

'Because he has to be?'

'Because he wants to be.'

'You're sure?'

Patrick nodded. 'This is Jed we're talking about. When has he ever let you down?'

'I don't want him to be there because he's worried he's letting me down. I need him to be there because he wants to be. Wants to get married. To me.'

'He does. It just . . . hadn't occurred to him that he did.'

'I'll take that. I suppose.'

'Hey!' Patrick took her face gently in his hands. 'For someone who's about to get everything they ever wanted, you don't seem all that excited.'

'I am. It's just . . .' Livia sighed. 'This wasn't how I pictured it.'

'Life seldom is.'

'No, but . . .' Livia thought for a moment, and Patrick kept quiet, trying to work out whether this was last-minute nerves or something more serious than that. 'I planned all of this thinking it'd make Jed and me closer, you know? Hoping we'd have an amazing weekend, and instead . . .' She shook her head. 'I don't know what I'm trying to say. I think I'm just feeling a little disappointed.'

'In Jed?'

'In myself. For not managing today a little better.'

'And better would have been?'

'Jed and I not spending most of the morning sniping at each other, or him doing his best to avoid me for the rest of the day.'

'Welcome to marriage!'

'Ha ha.' Livia smiled, though there wasn't a lot of humour behind it. 'You're serious?'

'Of course not. Well, a bit. But marriage, life, married life . . . it's complicated. There are some things you just can't control. Even you. So you've got to let them go, and . . .'

'Keep your eye on the prize?'

'Exactly.'

Livia puffed air out of her cheeks, then she glanced at her watch. 'Any last-minute tips?'

Patrick shrugged. 'Don't trip over your dress, repeat what the official says, and—'

'No. For marriage.'

'I'm the last person to—'

'You had twenty good years. And a lovely daughter. You must have done something right.'

'Evidently not. I'm never getting married again . . .' He hesitated when he saw how Livia's expression had fallen. 'But you and Jed totally should.'

'Even so, I'd rather not learn from my mistakes, so . . .'

' . . . you want to learn from mine?' Patrick let out a short laugh. 'Liv, every relationship's different. Because every*one* is different – you just need to look around you. So there's no generic advice I can really give you that . . .' He stopped talking for a moment. 'Actually, there is.'

'Which is?'

He gently rested a palm on Livia's belly. 'In a few months, something's going to happen to you both that's the most bewildering, wonderful, tiring, rewarding, amazing, frustrating thing that can happen to anyone. And no one teaches you how to be a parent, which is possibly just as well, because there's no one way of doing it. Right now, you and Jed are a couple. Soon, you, Jed and little *Patrick* here,' he said with a wink, 'are going to be a *family*. And that's the best, most precious, most special, most *valuable* thing in the entire world. Never forget that, and I think you'll be okay.'

'Wow. That's . . . something to think about.'

'Isn't it?' Patrick tapped his watch and motioned towards the door. 'So – and I've said this to Jed too – the most important thing you need to do is ensure you don't fuck it up.'

Livia laughed. 'Right. And how do I make sure of that?'

'If I knew that, I wouldn't be here with Izzy, would I?' He patted his pockets, retrieved Livia's key card from the slot on the wall, then opened the door. 'But just promise me something.'

'What?' said Livia as she followed him out into the corridor.

'When you work it out, let me know, will you?'

'Deal!' She smiled. 'Things clearer with Izzy?'

'I think so. We had a . . . *talk*, this afternoon, and . . . she and I . . . let's just say we reached an understanding.'

'I heard you. Twice!'

Patrick blushed. 'Says the woman who almost blew the door off her room earlier!'

Livia burst out laughing. 'Well, good for you.'

'She told me she loved me, though.'

Livia made a face. 'Oops. Awkward.'

'Except it wasn't.'

'No?'

'No.' Patrick pressed the lift's call button. 'Mainly because I had to hightail it out of there to come and get you. Besides, she's young. She doesn't know what love is. Not real love, anyway.'

'And what is "real love", exactly?'

'Something you have to be a lot older than twenty-two to know about.' He jabbed impatiently at the button again. This wasn't a conversation he wanted to get into right now. 'Like you and Jed have.'

'Here's hoping.' Livia mimed biting her nails, and then, as the lift doors pinged open, she stood on tiptoe and kissed him on the cheek. 'Thanks,' she said.

'For what?'

'For doing this. For trying to put me at ease with that rather unkind reminder about my earlier, ahem, gastric issues. And for doing whatever it is I'm sure you did to make Jed see sense.'

'I didn't make Jed see anything he couldn't already. I'm sure of that. All I did was . . . remind him.'

'Even so.'

They stepped into the lift, Patrick checking his reflection in the mirror on the back wall and hastily wiping off the traces of Livia's lipstick, then – suddenly all serious – they rode silently down to the ground floor. As the doors opened, following Patrick's formal 'Shall we?' they linked arms, and he walked her through reception, smiling proudly at the other hotel guests and the handful of staff who were grinning inanely at them as they passed. After a quick peek through the doors – to make sure Jed was actually there, though Patrick didn't dare tell Livia that was why he was looking – he turned to her one final time.

'Good luck,' whispered Patrick.

'Same to you,' said Livia.

'And try to have fun.'

'You too!'

'I will.' He grinned. 'I've got a daughter, remember. This is probably my only chance to take centre stage at a wedding when I'm not paying for the whole show.'

Livia nudged him. 'Maybe not your *only* chance . . .'

As Patrick blanched, she laughed. 'Your *face*!' she said, and he smiled sarcastically.

'Very funny,' he said, resting a hand on the door handle. Though Patrick didn't think it was funny at all.

'Are you all right?'

Jed fingered the side of his face as he and Liam stood in the court-yard, waiting for Livia to make an appearance. 'Apart from the black eye, you mean?'

'Yeah,' said Liam with a grin, though to his credit, Jed thought he sounded at least a *little* guilty. The side of Jed's face was still visibly swollen, though thanks to some hastily applied foundation from Izzy, he should be able to get through the wedding without looking like he'd gone fifteen rounds. Even though, after the day he'd had, that was how he was feeling.

He gazed around the terrace. Where they stood, and where earlier a handful of sunbeds had been lined up by the old stone wall, now there was a small table with a couple of chairs for him and Livia, and a row of seats arranged behind for their friends, where Rachel and Izzy were patiently waiting. The potted olive trees that dotted the courtyard were bedecked with as-yet unlit lanterns, which were swinging gently in the light breeze coming in from the Mediterranean. The open dining area on the other side of the pool had a long table set for eight at one end, which was decorated with simple white floral arrangements. It couldn't have been more perfect. He only hoped Livia would feel the same.

The sun had baked the flagstones all day, which meant there was a pleasant, bearable warmth emanating from them, so why Jed was sweating so much was beyond him . . . Then it hit him. This was *real*. He and Livia were getting *married*. And he was actually feeling *excited* about it.

Liam nudged him. 'Set up nicely, eh?'

'The courtyard? Or were you referring to what Livia did to me?'

'Both.' Liam grinned. The sky was a deep blue, with not a cloud visible, which Jed had to see as a good omen. It looked like it should stay that way too – last night, even from the hotel's position slap bang in the centre of the city, the constellations had been visible, stunningly so, and Jed was looking forward to a repeat performance.

'Sorry, Liam.'

'What for?'

'You might not be the only star putting in an appearance this evening.'

'Biggest, though,' said Liam.

'Biggest something.' Jed grabbed his brother in a playful headlock. 'And no, I'm not being complimentary.'

A man in a suit was making his way towards them – the official who'd be marrying them, Jed guessed, so he held out his hand. 'Hi,' he said, nervously introducing himself. 'I'm the groom.'

'Ah, Jed. It is nice to meet you. My name is Miguel,' said the man, shaking his hand formally. 'I'll be marrying you this evening.'

Jed narrowed his eyes at Liam, hoping to prevent the inevitable attempt at a joke. 'And this is Liam. My brother.'

'Aha. The best man.'

Liam gave Jed a look, as if to say 'See?' – then, as Miguel excused himself to get ready for the ceremony, he frowned. 'You're sure you're okay?'

'What do you mean?' said Jed, surprised to find his voice was trembling.

Liam rolled his eyes. 'You look like . . . well, like you need the toilet. Badly.'

'Yeah, well, *you* look like . . .' Jed grinned. It was a game they used to play as kids, upping the insults until one or both of them collapsed in fits of laughter, and he could do with a laugh right now to calm his nerves. He looked his brother up and down, taking in the slightly shiny suit, trousers with legs so tight he wondered how Liam had managed to pull them on over his feet, the white shirt open almost to his belly button, displaying the Chinese tattoo across his chest that Jed had once (unkindly) managed to convince Liam actually spelled out 'egg fried rice' rather than the Cantonese translation of his name. 'A bloody Premiership footballer. And that's not a good look.'

'For you, maybe not. For me . . . it's what the women want.'

Jed glanced over his shoulder, smiling nervously at Rachel and Izzy. 'And your date for this evening is where, exactly?' he whispered.

Liam shrugged. 'Thought I'd give it a miss.'

'Slipping?'

'Not really. I've just decided . . .' Liam took a deep breath. 'I want a Livia.'

'Well, you can't *have* Olivia. She's mine.'

'Not O-Livia. *A* Livia. Someone like her, at least. Or rather, to have something like you guys have.'

'Wow – my little brother's finally growing up. What on earth's prompted this?'

Liam shrugged. 'Dunno. Maybe because . . .' He stopped talking, because Jed had glanced over his shoulder again then turned ashen: Rachel was holding her phone up in the air, the 'Wedding March' blasting tinnily out of the speaker.

'Is it her?'

'Who else were you expecting to appear to the strains of "Here Comes the Bride"?' Liam nudged him. 'Have a look for yourself.'

'I can't.'

'Why not?'

'I can't move.'

'Bro, if you don't, you'll miss one of the most amazing sights you'll ever have the chance to see.' He reached across and adjusted Jed's shirt collar. 'It's not like if you lock eyes with her, you'll turn to stone, like in that film.'

'What film?'

'The one you used to love when we were kids. Something to do with Argos.'

Jed thought for a moment. '*Jason and the Argonauts?*'

'That's the one.' Liam nodded. 'Now relax. Most grooms worry the bride isn't going to turn up. You're looking like you're worried she *has!*'

'No, it's not that. I just . . . I'm getting *married.*'

'Hold on.' Liam pulled his phone out of his pocket and – making sure Livia was visible in the shot – took a quick selfie of them all, then stuck the phone in front of Jed's nose. 'See? Nothing to be scared of. Just your wife-to-be walking up the aisle, looking abso-fucking-lutely amazing in her wedding dress.' He peered closely at the screen. 'At least, I *think* it's Livia. Or maybe there's another wedding going on here, and there's been a bit of a mix-up . . .'

'What?' Jed wheeled round, not getting – or appreciating – the fact that Liam was joking, to be greeted with the most incredible sight he'd ever seen. Livia looked . . . well, 'stunning' didn't quite do her justice. Her dress . . . The simple band of white flowers in her hair . . . No wonder Patrick was looking so emotional as he escorted her past the pool.

At once, he knew this was what he wanted, and that he'd been stupid. He was getting to marry the woman who'd knocked him off his feet all those years ago – and still did, if he was honest, on a regular basis. He couldn't believe his luck. And what was more, *she'd* asked *him*! Arranged all of this. And it couldn't have been more perfect.

He felt his chest swell with pride, then his legs started to buckle and he grabbed Liam's arm for support. 'Pinch me, will you?'

'She looks good, doesn't she?'

'She does,' agreed Jed. 'She always does.'

Liam took him gently by the shoulders. 'Now you're absolutely, one hundred per cent sure you want to go through with this?'

Jed stared at him for approximately a nanosecond, then he nodded, surprised at himself, because he'd never been more sure of anything else in his life. Yet as he looked round at Livia again, she seemed to be – well, 'not that happy' just about summed it up, and Jed's heart lurched. How could he have been so unfeeling? So unenthusiastic. This was their wedding day, and he'd spent most of it away from her, or sulking, or provoking a stupid argument, then she'd been ill, and to cap it all he'd gone and got into a . . . not a fight, exactly, but he had a black eye. And it wasn't something he was proud of. Any of it. He should have behaved more enthusiastically from the start. Been smart enough to realise it was a big deal to her, and that she might actually resent him for making her go through all of this, rather than the other way round. And feel a little embarrassed that she'd had to.

Suddenly, Jed felt awful. He'd been thinking he'd have to try to apologise somehow, but the look on her face right now – if he could turn back time, go back to last night's proposal, act just a little differently, be honest with her about his doubts, his dad . . .

Jed sighed, suspecting it was already too late. He'd blown it. And Livia would probably never forgive him. He reached up and touched his eye again, wincing as his fingers found the tender part above his cheekbone. Still, it would be a talking point in the photos, he realised.

'Sorry again,' said Liam.

'Some best man you turned out to be,' Jed whispered, and Liam made a face.

'I'll do better next time, I promise.'

'You'd better!' said Jed, then he did a double take. 'Wait. What?'

'Nothing.'

Liam had turned white – quite a feat in a man whose daily mois-turiser included a significant percentage of fake tan, so Jed narrowed his eyes at him, wincing again at the throbbing from the side of his face. 'What do you mean, "next time"?'

'Nothing. Slip of the—'

'Liam!' he hissed.

'Well, *Patrick* said . . .'

Jed shook his head. Liam used to do this as a kid whenever he felt he was in trouble, try and deflect the focus of the conversation, the *blame*, onto someone else, and in that moment, Jed knew something was up.

'Patrick said what?'

Liam was staring at his shoes. 'Livia's going to kill me.'

'She won't. Because I already will have. Unless you spill *right now* . . .'

His brother glanced round at the slowly approaching Livia, then back at Jed. 'Well, you're going to have to do all this again, aren't you?'

'Am I?'

'Yeah. On account of today not being legal.'

'What?'

'I said, on account of this not—'

'Not "what?" what, Liam. I meant *explain*.'

'This wedding. It's not really a wedding, is it? Not legally. I mean, I dunno, maybe it is in Spain, like if you were to do something illegal on holiday in, say, America, like get caught with drugs – nothing heavy, mind – then when you went back there, they could like arrest you for it, so perhaps if you and Liv come back here you might find yourselves actually Mr and Mrs . . .'

'Liam!'

'This bloke.' Liam jabbed a thumb at Miguel. 'He could be anyone, really. Could be me, for all it matters back home.'

'I don't . . .'

'Jed, normally I'm the thick one. What part of "what you're about to do here doesn't mean you're legally married in England" don't you understand? You're going to have to do this for real when you get back home. Properly. At a register office or something. Which means you can have a proper stag night. And I know just the place to go. Gets great reviews on TripAdvisor. Though *Strip*Advisor would be more appropriate.'

Jed stared at Liam for a moment, looked round at where Patrick was about to deliver Livia to his side, then – like he used to do when they were kids – grabbed his brother by the ears, pulled his head forward and kissed him squarely on the forehead. 'Liam, you *beauty*!' he said.

Because suddenly, he knew how he was going to make everything right.

Livia took her place next to Jed, her head spinning with a range of emotions. And though he'd smiled down at her when she'd arrived, his face was . . . it was hard to read. Then again, he was probably nervous. God knew she was.

She reached up and tenderly rested a hand on his cheek, then withdrew it sharply. 'What happened to your eye?' she whispered.

'Liam,' was all Jed said in response, and Livia knew better than to ask any more. As a hush fell over the assembled guests, she felt Jed grab her hand, and she returned his squeeze gratefully.

'You okay?' she asked, concerned Jed hadn't seemed able to meet her gaze.

'Yeah,' he mumbled. 'Actually, no.'

'*No?*' Livia felt her legs almost give way. Surely Jed wasn't about to call the wedding off – and in front of everyone? 'What do you mean, "no"?'

She stared at him for a moment, registered Liam's look of horror and spun round to lock eyes with Rachel, but when she turned back again, Jed was nowhere to be seen. Then she heard a familiar voice whisper, 'Liv?' and she looked past her stomach to see him kneeling at her feet.

'What are you doing down there?'

'Bro . . .' said Liam, attempting to haul him up again, but Jed shook him off.

'Hang on.' He grabbed Liam's wrist and pulled a ring off his brother's index finger. When he presented it to her, Livia's mouth dropped open.

'What's this?'

'An engagement ring.'

'What?'

'Well, it's symbolic. I'll get you a proper one when—'

'I heard you the first time. I just . . . I don't understand.'

'Olivia Wilson, will you marry me?'

'Um . . . I was just about to?'

'Properly.'

'What?' Livia had started to colour, and Jed grinned.

'I may not have seen this coming, Liv, but I'm not completely blind. We're going to have to do this for real when we get back. Aren't we?'

'Are we? I don't know, I—'

'Liv!'

'When did you find out?'

Jed glanced up at Liam, who was trying his best to look innocent. 'That's not important. Were you ever going to tell me? Or was the plan to wait until we got back, then do some grand Scooby-Doo-type reveal?'

'I . . . I just thought it'd be easier this way. To make you see that marrying me wasn't so bad.'

Jed shook his head. 'Liv, I never thought it'd be bad. I just thought I'd be bad at it. Besides, I didn't think it was something you wanted. Something *we* wanted.'

'And you do now?'

'I'm on one knee in front of you, in front of everyone, holding a borrowed ring. I'll leave you to work that one out.' He grimaced up at her. 'But don't take too long, will you? I'm in danger of getting cramp.'

'Oh, Jed. I don't know what to say.'

'Well, that's a first,' said Jed with a smile.

Livia stared at him for a moment, then she peered at the ring and – ignoring a surly 'I want that back' from Liam – slipped it onto her finger. She hauled Jed back up and, to a round of applause from Patrick, Rachel and Izzy, turned back to face the front.

'Sorry about that,' she said, and Miguel smiled.

'This is, I think, going to be the shortest engagement in the whole of history.'

'But possibly the best proposal,' said Livia.

'So . . .' Miguel looked at them both in turn. 'Are we ready?'

'We are,' said Jed.

'Okay. Well, thank you all for coming,' Miguel said, though Livia thought it was perhaps a little over the top for the three people gathered behind them. 'We are here this evening to celebrate the marriage of Olivia and Jeremy . . .' Liam coughed loudly at the mention of Jed's full name, and both she and Jed turned to shush him. 'Now, marriage, as I am sure you all know, is the union of two people, voluntarily entered into for life' – Livia cringed a little at the 'voluntarily' part – 'to the exclusion of all others. The purpose of marriage is that you may always love, care for and support each other through all the joys and sorrows of life. It is a partnership in which two people can pledge their love and commitment to each other; a solemn union providing love, friendship, help and comfort to you both through your life together.'

'Sounds fine to me,' said Jed, to a ripple of laughter.

'Now, I am going to ask you both whether you know of any lawful reason why you should not be married to each other.'

Jed hesitated, and Livia nudged him. 'Sorry,' he said. 'You said "I'm going to ask you." I didn't realise that was you *actually* doing the asking just then.'

'No,' said Livia. 'We don't.'

Miguel laughed. 'In that case, I am going to ask you, Livia, if you take Jed to be your husband, and whether you promise to be loving, faithful and loyal to him for the rest of your life together?'

Livia turned to face Jed, and tried to ignore the fact he'd turned a shade of white. 'I do,' she said.

'And do you, Jed, take Livia to be your wife. And do you promise—'

'I do,' said Jed, loudly, followed by, 'Sorry, just got a little ahead of myself there.'

'Can I have the rings, please?'

Jed cleared his throat and glanced at his brother, and Liam stood there for a second or two, as if he didn't realise Miguel was addressing him. He looked at Jed, then at Livia, then he paled and began frantically rummaging through his pockets. 'Hang on,' he said, after a moment. 'You didn't give me them.'

'Gotcha!' whispered Jed.

'You *bastard*,' Liam whispered back, as Patrick stepped forward and passed the officiant the ring Livia had collected earlier. Then Jed reached into his jacket pocket and handed Miguel a jewellery box. Although Livia thought it looked a little big for a ring.

She raised an eyebrow at him. 'What's that?'

'I went back to the shop. They said I could exchange mine for anything I wanted, so . . .'

Miguel opened the box, and Livia peered at the contents. 'With this watch I thee wed?' She frowned. 'It's not exactly traditional, is it?'

Jed glanced at the assembled guests. 'Given the whole nature of this wedding, I didn't think that would be an issue.'

Miguel cleared his throat politely. 'Okay,' he said. 'Jed, please repeat after me: Livia, I give you this ring as a symbol of our commitment to each other.'

'Livia, I give you this ring as a symbol of our commitment to each other.'

'As a sign of our marriage. And as a token of our love and affection.'

'As a sign of our marriage. And as a token of our love and affection.'

'And I call upon all persons present to witness that I, Jed, take you, Livia, to be my wife.'

'And I call upon all persons present to witness that I, Jed, take you, Livia, to be my wife.'

'I promise to love, care and honour you, for richer, for poorer, in sickness and in health, till death do us part.'

'I promise to love, care and honour you, for richer, for poorer, in sickness and in health, till death do us part.'

Jed's voice was cracking, and Livia felt her heart swell. At least, she hoped it was that, and not a repeat of her earlier *patatas bravas* experience.

'And Livia?' said Miguel. She looked up at Jed. She couldn't wait to be married to him.

'Ditto,' she said.

Jed slipped the ring on her finger, and Livia felt her heart skip a beat. It was as if she'd just crossed the finish line, and it was all she could do to stop herself from punching the air in celebration; instead, she turned to her guests and held her hand up, proudly showing off her ring finger to a smattering of applause. Then she took the watch and slipped it around Jed's wrist, and clicked the clasp shut.

'Ouch.'

'What?'

'Sorry – you've caught a few hairs . . .'

Jed reached down and adjusted the bracelet, and Livia rolled her eyes, and Miguel laughed again. 'Well, in that case, I now pronounce you man and wife.'

There was a loud sob from behind them – Rachel, Livia guessed, and she told herself it was because her best friend was happy for them. Then Jed took her hand again, and Livia finally knew she'd done the right thing. And hoped he was feeling the same way.

'Is that it?' Liam asked, and Miguel smiled.

'Not quite,' he said. 'You may now kiss the bride.'

There was a smattering of applause, then: 'Not *you*,' said Jed, as Liam made to elbow him out of the way.

Chapter 9

'What's the matter, Liam?'

Patrick had appeared at his shoulder with a couple of glasses of cava, so Liam took one and downed half of it gratefully. 'Thanks.'

'That was actually for Izzy.'

'Ah. Sorry,' said Liam, offering him the glass back.

'Why don't you keep it?'

'Will do,' he said, sheepishly. 'And what do you mean, "what's the matter"?'

'This is not a wake. Yet you look like it is.'

'Yeah?'

'Yeah,' said Patrick, mimicking him.

'It's this whole marriage thing. It's made me think a bit. A lot, actually.'

'About?'

'Me. My life. And how, despite all this . . .' With a sweep of his hand, Liam indicated his own face and body. 'I'm here at my brother's wedding without a date.'

Patrick put an arm around his shoulders. 'Hey – the night's still young.'

'Yeah, but I'm not. I mean, I'm a lot younger than *you*, obviously, but I'm going to be *twenty-eight* soon.'

Patrick had opened his mouth to say something but evidently changed his mind, and he gave Liam an affectionate squeeze. 'Well, like I said, the night's young. And loads of people meet their future partner *at* a wedding, apparently.'

'That's true, is it?'

'According to *Four Weddings and a Funeral*, yes.'

Liam sighed. 'Yeah, well, the way things are going, I'm more likely to meet someone at *my* funeral.'

Patrick nudged him. 'What about Rachel?' he said, and Liam followed his gaze to the table where they'd be eating shortly. She was properly single now, judging by how Rich seemed to have disappeared from the scene an hour or so ago, and while, perversely, that made her a bit less of an attractive option in Liam's book, she was still as hot as he'd informed her earlier. Plus there was something quite sexy about the way her forehead crinkled as she sipped her cava and frowned at the seating plan . . . Liam hadn't seen many crinkled foreheads recently. When everyone around you had Botox, it was an occupational hazard.

'How does Livia know her again?'

'Friends from college, if I remember rightly.'

Liam peered at her, as if studying a racehorse in the paddock before deciding whether to place a bet. 'And what's wrong with her?'

'Pardon?'

'What's wrong with her. She's Livia's age and not married. She's not even been able to hang on to that Rich wanker . . .'

There was a pause. 'Oh, you mean *Richard*. And not . . .' Patrick sniggered. 'There could be a hundred reasons for why that's the case – and none of them have to be negative. Besides, the same question could be asked of you.'

Liam gave him a look. 'So should I just go and talk to her, then?'

'Why on earth would you want to do a thing like that?' Patrick was looking horrified, then he grinned and clapped Liam on the back. '*Of course* you should go and talk to her!'

'Right.'

'Now.'

'Now?'

'Right now. And you may want to turn down that Liam knob a few notches.'

'That's not a very nice thing to—'

'I meant "knob" as in the kind of thing you'd find on, say, a hi-fi. Though to be honest . . .'

'Okay, okay.' Liam adjusted his jacket, removed a stray hair from his sleeve and checked his breath in his cupped hand. 'Here I go.'

'Remember. Play nice.'

'Sure. And, um, what should I say?'

'Say?'

'We didn't really meet properly earlier. How should I introduce myself?'

'I don't know. How about something like, "Hi, we didn't really meet properly earlier"? Followed by "I'm Liam, the groom's clueless idiot brother" . . .'

'Ha ha. Yeah, very good.'

'Here.' Patrick picked up what he assumed must be Livia's untouched glass of cava from the table, and handed it to him. 'Wait until she's finished her drink, then take her this.'

'Why can't I do it now?'

'Because she hasn't finished the one she has yet. And it's polite to wait for someone to finish what they already have before offering them a new one . . .' He let the sentence hang. 'Did you want *me* to introduce you?'

'Would you?'

Patrick sighed exasperatedly. 'No.'

'Right. Sure.'

Liam watched as Rachel downed the rest of her cava, then he took the glass Patrick had handed him and strode purposefully over to where she was standing. He stood there for a moment, watching while she picked up one of the place cards, crumpled it into a ball and threw it on the floor, then he took a deep breath. 'Trying to find yourself?'

'That's pretty deep!'

'On the seating plan.' Liam nodded at the table. 'Sometimes you need a degree in maths to work out who should sit next to who at these things . . .'

'I've got a degree in maths. In any case, it's not that complicated, seeing as there are only six of us now, despite the two extra settings.' She pointed to the place card in front of her. 'I seem to be here. At the sad singles end. Next to, well, *you*.' Rachel smothered a giggle. 'Sorry about the "sad singles" thing.'

'No, that'd be about right.' Liam suddenly remembered he was holding two glasses, so he passed her one. 'We didn't really get a chance to talk earlier.'

'No.' Rachel cheersed him, then took a huge gulp of cava. 'I was too busy telling my loser of a boyfriend to piss off.'

'Right,' said Liam, unsure whether that was a good thing. 'So you know Livia from . . . ?'

'College. She and I were roomies.'

'*Bed* roomies? Or . . . ?'

'Always on, eh? Impressive!' She looked him up and down. 'Hard to believe you're Jed's brother.'

'I'll take that as a compliment. Though actually . . .' He lowered his voice, using it as an excuse to lean in closer to her. 'We're not really brothers. That's just a cover story. We actually met in prison. He and I . . .' Rachel had taken half a step backwards, so he smiled quickly. 'Sorry. Joking. He *is* my brother.' He pulled an imaginary notepad and pen from his pocket, and pretended to jot something down as he said, 'Don't use the prison line again.'

'No. Good idea.' Rachel smiled. 'Though prison is a bit more of an interesting opening gambit.'

'In that case, yes, it *was* prison.'

'And what were you and Jed in for?' said Rachel, playing along.

'Um . . .' Liam laughed. 'You'd have thought I'd have worked that one out. Right now, I can't think of anything that'd show me in a positive light.'

'Hard to spin a prison sentence, really.'

'Exactly.'

'So . . .'

'So?'

'Nice ceremony.'

'Wasn't it?'

'Funny, though.' Rachel had finished the last of her second drink, so Liam passed her his glass. 'Jed having a wedding watch instead of a ring.'

'I think it's so he always knows when it's time to come home . . .' He elbowed Rachel gently in the ribs to reinforce his attempt at humour, then noticed she was wiping away a tear. 'It wasn't that bad a joke, surely?'

Rachel shook her head, she fished a tissue out of her handbag, and dabbed at her eyes. 'No. Sorry. Weddings always make me cry.'

'Because they're so romantic?'

'Because it's never me!' said Rachel, downing half of Liam's glass of cava in one go, and he had to resist the impulse to reach across and take the glass back.

'You've never been asked? I'd have thought someone as beautiful as you would have a queue of—'

Rachel silenced him with a look. 'Eleven weddings, I've been to in the last four years. *Eleven*. And not one of them mine.'

'Yeah, but . . .' Liam thought for a moment. The 'but' was proving tricky – then something occurred to him. 'Remember, though. It took Livia asking Jed for this one to happen.'

'I'd need a boyfriend for that.'

'For what?'

'To ask him!' Rachel almost shouted, and Liam flinched.

'Yeah, well, if you ask me . . . I don't actually mean ask me . . .'

'Thank you for clarifying that,' said Rachel, testily.

' . . . the whole concept of being tied down . . . I mean, I don't mind actually *being* tied down, if that's your kind of thing. I did it once. Got off my tits in a club, went back to this woman's house, next thing I know she's got the handcuffs out.' He smiled wistfully at the memory. 'But in the marriage sense . . . So many women, so little time!'

'If that's supposed to make me feel better . . .'

'Okay, okay.' He grinned sheepishly. 'I'll let you into a secret,' he said, gesturing across the terrace to where Livia and Jed were sitting by the pool, hand in hand, as Izzy snapped a series of photographs on her phone. 'This is what I want more than anything. To meet someone, to fall in love with them, have kids.'

'Oh no!' said Rachel, facepalming. 'And on the day I decide to start enjoying the single life . . .'

Liam stared at her for a moment, then broke into a grin. 'Yeah. Good one, Rach,' he said.

'I'm serious! About enjoying singledom, that is, and not . . .'

'So am I. It's just . . . a million miles away from how I live, isn't it?'

'It doesn't have to be.'

'What do you mean?'

'Have you tried this thing called dating? Meeting someone, doing things the traditional way, rather than swiping right or getting – to use your wonderful phrase – off your tits in a club and going home with someone whose name you don't remember the next morning. If you even knew it in the first place.'

'I don't know, Rach . . .' Liam scratched his head. 'My way's just . . . easier.'

'And how's that working out for you?'

'Huh?'

'Where's your date this evening?'

'Well . . .'

'In fact, that's probably why you're over here now, isn't it? To see whether I'm that depressed and vulnerable – or drunk – that you might have a chance. Well, hang on . . .' She downed the rest of Liam's cava, then handed him back his glass. 'Tell you what – fetch me another couple of these, and maybe you might.'

Rachel was looking at him strangely – either with amusement or anger, Liam couldn't tell – so he glanced around the room. Patrick and Izzy seemed to be watching him intently, and the last thing he wanted was for everyone to know he'd got Rachel drunk and slept with her – or even that he'd tried to. And while that sort of had been on his mind, he was beginning to realise he couldn't go on like this. Not indefinitely. Not without people getting hurt, he thought, remembering how Jed got his black eye. And certainly not if he did want what he'd told Rachel just now.

'Not at all,' he said, as sincerely as he could muster. 'You were just looking a bit sad, so I thought I'd come over and cheer you up with a bit of banter. Have a bit of a laugh. We could just console ourselves as the two singletons here.' Rachel was looking at him as if he should have referred to himself as simpleton instead, so he fixed a sympathetic smile on his face and pulled out her chair, indicating she should sit down. Dinner was due to start, and as the others made their way towards the table, he sat down next to her and lowered his voice. 'In fact, tell you what. How about you and me have a pact?'

'A pact?'

'Yeah. If neither of us is married by the time we're thirty . . .'

'What?'

'I saw it on this TV programme once. This couple had this pact that said if they weren't married to anyone else by the time they were thirty, then they'd get married. To each other,' he added, in case she hadn't understood, then he stopped talking. There was no mistaking it – Rachel looked like she was about to explode. 'What's the matter?'

'I'm *already* thirty!'

'Oh. Right. Well, um . . .' He looked around desperately. Jed and Livia were approaching, Livia giving him daggers, and judging by the look on Patrick's face as he lowered himself into the seat opposite, Liam suspected he wasn't too pleased with him either. 'If it's any consolation, you don't look any older than . . .' He swallowed hard. 'Twenty-eight, twenty-nine, tops.'

Rachel burst out laughing, then mimed shooting herself in the temple, and though Liam was useless at reading women, he could tell it was no consolation at all.

Livia waggled her ring finger, smiling at the contrast between her elegant wedding band and the somewhat masculine 'engagement' one Jed had borrowed from Liam, then when she caught Jed looking at her and slowly shaking his head, she tried – and failed – to stop her cheeks from reddening. She still couldn't believe her luck – Jed's proposal was something she'd remember for ever, and not only because it had rid her of any doubts she'd had that he was just going through the motions. And the ceremony itself had been . . . well, Livia knew it didn't really mean anything, and yet somehow it had felt like it meant *everything*.

She cast her eyes around the table – Izzy and Patrick were locked in conversation, god knows about what; Liam staring at them across the table from where he was sitting next to Rachel, trying to appear interested, but, she suspected, more interested in peeking down Izzy's rather revealing dress. To her left, Rachel was sitting, picking the slice of cake on her plate apart with her fork, so she leaned across to whisper in her ear.

'Are you eating that, or trying to find out how it died?'

'Huh?'

'You look like you're performing an autopsy, rather than enjoying my wedding dinner.'

'What? No, sorry, Liv. I'm just . . . thinking.'

'About?'

'Rich and I . . . just before . . .' She swallowed hard. 'I told him it was over.'

Livia smiled sympathetically. 'I guessed.'

'How did you . . . ?'

'The empty seat next to you during the ceremony was a bit of a giveaway. As was the crying. But good for you. It was a very brave thing to do. Though I'm still a little puzzled as to why you took him back in the first place?'

Rachel thought for a moment. 'Like I said earlier, I didn't want to just throw away the last two years. But then when Rich showed his true colours, I realised that was better than throwing away the rest of my life.' She put her fork down and pushed her plate away. 'I just don't know why I didn't see it.'

'See what?'

'What a . . . *plonker* he was.'

Livia took her hand. 'Maybe because you didn't want to?'

Rachel stared at her for a moment, then she smiled. 'Maybe you're right. Though he was right too, when he said, "It's not me, it's you." It *was* me.'

'How so?'

'In that I deserved better than him.' She smiled, wistfully. 'And I'm sorry about the tears. Though that wasn't because of Rich.'

'No?'

'No. It was just . . . weddings always make me cry.' Rachel forced a smile. 'All the emotion. The commitment. The vows. Those promises. There's something about them that's just so . . .'

'I know.'

'And Jed's proposal. That was so romantic.'

'If a bit last-minute.' Livia grinned. 'Took me rather by surprise, I can tell you. I actually thought he was going to call the whole thing off!'

'You're kidding?'

'Given the day I've had, nothing would have surprised me. Lots of ups and downs. Especially with *my* emotions. For a moment, I thought I was going to blub in front of everybody.'

'You? You never cry.'

'Maybe it was just my hormones.' Livia shrugged. 'You sure you're okay?'

'Yeah.' Rachel stared at her glass for a moment, went to take a drink, and then, as if making some momentous decision, put it back down on the table. 'You were right earlier. I need to just get on with my life, have fun, see what happens. Who cares if I'm the last one standing?'

'What about Izzy? I don't see Patrick getting down on one knee any time soon.'

'She's twenty-two! In any case, she's already got him wrapped around her little finger. And several other body parts, by the looks of things.'

Livia lowered her voice. 'There's always Liam?'

'No thank you!'

Livia glanced across to where he was sitting, just the other side of Rachel, blatantly staring at Izzy's cleavage. 'No, I meant that he's around our age and still single, and nowhere near settling down.'

'Are you surprised? Besides, that's through choice.'

'You're single through choice. You chose not to let Rich treat you like that. And you're being choosy as to who you meet. I rest my case.'

'Yes, well, that's because—'

'In any case, Liam's not that bad, once you get through the top layer of, well, Liamness.' Livia lowered her voice. 'Which was why we sat the two of you together, so . . .'

'Is this some kind of set-up?'

Livia gave her a look. 'Sure, Rachel. Jed's actually been in on this the whole time, and he and I planned this whole weekend in Barcelona as a ruse to get you and Liam together, instead of just arranging a night out down the pub back home. I meant so he can give you some tips.'

As Rachel grinned, perhaps at the absurdity of the both of those ideas, Livia reached over and gave her friend a hug.

'What was that for?'

'Thanks, Rach.'

'What for?'

'For coming. And staying. I know this can't be easy for you right now.'

'How do you mean?' said Rachel, though she looked like she knew full well what Livia meant.

'Being the only single person at a wedding. Apart from Liam. Though give him half an hour, and he won't be.'

'I'm not so sure.'

'How do you mean?'

'Like I said. Weddings make you think, don't they? And by the looks of Liam, he's been doing some thinking.'

Livia laughed. 'You have to have a brain to do that.'

'Well, I gave him a bit of a hard time earlier, and . . . let's just say he might surprise you.'

'Liam surprises me quite often. Usually not in a good way.' Livia smiled at her, then nodded at Rachel's plate. 'Now, are you going to eat that?'

'I don't think so.'

'Great!' Livia helped herself to Rachel's leftovers. 'Keep this up, and you'll be the best maid of honour ever. Though after your little adventure this afternoon, perhaps "honour" isn't the most appropriate word.'

Rachel stuck her tongue out, but before she could say anything back, the tapping of a spoon against a glass from behind her made her swivel round.

'Oh good,' said Livia, sarcastically. 'The speeches.'

'Are you going to say something?' asked Rachel.

Livia thought for a moment, then she hauled herself to her feet, causing Liam to tap his glass so hard he cracked it.

'Before Liam starts, I'd just like to say . . .' Livia looked round at her friends, then she smiled at – and the revelation almost took her breath away – her *husband*. 'If anyone doesn't want their cake, I'll have it!'

She sat back down to a smattering of applause, and as Jed slid his barely touched plate across the table towards her, Rachel smiled.

'Well, that disproves *that*.'

'Huh?'

'You *can* have your cake and eat it,' she said.

Livia picked up her fork, speared a piece of icing and popped it into her mouth, then she picked up her glass and clinked it against Rachel's.

'Here's to not being the only one,' she said.

'Guys and gals, the groom!'

Jed breathed a silent sigh of relief. Liam had just finished his speech – though 'speech' would suggest it had some sort of structure. In reality, it had been little more than a ramble: an attempted joke about incest, followed by a comment about Jed having been 'groomed', which had fallen rather flat, even though Liam had gone on to insist he hadn't meant in the paedophile sense. To his credit, he had soldiered on regardless, even getting quite emotional towards the end – though that was possibly a result of the double tequila he'd downed at the bar beforehand to steady his nerves (or, to use Liam's delightful phrase, because he didn't want to cack himself in front of everyone).

There was a smattering of applause, along with a loud 'Hear hear' from Patrick (followed by an even-louder wolf whistle from Izzy), and Jed sat there, wondering what was supposed to be happening, until (and ironically, only thanks to Liam's joke) he remembered 'the groom' actually meant *him*. He gave a sheepish wave, adjusted his tie and hauled himself to his feet.

'Yes, so, ladies, gentlemen . . . and Liam.' He paused to peer around the table, taking in the familiar faces, his nervousness evaporating when he realised whatever he said, it couldn't be worse than his brother's performance. 'I didn't know I had to give a speech. But then again, I didn't know I was getting married, so I guess that's not surprising. Anyway, thank you all for coming. You complete and utter bastards!' He paused for the ripple of laughter to die down, took a quick swig from his wine glass and soldiered on.

'I say "bastards", but I'd like you all to know that as bastards go, you're a pretty special lot. Liam, Rachel, Patrick and Izzy . . .' – Jed toasted them as he mentioned their names – 'I couldn't think of a nicer bunch of people to be sharing this evening with. And I want all of you to know that I *will* have my revenge.

'Anyway, now it's time to introduce a serious note, like Liam's "jokes"' – Jed made the air quotes gesture – 'did earlier. So, you're all possibly wondering why Livia proposed to me. I'm sure there were times today when she felt that way too. And you're probably asking yourselves why I didn't ever get down on one knee in front of her. She's amazing, and funny, and clever, and sexy, and kind, and . . . I could go on.'

'Please do!' interrupted Livia.

'And the answer is – I don't know, really. But I have been thinking about it today. A lot.' He reached down and took Livia's hand. 'Livia. Back when I first saw you, ten years ago – in fact, right about . . .' He looked at his watch, mouthed a brief countdown, then added . . . '*Now*, do you remember what you were doing?'

'No. Though only because I was very, very drunk.'

'Well, I do. As if it was yesterday. You were dancing, on a table, in a bar not that far from here, and I couldn't believe how beautiful you were . . .'

'That's because *he* was very, very drunk,' said Livia in a stage whisper, to another round of guffawing from the table.

'True,' said Patrick.

'Anyway, I thought to myself, "There's no way a girl like that would ever go out with me," but I asked you if I could buy you a drink anyway – and do you remember what you said to me?'

Livia frowned. '"Get lost, creep"?'

Jed waited until the laughter had died down, which took a while. 'That's not quite how I remember . . .' Livia was shaking her head, so he smiled. 'You said, "I thought you'd never ask." And how prophetic that turned out to be. Because I never asked. But that's the problem with us men. Sometimes we're so stupid, or so blind to what's right in front of us, that we simply don't give any of it a second thought. Equally, we're so afraid of rocking the boat, of upsetting the status quo, that we don't dare change anything. Back then, it took me ages to pluck up the courage to walk the ten metres across that bar to speak to you, because I was convinced you would tell me to get lost. And while I think you might have been more of a safe bet this time round . . .'

'Given that she's up the duff?' suggested Liam, and Jed paused for a moment, wondering whether he should give the chivalrous answer, then deciding to play the comedy card.

'Well, *yes*. Anyway, people change. Circumstances change. But the fact is this: Livia, I love you. The moment I saw you, I knew I wanted to spend the rest of my life with you, and while I kind of thought that's what I *was* doing, after tonight I'm finally sure that's what's going to happen, and it makes me so, so happy. And while I might not have done the best job so far today of giving that precise impression, I want you to know that this' – Jed gestured around the courtyard – 'is quite possibly the nicest, most thoughtful, best, most incredibly wonderful thing that anyone's done to me.' He winked at Livia. 'Sorry, *for* me. Ever.'

Jed gave Livia's hand another squeeze, found the bottle of cava he'd been guarding for this precise moment and circled the table, making sure everyone had a full glass, then he picked up his own drink and motioned for everyone else to do the same. 'A toast, please, on this most fabulous of occasions, in the most perfect of settings, with the best friends – and brother – anyone could hope to have. To Livia. My *wife*.'

'To Livia,' the table chorused.

And when Jed turned and smiled down at her, for the briefest of moments, and for the first time since they'd met, he'd swear Livia was wiping away a tear.

'You coming?'

Livia had just finished another of the rather large pieces of wedding cake from the plate she'd been balancing on her stomach, and her nudge startled Rachel.

'Coming where?'

'To catch the bouquet!' said Livia, excitedly. 'I'm about to throw it.' She stifled a burp. 'Or possibly throw up, if I try and move too quickly.'

'And, um, who are you going to throw it to? Because by my estimation, there's only me and Izzy here to catch it.'

'Nonsense!' Livia waved her hand in the general direction of the other tables by the pool, where a number of hotel guests were sitting, enjoying an al fresco dinner. 'I'll get Liam to go and round up the women from over there. Make it a bit more of an event.'

'Good idea.' Rachel sighed. 'But perhaps I'll just sit this one out.'

'This isn't that "I'll never meet someone so what's the point" stuff again?'

Rachel gave her a look. 'No, it's just . . . forgetting for one moment that catching it is supposed to signify who gets married next, don't you think it's a bit . . .'

'A bit what?'

'Well, to be honest, a bit "I'm a smug married now, so all you single losers go and stand over there, and I'll lob some second-hand flowers at you"?'

Livia laughed. 'Well, that's one way of looking at it. Come on. It'll be fun.'

'I'll tell you what'll be fun. Seeing the look on Patrick's face if Izzy catches it!'

'What do you mean, "if"?'

'What's that supposed to mean?'

'Nothing,' said Livia, mischievously. 'It's just that Izzy's younger, fitter, taller and probably a *lot* springier than you. And when you factor in any random last-minute entries that Liam manages to coerce into joining in . . .'

She reached for the nearest bottle of cava to top up Rachel's glass, but Rachel stopped her mid-pour, surprised to find her competitive streak bubbling up. While everything Livia had said was true, why couldn't she catch the bouquet? She'd managed to 'catch' Jay earlier. Dumping Rich the way she had today had felt incredibly empowering. So wresting a bunch of peonies from a tipsy twenty-two-year-old should be a piece of cake.

'Fine,' she said, then she lowered her voice. 'You couldn't perhaps aim it at me, could you?'

'Don't you think I've got enough on my plate,' Livia said, glancing down at her stomach.

'Oh, you mean because of the *baby*.' Rachel grinned. 'And not those two slices of cake.'

'One's Jed's,' said Livia. 'I'm saving it for him. And even if it wasn't, I am eating for two, remember?'

'You're sure you're not expecting triplets?'

'Cheeky b—'

Rachel fixed a smile on her face and hauled herself out of her chair. 'Just off to the ladies',' she said.

'I'll get Liam to do the same,' said Livia, nodding towards the hotel's other guests.

'No throwing while I'm gone.'

'I haven't had *that* much cake!'

Rachel nipped off to the toilets and composed herself in front of the mirror, and by the time she returned, a crowd of a dozen or so women had gathered in front of the pool. She helped Livia up, escorted her to the front of the terrace and – following the clamour of excitement at Liam's on-cue announcement of 'It's time to throw the bouquet!' – hurried over to join the group.

With a sly glance to either side, Rachel sussed out her competition. The ladies next to her shouldn't present much of a problem – that they were still trying to catch bouquets at their age suggested they weren't much good at it. The two red-faced (and from what she could see, red-everything'd) English women chattering excitedly to each other (and who Liam seemed keen to avoid) were so drunk that Rachel didn't think their hand-eye coordination would be up to the job – if, indeed, they could move in the towering heels they were tottering about on. A couple of teen girls were there too, vacantly staring at each other, their mother – camera at the ready – egging them on from the sidelines, and Rachel considered pointing out that they shouldn't be allowed to take part, seeing as they were too young to get married, but she stopped herself. That would seem desperate. And besides, that was more of an incentive to win – if catching the bouquet did, in fact, signify the next person to get married, and either of these two teenagers caught it, then Rachel's chances were well and truly scuppered.

No – Patrick's girlfriend Izzy was probably her main rival: she looked like she exercised *a lot*, and that she had a point to prove. But she also looked like she'd drunk a lot too, plus she might be exhausted from the shag-fest she and Patrick had been involved in this afternoon, according to Livia. In any case, Patrick looked like he was desperate to put her off, and to be honest, would Izzy really want to catch it in front of him knowing his feelings about marriage? These things were all about desire, weren't they? And right now, Rachel wanted this more than she'd wanted anything in a long time. Besides, she'd played a lot of netball at school. Had been quite good at it. And had sharp elbows.

She narrowed her eyes in concentration as she watched Livia walk towards the far side of the deck area, mentally pictured the arc the flowers might take through the air, and tried to work out whereabouts in the group was the best place for her to stand. In the middle would be playing the law of averages, but then again, she might get blocked in, and she didn't think she'd be able to barge past the larger ladies if it came to it. She could pick a side – but which side? Livia's stomach was too large to allow her to throw with both hands, and she was left-handed, which would suggest – assuming she threw with her back to everyone – the bouquet would land somewhere in the right of the group. But that would assume Livia would throw left-handed, and if she didn't, and Rachel was stuck on the left of the group, then she'd be in even more trouble.

At the front might work, particularly if Livia underthrew – Rachel would be nearest, and could simply pounce on the bouquet like a rugby player going after a loose ball and claim her prize. But Livia was a powerful girl – Rachel had been to Boxercise with her once, and had seen the way she'd rattled the punchbag – and was therefore more likely to give it more of a heave. Plus, how much did a bridal bouquet weigh?

The thought that she didn't know only reminded Rachel she'd never been in a position to find out, and made her even more determined. For a moment, she considered nipping across to where Livia was standing to ask if she could suss it out, but that would open up a whole new calculation involving mass, surface area and aerodynamics, and even with her maths degree, Rachel suspected she was too tipsy to work that one out.

In any case, maybe behind everyone else was the better option. That way, she'd be well placed for any overthrow – or, if she saw it landing mid-crowd, she could swoop in from behind, take the other girls by surprise, elbow them aside and get there first. And if it landed in front of everyone, someone else might get their hands on it first, but it didn't mean Rachel couldn't snatch it off her.

Decision made, she pushed her way to the back of the group, wondering whether she should remove her heels, though the extra manoeuvrability that might give her could be negated by the loss of height. She was already an inch or two shorter than Izzy, and Rachel didn't want to give her any more of an advantage. No, she'd keep them on. She might need them as a weapon, too, if things got nasty.

Surreptitiously, she bent over and did a couple of stretches, under the pretence of adjusting her shoe straps, though she didn't really care if anyone noticed – this bouquet was going to be hers, and if she had to utilise some pre-Olympic-hundred-metre-final-psych-out tactics, then so be it.

As a giggling Livia took up position in front of them, Rachel considered sticking one arm up in the air, like she'd seen footballers do to signal their desire to be passed the ball, but that might be a bit too obvious. Besides, this was a competition. A trial. She needed to win on merit. By catching the bouquet, Rachel would prove to all these other women that she was the alpha female, and show any men watching that *she* was the catch. If Livia simply lobbed the bouquet to her on some prearranged signal, it would look like a fix. A set-up. No, she'd have to be prepared to jump, fight, elbow, push . . . whatever it took to get her hands on the thing.

Izzy had sidled up next to her, and Rachel readied herself to shove her away if required, to give herself the necessary space, again like a footballer might – perhaps those boring Saturday nights sitting in front of *Match of the Day* with Rich were all leading up to this moment, and if that was the case, at least she'd got something out of the relationship.

'Good luck!' whispered Izzy, and Rachel smiled humourlessly back at her. *Luck has nothing to do with it*, she thought.

'You too,' she said, her fingers crossed behind her back.

She took a couple of deep breaths as a beaming Livia turned her back on the group. 'Ready?' she said, and Rachel nodded determinedly.

I was born ready, she thought, before realising she'd said that out loud.

'One . . .' said Livia, as Rachel shushed the women standing in front of her.

'Two . . .'

Rachel tensed. But was Livia going to throw *on* 'three', or would it be one-two-three-throw?

She considered bringing a halt to the proceedings so she could ask her, but surely that would sound a little desperate? And besides, Livia's loud 'Three!' combined with her heaving the bouquet up and over her head in a soaring arc pretty much answered her question.

Rachel shaded her eyes against the lights that dotted the terrace, careful not to lose sight of the bouquet's trajectory – NASA mission control couldn't have kept a closer eye on its flight – and prepared herself to leap for all she was worth. But Livia had put her *and* her baby's combined weight behind her throw, and instead of landing mid-group, it was looking like the bouquet might soar over all their heads.

As if of one mind, the women surged towards her, and Rachel feared she might be trampled in the stampede, so she began running backwards as fast as she could, her feet kicking up, her fists flying to stop her pursuers getting too close, while keeping both eyes determinedly on the bouquet as it flew over her, agonisingly just out of reach. Then, suddenly, one of the red-faced English women seemed to snap the heel on her towering stiletto, and with an agonised cry of 'Sooz, no!' from her friend, went down heavily in front of the chasing pack, causing the sort of pile-up you saw on those comedy video shows on TV.

Rachel mentally punched the air. The bouquet was surely hers now. She could wait for it to land, just pick it up off the floor – a hollow victory, perhaps . . . But then again, didn't you have to actually *catch* the thing for it to count? And besides, if she stretched, maybe jumped, there was a distinct possibility that she still could.

Her adrenaline pumping, it seemed as if everything was happening in slow motion, and with a desperate leap Rachel reached up, stretching her arm almost out of its socket, and by some miracle she managed to close her fingers around the bouquet's foil-wrapped stems. It was *hers*. She'd done it! *Take that, Izzy. You snooze, you lose, you other women. Tough titty, teenagers.* She was the one who'd caught it, fair and square. And now she'd be the next one to get married.

Out of the corner of her eye, she caught sight of Izzy, trapped in the middle of the pile of scuffed knees, sunburnt flesh and mussed-up hair the chasing pack had ended up in, and smiled smugly. Younger wasn't always better, and Rachel felt buoyed by the expression of horror on her face. Although what did Izzy mean by shouting 'Rachel, no!'? Talk about a sore loser.

With the agility of the cat she refused to get, Rachel swivelled round in mid-air and began her descent, hoping she could pull off the same graceful three-point landing Scarlett Johansson always seemed to manage in the *Avengers* movies. That would be her crowning glory. The thing that would make all the men watching look at her with desire in their eyes. Pull this off, and she was sure she only had to parade around the tables on the terrace, click her fingers, and any man she wanted would be hers.

Trouble was, as Rachel quickly realised to her dismay, to achieve any kind of landing – graceful or otherwise – you needed to be landing on *actual* land.

And not, as she was about to do, slap-bang in the middle of the hotel's swimming pool.

Patrick had sat through the speeches, wondering whether he was going to have to make one of his own later. Izzy hadn't let him out of her sight since the ceremony, and he knew he'd have to address her declaration of love at some point. Trouble was, when – and more importantly, how?

Still, at least she hadn't caught the bouquet. He had to think that was a good omen. As was the fact that the person who did had ended up making a fool of themselves in front of everyone. Which pretty much summed up how Patrick felt about marriage.

Though Jed's speech had made him think. Particularly the line about being blind to what's in front of us. Yes, he and Izzy were different, but since things had turned out so disastrously with him and his ex-wife, he truly believed in the whole 'opposites attract' thing. Why would you want to date someone exactly the same as you? Where would be the fun in that? And as for the age gap . . . Patrick kept himself in shape. Had regular medical check-ups. And even though he sometimes thought it was the sex that might kill him, on balance the stamina and flexibility it required was probably doing him a few favours too.

He glanced across at her – she'd spent the last ten minutes picking the icing off her slice of wedding cake, and while Patrick had assumed that was because she didn't want to overload on sugar, she'd actually ended up leaving the fruity interior and devoured all of the sweet bits. But that was Izzy. She could surprise you. And unlike Jed, Patrick actually quite liked surprises.

'Having fun?'

Izzy mimed a yawn, then followed it up quickly with a smile. 'Just kidding. It's all right.'

'You not a fan of weddings, then?'

'I prefer them to funerals.'

'I should hope so.'

'Actually, it's my first one. Of either of those things.'

'You're kidding?'

'How old do you think I am?'

Patrick's heart skipped a beat, then he relaxed when he realised she'd have to be at least sixteen to be working in Selfridges. 'None of your friends ever . . . ?'

'Nope.' Izzy popped the last piece of cake icing into her mouth. 'Most of my friends think marriage is kind of over. No offence.'

Patrick made a face. His certainly was. 'None taken. Though you better not let Jed and Livia hear you say that.'

'Yeah, well, they've been together for, like, a hundred years. So it doesn't really make that much difference to the likes of them, does it?'

Patrick opened his mouth to argue, then realised it wouldn't achieve anything. 'Perhaps not.'

Izzy turned her attention to Liam, who seemed to be fussing with a pair of giant speakers at the far end of the terrace. 'When does this party actually start?'

'Once everyone's eaten, I guess. The hotel normally has a DJ in on a Saturday night for a bit of a poolside disco . . .' Izzy had started to snigger, so Patrick stopped talking. 'What?'

'*Disco.*'

'What would you prefer? Rave?'

Izzy nodded enthusiastically. 'I would, actually!'

'Anyway, we're going to join in with that. Or rather, we were going to, until the DJ did a runner. So Liam's stepping in.'

'Excellent!'

'Why is that excellent?'

'At least we'll get some decent music.'

'Right.'

As Izzy sat there, impatiently tapping a fingernail on the table, looking a little too much like a bored teenager for Patrick's liking (and which, he reminded himself, wasn't far off an accurate description), he took a deep breath. Now would be as good a time as any for them to finish their little talk. Although 'as good as any' didn't necessarily mean 'good'.

'Izzy, about what you said earlier.'

She smiled innocently at him. 'What did I say?'

'You know what you said. And if this is what you want . . .' He gestured around the room. 'Marriage. Me saying "I do". And kids . . . I'm sorry, but I just can't do it again.'

'Why not?'

'Well, because . . .' Patrick hesitated. He'd only worked this answer out recently. Just before he'd met Izzy, in fact. But to admit that the actions of one woman, his ex-wife, had caused him to doubt everything he knew about human nature, made him question whether he could ever love – or trust – anyone ever again, made him fear that loyalty and commitment were just made-up constraints that were there to be discarded as soon as someone better came along, and that family ties weren't actually that strong at all . . . that sounded really melodramatic, and to be honest, a bit pathetic, especially at someone else's wedding, right when *they* were about to have a baby . . .

He took Izzy by the hand, grateful when she didn't pull away. 'Because I'm too old.'

It was a cop-out, and he knew it, but by the incredulous look on her face, Izzy didn't seem to be having any of it. 'Surely I'm the judge of that? And you didn't seem that old earlier.'

'I'm nearly fifty now. If I had another baby, it'd probably kill me.'

'You mean the effort of raising it, right, and not in an "it'll murder you when it grows up" way?'

He smiled, relieved Izzy could make a joke at a time like this. 'Right,' he said, as she let his hand go, but only to help herself to a piece of icing from his plate. 'And even if it didn't, I don't want to be the oldest dad at the school gates. Don't want people to think when we all went out together, it'd be grandson, mum and granddad.'

'Hardly,' said Izzy, and Patrick smiled grimly. Because while that was one of his fears, he couldn't tell her that 'I don't want to do it with you' was perhaps the most appropriate reason – not that he didn't think Izzy could be a good mother, just that he suspected she wasn't ready to be one any time soon. And he certainly didn't have the luxury of waiting until she was.

'Tell me something,' he said, leaning in so he could talk to her without anyone else overhearing. 'Back when we met. How did you think this would go?'

Izzy popped another piece of icing into her mouth. 'I didn't. I just thought we'd have a good time and see what happened. Besides, you can't live your life thinking "what if?", especially if you do the numbers and realise the relationship is doomed to failure, statistically, so what was the point of trying to make any plans whatsoever?'

'That sounds a bit . . .' Patrick remembered Livia's comment from earlier. 'Cynical.'

'Look who's talking! And it's not cynical. It's called getting real. People generally have loads of relationships, and they *all* fail, until one doesn't.' She shifted uncomfortably in her chair, her expression the same as when she feared Patrick might be breaking up with her earlier. 'Baby, do we really have to talk about this *now*?'

'We do, if this' – he waved a hand around in an attempt to indicate the evening's events – 'is where you see things going.'

Izzy stared at him for a moment. 'I don't *know* where I see things going,' she said, sulkily. 'Not yet, anyway. What are you so worried about?'

He raised his voice a little, though only so she could hear him above the music that had started to boom out from the speakers. 'That I might be stopping you from doing what you really want.'

'Haven't you learned by now?' Izzy inspected her fingertips, locking eyes with him as she suggestively sucked the icing from them. 'There's actually very little that stops me from doing what I really want.'

'And what do you really want, Izzy?'

She got up from her chair, then straddled him in his. 'You.'

And despite his best intentions, Patrick didn't have an answer for that.

Chapter 10

Rachel had spluttered to the surface, just in time to see another, fully clothed body jump in beside her, followed by another, then another, until perhaps half the hotel guests were floating beside her in the pool, playfully splashing and ducking each other. As she'd struggled to touch the bottom, she'd felt a strong arm encircle her waist, and she gratefully allowed herself to be towed to the side of the pool. Then, to her horror, she realised the arm was attached to someone she knew. Someone she'd met earlier, in fact. And the last person she wanted to see her like this.

'Jay?'

'We must stop meeting like this.' He put both hands on the edge of the pool, and hoisted himself athletically up and out. 'Actually, we mustn't. I'm quite enjoying it.'

'Wh – What are you doing here?'

'Here as in "at the wedding", or here as in "in the pool"?'

'Either. Both. I don't . . .' Rachel reached up and grabbed the hand he was offering her, marvelling at his firm grip as he hauled her out of the water and lowered her down next to him with a loud, soggy squelch.

'I got here just in time to see you launch yourself into the water. I guessed it wasn't on purpose, so I thought if I jumped in too, people might think it was a thing to do.' He nodded at the still-full pool, where the guests seemed to be enjoying a respite from the warm evening. 'And it looks like they did.'

'So you did that just to spare my blushes?' said Rachel, realising she was probably blushing now, and Jay shrugged.

'Well, yeah.'

'That's . . . That's possibly the nicest thing anyone's done for me. Ever.'

Jay shrugged again, then he helped her to her feet. 'In that case, you've been hanging round with the wrong kind of people.'

'You're telling me!'

He reached down and removed his shoes, emptying the water from each of them back into the pool. 'That was some jump.'

'Thanks. Though I don't think Tom Daley's got anything to worry about.'

'Maybe not.' Jay leaned across and brushed a wet strand of hair from her face. 'Having a nice time?'

'Up until a moment ago.'

'When I arrived?' he said, pretending to be hurt.

'No, silly. When I fell in the pool.'

'Fell?' Jay smiled as he wrapped her in a towel he'd grabbed from a pile on a nearby sun lounger. 'I think "leapt" might be a more accurate description.'

'Maybe.' Rachel pulled the towel tightly around her shoulders, partly because she was cold, but mainly because her dress had gone see-through.

'Still, at least you caught the bouquet.'

Rachel realised to her horror she was still clutching tightly onto the (somewhat bedraggled) bunch of flowers. 'This?' she said, putting it down hurriedly on the nearest table. 'Oh, that was just a bit of fun.'

'Right,' said Jay, mischievously. 'Where are the happy couple?'

Rachel scanned the terrace. 'See those two over there doing a bad job of pretending not to be watching us?'

'Which ones?'

'By the bar. The heavily pregnant woman, and the rather embarrassed-looking chap standing next to her.'

'Crikey. She looks about to burst.'

'That'll be the amount of wedding cake she's eaten.'

Jay found himself a towel and began drying his hair. 'I can see why they were in a hurry to get married.'

'Well, one of them was.'

'Huh?'

'Long story.'

'I've got all night,' said Jay, then he blushed, though Rachel was too busy trying to wring the water out of her dress to notice. 'Should we perhaps get a drink?'

Rachel decided not to point out she'd just had one, so she allowed herself to be helped to her feet, then she steered him towards the bar, trying to stop her mind racing. *Jay* was here. Jay was *here*! And while she didn't know how, or why, what was more important was that he hadn't left when he'd see her perform the worst of bombs into the swimming pool . . .

As she ordered them each a beer, Rachel reminded herself not to get too excited. They'd had a holiday fling, nothing more. Then again, it wasn't as if Rich was waiting for her at home, and not only because he wasn't *at* home.

It wasn't as if *anyone* was waiting for her back in England, come to think of it.

A tap on her shoulder made her spin round, though before she could say anything, Livia's 'Good catch!' made her smile. Particularly since, by the way she was eyeing Jay up, Rachel suspected she wasn't referring to the bouquet.

'Livia,' she said, awkwardly. 'This is . . .'

'Jay?' said Livia.

'How did you know it was him?'

'It wasn't that hard to guess.' Livia stood up on tiptoe to give him a kiss on the cheek, then she looked Rachel up and down. 'That's a good look for you. Though isn't it the bride who's supposed to change outfits at the end of the wedding, rather than the maid of honour?'

'Yes, well, the maid of honour isn't supposed to go for a swim mid-reception either. Then again, this is quite an unconventional wedding.'

'Unconventional?' said Jay. 'How so?'

'Livia asked Jed to marry her.'

'Oh. Right.' Jay had raised both eyebrows. 'Good for you. Was he surprised?'

'Oh yes.' Livia grinned. 'Seeing as I only asked him yesterday.'

Jay's mouth fell open in shock, then he burst out laughing. 'Double good for you! I like a forward woman.'

Livia was smiling at her, though Rachel couldn't meet her eyes. 'So, Jay, what brings you here?'

'I, um . . .' Jay gave Rachel a look. 'Rachel left her . . . *something* at my flat earlier. I'm just returning, you know, *it*.'

'That's good of you,' said Livia, though Rachel's heart was sinking faster than she'd been about to in the pool before Jay had saved her. She'd thought – *hoped* – he'd come here to see her, but in reality he was just returning an item that – yet again – Rachel had been stupid enough to lose. And even now, she was too stupid to remember what she'd left there. As far as she knew, she'd had everything with her when she left his place. Except, perhaps, for a small piece of her heart.

'You should have come earlier,' Livia said. 'You could have had some food.'

'Sorry. Rachel told me you were staying at the "something" Catalonia. Do you know how many hotels in Barcelona have the word "Catalonia" in their name? I tried four different places before I realised that "something" was actually just "hotel".' He grinned. 'I was beginning to worry she'd done the hotel-name equivalent of giving me a one-digit-wrong phone number.'

'Persistent.' Livia raised an eyebrow in Rachel's direction. 'Well, you're here now.'

'I am.'

The three of them stood there awkwardly for a moment, then Livia grinned. 'Well, I need to go and find my, you know, "husband".' She'd made air quotes around the word, as if still getting used to it. 'You two have fun. And don't do anything I wouldn't do.'

Jay let out a short laugh. 'By the sounds of things, that gives us quite a lot of leeway!'

'So . . .' said Rachel, brusquely, once Livia was out of earshot. 'What is it you're returning?'

'Um . . .' Jay was patting his pockets, which made a squelching sound, then he grinned guiltily. 'I made that bit up. I was desperate to see you again, and I didn't want Livia to think I was crashing her wedding.'

'*What?*'

'I said I didn't want Livia to think . . .'

'No . . .' Rachel couldn't believe what she was hearing. Jay *had* come to see her after all. She shook her head to clear any swimming pool water out of her ears, just in case. 'So . . . you're not actually returning anything?' she said, trying to keep the excitement from her voice.

'No. Sorry.'

'Don't be. It's great to see you.'

'Likewise. Though I wasn't sure I was going to. Especially by the time I'd tried the third hotel.'

'Sorry about that. I just . . . I was a bit confused after what happened this afternoon . . .' Jay was looking startled, and Rachel suddenly realised why. 'In a good way.'

'Right.'

They stood there for a moment, listening to Liam skip through the music on his phone in an attempt to get everyone dancing again.

'So,' said Rachel, again.

'So . . .'

'Did you want some wedding cake? That's if Livia's left any.'

'No, I'm fine.' Jay took a mouthful of beer, closely followed by another. 'Listen, I—'

Rachel raised a hand, and rested a finger on his lips. 'Don't.'

'Why not?'

'*Because*,' said Rachel, hoping that one word would sum up, well, *everything*. 'What happened this afternoon . . . It's not the kind of thing that happens to me all the time.'

'I should hope not,' said Jay. 'Otherwise it'd cost you a fortune in replacement phones.'

'Not *getting robbed*!' Rachel slapped him playfully on the chest. 'The *sex*,' she said, a little too loudly, seeing as Liam had chosen that exact moment to swap songs and left an unprofessional couple of seconds of silence between them.

'Me neither. And that's the real reason I came tonight. Because I thought we had a real connection.'

'Me too. Otherwise I wouldn't have . . . you know . . .'

'I get it,' said Jay, giving her another one of those smiles.

Liam had changed the music to something slower, so Jay put his beer down on the nearest table, took Rachel by the hand and led her to the dance floor. 'So, at the risk of asking a question I'm probably not going to like the answer to, what time's your flight tomorrow?'

'Six,' said Rachel, careful to enunciate the word properly.

'Right.' Jay held her a little tighter. 'Maybe we could . . . do something? Before you go?'

'I'd love to! What did you have in mind?' said Rachel, then she realised she'd sounded a little more suggestive than perhaps she'd meant to, and the thought of what Jay might have in mind made her shiver in anticipation.

'Hey,' he said. 'Are you cold? Maybe you need to get out of these wet things. I don't want you catching a chill. Especially if we do only have one more day together.'

'I'm fine.' Rachel reached up and looped her arms around his neck. The heat between her and Jay meant a chill was the last thing she was going to catch. 'Although . . .'

'Although?'

'What are you doing for the next few days?' she said, impulsively.

'Nothing. School's closed until . . . Why?'

'It's just that . . .' She shivered again, though for effect this time. 'I think I *do* feel a chill coming on. So I might have to change my flight. Call in sick at work on Monday.'

'Excellent!' Jay was looking at her like . . . almost like Livia had looked at Jed when he'd been down on one knee earlier, and for the second time that day, Rachel couldn't keep the smile from her face. 'Though you'll have to make sure you don't go back to work with a tan.'

'Good point,' Rachel said. Though there wouldn't be much danger of that. Especially since she wasn't planning on the two of them leaving her hotel room, except perhaps to change venue to Jay's apartment. 'But . . .'

'But?'

'No promises. No making commitments that we can't keep.' She took him by both hands, and – leaving a soggy trail behind them – steered him towards the elevator. 'No asking where this is going.'

'Um . . . where are *we* going?' he said, as she stabbed at the up button.

'Like you suggested earlier. To get out of these wet things.'

'But I don't have a change of clothes.'

The doors opened with a ping, and Rachel followed Jay into the lift, then stood up on tiptoe and kissed him on the lips. 'You won't need one,' she said, with a smile.

Livia's feet were killing her. Her back was killing her too, but she didn't care. A few short hours ago, she'd been worried that Jed was going to be thinking of killing her for dropping this whole surprise wedding thing on him, and yet, somehow, it had worked out even better than she'd dreamed. Jed had turned out to be amazing – or rather, reminded her how amazing he was. And going forward, she needed that – needed *him* – more than ever.

She had Liam to thank too. And Patrick – though she'd always known she could rely on him. The thing was, now she was sure she could rely on Jed, because of what she'd put him through. Because she understood him a little better. And hopefully, because he understood her better too. They'd need to talk more, of course, once they got back home – about his past, and how it might affect their future. But there was no rush. Because now, Livia was sure, they had the rest of their lives for that.

She leant heavily back in her chair, and glanced across to where Rachel and Jay were making for the lift, a look on Jay's face that . . . well, Livia had never seen Rich look at Rachel like that. And maybe this one would work out for her. Livia had a feeling that today was all about new beginnings, new chapters. Patrick and Izzy seemed to have . . . 'reached an understanding' was what she was going to go with. And even Liam seemed to be revelling in his best man/DJ role, as opposed to his TV role. You had to see that as progress.

She rested a hand on her stomach as the baby kicked – at least, she assumed that was what it was, rather than another adverse reaction to something she'd eaten. She'd be glad when it was out. She could only hope Jed would be too, though given that he'd have had almost nine months to get used to the idea, as opposed to the one day she'd allowed him for the wedding, she was pretty confident about that. And while she wasn't sure that being married would change their lives that much, she was sure that being parents would. In a good way. She hoped.

'Hey, sis!'

Liam's exclamation startled her, but she smiled up at him. He'd done her proud today, what with finding a doctor so quickly earlier, and stepping in for the DJ, and his speech . . . Though, to be honest, that hadn't been his finest hour – or even five minutes. But they'd laugh about it in years to come, she was sure.

'Bro!' she said, mimicking the way Liam always greeted Jed, then fist-bumping him for good measure.

'Looking *muy guapa*!' he said, looking her up and down, his eyes lingering on her chest. 'That's how they say "very beautiful" here.'

'Speaking Spanish now, Liam? I'm impressed.'

Liam shrugged nonchalantly. 'I'm like a sponge.'

'That's what Jed's been saying for years.' She winked at him. 'Having a good time?'

'Yeah, actually.' He cast an eye proudly over the dance floor, where most of the hotel guests seemed to have ended up, then returned his gaze to her. 'Normally I'd be off my tits about now . . .'

'Instead of staring at mine?'

'Sorry. It's just . . . with the baby and everything . . . they're *huge*! Anyway,' he said, sinking into the chair next to her. 'I just wanted to say congratulations, you know? This has all been . . .' He waved a hand in the air, as if dismissing a bad waiter. 'Inspirational.'

'Jed's baby brother's growing up at last,' said Livia, reaching over to ruffle his hair, then immediately regretting it, given the amount of product that came off on her hand. 'Dance with me?' she said, surreptitiously wiping her fingers on her napkin.

'I'm not sure you should, in your condition.'

'Don't worry. It's perfectly safe for pregnant women to—'

'*Married*, I meant!'

Livia reached over and poked him sharply in the ribs. 'Come on. It's traditional for the bride to take a turn with the best man. Not like *that*, Liam,' she added, at the look on his face.

'Go on, then.' Liam leapt up and offered her his hands, then hoisted her out of her chair (Livia was grateful she wasn't that wedged in, so it didn't come up with her), and the two of them took to the dance floor.

'It'll have to be a slow one, on account of my . . .'

'Condition?'

'Exactly,' said Livia. 'Oh, and don't squeeze me too tightly.'

Liam nodded. 'Sure,' he said, holding her at arm's length. 'Don't want another false alarm. And just let me know if I need to go and find a gas mask . . .'

'Scratch earlier Liam-growing-up comment,' said Livia, grinning. 'Now c'mere!'

She grabbed him round the waist and pulled him close, only for him to recoil in horror. 'Jesus Christ!'

Liam had almost jumped a foot backwards, and Livia's first thought was that she must have stood on his foot – and at her current weight, and in these shoes, that wouldn't be pleasant.

'What's the matter?'

'Something . . . it . . . *moved!*'

'What?'

'In there.' Liam was staring in horror at her belly, and Livia laughed.

'If by "it" you mean your soon-to-make-an-appearance niece or nephew . . .'

'Yeah. Unless you're planning to asphyxiate us all again?'

Livia gave him a look. 'That's what they do, Liam. There's nothing to be scared of. Here. Have a feel.'

She grabbed his hand, but Liam resisted. 'I'll pass, thanks.'

'*Liam . . .*'

Reluctantly, he reached his hand out towards her, and Livia shook her head as he tentatively rested it on the front of her bump, then suddenly pulled it away, as if he'd just had an electric shock. 'It did it again!'

'Well, "it" obviously likes you!'

'Jesus! It's . . . *alive.*'

'It is.'

Liam carefully put his hand back onto the same spot, and as Livia felt the baby move obligingly, he looked down at her, a mixture of wonder and fear on his face. 'That's *amazing!*'

'Isn't it?'

'I mean, I'm still thinking it's a bit like that scene in *Alien*, but even so . . .'

Livia peered down at her stomach. 'Hey, little one,' she said, addressing her bump. 'This idiot is your *uncle*.'

'Christ, Liv.'

'What *now?*'

'Me and it are *related.*'

'Sadly, yes.'

'But that means . . . if you and Jed have an accident . . .'

'Well, that's a happy thought for my wedding day.'

'I didn't mean . . . you're not . . .'

'What's up?' A not-that-sober-looking Jed had sidled over to join them, so Livia smiled.

'Your brother's just discovered the miracle of life.'

'Finally.'

'You did have the birds-and-bees conversation with him, I take it?'

Jed grinned. 'There was no need. Since he turned fourteen, Liam's been using his personality as birth control . . .'

As Livia laughed at her husband's joke, Liam removed his hand from her stomach. 'Bro, I . . . and Liv – sorry . . . *sis* – I just want to say that . . . I'll, you know, be there. Just in case. I mean, obviously, I'll try my hardest to be the cool uncle. You know, play football with them in the park, teach them how to smoke, buy them their first pint, get them a hooker for their eighteenth birthday . . .'

'And if it's a boy?'

'That's what I . . . right. Good one, Liv. But seriously. I'll do my best.'

'To what?'

'Set a good example. I'm going to change my ways. Give up on Tinder. Think about settling down.'

'Blimey, Liam. What's brought this on?'

'I dunno. I just . . .' Liam shrugged. 'I'd wanted to be famous for ages, you know? But something was obviously stopping me . . .'

'That would be your lack of a thing called talent,' suggested Jed, though Livia quickly shushed him.

'And then finally I got on *Big Brother*.'

Livia shook her head. 'I never got why you did that.'

'It seemed like a good idea at the time.'

'So was getting on board the *Titanic*.' Jed laughed. 'Which is actually a pretty good metaphor, given what happened to your career afterwards.'

'Don't you see?' said Liam, desperately. 'That's my point. I thought it was the best thing that had ever happened to me. But it turned out to be just after everyone stopped watching it.'

'Right.' Livia nodded sagely, though she hadn't got his point. 'And?'

'Like your *Titanic* comment. Really I missed the boat. And not in a good way. So I kind of don't want that to be the case with everything else.'

'Are you drunk?' said Jed, though funnily enough, Livia thought Liam had never looked more sober.

'I must be,' said Liam, then he slipped an arm around his brother's shoulders, and Jed clapped him heartily on the back.

'Thanks, bro. Good speech, by the way.'

Liam narrowed his eyes at his brother. 'You mean the one at the table earlier, and not just now?'

'I do.'

'You think?' said Liam.

'We both do,' said Livia.

'What was your favourite bit?'

Jed was looking at her, desperately trying to find an answer, so Livia smiled. 'The end,' she said, and burst out laughing.

Then she grabbed Liam's face with both hands, pulled him down to her level and kissed him full on the lips. And the look he gave her as he headed back to the safety of the speakers made her laugh even harder still.

'Come and dance with me.'

It had sounded more like an order than a request, but even so, Patrick shook his head. Since their little chat, Izzy had been sulking, not to mention drinking . . . if not excessively, 'steadily' would probably sum it up – and she was enough of a handful sober.

'You go ahead,' he said, settling back into his chair.

As she stuck her tongue out at him, then flounced off towards the dance floor, he sighed. On their third date, he'd made the mistake of agreeing to Izzy's suggestion they go to a club, even though dancing wasn't something he enjoyed any more – he wasn't sure he ever had, to be honest. And when he'd foolishly tried to dance with Izzy . . . well, what he'd experienced wasn't like any dancing he knew how to do, it was more like trying to wrestle a snake. And one that seemed to be trying to have sex with you while fully clothed. Though where Izzy was concerned, 'fully' perhaps wasn't quite the right description.

He sipped his drink as he watched her stride confidently to the space in front of the speakers, then raise her arms above her head and start to move to the music. In truth, Izzy didn't appear to need a partner. She'd shut her eyes, lose herself to the beat, happy to put on a solo performance for song after song before returning, sweaty, to his table, where she'd look at him in the same way his daughter used to, aged five or six, checking he'd seen her, desperate for approval.

But not tonight. She shot a defiant glance in Patrick's direction, making sure he was watching her, and – keeping her eyes fixed on his – seductively ran her hands up from her waist, over her breasts and through what remained of her blonde tresses. Then, her hands on the sides of her head, elbows pointing outwards, she started to gyrate with such energy Patrick feared someone nearby might lose an eye.

Most of the other hotel guests on the dance floor had noticed her, some of the men even surreptitiously swivelling their wives and girlfriends round so they could get a better look. Though it was hard not to blame them – generally, the only way you'd get to see a show like this was by stuffing some twenty-pound notes down (what remained of) some stripper's underwear, but here, given her braless state, low-cut dress and the enthusiasm of her movements, Izzy was giving everyone almost as much of an eyeful. And for free.

He watched, part horrified, part hypnotised, as she shimmied over to where Liam was standing behind the speakers, his back to her, probably updating the evening's playlist with yet another song Patrick hadn't heard before, then – as if thanks to some sixth sense – Liam whirled round to see her. And before he knew what was happening, Izzy had grabbed his arm and pulled him to the centre of the dance floor.

Liam nervously flicked his eyes over to where Patrick was sitting, but seeing him simply shrug, he flashed him an awkward grin and began dancing, and Patrick nearly laughed out loud. It was like watching a Sunday footballer having a kick-around with Lionel Messi, and while Liam did his best – and wasn't a bad dancer – there was no way he could match Izzy's moves.

After a few more songs, just as Liam seemed on the verge of knowing when he was beaten, the music changed – a slower number – and before he could head back to the safety of the speakers, Izzy had fastened her arms around his neck and pulled him close.

It was almost comical. Liam was doing his best to angle his body away from her, as if trying to avoid a judo takedown, while Izzy seemed set on grinding her hips against his. Then – and Patrick couldn't tell whether he or Liam was the more surprised – she leapt up, and in one fluid movement wrapped her legs around his waist, as if performing some weird, vertical rodeo ride.

In an instant, Patrick was out of his chair and steaming towards the two of them, though to his credit Liam was pulling away, a horrified look on his face almost as soon as Izzy had made contact.

'What do you think you're doing?'

'I . . . Patrick . . .' Liam had both hands up, as if ready to fend off an attack, but Patrick just shook his head.

'Don't worry, Liam. You're not the one who's got anything to apologise for.'

'Relax!' said Izzy, mischievously, climbing off him like a small child ordered down from a tree. 'We were just dancing.'

'You call *that* dancing?'

'Yeah, granddad. And seeing as *you* wouldn't dance with me . . .'

Liam had taken the opportunity to sneak away, so Izzy slinked her arms round Patrick's waist and began grinding against him, but he shook her off.

'What's wrong, baby?'

'You're embarrassing yourself.'

Izzy shook her head. 'No. I'm embarrassing you!' she said angrily, and Patrick stared at her.

'And that's the last time you will, if you're not careful!'

'Finally!' Izzy rolled her eyes. 'A reaction!'

'What's that supposed to mean?'

'I told you I loved you, Patrick!' she said, her voice a little too loud for his liking. 'And you were out of the door like the hotel room was on fire. And then all that stuff about not wanting to get married again. Not wanting kids . . .'

Patrick glanced across towards the speakers, where Liam was doing a bad job of trying to simultaneously hide and not listen in on their conversation. 'I'm sorry, Izzy. But how does that relate to you . . . dry-humping Liam just now. And in front of everyone?'

Izzy was watching him intently, though Patrick couldn't interpret her look. 'You don't get it, do you?'

'No. I don't.'

'What you said.' Izzy ran her hands through her hair. 'I needed to know if it was because of *me*.'

'Izzy . . .' Patrick stared at her, dumbfounded, wondering how on earth she'd got the wrong end of the stick, though he realised almost immediately it could only be his fault. 'Of course it isn't.'

'And the love thing?'

'Well, I'm flattered, obviously . . .'

'Fuck off!'

Izzy stormed off the dance floor and into the poolside toilets, slamming the door behind her, and Patrick winced. Given how his wife had left him, and now this, he was starting to suspect relationships weren't his forte. Ignoring the stares from the hotel's other guests, he followed her to the toilet and knocked softly.

'Izzy?'

There was the sound of some rummaging, then a couple of sharp bangs, and Patrick started to get worried. 'Izzy,' he said again, a little louder this time, his knocking more insistent.

'What?'

'Come out.'

'No!'

'Hey . . .' He glanced around, conscious he appeared to be having a conversation with a toilet door. A few people were watching him intently, but he was past caring. 'You can't stay in there all evening.'

'Why not!'

'Well, for one thing, you're in the gents.'

'Just leave me alone!'

'Come on. Don't do anything stupid.'

'I think I already did. Earlier.'

'Izzy, let's just talk about—'

'What is there to talk about?' Izzy had cracked the door open, and her tear-stained face peering through the gap wasn't something Patrick was ready for. 'I open my heart to you, tell you how I feel and you say . . . nothing.'

'Just calm down, come out, and we'll—'

'We'll what? Have sex again? That'll shut Izzy up, because she knows she shouldn't talk with her mouth full.'

Patrick shook his head, though partly because after their earlier marathon session, he wasn't sure he'd be able to. 'Like I said. Talk. I need you to understand . . .'

'Understand what?'

'If you come out, I'll tell you.'

Izzy stared at him for a moment longer, then slowly, reluctantly, padded out from the toilets and flopped down onto a bench set against the wall. 'Well?'

'Not here,' he said, reaching for her hand. 'Let's walk and talk.'

She stared up at him for a moment, then wiped her eyes on the back of her arm. "K', she said, quietly, allowing herself to be helped up.

'Good girl.'

Patrick slipped an arm around her shoulders, steered her from the terrace and back out through reception. If she was going to make a scene – or rather, more of a scene – he didn't want it to spoil Livia and Jed's evening.

Wordlessly, they headed out of the hotel's front door, and along the dark, paved street towards Las Ramblas. The boulevard was busy – stag and hen groups moving excitedly between Barcelona's many bars and clubs, tourists on their way home from dinner, locals just heading out for theirs – and as Patrick led Izzy down towards the port, she cleared her throat.

'Las Ramblas isn't just the one street, you know?'

'Pardon?'

'It's a series of shorter streets that run into one another to form one long one, hence the plural.'

'Where did *that* come from?'

'That stupid woman on the satnav this afternoon. I was listening, you know?'

'But why . . . ?'

Izzy looked up at him and forced a smile. 'We seemed to be doing a lot of walking, and not that much talking. I thought I'd better get the ball rolling.'

'Sorry.' He mouthed a '*No, gracias*' as they sidestepped someone selling animal balloons, hoping Izzy hadn't understood their 'For your daughter?' in Spanish. 'This . . . us . . . it's difficult for me.'

'*Difficult?*'

Patrick noticed Izzy's expression darken, so he hurriedly corrected himself. '*New*, then. It's just so different. In a good way, I mean. You just . . . took me a bit by surprise earlier. That's all. And that stuff you said about me always trying to teach you things – remember, I'm learning from you too. All the time.'

'Learning *what*?'

'All kinds of things. How not to be so inhibited, for one. To live for the moment, for another. What selvedge jeans are.' Izzy smiled at this last point, so Patrick soldiered on. 'You're twenty-two, and you've been in love how many times?'

Izzy thought for a moment. 'A dozen or so.'

'*A dozen?*'

'If you count all of One Direction. Except for Niall.'

Patrick nodded, hoping Izzy wouldn't know he didn't have a clue who she was talking about. 'Well, I've been in love *once*. With Sarah. For *twenty-three years*. And look where that got me. What she did to me . . . I thought we were compatible, thought she loved me, but we evidently weren't, and she obviously didn't. And now . . .' He stared up at the night sky as they walked, resisting the temptation to point out the constellations. 'When someone does that to you, cheats on you, when you divorce them, you're supposed to forget just like that.' He clicked his fingers loudly for added effect. 'And that's hard. It's not like an on-off switch.'

'So you still love her?'

'No,' said Patrick, quickly, aware that would be a very dangerous direction for the conversation to take. 'But when you go through something like that, it makes you question what love is. Whether you got it right the first time. It's not a word you – *anyone* – should just bandy around willy-nilly . . . What's so funny?'

'*Willy-nilly?*'

'Anyway, my point is, something like that means you need to be doubly sure when – if – you ever say it again. So I suppose what I'm trying to explain is – and believe it or not, I've only just realised this – it's not you, it's me. I'm dealing with twenty-plus years of emotions, of incidents, of *life*. So much of what we do is new for you. But for me, it's . . .'

'Boring?'

Izzy had found his hand with hers, and he took the opportunity to give it a squeeze. 'No – I don't mean that at all. It's just . . . I've had someone tell me they loved me, and look where that went. And I know it might not seem fair, but . . . saying you love someone . . . it's not like it's some password that automatically gets you into the members' area, or a handshake that secret societies do to identify . . .' Not for the first time that day, Izzy's eyes had begun to glaze over, so Patrick decided to change tack. 'All I'm saying is . . .' He stopped to think. Izzy had swivelled around to face him, and was looking at him so expectantly he knew one misspoken word here could be a very big mistake. But fortunately – and at that precise moment he almost *did* love her for it – she put him out of his misery.

'Baby, the reason I told you I loved you was simply because it's how I *feel*. You're funny, and sexy, and smart, and generous, and clever, and kind . . .' She reached up and tenderly rested a hand on his cheek. 'And the Porsche's pretty cool too.'

'So it's not just because I, you know, buy you stuff?'

Izzy gave him a look. 'I let you buy me stuff because *you* seem to like doing it. Not that I'm saying you should stop . . .' She grinned. 'And I'm not expecting you to say you love me back. Not right now, at least. I just need to believe that there's the possibility that, one day, you *might*. Otherwise . . .' She sighed. 'Well, we'd just be wasting our time.'

'Well, that's . . . I suppose . . . it's not beyond the realms of . . . I mean, I possibly could . . .'

'Just let yourself *feel* it, Patrick. All this stuff about compatibility, suitability – whether, I don't know, you're a dog person or a cat person – is shit. There are loads of different types of dogs. And cats. Don't get me started on those Egyptian hairless things . . .' Izzy shuddered theatrically, then she grabbed his shoulders and stared deep into his eyes. 'You've got to *believe* it can be different. Each time. And that it's going to work, despite – or even *because of* – your differences. Otherwise you might as well go up to Jed and Livia and tell them not to bother.'

Patrick looked down at her with a new respect. He had to admit, Izzy had a point, though he didn't want to admit it just yet. Or that, when it came to Jed and Livia, the thought had occurred to him.

'So, do you?'

'Do I what?'

Izzy angled her head, the way a cute puppy might. 'Think you might? Feel it? One day?'

Patrick realised they were standing at the end of the road. Though as Izzy had reminded him, Las Ramblas was a *series* of roads, one after the other. And while he'd walked down it before, there was no reason he couldn't try going in a different direction.

He took her in his arms, and gave the only possible answer he could; though this time, he was sure he meant it.

'I do,' he said.

Liam checked over his shoulder that Izzy wasn't waiting to pounce on him again, then he finished putting together his 'smooch' playlist, hit 'Add to queue' and peered out at the dance floor. Most of the guests had gone now, though Livia and Jed were still dancing, holding each other close, and Liam smiled at the sight. Jed's back was going to be sore in the morning, given how he was having to work around Livia's distended stomach, but by the looks of him, he didn't care.

Liam had done a good job as stand-in DJ, he reckoned – although DJ-ing at this particular wedding had pretty much been compiling a list of his favourite tracks and hitting play. And while it had meant he'd had plenty of opportunities to dance himself, to be honest there hadn't been that many eligible women to dance with. He'd spent a considerable amount of time trying to hide from Sooz and Debs: they'd ended up getting so drunk that they'd marched straight up to him to ask outright if he fancied a threesome, and even if he hadn't replied 'You're about twenty-nine stone short, love' when Sooz had indicated herself and Debs and said 'Two birds, one stone,' he didn't think it would have happened. Right now they were both asleep on a nearby sun lounger. And looking like they'd be spending the night there.

He'd had a bit of fun earlier, he had to admit, with that girl from the gym, and while that had been a bit one-sided, that hadn't been his fault. Livia had been in trouble. And he'd more than made up for it by playing the hero this evening. Stepping in to save the day when the original DJ had run off – *and* when his playlist had looked like making everyone suicidal. Though what was his reward? Being the last man standing. Alone.

He'd thought he might have had a chance with that Rachel girl, but she'd disappeared off with some guy he didn't recognise, and while Patrick's bit of fluff had virtually tried to have sex with him in front of *everyone*, he suspected that hadn't been for his benefit.

He looked at his watch. Just gone midnight. The pool bar looked like it was shut, so Liam scanned the room, wondering if there was any point in doing a minesweep of any half-drunk glasses of wine on the tables, then decided against it. He'd drunk enough today, and he was already dreading his hangover.

He supposed he could head out to a club, but to be honest he wasn't in the mood. Today had given him a lot to think about, and he might just need to think about it sooner rather than later. Besides, he'd promised Jed and Livia he'd clean up his act. Turn over a new leaf. And right now was as good a time to start as any. With a wistful sigh, he made his way over to where the newlyweds were dancing – well, swaying gently, to be exact – and tapped his brother on the shoulder.

'I'm off.'

Livia wrinkled her nose. 'You don't smell that bad to me.'

'Ha ha. To bed.'

'On your own?' Jed was peering over Liam's shoulder, evidently wondering where the girl was who he was perhaps anxious to be with, so Liam smiled.

'Yeah. One night off won't kill me, eh?'

'I'm surprised all the nights "on" haven't.'

Liam rolled his eyes good-naturedly at Livia's comment. 'Anyway . . . I just wanted to say . . .' He swallowed hard. 'You know, if I hadn't said it before . . . I, ahem, um, love you both, and I'm made up that you and Jed have, you know, made up, and . . .' Jed was giving him a look, and Liam suddenly remembered that Livia had no idea about Jed's 'missing' period earlier. 'I mean, Jed's made an honest woman of you, and like I said earlier, it's made me think that, well . . .'

His voice trailed off. Jed was smiling at him. 'We get it, Liam. And thanks again. Like *I* said earlier, you've been the best best man a brother could ask for. Even though he didn't ask for – or know he was going to be needing – one.'

'Yeah, well, you'll be doing the same for me one day. Hopefully sooner, rather than later.'

Jed slipped an arm round his shoulders. 'I can't wait,' he said, and Liam grinned sheepishly. Neither, he realised, could he.

'Anyway,' Liam said again, then he leaned across and gave Livia a hug, and kissed his brother on the forehead. 'Like I said, I'm out of here.'

'I'm liking this new Liam,' said Livia, then she winced, and both Liam and Jed looked concerned, but then she smiled. 'It's okay. It just kicked me.'

'What did?' said Liam.

'The *baby*, Liam,' said Livia, then she widened her eyes. 'Baby Liam. How's that for a name?'

Jed laughed. 'I think one Liam Woodward is already more than enough, thank you.'

Liam grinned, and gave them both one of those salute-waves he'd seen people do in films (and that he'd practised in front of a mirror because it always looked pretty cool), then he headed out through reception and made his way back to his room. He'd be sad to be leaving Barcelona tomorrow. It had been an eventful couple of days. Perhaps a little too eventful, given everything that had happened today, but as Liam thought about it, he decided he wouldn't change a thing.

The lift doors pinged open, and he stepped out into the corridor, trying to remember which way to turn for his room, when he spotted a devastatingly pretty girl in a hotel uniform walking towards him.

'Well *ho-la!*' he said, before remembering he was trying to have what was left of the night off.

'*Como puedo ayudarte?*'

'I'm sorry.' Liam flashed her his best smile. 'I don't speak Spanish. And to be honest, after the amount I've drunk this evening, English is proving a bit tricky.'

The woman smiled back. 'It means "Can I help you?"' she said, her voice heavily – and to Liam's ear, *sexily* – accented. 'You look . . . lost.'

Liam stared at her. That was exactly it. He *was* lost. Or at least, he had been. Then he realised he was, in fact, standing right in front of his room. 'No. Thank you. I'm fine. This is me.'

The girl – Margarita, according to her name tag, and Liam had to stop himself from asking whether she was named after the pizza – looked him up and down. Or was she checking him out? He'd have bet money on it being the latter.

'I can see that.'

'No. It's an English expression. It means . . . never mind.' He pointed to his door. 'My room. Number thirteen. Unfortunately.'

'Why?'

'The number. Thirteen? It's bad luck.'

Margarita smiled, and Liam couldn't help but stare at her mouth. Her plump, kissable lips. The slight dimples that formed in her cheeks. Her perfect white teeth. How he'd love to . . .

He shook his head to clear it, and realised she was speaking again. 'Thirteen is a lucky number in Italy.'

'Right. Good to know. Although we're in Spain. Aren't we?'

'We are.' Margarita smiled again. 'But I am Italian.'

Liam shook his head. This was almost too good to be true. And if she was suggesting he'd just got lucky . . . He located his key card in his pocket, and with the greatest of efforts, forced himself to open his door. 'Well, *buenas* . . .' He hesitated. What was the word?

'*Noches*,' said Margarita, and Liam almost laughed. That was exactly what Livia had accused him of collecting on his bedpost. And, he'd decided, all that was going to stop. With a smile, he moved to slip through the doorway, but the woman followed him inside.

'Hold on. If you're some kind of best man gift organised by Jed and Livia, then thanks, but no thanks. You're very pretty, but I'm absolutely knackered, and I—' Liam stopped talking. Margarita was frowning at him.

'I'm sorry. I don't understand. I am a . . .' She thought for a moment. 'Turndown service.'

Liam made a face. 'I've been turned down enough today, thank you.'

'For the *bed*.'

'Huh?'

'I turn down your bed.'

'You wouldn't be the first,' said Liam, escorting her to the door.

Margarita paused, then she narrowed her eyes. 'You're him, aren't you?'

'Who?'

'The reality star.'

Liam smiled as he shook his head. 'I used to be,' he said.

And as he ushered Margarita back into the corridor, locked the door behind her and pressed the 'Do Not Disturb' button, he found himself hoping that was true.

Jed and Livia stood in the middle of the dance floor, arms around each other, rocking gently together, even though they were the last ones left – and the music had stopped when Liam took his phone with him. But they were moving to their own beat, rather than Liam's – excellent, it had to be said – choice of music, and right now, Jed knew he wouldn't have it any other way. After a moment, he angled his head back so Livia could see his face, and narrowed his eyes at her.

'What?' he said.

'What do you mean, "what?"'

'You've got that look on your face. Like you're desperate to ask me something.'

'Well, I was just wondering . . .'

'Come on, wife. Out with it.'

'How did you know?'

'Know what?'

'That it – this – wasn't legal.'

'I'm not stupid, you know?'

'No, I know, but . . . come on.'

Jed grinned. 'Liam let it slip. But don't tell him I told you. He's mortified enough.'

'No problem.'

They danced on for another moment, then Jed suddenly took a step backwards. 'Thank you,' he said, earnestly.

'For?'

He gestured around the terrace. 'All of this.'

'Says the man who didn't want to get married.' Livia reached up and adjusted his tie. 'And how does married life feel, exactly?'

Jed looked at his watch. His *new* watch. 'Early days yet. But I'll keep you posted.'

'You do that.'

'It has a nice ring to it, though.'

'I wouldn't mention rings if I were you.' Livia prodded him in the stomach. 'And what does?'

'Mr and Mrs Woodward.'

'Well, Mr Woodward and Ms Wilson.'

'What?'

'Don't think I'm automatically taking your surname.'

'But . . .'

'Hey, here's an idea. How about you take mine?'

'Well, I, er, um, suppose that . . .'

'Relax, Jed. I'm kidding.'

Jed shuddered involuntarily. After the events of this weekend, he wouldn't put anything past Livia. He flicked his eyes down at his wife's stomach. 'What about, you know, *it*?'

'What about it?'

'Who's he – or she – going to be?'

'That's a very deep question. And I think it's a bit early to tell . . .'

'No – whose surname are they going to have?'

'Well . . .' Livia thought for a moment. 'They could be double-barrelled?'

'They could. As would be the shotgun you'd have to hold to my head to get me to agree to let them sound like some posh twat. Besides, we haven't even talked about Christian names.'

'Okay – what about half and half?'

'Like a shandy?'

'Clara.'

'I quite like that. For a girl, obviously.'

'No, *clara* is what they call a shandy here in . . . Never mind.' Livia grabbed him again, and started moving to some imaginary song, then she looked up suddenly. 'I've got it,' she said. 'How about this first one has my surname, and the next one takes yours, and the third . . .' She broke into a huge grin, no doubt at the look of terror that Jed hadn't been able to stop creeping across his face. 'Anyway,' she said. 'Let's not worry about that right now. We've got a few more months of just the two of us. Including our honeymoon.'

'Honeymoon?'

'A week in a fantastic hotel right on the sea.' Livia retrieved her phone from where she'd stashed it down the front of her dress, and flicked through her emails to show him the booking confirmation. 'Menorca, rather than Thailand, on account of my condition. You and me. Just like in that Leonardo DiCaprio film.'

'*Titanic*?'

'*The Beach*, silly . . .' Livia stopped talking. Jed was sporting a particularly smug 'got you' expression.

'Well, that sounds lovely,' he said. 'Listen, Liv. About earlier . . .'

Livia reached up and put a finger on his lips. 'I get it, Jed.'

'Right.'

'And I should be the one to apologise.'

'I wasn't about to apologise!'

'But . . .' Livia seemed as if she was searching for the right words, so Jed winked at her and, for good measure, silenced her with a kiss.

'Finally. We've become one of those couples who finish each other's sentences.'

'Let's just promise ourselves we won't ever get to *starting* them.'

'Deal,' said Jed, then he scanned the terrace. There weren't that many people left outside at all – Patrick and Izzy had slunk off not long after Rachel had taken some man to the elevator, and Liam had just gone, *on his own*, so all the other people scattered round the few remaining occupied tables were hotel guests. With everyone they knew gone to bed, he and Livia wouldn't be missed. 'Tell you what. How about we go back to the room and celebrate?'

'*Celebrate.*'

'Yeah,' said Jed. 'It is our wedding night, after all.'

Livia looked at him, as if trying to work out exactly what 'celebrate' might mean, then she widened her eyes in surprise, and the sight almost made Jed burst out laughing.

'That sounds like a plan. But no trying to carry me over the threshold.'

Jed looked his wife up and down. 'Sorry, Liv,' he said, bracing himself for the poke in the ribs that was surely coming. 'But given the size of you, I'm not honestly sure I could.'

'Okay. But before we go . . .' Livia took his hand and led him towards the nearest table. 'Help me up, will you?'

'Huh?'

'For a dance!'

'Liv . . .'

'It's perfectly safe,' she said, clambering awkwardly up onto a chair, then onto the table, and beckoning for him to follow her.

'What if you fall off?'

'I won't. And even if I do . . .'

'What?'

'You'll be there to catch me.'

'I will,' said Jed. 'Always.'

'Promise?'

'I do,' said Jed, with a smile. Now he *knew* it was a promise he could keep.

ACKNOWLEDGMENTS

Thanks: To Emilie Marneur, Sana Chebaro, Victoria Pepe and the rest of the Amazon (though that really should read 'Amazing') Publishing team – without you, it'd all just be typing.

To super-editor Sophie 'I think we can lose this (translation: it's not funny)' Wilson.

To Gemma Wain, for her painstakingness and meticulosity (STET).

To Tina (for more than I can say).

To the usual suspects (Tony, Loz, John, and Dave & Nic) for being good friends/the material/not suing me.

To the (new, social media version of the) Board.

And finally, to everyone who's ever read, recommended or (nicely) reviewed one of my books. I couldn't – and wouldn't – do it without you.

ABOUT THE AUTHOR

Photo © 2014 Cassandra Nelson

British writer Matt Dunn is the author of twelve (and counting) romantic comedy novels, including *A Day at the Office* (a Kindle bestseller), *The Ex-Boyfriend's Handbook* (shortlisted for both the Romantic Novel of the Year Award and the Melissa Nathan Award for Comedy Romance) and *13 Dates*. He's also written about life, love and relationships for various publications including *The Times*, the *Guardian*, *Glamour*, *Cosmopolitan*, *Company*, *Elle* and the *Sun*. Before becoming a full-time writer, Matt worked as a lifeguard, a fitness-equipment salesman and an IT headhunter.